Wyndham Family Tree

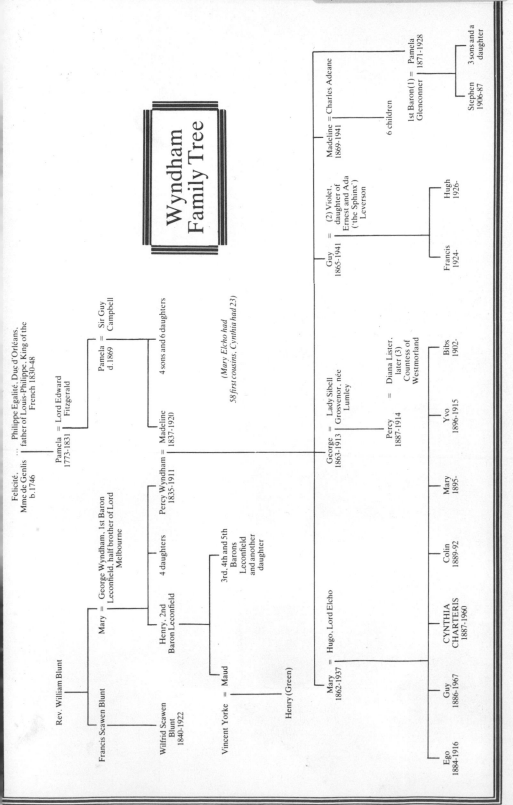

Cynthia Asquith

Cynthia Asquith

····≯· by ·≺····

Nicola Beauman

Hamish Hamilton : London

····◆ To Chris ◆····

HAMISH HAMILTON LTD

Penguin Books Ltd, 27 Wrights Lane, London W8 5TZ (Publishing & Editorial)
and Harmondsworth, Middlesex, England (Distribution & Warehouse)
Viking Penguin Inc., 40 West 23rd Street, New York, New York 10010, U.S.A.
Penguin Books Australia Ltd, Ringwood, Victoria, Australia
Penguin Books Canada Limited, 2801 John Street, Markham, Ontario,
Canada L3R 1B4
Penguin Books (N.Z.) Ltd, 182-190 Wairau Road, Auckland 10, New Zealand

First published in Great Britain 1987 by
Hamish Hamilton Ltd

Copyright © Nicola Beauman

British Library Cataloguing in Publication Data

Beauman, Nicola
    Cynthia Asquith.
    1. Asquith, Cynthia—Biography
    2. Authors, English—20th century
    —Biography
    I. Title
    828'.91209   PR6001.S68Z/

ISBN 0–241–12368–2

Typeset in Great Britain by
Input Typesetting Ltd, Wimbledon SW19 8DR

Printed in Great Britain by
Butler & Tanner Ltd, Frome and London

Contents

Contents

The publisher wishes to apologise to the author and the
reader for the incorrect order of the pictures. This occurred
during the binding. For the correct order, please see the
Picture Sources on page 366.

But there is a further value in this chronicle – one that the author herself shows no sign of realizing. It shows how one of the greatest revolutions in English history was met by an individual of flexible mind and stout heart, who belonged to the class least prepared to withstand it . . . There is no 'moaning at the bar' for our Cyynthia . . . She grabbed at commissions whenever they were offered and raced after deadlines, even when she had to meet them with a family gathering or extensive houseparty in full swing. And this strictly practical, professional attitude was taken naturally and unselfconsciously without the slightest sense of injury, class betrayal or self pity. This is in such striking contrast to the perennial wailing of the Russian aristocracy when suddenly forced to earn their own livings and otherwise behave like ordinary human beings, that we find ourselves doffing our hat and raising a cheer for the ex-ruling class of England.

Review of Cynthia Asquith *Haply I May Remember* in *Oakland Tribune* (California) 9 October 1950

There was a woman who was beautiful, who started with all the advantages, yet she had no luck. She married for love, and the love turned to dust. She had bonny children, yet she felt they had been thrust upon her, and she could not love them. They looked at her coldly, as if they were finding fault with her. And hurriedly she felt she must cover up some fault in herself. Yet what it was that she must cover up she never knew. Nevertheless, when her children were present, she always felt the centre of her heart go hard. This troubled her, and in her manner she was all the more gentle and anxious for her children, as if she loved them very much. Only she herself knew that at the centre of her heart was a hard little place that could not feel love, no, not for anybody.

'The Rocking-Horse Winner', D. H. Lawrence 1926

I went to see Dr R (on behalf of B) . . . I liked him very much. He seemed surprised at my not being a patient myself, especially when he asked me 'Lord Curzon was your father – wasn't he?' and I lost my head and said 'I don't *think* so'.

Cynthia Asquith's Diary 13 January 1932

I am beginning to rub my eyes at the prospect of peace. I think it will require more courage than anything that has gone before. It isn't until one leaves off spinning round that one realises how giddy one is. One will have to teach one's wincing eyes to look at long vistas again instead of short ones – and one will at last fully recognise that the dead are not only dead for the duration of the War.

Cynthia Asquith's Diary 7 October 1918

····✋· Chapter 1 ·✌····
Clouds, Stanway, Colin's Death:
1887–92

I thought dinner would never be over, went upstairs, sent for Dr ¼ to 11, played game of reversé with H in drawing room, went up to bed about 11. Mamma and Hugo sat in my room, he read Dickens – Dr came 3.15. Baby Heigh Presto as the clock struck four. She was a little girl to my great joy and yelled lustily almost before she was born.[1]

There is an endearing lack of fuss about this entry from Mary Elcho's diary: nothing about pain or chloroform or effort. It is curious, too, that dinner was endured and the drawing room sat in – and that the doctor took four and a half hours to arrive, appearing with only forty-five minutes to spare. (There were no telephones then and he must have been summoned to Clouds from Salisbury or Shaftesbury.)

The baby weighed 9lbs and 'does nothing but eat sleep & swell visibly.' Exactly four weeks to the day after the birth, which had been on Tuesday 27 September 1887, the christening took place.

We had a great deal of discussion as to name, after we got down to a certain number of names Madeline, Sylvia etc we put it to the vote, everyone in the house (Papa, Mamma, Fraulein, Madeline, Pamela, Guy, Hugo and I) wrote on a slip of paper the 3 names they liked best and the 3 names above got the most votes, this was the eve of

1

the Christening. We called her Cynthia because she came out of the Clouds, like the Moon in memory of her birthplace.[2]*

She was also called Mary and Evelyn, her third name being that of her father's sister Lady de Vesci; years later, with retrospective whimsy, Mary wrote that she had nearly called her 'Brunhild, Heaven help her!'[3]

The adult Cynthia was always intrigued when people were what she called 'typical', displaying their qualities to such extreme effect that they virtually parodied themselves. Certainly the circumstances of her birth were almost laughable intimations of the tenor of her life. First, there was the matter-of-factness on her mother's part and the glossing over of anything disagreeable. Then, there was the family interest, the concerted voice about the choice of name (which turned into a paper game) and the quaintness of the birth certificate – 'Name & Surname of father: Hugo Richard Wemyss Charteris, Occupation of father: Lord Elcho.' Finally there was Clouds – a house with such individuality that the baby's name was chosen as an act of homage to it, even though there was no precedent either of family or fashion.

Even the name – Clouds – has resonance. Completed at the end of the previous year, and costing £80,000 (£2 million)†, it took five years to build, but that was after a five year period of consultation and design (by Philip Webb, who received 5%) and, even before that, a further five years during which Cynthia's Wyndham grandparents had searched for a site. The house, although on the top of a hill with a slanting outlook to the south-west, does not have a wide view and is curiously hidden among woods, allowing privacy while linking it in a magic circle with its neighbours Wardour Castle, Fonthill Abbey and Stourhead. 'The site looks a perfect piece of the ideal England which we all love'[4] wrote Webb's biographer.

Percy and Madeline Wyndham did not feel it inappropriate to build themselves such a vast home with a high, wide terrace, a basement-full of pantries and service rooms, numerous bedrooms and all the usual apparatus of affluent Victorian life in the country.

The house itself marks the end of an epoch. It appears to have been imagined by its gifted hostess as a palace of week-ending for our politicians. It was planned to have the residential and reception part almost detached from the service block. The former is square and

---

*Cynthia is one of the titles of the moon goddess Artemis.
†Second figure will always be in 1987 terms.

high, and the latter is low, rambling away to the east, lighted mostly from its own court and half-veiled externally by trees. It was the affection of the time that work was done by magic; it was vulgar to recognize its existence or even to see anybody doing it.[5]

Yet in many respects the Wyndhams were ahead of their time, the contemporary fondness for over-decoration and for clutter being abandoned in favour of light, flowers, Oriental blue-and-white china, delicate plasterwork and light oak panelling. The white walls, William Morris carpet, chintz-covered armchairs and comfortable, light-filled atmosphere which are all apparent in the surviving photograph of the drawing-room at Clouds shows it as a room which would not appear old-fashioned nowadays. It was also a room which displayed, conspicuously, the Wyndham good taste.

But 'all gone. Alas! Alas!' Madeline wrote on a now tattered photograph of the mural which Burne-Jones had painted on the staircase wall. On 6 January 1889, during the Christmas visit of the baby Cynthia and her two brothers, Clouds was virtually destroyed by fire. She was to hear the descriptions of that night so often that they became part of her supposed childhood memories. She knew that it had been an unusually cold winter and that the fire spread from a candle left by mistake in a cupboard; and that the horse-drawn fire engines were tragically delayed because the roads were icy.

The children were all in the nursery at the top of the house: Cynthia, Ego and Guy, fifteen months, four years and two-and-a-half years respectively, were carried down the huge staircase wrapped in dampened blankets with wet sponges in their mouths. From the terrace they watched the flames roaring up through the great central hall and fanning out to the surrounding rooms. Later they were driven over to the Stalbridges at nearby Motcombe House. Four year-old Nellie Grosvenor remembered the excitement of that night (they had leaned out of the window to watch the fire-engines race past) being

sadly shattered by the arrival in *our* nursery of a batch of small Wyndham children snatched, I thought unnecessarily, from their burning nursery. We were told to welcome them: we did not. One, later to become the brilliant Edwardian socialite Cynthia Asquith, made a bee-line for *my* rocking-horse. I hit her, and disliked her ever afterwards.[6]

During the two years of re-building (paid for to the tune of £27,000 (£675,000) by Sun Insurance) Cynthia's grandparents managed to go on living in the servants' wing at Clouds because it was undamaged and had been designed by Webb on rather egalitarian and therefore spacious lines. 'It is a good thing that our architect was a Socialist, because we find ourselves just as comfortable . . . as we were'[7] Madeline wrote. Although the original workmen did the restoration work, a shadow hung over Clouds and the traditions of family life envisaged by the Wyndhams were never to be established. But Cynthia spent many childhood holidays there and liked to make much of her birthplace, though it was, in the end, less out of passion than sentiment.

Passion she reserved for Stanway, the Elcho* house in the North Cotswolds. It was her 'core of the world', as it must be for anyone brought up in such a uniquely beautiful village with its great house, little church, surrounding cottages and barns (one mentioned in the Domesday book) and steep hill leading to a duckpond, the lawn with its 'tulip' tree under which Edward VII enjoyed tea until forced indoors by a thunderstorm, the gentle slope up to the folly called 'the Pyramid' which was just the right distance for a walk before lunch. Cynthia was to describe Stanway rather memorably, and her turns of phrase were to be 'lifted' unscrupulously by later writers.

> The house is built of time-tinted golden Cotswold stone. Approached through the arch of the beautiful Inigo Jones Gatehouse, the west front of the house with its four wide sixteenth-century gables, numerous mullioned windows, and one huge oriel, closely overlooks the village church and the huddled graves of the rude forefathers. The southern wing faces a lawn skirted by a wood of yew trees that makes a dark background in the spring for the brief, shimmering, waxen glory of a large magnolia tree.[8]

Stanway Manor was originally owned by the monks of Tewkesbury Abbey and was leased to the Tracys at the dissolution of the monasteries; they rebuilt the house from 1580–1640. Then, in 1771, one of the two daughters of the last Viscount Tracy married Francis Charteris, Lord Elcho, son of the 7th Earl of Wemyss; thus, as the Stanway House Guide Book observes, the house is 'notable for having changed hands only once, other than by

---

*Cynthia's surname was Charteris; her parents, Hugo and Mary, were Lord and Lady Elcho, which they became in 1883 when Hugo's father succeeded to the title, Earl of Wemyss. In 1914 they became the Earl and Countess of Wemyss and Cynthia became 'Lady' instead of 'the Hon.'

inheritance, in the last 1260 years'. Until the 1880s the family lived mainly in Scotland and so the house escaped 'Victorian uglification': as one frequent guest (Eddie Marsh) put it, though there was 'electric light and very good hot water, all up-to-date spickness and spanness had been held at bay'.[9] The corollary of this was the cold. Diana Manners, later Cooper, went so far as to evoke 'lukewarm water, blankets that are no prison to one's wayward toes, and every horizontal object wears a coat of dust, like a chinchilla'.[10]

The draughts and cold bathrooms and rather spartan meals were less important than the atmosphere of books and sofas and window-seats and chow dogs and informal human pleasures (amateur theatricals, walks, firelit evenings). Stanway's beauty has a self-contained quality foreign to houses that depend on human attention. It has never been neglected yet Cynthia once described the house as seeming to 'repudiate human ownership'.[11]

It was at Stanway, the summer after the Clouds fire, that a new baby, to be called Colin, was born. There were now four children under five in the nursery and here all the rituals of late Victorian childhood were peacefully enacted: well out of the adults' way, of course (in 1911 *Country Life* commended a recently built house because 'the whole of the nursery quarters are isolated, as they should be, and served by a separate corridor')[12]. For the Charteris children there were well-wrapped up walks, simple food sent up from the kitchen on trays and eaten round the deal table, games with spinning tops and bricks, much dressing and undressing in front of the open fire which was at all times guarded by a brass-edged fender fixed to the wall by hooks and, at appointed hours, visits downstairs. There were as well holidays by the sea (Ramsgate or Margate) and visits to relations.

In early 1890 Mary went to Pau, in the South of France, for four months, taking only her eldest child Ego with her. This was quite normal behaviour for a woman of her time and class; Ego's plea that 'I can't leave this Baby [Colin], oh no, we've got a *good* Baby in the nursery here and I mustn't leave him'[13] was ignored. Nor would Cynthia's feelings have been considered. Well-off mothers of the period expected to be away from their children a great deal and when with them wished only to see their more agreeable aspects, leaving the day-to-day chores to nannies and house-maids. Even so, 'it *was* joy being back again and finding the children safe and well. Mrs Fry is a trump and takes splendid care of them'.[14]

That summer Mary's journal records the first instance of 'acute jealousy' between governess and nanny: 'I wrote a long letter in the train of exhortation to Mrs Fry, intended to help her get on with [the governess] who goes with them to Stanway and whose advent she views with unmitigated dislike'.[15] Mary longed rather fervently for nursery harmony since she was planning to be away for ten weeks during the late summer of 1890, five at Bad Kissingen, three in the Tyrol and one in London buying clothes. Even when she came home she spent only a month with the children at Stanway; on 8 November they were taken to Clouds and spent nearly four weeks there because there was a shooting party at Stanway, and Mary was visiting Longleat, Studley and so on. When Mary did join them 'the little ones lived at Prospect House, Mr and Mrs Russell's, and were very comfy there and came over every day to Clouds. The little boys dined with us each day at 1.30 and the others came up later and often had tea'.[16]

But Mary was considered a devoted mother. She could not have looked after her children more without being thought definitely eccentric (it was odd enough to breast-feed them for six weeks). In 1891, as in 1890, Mary spent six months *in toto* away from her children, either being ill or staying in a house party or taking another cure at Bad Kissingen. Yet, despite her long absence over the summer, and the children's obvious good health and spirits, her first action upon arriving in Scotland was to dismiss the governess because her mother-in-law was of the opinion that 'she talks too much and is too nervous'. As was the pattern with all Elcho dismissals it was not a callous parting and there was much note-writing and self-explaining on both sides.

At the age of two-and-a-half Colin's talking remained 'unintelligible to the stranger, but Cynthia understands and can interpret every word . . . Cynthia was his little interpreter, she had taught him her own language (she speaks plainly now) and she best understood it. I understood nearly everything that he said, but if there was a doubt as to a word, she was unfailing.' Mary added, 'deeply must I always regret the many many hours of that short, short life I spent away from him'.[17]

At Clouds on Christmas Day 1892 'poor Cincie', now five and a quarter, was ill with scarlet fever; by the next day Colin was too. Mary was kept away from the children for fear of catching the infection and sat impotently at her writing table listening to people coming and going, fetching aconite to bring the temperature down, fetching the Shaftesbury doctor.

At ten they were to see the result of the sponging. We waited there, Mamma, I, Hugo, the others were then downstairs. Berta, the Messenger of Woe, came down with her poor dear sodden countenance. 'He is less well,' she said; poor dear, it was she who had to give these strokes. Silence for a few moments, I stiffened myself against the doorpost, scrunched my hands behind my back, swallowed down everything and said 'What?'

I remember all like a strange awful dream, after a point sensation ceases. 'He is in convulsions and his temperature has risen to 107.'[18]

Colin died on 27 December and was buried two days later. Mary's description of the funeral has a sparseness and directness quite different from the sentimentality more usual at this period. She was in agony but not out of control. Life went on much as usual with the children appearing to accept that Colin had been carried away by the Angels. During the quarantine period 'I went round and saw Cincie at her window, with her face like the full moon and pink and white, she writes many letters, works very hard and does 'crocussing' (crochet), sticks scraps etc and is in excellent spirits with ringing and robust voice.' In a letter to Hugo, Mary's true feelings were revealed: 'Guy and Ego are very interesting in their ways and Cynthia will, I'm sure, develop charm, I like her the least now but that is my fault'.[19]

Cynthia was immured in her room for the whole of January and when she was allowed out Colin was not much talked about. It was not as if he had never been, but there was a fierce awareness that life must go on and heads be held high. (The death of children was, sadly, an inherent part of Victorian family life.) 'She would miss her little companion cruelly *if one let her*' wrote Mary, at one point referring to Cincie turning her head away from her to prevent herself from crying and thereby getting very pink (this in a child of five). However, the need for bravery did not prevent Mary from recording Cynthia's muttered words to herself in bed: 'Oh, but my dear Colin I want you to play with me, I wish you would come to me, who shall I have to play with?'[20]

Mary's journal about the children ends with the death of Colin, which is in itself significant, as though something irreplaceable had departed with his death. It might seem odd that Colin was so especially mourned – there were, after all, Ego and Guy still safe and well – as well as Cynthia. But he had a character of particular sweetness, or so the adults appeared to think. On Boxing Day, during his illness, 'poor Nanah looked tearfully and said, "Oh, why is *he* the worst?" ' Mary recorded this remark in a quite matter-of-fact tone; and, when writing her reminiscences, Cynthia wrote that 'Nannie, who had never tried to conceal her preference for Colin, had not been very kind to me. One day

7

shortly after his death, just because I could not eat my pudding, she actually said, "God had taken the good one and left me the bad". The words seared my very soul'.[21]

This 'searing' had perhaps an edge of poetic licence: Cynthia might have been a little envious of her younger brother, and aware of her own deficiencies (visitors to the drawing-room always said 'what a lovely little *boy*!') but she seemed unquestioningly to have accepted Colin's superiority.

> Neither did I mind Nannie declaring Colin's to be the sweetest nature of any child she had ever brought up.
> Apart from his beauty – delicate as that of flowers and shells – which even had I not continually heard it exclaimed at, I am sure I should have perceived, Colin was a singularly loving quicksilver child, with an unforgettable gentleness and some quality that, for want of a better phrase, I suppose I should now call fineness of grain.[22]

Cynthia thought that her brother's death destroyed forever her sense of security ('no child had ever been more loved than Colin, yet it had not kept him safe') but it also, because of the glow with which the dead child came to be endowed, contributed to Cynthia's lifelong belief in the superiority of males. She already revered her elder brothers, but Colin could never be a disillusionment: his death ensured that his mattering most could not be questioned.

'I wanted to be like "The Big Boys", as they were always called, as tall, strong, swift and rough. Above all I wanted like them to be trousered. As the only girl, I was ashamed of the singularity of my attire. Besides, petticoats got terribly in my way.'[23] The boys were brought up quite differently: 'they came and went, had larger concerns of their own'. This was another reason for Cynthia's attachment to Colin: he was a boy and yet he and she had been treated exactly the same, nor was this paradise ever shattered, as would have happened eventually, by his departure for prep school.

····✣· Chapter 2 ·✣····
Hugo, Mary and Balfour

Her brothers, both elder and younger, were the ones that Cynthia was to venerate: certainly not her father, nor indeed her mother and sisters with whom she was on terms both affectionate and intimate, but never deferential. (After Colin's death Mary and Hugo were to have two daughters and one more son.) The boys were her models since Hugo had flaws too apparent to allow for respect – fear was a different matter. He was thirty when his third child Cynthia was born, five years older than his wife to whom he had been married for four years. Conventionally educated at Harrow and Balliol, and heir to his father the 10th Earl of Wemyss, he was a Tory Member of Parliament for most of the 1880s and 1890s. He always had a reputation as a wit but it is likely that this is because of the enthusiastic loyalty of his friends; undoubtedly Hugo was sarcastic, but this is not quite the same as being witty, relying more on an imperviousness to others' feelings, on a wish to shock, than on making people laugh or being perceptive.

For a child, sarcasm is a terrifying quality. One day something Cynthia said could provoke laughter, the next, 'though I had acted in precisely the same way, he might be completely unnoticing. His receiver would be off'.[1] She could not ignore this weather-vane behaviour and her longing to please him, the first adult male she knew, was to be another factor in her relationships with men. She was to *expect* them to be unpredictable and to have moods; and her long practice at smoothing away bad temper was

9

to be useful when it came to handling the mildly as well as the famously sullen.

Hugo was acknowledged by his friends as someone both amusing and unscrupulous. He was remembered by the House of Commons for his often repeated suggestion that it should adjourn on Derby Day. He did have charm and kindliness, but the camera would catch his sulks: and he had no objection to playing chess with his grandchildren and cheating in order to win. Blanche Dugdale remembered him enticing her to play back-gammon for money one Sunday while the others were at church and then awaiting with 'mischievous curiousity'[2] the wrath of Blanche's mother. And Laura Charteris, the present Laura, Duchess of Marlborough, has described him as encouraging her to

> think of everything as one huge roulette table. He spent many hours playing games of chance and skill and if I mastered them too well, he cheated to win. This cheating, no doubt inherited from the notorious Colonel [the seventeenth-century 'wicked' Colonel Charteris] came into force in *L'Attaque* where he would place me in front of a mirror so that he could spy on the identities of my men.[3]

Cynthia defended her father by referring to him as the only truly natural person she ever knew: whatever mood he happened to be in, he could not possibly dissimulate. This honesty was endearing, and it is true that Hugo's moodiness was caused by boredom so acute that it was almost an illness. His occupation, apart from being Lord Elcho, was waiting to be Lord Wemyss. Although born the fourth son, by 1873 he had become his father's heir, a situation which is notoriously unconducive to hard work. When she was seventeen and first saw *Peter Pan* Cynthia must have been reminded of her father by the character of Mr Darling who, when he could not tie his tie, 'became dangerously sarcastic'; when he collides with Nana, thereby covering his new braided trousers with hair, 'he had to bite his lip to prevent the tears coming' and when he ties Nana up outside 'he was ashamed of himself, and yet he did it. It was all owing to his too affectionate nature, which craved for admiration'.

Mr Darling, at least, 'was one of those deep ones who know about stocks and shares'.[4] Hugo, being highly intelligent, must also have known about them but, treating life as a huge roulette table, speculated rashly on the Stock Market. He was not that young when he did this, for it was in 1899 when he was forty-two that he lost £80,000 (£2,500,000) and he had already had

£12,000 (£350,000) advanced from his inheritance when he had first run up massive debts five years previously.[5] He was disinherited by his father and a trust fund was set up with Alfred Lyttelton, Maurice Yorke and Arthur Balfour as trustees (later Alfred's son Oliver replaced Balfour). The fund was a generous one of £100,000 (£3 million), paying Hugo a substantial annual income. Nevertheless financial discussion and economies were a feature of Cynthia's childhood: her parents and their friends had first begun to deplore the hedonism of 'the smart set' partly because they could not afford to own horses or throw extravagant parties; the simple virtues are cheaper.

There were also other reasons why they were preferable. Hugo and Mary did the same as their parents which was to stress family and home life, intelligent conversation, the pleasures of friendship. To appear to have too much money was vulgar – at Stanway or Gosford the carpets may have been valuable but they were worn ('only the middle classes have new carpets'). Possessions, both accumulated and inherited, were valued, but they mattered for their intrinsic beauty or sentimental value rather than their status or monetary value. This was self-evident to Angela Thirkell, who knew the Charteris family through her mother Margaret Mackail (née Burne-Jones) and wrote novels in which her characters bore a marked but flattering resemblance to some of its members. Mary was elderly when *Wild Strawberries* (1934) was written and had been dead for ten years when *Love Among the Ruins* (1948) appeared, but things could not have been very different thirty years earlier: the novels' descriptions of the Charteris, alias Leslie, family at Stanway caused enough fluster for us to be convinced of their accuracy.

On her [Lady Elcho, alias Lady Leslie's] bed were a breakfast tray, the large flat basket of letters, the small round basket with the green edge which contained unanswered correspondence, a large piece of embroidery, several books, another basket of combs and pins, and some newspapers. On the table by her side were a paint-box, a glass of water, and a white paper fan, which she was decorating with a dashing design of fishes and seaweed. The large bedroom was crammed to overflowing with family relics . . . Watts's beautiful head of Lady Emily soon after her marriage; hundreds of photographs, from studio portraits signed by crowned heads and great statesmen and the Leslie children at every stage to snap-shots of the third housemaid's wedding . . . a large bureau covered with letters and bills with corners of papers sticking out of every drawer, occasional tables covered with flowers, pencils, paints and stationery, a canary in a cage . . . Part of one wall was decorated with a romantic landscape

painted on the plaster, the fourpost bed was hung with her own
skilful embroidery, water-colour drawings in which a touch of genius
fought and worsted an entire want of technique hung on the walls
. . . in spite of the muddle such a triumphal sense of the fullness of
life, such a bringing together of time past and present, that the rash
beholder felt the spirit of the room even more than she saw its
untidiness.[6,7]

Mary Elcho was charming and unselfconscious. The worst thing
that could be said about her was that she was so interested in
everything and everybody that she had a quality defined by
Margot Asquith as 'maddeningly impartial'[8] – an all-embracing
kindness which annoyed those of a more censorious temperament. Cynthia was to be more critical of people but like her
mother could find qualities she admired in apparently unlikely
people, with the result that some of her friends considered her
other friends 'odd' and Cynthia to be 'curiously undiscrimi-
nating'.[9] Mary, being a product of a more rigid society, was forced
to be more selective socially but nevertheless tended to welcome
all comers. Many hours of Cynthia's girlhood were spent being
agreeable to visitors invited by Mary while even more hours were
spent 'arranging', namely organising activities to the best advantage of everyone. When Mary went to Whittingehame in Scotland
to stay with Balfour his niece Blanche Dugdale could never quite
believe 'the amount of arranging that went on about the simplest
things, such as who should be Uncle Arthur's partner at garden
golf, and who should go for a walk with whom'.[10] And Cynthia
was to describe the effort involved in 'coping':

Mamma never seemed to have her own house to herself, or to be
able to enjoy the immediate present unpreoccupied by plans for the
future . . . What with family, incessant village duties, visitors, neighbours and household, how seldom did she have a disengaged
hour . . . Kindness of heart, combined with total lack of system made
her utterly defenceless . . . Yet she had an intense enjoyment of planning for planning's sake and always wanted to know not only what
everyone in the house was doing just at that moment, but also what
they would be doing at every hour of the week.[11]

Cynthia suffered in childhood from her mother's 'general avail-
ability'; when she was in her fifties she wrote a novel about
someone whose nickname was 'Available' and was lightly
sarcastic about the effects of endemic unselfishness on others.
Mary *was* interested in her children, but she was just as much
interested in her numerous relations and in her friends, with the

result that she often gave so much to others that by the time she got round to her children she was quite exhausted. Yet she loved them dearly and proved understanding throughout their lives. If she had a flaw it was that she too often reacted sympathetically instead of thoughtfully (though herein lay much of her charm).

Nanny, Fräulein, the governess – they were the ones who were expected to be the child's bastions of rationality: and this was a good system if the child could also rely on its parents' unstinting love. So many upper-class children have described the magical memory of their mother gliding in, scented and rustling, to kiss them good night on her way 'downstairs' or out to dinner. This was not a mere good-night peck – it was almost an affirmation that Love was always there, if not in the foreground of life in the nursery wing, at least constant.

With Mary away so much during Cynthia's infancy she had little option but to believe in Love's Constancy. But why *was* she away so much? Partly because she believed that the maintenance of good health depended on cures. Partly because she saw little reason not to be – until, that is, the death of Colin and the events of 1895, after which she went away less. But mostly her absence was to do with her relationship with Hugo.

There was rarely any overt sign of discord, and loving letters were exchanged almost daily whenever they were away from each other. At Stanway there are hundreds of surviving letters between Mary and Hugo ('Migs' and 'Wigs') which are evidence of how much they were apart. His are formal but affectionate, hers are impetuous, rambling and loving, written in a very difficult hand-writing like zig-zag sewing machine stitches which criss-cross each other (in order to save paper). Sometimes Mary berated Hugo for *not* writing which shows how much she relied on his letters: 'I don't believe you would give up one little pleasure to write and I can't think why you do not write from the House of Commons where you have every convenience and it looks well to boot but I don't believe you have been *near* the House of Commons!'[12] she wrote sharply in the April before Cynthia was born.

Yet there is little doubt that if the Elcho marriage had been happy they would have spent far more of the year together at Stanway, together at country house parties or, in the season, in London. Hugo, being charming and easily bored, always had a mistress and had extended liaisons first with Charty Ribblesdale, later on with the Duchess of Leinster, whose last son, born in 1892, was known to be Hugo's, and finally, for over twenty years,

13

with Lady Angela Forbes. Mary, despite being warm and loyal, was forced early on in their marriage to turn elsewhere.

She would have preferred not to, since family affection was firmly part of her inheritance on both her Wyndham and her Campbell side. But aristocratic marriages in nineteenth-century England were not often inspired by love. Hugo was, after all, one day to inherit sixty thousand acres in Scotland and, before his hair started to thin, was very attractive, at least to women (it was Cynthia's future brother-in-law who was to call him 'one of the ugliest men in the Empire, though by no means the least witty, but that was after he went bald'[13]). Yet 'her mother pushed her into marrying Lord Elcho – so one used to be told at least'[14] a Wyndham relation wrote years later, and Mary herself told Wilfrid Blunt that 'her marriage with Hugo was her mother's doing – she would have been happier with Arthur [Balfour] who has a perfect belief in her and devotion to her.'[15]

Early on in their engagement Mary did make an attempt to break things off and wrote Hugo a letter beginning 'I have hour by hour become more forcibly, painfully and unmistakably convinced that when I accepted you a fortnight ago I did *not* rightly understand my own mind'.[16] But she had a change of heart and then, just before the wedding on 9 August 1883 ('we went to the church at three and were married' she wrote laconically in her diary) warned Hugo that she was an 'undisciplined creature' who was

> not used to being dictated to or *crowed* over. However patience! courage! the task though long is not altogether hopeless! difficulties and obstacles should but fire your ambition, for bright and glorious is the victory that comes after a hard fight! and I do not doubt but that protracted patience and judicial firmness and above all great circumspection of *action* will not fail to imbue me with a perfect respect for all your thoughts and deeds.[17]

Mary could not respect Hugo's gambling or his interest in other women or his unsociability, but she adapted quickly and perfected a 'highfaluting purely intellectual romantic mystic kind'[18] of relationship with other men, for example with 'Tommy' Lord Ribblesdale and with Harry Cust ('went through a lot of Mamma's letters including Harry Cust affair . . . I think I should destroy them'[19] noted Cynthia in 1938). In a letter to Hugo written the month before Cynthia was born Mary defined her philosophy: it is a rather neat summing-up of the courtly, asexual type of romantic love that Cynthia was to re-define and to adapt, as far as possible, to the twentieth century.

> Migs in practice (flirtation practice) dwells on the ambiguity of implications the possibility of a backdoor or loophole that Tommy considers the word to contain. Migs thinks it doesn't matter *what* she says in her letters to men conks, provided she only *implies* it she still thinks that she possesses a means of escape for if brought to book she can say that they have misunderstood her – and nice men conks never take one to task.[20]

There was a crisis in 1891 when Hugo admitted that Hermione Leinster was expecting his child (a son who, as Edward, 7th Duke of Leinster, was to have a scandalous reputation and early on to run up vast debts). And there was another crisis in 1895 when Mary became pregnant by Wilfrid Blunt (proof, if such were needed, that men conks could sometimes take one to task), yet Hugo and Mary were always, even when apart for months at a time, held together on terms of weary affection and concern.

The real love of Mary's life was the politician Arthur Balfour. They had met before her marriage when she was seventeen and he was thirty-one, and they continued to be friends. But he did not propose. In middle age Mary remembered their (chaperoned) visit on Valentine's Day to *Much Ado about Nothing*:

> Had there been beneficient mischief makers – match making plotters – in the case of one gentle girl and busy political 'boy' or had *she* been as audacious as Margot or Laura or many a maid then might you have been after all 'Benedict the *married man*'! but she was too proud and shy and wanted as much luring as Beatrice and he was too busy and captious and so the tale had another ending – or rather it isn't over yet . . . and though B is not a married man – and may still flout the matrimonial state yet I flatter myself that B is not absolutely *free*.[21]

But Balfour was to remain a lifelong bachelor; as H. G. Wells put it, 'he had it seemed no hot passions, but only interests and fine affections and indolences'.[22] Beatrice Webb was fiercer: 'For philanderer, refined and consummate, is "Prince Arthur", accustomed always to make others feel what he fails to feel himself. How many women has he inspired with a discontent for their life and life companion, haunted with the perpetual refrain, "If only it had been so?"'[23]

Balfour's 'detachment' became a by-word, and his effeteness was also commented on, though more discreetly. Cynthia's governess once wrote to Mary: 'Poor Mr Balfour! His health seems rather feminine'[24] and Walter Raleigh saw him at a June Friday-to-Monday watching a tennis game 'in wraps, lying under the low terrace wall'.[25] Possibly Balfour was impotent (though certainly not asexual). It was a possibility that must often have occurred to Cynthia as she wondered whether Balfour might really have been her father. And it cannot have been mere coincidence that one of the closest friendships of her life, that with J. M. Barrie, recreated the kind of intimate, loving, sexless relationship that has to result from a man's impotence.

Mary and Balfour loved each other, in their fashion, for forty-five years. Many have speculated what this fashion was. In the early 1960s Balfour's biographer took it for granted that their intimacy was sexual, causing great distress to Mary's three surviving children who denied his assumptions. Nevertheless their relationship was certainly physical to some degree: even though many letters have been destroyed and a few sentences in the surviving ones blacked out, enough remains to show that there was a form of sexual passion.

The affair began in mid-February 1886 when Mary had been married for nearly three years and had provided Hugo with an heir. She was expecting another baby in May. By the autumn of that year Balfour and Mary were very close (a letter of 20 November ends intimately if discreetly 'yours in haste Mary') and they often stayed in the same country houses. Mary's diary was always enigmatic but occasionally an entry is decorated with flowers, hearts with angels' wings and so on, signifying kisses and caresses.

Mary was to tell Blunt that relations between her and Balfour 'are not those of absolute lovers.'[26] But from her babyhood onwards he was part of Cynthia's life. Cynthia used to joke about the possibility of her being Balfour's daughter (her youngest son liked to think she was, her middle, surviving son, believes firmly that she was not) and both her novels feature illegitimacy. As a child she must have been aware that Mary and Balfour's relationship was not 'purely intellectual' and must sometimes have had a glimpse of letters like the following, written by Mary from a *Kurhaus* in Germany. (Her mother was far too vague to have been scrupulous about hiding all her letters and sometimes Cynthia accompanied her to Germany – though what she did while Mary took the waters is unclear.)

I do look *very pretty* in my bath, thousands of nestling bubbles that show off the modelling – breasts supported by water, of perfect shape with rosy tips! limbs of a ghostly whiteness – Really like a Venus or a Rhein maiden – Goodbye . . . Yesterday while reading George's Introduction I slipped into Venus and Adonis – my dear! *You* may consider yourself lucky – that's all I say!!! Write to me freely – I will destroy your letters.[27]

She did not, of course, destroy them all and hundreds still survive at Stanway, covering all the years of their relationship (with the unaccountable absence, that is, of the months in 1887 when Mary was pregnant with Cynthia). Some of the letters are suggestive ('Did I behave nicely to you yesterday in the brougham?'[28] inquired Mary) and some are more than suggestive. In August 1897 Balfour told Mary that while in Germany he had found the booksellers to have little but books on the manufacturing industry, a few French novels and 'manuals of instruction in Latin on the best way to become a wife without also becoming a mother! I bought one of these last as a curiosity – I hope you are not going to allow all the blood to be sucked out of you by that Vampire Balfour'[29] (six lines scratched out by Mary).

But all too often Mary did become both wife and mother. On 10 December 1886 she was 'ill and wretched' and had her monthly ritual of 'hot bath and bed'; from this gynaecological detail it is easy to deduce that Cynthia was conceived when the Elchos were at Clouds for Christmas. Balfour was there with them from 18–20 December and then went to Whittingehame until mid January, when he and Mary often met in London. Soon she began to feel unwell and during February was often on the sofa or in bed until lunchtime. She was not, however, idle and had begun to read philosophy (Sorley's *Ethics of Naturalism*) – presumably under Balfour's influence. Even during Ascot week in June, when Mary was six months pregnant, she and the Ribblesdales (Charty was five months pregnant) had 'ethical readings' with Ettie Grenfell and went punting on the Thames while Willie Grenfell talked to them about Aristotle. One of Mary's 'men conks' (Harry Cust) observed in a letter written to her just as the sofa-till-lunchtime ritual was being established: 'It's humanity's loss that people like you . . . shouldn't have had to work for your living . . . with all these faculties running to lettuce seed'.[30] No-one could accuse Mary of allowing her pregnancy to impinge on her normal activities.

Yet, unspokenly, everyone was well aware of her condition. In March Balfour went to Ireland as Chief Secretary and, aware that assassination was a possibility, gave his sister-in-law Frances a small locked despatch bag to be opened in the event of his death. This was not to occur for forty-three years when, in 1930, Frances and Mary cut open the bag and 'took out letter & brooch from where they had lain for 43 years quite unsuspected by *anyone* but the writer'.[31] The letter was as follows:

My dear Frances,
   I write this in a great hurry: but as you will only have to read it in the event of my death you will forgive my hand writing – I think you and all whom I love will be sorry that I am not to be any longer with you.
   But you will be able to talk it freely over with each other and all whom such an event may concern – There is however one who will not be in this position. I want you to give her *as from yourself* this little brooch which you will find herewith: and to tell her that, at the end, if I was able to think at all, I thought of her.
   If I was the means of introducing any unhappiness into her life I hope God will forgive me. I know *she* will –[32]

Balfour did introduce some unhappiness into Mary's life, and she did forgive him. But he also brought her the greatest possible joy. The unhappiness was caused by Mary's very natural feelings of jealousy, which she could not always suppress, and by the exhaustion caused by the constraints of her relationship with Balfour. She knew that in order to keep his attentions she had above all to be discreet – the political careers of Parnell and Dilke were destroyed at precisely this period, nor did she wish to jeopardise her and her children's domestic security. The catastrophic effect that the discovery of a Balfour bastard would have had on his career is the strongest reason why he and Mary would not have risked this possibility. Cynthia was very unlikely to have been Balfour's daughter – but she was never quite sure.

····✎· Chapter 3 ·✎····
Miss Jourdain, Egypt:
1895

Cynthia's first book was to be called *The Child at Home* and was about how to bring up children. Rather absurdly, it starts off by stating the vital necessity of choosing the right nanny. Caring for a baby is 'so exacting a task that it demands complete dedication' – and the full-time mother runs the risk of not being fit for much *after* the nursery stage.

> Constantly occupied and tired, how will you find the necessary leisure for self-equipment as a satisfactory companion to a son who has outgrown the nursery? Can you afford thus to specialize? Will it not be to risk partial atrophy of other faculties he will need in you when he is older?[1]

Ideally, the mother should be 'something to be grown up to, not out of, like the perambulator and the rocking-horse'. It is the nanny who must be left behind, the mother is someone who is to be stretched towards, an ideal which the little legs are struggling to reach. But the nanny becomes a thing of the past – like the Stanway nanny.

In her reminiscences Cynthia wrote about her own nanny rather little, but tells three of four short anecdotes (including the one about 'God has taken the good one and left me the bad') which makes it clear that she was not particularly fond of her. She was 'almighty, vigilantly protective, but by no means always kind'. She was not always in a good temper. Although she slept in a bed between Colin and Cynthia, a 'cosy happy sense' came from 'being alone with Colin, that gentle nestling little creature, so near to me that he was part of myself and yet was delicious "company", someone to cuddle and with whom I loved to talk and to giggle'. Nanny tended forcibly to feed her charges with milk puddings and when Cynthia, locked up until she had finished, once scraped the leftovers into the fireplace, the punishment was incarceration in a built-in clothes cupboard. Most poignantly, Nanny would come to fetch the children from their after-tea visits to Mary's boudoir and Cynthia would endure 'a little daily death'[2] as the nursery reclaimed her.

With Colin's death Cynthia's babyhood had come to an end and, simultaneously, Nanny's influence became less absolute. In the previous summer of 1892, Fräulein Matzke had been replaced by an English governess of twenty-seven, Miss Jourdain. It was partly Cynthia's understandable but suppressed grief for her brother that caused her affection for the new member of the household to become so intense and eventually, in her mother's eyes, extreme. But it was mostly the extraordinary and unusual nature of the governess.

Charlotte Jourdain was the third child of the impoverished vicar of Ashbourne in Derbyshire. All his ten children were clever and spirited, among them two became distinguished soldiers, one a clergyman and notable ornithologist and another, Philip, a brilliant mathematician. The eldest daughter Eleanor became Principal of St Hugh's College, Oxford and, with her friend Miss Moberly, co-authored *An Adventure* (1911), the story of their famous 'encounter' with Marie Antoinette and her *entourage* in the grounds of Versailles in 1901. Margaret became a furniture expert and, later, friend and companion of Ivy Compton-Burnett the novelist.

The Jourdains were self-contained, austere and academic. They rather cultivated the macabre and were thought 'queer' by local people. Charlotte's upbringing was fiercely anti-sentimental and stressed accuracy and truth over the woolly-edged and the fudged; hers was a family of painfully high ideals that never allowed itself to compromise by forgiveness, but instead favoured tight-lipped silence.

Charlotte had been the first on the list of students accepted by the newly-formed St Hugh's Hall which was under the Principalship of the Miss Moberly who was later to be Eleanor's friend. She went up to Oxford in 1886 when she was twenty; she was considered 'psychic' by her fellow students as had Eleanor been three years earlier. Charlotte has been described as 'a plain and

20

rather unobtrusive girl with none of her sister's forcefulness, easily forgotten by those who knew her'.[3] But by the Charteris children she was not easily forgotten.

Miss Jourdain was in Derbyshire for the autumn of 1893; Mary and the three children were abroad a good deal of the year, perhaps because Stanway and Clouds were too imbued with memories of Colin. But that Christmas, a year after Colin's death, the six-year old Cynthia's infancy was over and she was, as she put it, 'precipitated' from the nursery. This was (for the moment) empty and Cynthia started lessons in the schoolroom. Until then Nanny had 'learned me out of the antiquated primer *Reading without Tears*: we used to call it Tears without Reading'.[4] Now she began lessons with Miss Jourdain who at once started her on Latin. 'This filled me with pride for I thought Latin a boyish study and my great ambition was always to do whatever my brothers did.'[5]

But Cynthia was also proud of being taught and of being taken seriously. Miss Jourdain may have appeared strictly plain, with receding chin, pince-nez, prominent Adam's apple above starched, mannish collar – yet she had a great gift for teaching and a charismatic personality. The five years of her reign in the Stanway schoolroom were to affect Cynthia for the rest of her life.

There are no records of what Miss Jourdain taught Cynthia. Latin, certainly. But not modern languages ('her French accent was staunchly patriotic') nor fiction – it was left to Mary to inculcate Cynthia's lifelong passion for Dickens and to her aunt, Lady de Vesci, to introduce her to the Waverley novels, required reading in those days, especially for someone with Scots blood. As well as Latin, Miss Jourdain put maths, history, geography and grammar somewhere in the curriculum, but not very much of any of them.

Her main influence was undoubtedly spiritual. Religion played little part in Cynthia's adult life yet during the Miss Jourdain years it 'permeated the whole of life and every night, instead of a bedtime story, an informal confession was held, after which I would fall asleep with a lovely spiritually cleansed feeling and would awake to a sense of beatitude'.[6] *Pilgrim's Progress* was read again and again and Cynthia would picture herself as a fervent pilgrim with a large bundle of sins on her back – either tramping up the Hill of Difficulty or dragging her feet out of the Slough of Despond.

Miss Jourdain's longest-lasting effect was on Cynthia's character. She taught her to question and to explore and to pursue a train of thought, with the result that Cynthia firmly eschewed

21

the 'bird brain' that was characteristic of some women of her class
and upbringing. It is true that she was born with a high level of
intelligence, but during these years she learnt to use it and to
value clear thought. Yet, later on, the conflict between her intellectual inclinations and her position as a woman in society was
often to create a good deal of difficulty, suppressed (usually) and
therefore a cause of unacknowledged frustration. For Cynthia the
great joy of her schoolroom years was that she woke up each day
with a purpose.

In the summer of 1894 Mary and Hugo took Ego abroad with
them for five weeks, leaving Guy and Cynthia in the charge of
Miss Jourdain. But then, in December, Cynthia accompanied Ego,
Guy, Mary and Miss Jourdain to Egypt. It is unclear why Mary
took the children on a visit which she knew in advance, at least
subconsciously, was for more than purposes of tourism: presumably she viewed them as chaperones, easily manipulated cloaks
of respectability, while she must partly have been swayed by
Cynthia having been ill all November with whooping cough.
She may also have hoped that the trip would be an educational
experience for the children; but later in life Cynthia was never to
mention that she had been to Egypt when she was seven, not
even when she returned there in the 1930s with her husband,
youngest son and a friend.

Mary's reason for going to Egypt was Wilfrid Blunt. He was
her father Percy Wyndham's first cousin who often visited her
parents in Wiltshire and during the mid–1870s appears to have
had a long affair with her mother Madeline. The evidence for this
affair is his surviving diaries, and his memoirs, *Arms to Oblivion*.
They are at times hard to believe, but since in Mary Elcho's case
there is living proof of her affair with Blunt, and the course of
this affair is described in the same tone as Blunt's other affairs,
there are no grounds for believing one episode and disbelieving
another. Anyone who has seen, in the Fitzwilliam Museum,
Blunt's original pencil-scrawled diaries*, must find it hard to label
them either fantasy *or* truth (although a recent biographer of

---

*The Blunt papers in the Fitzwilliam consist of a) letters b) the unpub-
lished *Alms to Oblivion* series which goes up to 1883; this consists of
exercise books divided into chapters, they are a re-working of earlier
diaries which Blunt destroyed because he considered their style imma-
ture c) little lined marbled-covered exercise books written in pale purple
pencil d) big white vellum bound volumes called the *Secret Memoirs*
copied out in 1914–15 to Blunt's dictation from the little exercise books;
they have pencilled passages added by Blunt and are the basis for the

Margot Asquith is so sceptical that she blandly leaves out Blunt's rather charming description of his night at Glen with Margot). It is, nevertheless, rather hard to believe Blunt's account of his affair with Madeline since she and Percy were known to have had a very happy marriage: but her romantic and exotic ancestry endowed her with an unusually open-minded outlook on life.

Wilfrid Blunt was fascinated by the family from the moment when, in 1867, Percy first introduced him to his wife. He wrote about Madeline visiting Paris and being able to shake off some of the constrictions of English domestic life, and commented how rare it was for a married woman of thirty to venture out, even in the streets of London, without a maid, and that it was difficult 'for those who had serious love affairs to arrange matters to their liking without infinite trouble, risk and small vexations'.[8] In his cousinly view a trip to Paris was 'a licensed moment when opportunities occurred and opinion to a certain extent excused irregularities of conduct'.

Despite Blunt's hyperbolic language it is doubtful whether the affair was really consummated in 1867. But five years later he and Madeline were brought together by sharing a three-day vigil at the death-bed of Blunt's brother Francis. The next year their long-standing 'intimate relations' found 'their passionate fulfilment'.

> Of all the women I have loved, Madeline was the one who most appreciated my artistic side being herself an artist, and with whom aesthetically I was most in sympathy. It was my poetry she loved and the appeal I made to her aesthetic sense, a bodily and spiritual concordance she recognised in me as something apart from her domestic life, overpowering at certain moments while it took nothing from the love she habitually lavished on husband and on children.[9]

They felt no remorse or insistent longings when apart: 'This is perhaps that most worthy form of love, though short in its heroics of the love which causes pain'.[10]

During December 1873 Blunt stayed with Madeline and the children at Hyères in the South of France. Percy was not to arrive until Christmas Eve, and they stayed for a fortnight 'of love in

---

published *My Diaries* 1888–1914. They have letters and photographs stuck in and have been heavily 'edited' by Blunt. The 1895 period comes under category c), although Blunt had many changes of heart about it, first expurgating it, then using the original, then nearly destroying it, 'finally the original, after being cut out of the Secret Memoirs (d) was sewn together again'[7] as in c).

idleness under a blue sky', sketching, reading poetry and talking, 'the children shouting through the woods with her'. 'It was a merry Christmassing the children had. Mary was the eldest, a beautiful dark-eyed girl of ten' (actually she was eleven, George was then ten). A few months later, while spending a week with Madeline in the Lake District, Blunt expanded his description of Mary as being 'full of imagination, life and happiness, very beautiful with her great dark eyes and complexion of ivory, her hair cut straight across her forehead, a new fashion then, but otherwise rough as a colt and a scaramouch of a girl, carrying white rats in her pockets and scrambling with me everywhere among rocks'.[11]

This was the background to Mary Elcho's upbringing and it explains not just her own maternal attitudes but also her relationship with Blunt. She, like her mother, believed that love could be separated from domestic life and (presumably) from life with an established lover (Balfour). (She was, however, less lucky than her mother who apparently survived her affair with Blunt without conceiving a child.) At the time of the Hyères Christmas idyll the eleven-year old Mary cannot have been oblivious of the relationship between her mother and her lover – just as Cynthia, at the age of seven, cannot have been oblivious of what was going on between *her* mother and the same lover.

Blunt first noticed Mary as a woman rather than a frolicking child when she was fifteen and living at home at Wilbury, the house the Wyndhams leased before building Clouds. She is alleged, by him, to have blushed when he kissed her goodbye and to have told him later that she first fell in love with him on that occasion. In 1885 they used to ride together, then, in September 1887, when Mary was heavily pregnant with Cynthia, Blunt came to stay at Clouds. During that weekend he was rather more interested in Mary's very close relationship with Balfour than in Mary herself, wondering, as did so many others, about its exact nature.

The next year came Blunt's imprisonment in Ireland after he provoked his arrest at an illegal political meeting. His attitude to Balfour quickly changed since, being Irish Chief Secretary at the time, Balfour was now his political opponent. Blunt felt particular resentment that, on the day he returned to prison for a second stint, Balfour, Mary and George Wyndham arrived in Ireland to stay at the Secretary's Lodge. There can be no doubt that Blunt's feelings gave his eventual seduction of Mary an added *frisson*.

But there was no open ill-feeling and in August 1892 Blunt

Cynthia in 1915, drawn by Norah Brassey
(p.219).

Sylvia Llewelyn Davies c. 1900 photographed
by Barrie.

Cynthia and John in August 1913 when John
was two and a quarter: at Kingsgate where
Lawrence dubbed him 'the fat and smiling
John'.

Cynthia c. 1918 in her winged hat which at
first appeared in the McEvoy oil painting
(p.223).

Oil painting by Augustus John 1917 (p.223). 'He said my expression
"intrigued" him – certainly I think he has given me a very evil one – a sort of
listening look as though I were hearkening to bad advice.'

went to stay at Stanway, the only other visitor being Balfour. Mary and Balfour

> went off to sit together in the Monument summer house [the Pyramid] at the top of the hill nor came back till it was night fall. It is touching to see two people so happy . . . Hugo goes his own way cynically, idles on the lawn, talks to the children . . . It is certainly the strangest of ménages, for Mary and Hugo are not on bad terms, only all her love is openly for Arthur. The children are certainly Hugo's, for they resemble him, especially Guy, who is Arthur's godson. There is a new governess, a clergyman's daughter who has been living with a bishop and it is amusing to see how puzzled she is at it all . . . Mary is an agnostic like Arthur, but thinks that all old-fashioned prejudices should be encouraged. She is a dear creature with it all, large minded, unaffected, affectionate, sincere, and with a playful wit which makes all she does seem right.[12]

In 1893 Blunt again visited Mary. She spoke enviously of his life in Egypt, where he was an Arabist* and an explorer, and, it appears, promised to bring her children there to see him. Perhaps, in all innocence, she wanted a holiday; and perhaps part of her knew what she was doing. It was after all only a year after the birth of Hermione Leinster's son, when Mary had briefly thought about leaving Hugo; she had thought, too, about the ethics of adultery (*Anna Karenina* is *very* interesting – I wonder you never cut your pages'[13] Miss Jourdain wrote to her that summer). Then, in the summer of the following year, Blunt stayed at Stanway once more. 'By a sudden inspiration in the evening, when we were once more alone, I kissed Mary's hand. She turned pale, said nothing and went away to Arthur.'[14]

We know exactly what Cynthia looked like at this time, the winter of the trip to Egypt, because she was drawn by Burne-Jones. During the sitting an 'odiously gushing' woman came into the room 'and bleated out, "Oh, what a dear little damsel in white! But she *is* a Burne-Jones!" ' Cynthia, writing about this incident sixty years later, added:

> I still possess his lovely drawing, and I find it terribly touching. Indeed, I confess I can scarcely look at that little girl, all unconscious of her doom – such a podgy somnambulistic little girl with her curtains of straight hair, wide wavy mouth, and no nose to speak of – without my eye-lids pricking.[15]

*A word that would have had an erotic resonance for Mary ever since the publication a few years before of Sir Richard Burton's unexpurgated version of *Arabian Nights*.

Soon after the drawing was completed Mary and the children left for Egypt. It was a difficult journey since the sea was very rough throughout the ten-day voyage from Tilbury to Alexandria. Apart from sickness, the main event was Miss Jourdain demonstrating her psychic powers: one night, wrote Mary, she 'looked into the cabin where Cincie and I were asleep and saw a small grey figure leaning over my berth, which vanished as she looked at it'.[16]

They arrived at Blunt's desert house Sheyk Obeyd near Heliopolis, a few miles east of Cairo, on 4 January. Four days later, after they had kissed and talked, Blunt took Mary into the magical walled garden full of apricot trees (they were at their best in February) and gave her a love-sonnet written for her. He wrote in his diary:

> One reads in her a mystery, and not one of her woman friends I know has pretended to be her confidante. Her secrets are shut close and guarded with a little laugh of unconcern baffling the curious – in many ways she reminds me of her mother whom I also loved, it is now nearly 30 years ago. She has the same large-minded view of things, and when at last her reserve is broken the same sincerity. But her nature is a finer one, being without the worldly touch. She is an ideal woman for a life-long passion – and with the subtle extra charm for me of blood relationship.[17]

By the 14th Mary had surrendered. She had sent Miss Jourdain and the children donkey riding and was resting on her bed; a letter to Balfour was waiting on the bedside table to be taken to the post in Cairo. Blunt came with his poetry book but there was to be no reading aloud. The seduction is beautifully described – Mary's pale skin and dark eyes and the fact that she is the kind of woman who is even more beautiful in bed. 'She did not certainly intend it all though she let me kiss her where I would – and it was but after much supplication that I was allowed the sweeter privilege . . . I was with her for an hour and a half . . . Then the rest came in and I went away . . . distracted with my happiness.'[18]

One can only guess at what the 'rest' thought. That there must have been a heavily erotic atmosphere can hardly be doubted. Not only was Mary in the throes of a passionate sexual relationship, but it had its pagan aspects – she was Blunt's 'Oriental woman whose life is to be kissed and kiss' and she was his cousin ('How right the Arabs have been always to marry the daughters of their uncles'[19]). Moreover, as she soon accepted, he had been her mother's lover: on 25 January Mary 'asked me about my recollections of her mother and I think she suspects something of the truth, but I cannot tell her yet – though I do not think that she would mind if she knew all'.[20]

Soon Ego had to leave Egypt to return to his private school, and the rest of the party made an expedition into the desert. The children, 'in high delight', were on donkeys, Miss Jourdain, who 'turned out a good traveller', on a camel and Blunt and Mary on Arab mares. On 26 January the unfortunate Cincie 'fell off her donkey onto her head so rested with Miss Jourdain'.[21] She was still mourning the sister who had died two years before and was to write to Mary ten years later telling her that

I had rather a bad time in Egypt, & I suppose I was quite stunned. I never seemed to feel or realize *anything* except the one fact – Then one day when we had all been having tea together in the garden the post came in, and you and Mr Blunt went off to ride & you turned over your copy of Mr Balfour's book to me to look at. I had read all but the last chapter in proofs before, so I turned to the end & fell upon the page which sums up rather shortly what a vivid realization of Christianity does for people who have faith. I didn't feel as if I had got much myself just then, but I did feel that page had been written with faith & it was the first thing for weeks that I had realized or understood.[22]

Another, longer expedition took place in February, the tents being pitched in a different place each night but with Blunt strategically distanced in his carpet-shelter so that Mary could come to him. ('What if there had been one wakeful child?'[23] asked Blunt's biographer.) Not only was Mary 'now my true Bedouin wife' but the children too had gone somewhat native: according to Miss Jourdain they 'have become "demoralised" by their camel journey and are in a state almost of rebellion against her – they have caught up my words and will hear of nothing European'.[24]

Every post brought up from Cairo meant reminders of England, including a protestation from Balfour (replying to the letter from Mary that had been lying on the table on 14 January) that he rather did mind the idea of Blunt making 'a little love' to Mary. By the second week in February it seemed that Mary was pregnant. 'For me it is a pure gift from heaven' wrote Blunt. Mary, being more practical, tried to use the rather opportunely timed fact of a visit from Hugo to make the baby appear to be his. But Hugo's mind was on the dying Hermione at whose bedside in the Hotel des Iles Britanniques in Menton he had been and to whom he would immediately return. Since Mary and Hugo 'do not lie together – this for the last six years' it was rather unlikely that they would start to do so in these circumstances. Hugo tended to spend the days going off 'after the fashion of Englishmen to shoot something'. On 17 February Blunt recorded that 'again *nothing* has happened and I found her worried and perplexed what to do'. Blunt himself was rather perplexed by the meeting between Hugo and the children.

> They were playing near the house but when they saw him they hung back as though to hide. Anne called to him eagerly, 'don't you see the children' and he went to them but there was no demonstration on either side more than between strangers. He neither kissed them nor spoke a word. This is probably in part affectation with him for I have seen him nice with them at Stanway, but the servants standing round with their Eastern love for children and reverence for parental authority were terribly astonished.[25]

Mary decided to tell Hugo nothing until they met in Florence in April and he went off after ten days without having 'fulfilled his conjugal duty – a matter to her of trouble, to me of very great joy'. Mary told Blunt that she and Hugo had planned a reconciliation after the Duchess's death but now this would not be possible. Hugo wrote from Alexandria:

> My darling Migs,
>   I am wretched still and I don't like this desert expedition at all. It will give me more anxiety than it can possibly give you pleasure. I felt I had a lot to say to Migs – but I didn't say – perhaps I made her feel how I loved her – I have loved her all the time more than she knew and more than even perhaps I knew – perhaps it is not too late to show her even now – though I don't deserve that she should care for me at all . . . If you can find an excuse chuck the expedition.[26]

But the lovers had already set out on another idyllic journey. They left the children behind this time because they knew they were going into the extreme wilds of the Eastern Desert. It was a sensible decision – it *was* a difficult journey and Mary had begun to worry Blunt by feeling sick; nevertheless she was staunch, despite the slight thinness of provisions. They arrived back at Sheyk Obeyd very tired. There were a few more days of 'quiet happiness'. Then came a telegram from Hugo ('I am unhappy. Shall wait for you at Rome') 'so we think the Duchess must be dead', and indeed she had died on 20 March. Mary began to make plans for leaving. There was a last wonderful night in Room 31 of the Hotel Abbot at Alexandria and on 26 March she, the children and Miss Jourdain sailed for Italy. 'I think no lovers since the world began had ever a more perfect season of love.'

Mary was trying, and managed, to reach Stanway by Easter because *in absentia* she had been elected a parish councillor and wanted to attend the 16 April meeting. On Easter Saturday she confessed to Hugo; her diary entry for the Sunday reads merely 'sad day, better evening'. (All Mary's diaries are similarly bland and no-one would ever know, reading the 1895 volume, that there had been an upheaval in her life. She liked to write about arrangements rather than feelings.*)

Soon Mary was writing to Blunt to tell him that 'the end has come . . . you *did* try and wreck my life'. Hugo wrote too: 'You have wrecked the life and destroyed the happiness of a woman whom a spark of chivalry would have made you protect . . . She was a happy woman when she went to Egypt and her misery now would touch a heart of stone'.[28] (It is taken for granted that if Mary had not conceived no lives would have been wrecked and that Hugo's fathering of Hermione's last son was *quite* different.)

Mary had to promise not to see Blunt again, but they met on a train in the August before the baby was born and went on meeting at family occasions, for example on 20 June 1897 when Blunt formed a circle with Mary, Balfour and Burne-Jones at Madeline's birthday party. By the time Blunt returned from a winter in Egypt and first saw his nine-month old daughter, who was born in October 1895 and was called Mary, Mary Elcho was once more pregnant, she and Hugo having had their promised reconciliation. Within a year and a half of her return from Egypt Yvo had been born: the nursery at Stanway was full again and Cynthia was elder sister to both a sister and brother.

---

*From April 1878, when she was fifteen, until December 1888 Mary kept diaries in large black leather notebooks. She wrote only a few lines a day, largely a record of dinner parties, expeditions (shooting, skating), names of friends. In 1890 she went over to red leather volumes of page-a-day diaries of the kind that can still be bought at Smythsons in Bond Street. These she used until three days before she died in May 1937. Only the diaries for 1885 and 1889 are missing. Cynthia observed: 'The brief unintrospective diary, kept every single day of her life from the age of sixteen onwards, chronicled every other member of the family's doings as well as her own. This diary was for ever falling grievously into arrears – "Do tell me what you did between luncheon and tea the Monday before last, Cincie," she would plead. "*Can't* you remember?"'[27]

····> Chapter 4 <····
Madame de Genlis,
Fitzgeralds, Campbells,
Wyndhams

Just after she returned from Egypt Cynthia visited Oxford for the day. Miss Jourdain told Mary:

> Cincie walked through the Oxford streets like a pilgrim – she is a funny child. She didn't say much, but looked as if she was walking on holy ground. Guy didn't. On the way to London we were in the Carriage with one man – Cincie asked in a distinct voice if you could get a baby without being married![1]

Yet Cynthia was to claim as an adult that she had no idea at all of her sister's impending arrival until Miss Jourdain announced that she had a surprise for her. 'That, I assure you, was my very first intimation of an utterly changed home.'[2]

The concept of Innocence, as Childhood as a State of Being or, more accurately, a State of Grace, was central to Cynthia's outlook on life: it was to affect her retrospective attitude to her own upbringing, to adulthood and to her rather chequered relationship with her sons. As a child she behaved, and remembered herself behaving, as a child: not as a miniature adult, or as a naïve one, but as a creature inhabiting a different world. These worlds were never really united. Cynthia might be brought, brushed, into Mary's boudoir or the drawing-room, she might go to the desert for three months, yet in so doing she was meant to be instinctive not intuitive, quick to react not deep in understanding. It was by presupposing these qualities, and teaching her children to

30

presuppose them in themselves, that Mary could keep them oblivious of so much of what was going on around them.

There was a phrase of which grown-ups of the period were very fond: it was 'for your own good'. And the thing which was deemed most clearly for a child's own good was unawareness – or innocence depending on which way one looked at these things. If one thinks of the sayings of old-fashioned nannies they are all connected with keeping the child blinkered, innocent, until the climax of adulthood bursts upon them – 'all in due time', 'don't care was made to care' (you may not mind now but you will one day), 'jam yesterday, jam tomorrow, but never jam today' and so on.

It was this for-your-own-good over-protectiveness that caused so much trouble when the boy went to school or the girl 'came out'. They were meant, from one day to the next, to cast off all things childish and not only *be* adults but understand as adults. For some this rapid switch led to severe mental strain. To begin with 'she never doubted that with long dresses and piled-up hair, her whole personality would change, and the meaningless chaos of life reduce itself to some incomprehensible solution . . . Everything that she was taught at home impressed the theory that her "coming out" would usher in the realities of life.'[3] But for the unlucky few, gradually, the adjustment process proved itself too tortuous; they failed to shake off the schoolroom and turn, chameleon-like, into the equals of their elders.

Cynthia was luckier than some because she was often allowed to listen to adult conversation and thus acquired a superficial sophistication. Where she was unlucky was in Mary's image of The Child as something spawned by romantic legend, filtering through the Pre-Raphaelites and culminating in the chivalric imagery of late-Victorianism. It is not coincidental that one of the few surviving photographs of Cynthia as a child show her dressed up as a crusader. Thus boys were taught to be loyal to some kind of Arthurian ideal (Arthur Balfour was even nicknamed 'King Arthur') and the girls too were taught to admire Burne-Jones, *Morte d'Arthur* and romantic love. Wilfrid Blunt wrote of the kind of women he made love to, including Cynthia's mother and grandmother, that they were 'in a phase of poetic romance of the neo-pagan kind then beginning to be popular with our fine London ladies, whose Bible was Morris's *Earthly Paradise* and book of hours the Pre-Raphaelite art revival as preached by Rossetti'.[4]

Even if Cynthia's childhood proved difficult to grow out of it was, in retrospect, idyllic:

Unlike most girls, I was in no hurry to 'come out'. I knew I was well off as I was; guessed that in the different life awaiting me, though, of course, there would be much to enjoy, there would also be much that would irk me. You can't blame Barrie for this – I hadn't been to *Peter Pan* yet – but I assure you I never wanted to grow up. Poised tiptoe in the wings of the stage on to which they were so impatient to rush, other girls told me my present existence was merely the prelude to the Real Thing; but their eagerness failed to kindle mine.[5]

For four years Miss Jourdain's reign in the schoolroom was smooth, except for occasional small incidents (like once, for example, when she had returned to Derbyshire for a holiday, Mary and her mother-in-law allowed the children to slip into lax habits e.g. *asking* for pudding instead of fruit). But in the autumn of 1896, when Cynthia was nine, there were signs of real dissent. Miss Jourdain was staying with Cynthia in Ireland at the home of Hugo's sister Evelyn de Vesci. Mary was in London (she was awaiting the birth of Yvo) and deputed her sister-in-law to explain to Miss Jourdain how she felt. Evelyn must have shirked doing this in person, preferring instead to slip a letter under the bedroom door (quite a lot of the letters among the Stanway papers were written to be delivered surreptitiously by hand rather than posted). She had the unenviable task of trying to explain Mary's views on Cynthia's upbringing.

She feels that when very young she came out of the quite simple form of child's life and has developed a sort of ultra sensitiveness – almost self-consciousness – and I am *sure* that the feeling working in her mind is 'I should like Cynthia to have the chance of having a very *primitive* sort of nature in daily contact with her now – for a time – that a sort of vigorous animal spirits should have a chance of developing and the sensitiveness etc. fall into the background.'

In fact she dimly feels that, from you, too much thought, too much love – *too much* altogether is concentrated on the one child – given the tendencies of her own nature to extra sensitiveness etc and that your mind is unconsciously influencing her at this moment of her life more than should be – *because* she came so soon out of baby life – and has missed something out therefore – and been at once with you and with her.

It is torturing to her to think this – and to try and say it – for how can she say it without seeming to say that your influence is not good for her – and yet she loves you and everything about you – when she thinks of *you*.

When she thinks of the *Child there is no feeling*. 'I want her for a bit to have just a very primitive simple minded vigorous sheer physical animal spirits influence about her and I should like to combine that for a bit with some learning of foreign languages and music.'[6]

Miss Jourdain replied to this directly to Mary in London, a long and interesting letter (still at Stanway) which, however, reveals much more about Miss Jourdain's complex, intelligent and sensitive personality than it does about her charge. Things must have limped on for another year and then, in the February of 1898 when Cynthia was ten, she left. On the 3rd Mary noted in her diary that 'Cincie came to show me her stocking [that she was darning]. I told her Miss Jourdain was going away. She was very dear and gentle and brave'. Later she was weepy, and the next day Mary 'woke up at 6 to sound of sobs, held Cincie in my arms till 7.30'. On 6 February 'C rather pale and weepy all day', a state of affairs which continued for another week.

We can only guess at the real reasons for Miss Jourdain's dismissal. She seemed to have been making Cynthia too sensitive, and ignoring her 'animal spirits'. And there were minor tiffs, for example Hugo announced that he did not after all want her to dine with them but Mary avoided telling her herself and asked the butler to say 'your dinner is in the schoolroom, Miss', so that she was hurt.

Miss Jourdain's influence had not merely been intellectual; her reassuring presence had been like scaffolding ('she was so single-minded, her sense of direction so strong'[7]). Without her Cynthia felt 'rudderless – utterly adrift – lost' and undoubtedly the hours the two spent together in the schoolroom were among the happiest of Cynthia's life. As Mary had feared they fostered her academic leanings at the expense of her physical nature: although Cynthia rode and hunted until she was married, and played tennis, swam and rode a bicycle, she never did acquire the animal spirits that Mary would have liked. But this may have been less to do with physique than with her personality. When Margot Asquith criticised Cynthia for lack of vitality she meant a lack of aggressiveness as much as a physical liveliness – a quality that no amount of lacrosse, physical jerks or romping would have affected.

If Cynthia had not been given the chance to discover her intelligence, there would have been less conflict in her life. Mary must have had premonitions of future difficulties, for she was at one with her era in her belief that her sons should be educated and her daughters merely occupied, exercised, finished, brought out and married off suitably. Cynthia's view was that had [Miss Jourdain] stayed on until I grew up, I should, I think, for better for worse, for richer for poorer, have turned into something quite different, but she left when I was only ten and after her departure there was no follow-through, no continuity, no discernible system of any kind in my so-called education.[8]

Miss Jourdain possessed great strength of character and deep devotion to Cynthia. She herself was never clear why her five happy years at Stanway had had to come to an end. A year afterwards she wrote, 'I can't help feeling like a person who has lost nearly all their capital' and (untruthfully) 'I've quite given up trying to understand what happened, or why you did things or why I didn't see things then that I do now'.[9]

The Elchos never lost touch with Miss Jourdain and indeed, after she left, the friendship between Mary and Charlotte, as they had now become to each other, grew much closer. For a while she assisted at the Women's University Settlement in Blackfriars, then for two years was a governess in Marlborough. Some time around 1903 Charlotte joined the Community of the Epiphany in Truro and as one of the sisterhood spent three years in Tokyo in the 1920s.* She and Mary exchanged letters regularly, and she and Cynthia never forgot each other. Her influence had been so strong that the child she had brought into being never entirely vanished.

Miss Jourdain had nurtured one aspect of Cynthia's character. Mary, Hugo, Balfour, Cynthia's brothers and small sisters, and her friends nurtured another. But there was a third, equally important, which was her female Wyndham antecedents, of whom the most notorious was her great-great-great grandmother.

She is generally assumed to be Madame de Genlis (1746–1830), the mistress of Philippe Egalité, Duc d'Orléans, and the governess of his children (who included Louis-Phillippe, King of the French 1830–48). This assumption is controversial. For example, the biography of Edward and Pamela Fitzgerald written by Gerald Campbell in 1904 devotes a whole chapter to 'the question of parentage', and her most recent biographer, Gabriel de Broglie in 1985, is against the theory that the two daughters she adopted were in fact her own by Philippe Egalité. No-one will ever know for certain, and even her descendants had to question their exact

---

*Miss Moberly wrote: 'Though at the actual moment of its occurrence she was in the north of the island, on hearing of the tremendous earthquake she hurried back to Tokyo and took a full part in tending the wounded and dying'.[10]

relation to her: from Lady Campbell to Lady Edward Fitzgerald, 3 February 1831, 'Dear Mama, I suffered with thee, I knew how much thou wouldst feel the loss of Mme de Genlis, thy mother, in short, for was not that the tie?'[11]

Félicité Ducrest, later de Genlis, was born into an unconventional household and her childhood in some ways foreshadowed that of her descendants, for example she was encouraged to be tough and adventurous and to wear either boys' clothes or to run around without the constriction of hoop petticoats. Philippe Egalité met Félicité during a danced version of Proverbs, when the players mime a proverb for the audience to guess. (Word and acting games were also to be a great passion of their nineteenth- and twentieth-century descendants.) Their affair lasted twenty-five years; it brought great happiness to both of them, although it involved the constant deception of Philippe's wife, to whom Félicité was lady-in-waiting. It seems likely that in 1773 the first of their two daughters was born and sent to England; she returned to France seven years later, an 'orphan' who was to be a companion to the two royal princesses.

Inherent in the life of Madame de Genlis is the paradox that was to be part of the lives of some of her female descendants: the contrast between professed behaviour, the public reputation, and the secrecy and self-delusion that made a private life possible. Well-known in Europe as an educational theorist (she wrote over a hundred tracts, textbooks, plays and novels) she adopted a firm moral tone in her writing which was in severe contrast to her rather ambivalent position in the Orléans family. As Cynthia was to do, she revealed something of her true self in her novels which, as Violet Wyndham née Leverson (Cynthia's aunt by marriage) observed, 'frequently described the anguish of a mother obliged to be separated from an illegitimate daughter whose birth she wishes to conceal, in the most melodramatic language'.[12]

The little girl born during Madame de Genlis's absence from court life during 1773 was 'la belle Pamela' who, in 1792, married Lord Edward Fitzgerald, son of the Duchess of Leinster. They made a striking couple, the self-willed and temperamental Pamela and the sweet-natured Edward, who was loved and revered as a hero and patriot and who handed on to his descendants a deep love for family life and the eighteenth-century gift of letter-writing. ('Lord Edward Fitzgerald's letters are today as fresh as a rose. The gift has come down as well to this generation of the family' it was observed in 1917.[13]) But he only had six years of married life before he died in a Dublin prison in 1798, having been wounded when being arrested as leader of a revolutionary expedition. He left his wife with three young children; her life was not lonely: according to Violet Wyndham 'she was considered one of the most beautiful women of her day and her portrait was on sale in all the print shops of Hamburg'[14] where she lived.

Her daughter Pamela also married someone 'attractive and impecunious', a Scottish army officer called Sir Guy Campbell. She was a 'delightful, happy-go-lucky, unpractical creature' and was described by her friend Emily Eden as being 'full of Irish and English fun and misery, adventures and difficulties'.[15] She embroidered and made artificial flowers; a large portfolio of her water-colours, mostly of flower arrangements, survived at Clouds until the contents were sold in 1933.

Pamela Campbell had eleven children. Her seventh and youngest daughter was the Madeline who, in 1860, married Percy Wyndham, a younger son of the first Lord Leconfield. This was Cynthia's grandmother so much admired by Wilfrid Blunt, an unusual and interesting person who seemed to have taken all that was best out of her English, Scottish, Irish and French ancestry. She inherited her mother's artistic gifts and, being better off, could afford to use them in a more obvious way. The interior of Clouds was her masterpiece; she painted (and was painted, most famously by Watts in 1877) and did enamelwork. But fabrics, colour, flowers – these were her passions. This extract from a letter she wrote to her daughter Madeline, one of Mary Elcho's two sisters, is typical of her furious interest in house furnishings:

> I send you a bit of red which you can use anywhere in your sitting or bedroom – a *remnant*, and also two turkish embroidered squares for *anywhere* – tablecloths, or just to put over any of the red chairs, that stand near and swear with *the greens*! I send a bit of green silk, seven yards, and some thin flannel to line it with, to cover the *long seat* if you cannot use the cream damask. You will have to join the flannel. It is all I had. *It is safest* to make up one *big* tablecloth with the cream damask, big enough for the big table one width in middle half width on each side in case the green one *does not come in time* . . .[16]

And so on.

Madeline was reputed to be the first woman in London society who dared to bring foxgloves and marsh marigolds and bull rushes and boughs of oak into her house for its decoration during the London Season. And she would have one single beautiful bowl of flowers, of the same kind or the same colour, as the centrepiece on a table, rather than the multi-coloured profusion which was more usual in Victorian households. She was, in fact, charmingly unconventional, a home-loving and maternal woman whose affair with Blunt arose out of her loving nature, her passion for beauty and originality, but did not make her love Percy the less. Like all the other women in her family before and after she wanted to make both her husband and lover happy. She was unfaithful out of love of life not dissatisfaction with it. Yet, and unsurprisingly, it was not easy to distribute her *largesse* without sometimes feeling the strain. Blunt remembered their love as something frolicksome, extraneous to Madeline's marriage; she, meanwhile, wrote rather anguished notes: 'It must be after lunch do not come till 12 as I have things to do with Percy I think he is not happy at finding me not alone, he has not said it but I think it, my heart fails me but I will do it as I said, you have chosen to [illegible] oh it makes me so sad – I don't know why my heart is not up to it I have no courage'.[17]

Madeline and Percy had five children who were brought up in the unstuffy way one might expect. They were dressed quite differently from their contemporaries, being allowed to wear very simple clothes such as guernsey sweaters. They painted and drew and made things: their mother's

> useful hands had learned so many crafts, that wet days were brightened, and indisposed and resourceless children beguiled by her wealth of contrivance. A few yards of stuff, a few sheets of cardboard and gilt paper, a canvass hanging, a paint-box, a large brush and a pint of water, evolved the theatrical equipment of the Princess, the Ogre, and Belted Knight of the Fairy Tale. Her brain had contrived it all, her hands had fashioned it all, her spirit had revealed to them all that there were giants to be slain, enemies to be overcome, and castles to be defended.[18]

(The elaborate prose belongs to the biographer of Mary's brother George Wyndham.) There were Shakespeare performances, with the children's friends and relations being called upon to act: the Burne-Jones children, Philip and Margaret, often had parts, as did some of the Wyndhams' first cousins (they had fifty-eight). Madeline produced and painted scenery while the German governess, Fräulein Schneider, was her assistant and inspired character actress. 'Bun', as the governess was always called, had for a while been with another family in Belgrave Square and once 'confessed that she had then had strict orders not to let her charges play with "those wild Wyndham children" '.[19] She stayed with the Wyndhams from the 1870s until 1912, when she returned to Germany, and was such a close member of the family that Mary asked her to be one of Cynthia's godmothers.

Percy Wyndham was shy, tolerant and brave, with all the marks of a 'character'. His eccentricity extended to finding, early in life, a rather unusual pair of coat and trousers and sticking to their cut all his life. He was the best type of Victorian *pater familias* and it is quite unsurprising that he and Madeline should have had five such remarkable children: not only Mary, Madeline and Pamela ('The Three Graces' of Sargent's famous painting) but also Guy – and George, widely thought of as the most brilliant young Conservative since Balfour and so admired by his father that he 'would hold up his hand to silence any other talker who interrupted, or even one that he feared might be about to interrupt the flow of George's eloquence!'[20] George's memorial at Clouds describes him as 'Statesman, Orator, Man of Letters, Soldier'. 'Had Balfour been able to add the words, inappropriate to memorial inscription, "Sportsman, Wit, Handsome Charmer", he would have not only rounded off the description of George Wyndham, but at the same time defined the qualities of an ideal male Soul.'[21]

Chapter 5
The Souls, Squidge

It was not by chance that the label stuck when, in the summer of 1888, Lord Charles Beresford 'declared, amid laughter, "You all sit and talk about each other's souls, I shall call you the 'Souls' " '.[1]* Conversation about each other and each other's interests was what drew the Elchos' friends and relations together, for 'as a group they were particularly literate, self-consciously clever and endlessly self-admiring'.[3] The Gang (they preferred this word with its overtones of shared intimacy rather than organised, cliquey aloofness) had reacted against the hedonism of the Marlborough Set grouped around the Prince of Wales but it was a reaction of mutual affinity rather than deliberate exclusiveness. The fifty or so people who came to be known as the Souls ('It is true that *we* did not call ourselves "Souls" '[4]) had the good luck to have many friends in common. And it was these friends, 'personal relationships', they were primarily loyal to rather than hunting or cards or politics. They were also loyal to an ideal, one which was defined by Mrs Humphrey Ward as 'disinterestedness' because 'they were certainly no seekers after wealth, or courters of the great . . . It might be said, of course, that they had no

*People used to latch on to Beresford's sayings. Walter Raleigh met him at Hackwood in December 1907 and wrote of him to his wife: 'He's simply heavenly. He says he is 62, has one foot in the grave and the other going strong. But I must try to remember the things he says.'[2]

occasion; they had as much birth and wealth as anyone need want, among themselves. But that does not explain it. For push and greed are among the commonest faults of an aristocracy'.[5]

The core of the group were Wyndhams, Charterises, Tennants, Balfours, Lytteltons and Grenfells. Arthur Balfour and George Curzon were the stars. Almost all were in some way related, almost all were aristocratic, the Tennant sisters being the obvious exception. Most owned land; the Cowper, Brownlow, Pembroke, Windsor and Wemyss fortunes were among the largest based on land (rather than trade or manufacturing). Yet, although the Souls could afford to entertain each other from Saturday to Monday, to meet in London during the Season and so on, austerity was the keynote rather than lavishness: the newly-invented bicycle was taken up enthusiastically and was one reason the women kept their figures (another was their puritan attitude to food which was often frugal and inedible). Souls' houses tended to be cold, the furnishings based on sparseness rather than clutter, on a few good (if rather tattered) pieces rather than the kind of profusion that is considered typically Victorian – the chenille tablecloths, heavily curtained windows, tassled bell-pulls, tables with orna-ments and thick carpeting.

It was the same with clothes: one of the reasons that Mary Elcho or Ettie Grenfell tended to the floating or the draped was that visits to couturiers were not part of their life and they would rather re-make or disguise with shawls before resorting to a little dressmaker. In *Wild Strawberries* Angela Thirkell described Mary/ Lady Emily 'wrapped in two large Shetland shawls, her head swathed in folds of soft cashmere pinned with diamond brooches',[6] while Blanche Dugdale's mother would go around Whittingehame after every one had gone on Monday morning and her two refrains would be 'Here is Mary Elcho's bag, forgotten as usual' or 'This must be Ettie's veil; why must these women trail these things about with them?'[7] Pre-Raphaelite painting was the inspiration for this trailing look while the Arts and Crafts Movement influenced the simple, unfussy interior style.

The friends grouped around Hugo and Mary were unconven-tional and clever, some more than others: Ettie would spend the long winter afternoons at Taplow reading and making notes on what she read and, having an excellent memory, could make use of what she learnt. Walter Raleigh mentioned her to his wife and said: 'We talked about most things. She knew all my books quite well – having read them from real interest, no bunkum. Indeed if you mentioned any poem, she could quote it mostly.'[8] Yet by other standards the Souls were philistines, even though they tried to appear cerebral and artistic and some of them were (most of them wrote a book at some stage in their lives). For they were not intellectual – theirs was a cleverness of wit and liveliness rather than depth, despite their reputation for deep discussions about the meaning of life even before the soup course was removed. Nor did they approve of overt serious mindedness. Non-Souls were often disconcerted by their habit of taking serious subjects lightly and light ones seriously. It was this tendency to flippancy, when the normal attitude was one of *gravitas*, that was to be part of Cynthia's character and was to cause her to be so misunderstood. And since her Charteris inheritance had also bequeathed her a rather unusual sense of humour, defined by Mary as one which 'swallows up feelings', she was to cause quite a lot of hurt feelings in her lifetime, always quite unintentionally.

The Souls were famous as conversationalists. Their talk was 'good' and rarely dull. Cynthia heard it and joined in; she grew up with very high expectations of conversation and of social life, and of the former in particular. In her reminiscences she answered the question 'What did we talk about?'

> We debated the rights and wrongs of blood sports, votes for women, monogamy, vivisection, bull-fights and censorship; we argued over vaccination, divorce-law reform, and euthanasia; we questioned whether the Man made the Century, or the Century made the Man, whether suicide was justifiable, Free Love to be advocated, Vegetarianism feasible; we discussed endlessly and inconclusively the Problem of Evil, the Omnipotence of God, the Immortality of the Soul, and Free Will; we compared Queen Elizabeth with Mary, Queen of Scots, Charles the First with Cromwell, Dickens with Thackeray, Keats with Shelley; we tried to define the distinction between Genius and Talent, Happiness and Pleasure, Intellect and Intelligence, Beauty and Prettiness; we asked one another where good manners left off, and insincerity began; whether we would choose to be widely popular or caviare to the general, whether we believed in Love at First Sight, Affinities, and Table-Turning; whether, if we could, we would abolish pain. And of course, over and over again, we tried to decide which six friends, six books and six pictures we would take to a desert island.[9]

The adults Cynthia knew did not generally care what 'people' thought. They preferred to be understated and 'had the aristocratic grandeur associated with reserve and refinement rather than with exuberance and display'.[10] But they cared about each other: they minded about making each other laugh and about making each other think. They preferred love and friendship to

41

scoring points. They conducted their affairs with sentiment and secrecy, yet felt that life was incomplete without love.

Because the Souls never officially formed themselves, they never officially fell apart as a group. Margot Asquith asserted that it was the death of her sister Laura in 1886 that drew her friends together, since they were so closely united by grief at her death. Mary Elcho considered that an occasion at Stanway in 1884 was the first real Souls gathering. In any case, by the middle of the 1890s, some of the Souls – those who were not related by blood or marriage – had begun to drift away. When Cynthia was adolescent she was more aware that her parents had *been* Souls than that they were still. Yet their everyday friendships did not change very much, so that the children of the Souls still felt that their parents were a cohesive enough group for *them* to feel a group.

'The Corrupt Coterie', as they called themselves rather cynically, began to form their friendships a few years after the turn of the century, though they had of course always met at children's occasions at houses such as Stanway, Taplow and Mells. Later on there were seven marriages between children of Souls' families – Percy Wyndham to Diana Lister, John Manners to Kakoo Tennant, Raymond Asquith to Katharine Horner, Guy Charteris to Frances Tennant, Bibs Charteris to Ivor Windsor, Ego Charteris to Letty Manners and Cynthia to Beb Asquith.

Raymond was the shining star of the Coterie, as Balfour was of the Souls. Yet, despite her admiration of Raymond, and her close friendship with others of the Coterie, Cynthia never felt quite at ease with any of them, being innately less frivolous and less flamboyant, as well as more conventional, than someone like Diana Manners. 'Fun is impossible with her but short of that she is perfect'[11] was Patrick Shaw Stewart's verdict on Cynthia, and she herself wrote:

> I'm sure there is an insidiously corruptive poison in their minds – brilliantly distilled by their inspiration, Raymond. I don't care a damn about their morals and manners, but I do think – what for want of a better word – I call their anti-cant is really suicidal to happiness. I am much more in sympathy with the elder generation – what one might call Ettyism – which is an object of ridicule to them.[12]

The Souls handed on mannerisms and assumptions to the Coterie, and, notoriously, a common language and a great fondness for games. 'Esoteric vocabularies were an occasional feature of upper class family life in Victorian England. The Gladstones and Lytteltons had a dictionary full of terms from their Glynne relations, and Burne-Jones shared a pool of phrases with the Wyndhams and the Grahams. The Ponsonby family had "a little language of its own" and the Souls developed their jargon from a mixture of these sources.'[13] There was a vocabulary of about two dozen words still in everyday use by the time Cynthia could take part in adult conversation. These included a 'dentist' (a tête-à-tête), a 'floater' (a gaffe), 'Heygate' (dull and conventional, what nowadays one might call, glibly, 'suburban'), 'spangle' and 'culte' (a romantic crush), 'relevage' (gossipy conservation), 'tigsy' (neat) 'spike' (insult) and so on.

Some words actually filled a gap in the language, for example 'dewdrop' which is not exactly a compliment because, for the Souls, the word had overtones of froth, early morning, unreality, and evanescence. When people gave Cynthia dewdrops, they were not dishonest but pleasurably exaggerated, and both parties realised this. In poetry, and early seventeenth-century poetry in particular, a dewdrop was a 'conceit', and indeed the word has a useful ambiguity. If Cynthia had collected conceits rather than the cloyingly-named dewdrops she would not so frequently have been accused of vanity.

Souls' games were to feature very large in Cynthia's life, some gaining, some waning in popularity. Some were a standard part of country house life, for example the 'Letter Game' which was a precursor of 'Scrabble'. 'Clumps', a forerunner of Twenty Questions, was popular in Cynthia's girlhood but was obviously on the wane by 1915 when she wrote in her diary: 'After dinner we played clumps for a little – it felt agreeably reactionary'.[14] Things to be guessed were often concepts – 'the eleventh hour', 'a lost cause', 'an interval' or 'the last golf ball Mr Arthur drove into a bunker'. 'Gibbets' was also very popular when Cynthia was young: 'we played it for hours on end, in and, many thought, out of season – even sometimes, to the general disapproval, in the bathroom. We even had special little gibbeting books made with our names and a little gallows printed on them.'[15] It was a version of 'Hangman' in which each player has a quotation to guess with six lives to do it in. This game also waned for a while, with Cynthia recording in 1916: 'We did gibbets after dinner. I *am* enjoying their revival. I can't think why I allowed them so long a slumber. About ten years ago the 'gibbeting' phase was the most marked of my life'.[16] She found she was 'still pretty good and went to bed un-hung'.

'Analogies' was a famous Souls game. Cynthia described it as 'guessing the person thought of by asking what flower – animal – musical instrument – shop – landscape – architecture, etc etc, they were like.'[17] In 'Styles' players were given a time limit to produce a piece of prose or poem in the style of, for example, Carlyle or Blake. 'Authorship' was a variation described by Cynthia in her diary in 1918:

> Played the game of inventing titles of books people might have written – the idea being to give the most anomalous, the one it would be most surprising to hear they had produced. *Aunt Tina's Bible Stories for Tiny Tots* was given to Papa; *Three Girls and a Horse* to Mr Balfour, and I gave Mamma *Who to Know and Where to Go*. Everyone denied the appropriateness of the one chosen for them – Mamma was quite piqued by someone giving her *Talks about Chaps*.[18]

Finally there were the games based on acting, not just charades but 'improvisations', when some imaginary drama was acted out; and there was its variant, 'breaking the news', which was to be one of Cynthia's favourite games when she was older. Margot Asquith described it in her *Autobiography*:

> It consisted of two people acting together and conveying to their audience various ways in which they would receive the news of the sudden death of a friend or a relation and was considered extraordinarily funny; it would never have amused any of the (older) Souls. The modern habit of pursuing, detecting and exposing what was ridiculous in simple people and the unkind and irreverent manner in which slips were made material for epigram were unbearable to me.[19]

In fact death was only one of the subjects on which 'breaking the news' was usually based. A favourite was telling someone that they were expecting a baby ('oh, I love babies') or that their engagement must be broken off because of halitosis ('oh, I adore raw onions'); the person receiving the news had to avoid accepting the truth for as long as possible.

The influence of the Souls was the headiest of Cynthia's youth. Nevertheless, the child created by Miss Jourdain never entirely vanished. Tending to the serious-minded, the ten-year old to whom Miss Jourdain said goodbye in the February of 1898 might have struck one as rather solemn, over-sensitive and dutiful. Her sense of responsibility was never to leave her and there was certainly little obvious trace of the 'wild' Fitzgerald ancestry or the Campbell high spirits. Yet if Cynthia had been sent to school (unthinkable until the 1920s) she would have worked intently. In a sense, it was a pity that her gifts were more verbal than artistic since there was far more scope for an Edwardian girl in terms of drawing, painting or embroidery than literature. Had her written skills been highly imaginative, she could have spent time 'scribbling'; but they were critical and analytical, and bound to be frustrated. So here was a child bright but deferential, eager to please but strong-willed, becoming, as adolescence approached, rather watchful and self-contained. Even at ten there was apparent that mix which was to be a characteristic part of Cynthia's temperament – the elusive, inward-looking combined with the lively and giving.

Cynthia was secure in the atmosphere of Stanway, doing the things one might expect, at times staid (darning stockings and reading aloud with Mary), at others noisy (William Rothenstein remembered her and Mrs Pat Campbell's daughter Stella as 'a lovely pair of children [who] ran wild together like hares on the mountains when they were not making sticky toffee in the playroom barn'[20]). Hers was a country house life that has virtually disappeared.

Mary was always the hub of Stanway life, especially after the birth of her younger children when she stopped going away so much. In January 1900 she wrote to Balfour describing a dance (held, presumably, in celebration of the new century):

> On Tuesday we had a wonderful school feast and last night *the* most *glorious* Tenants and Servants Ball that has *ever been*! You *never saw* people look *so* happy – or dance with so much spirit. It was *really* beautiful. The drawing room quite splendid, empty of furniture and decorated with wreaths and fairy lights – a rubber of whist in my sitting room . . . the darling farmers smoking all Hugo's cigars in the hall over a blazing fire and looking *utterly pleased*, billiards in the next room – supper in the dining room – I carved turkey till all was blue – a most cosy tea and coffee arrangement in the still room – all the servants looking beaming – Smithkins perspiring and dancing madly – bakers gardners farmers keepers clergymen, doctor, stablemen all mixed up and quite happy and I in my best gown and all my jewels – the children flying round. It really was *beautiful*. It was kept up from seven till past one. Hugo went to bed not so very early – and he behaved *very well* . . . The people here seem so full of character and identity. I think it is being so far from the station – the spirit is just what it was 100 years ago – and one feels one knows them all so well, now that we've known them 16 years and they've been here for 100s of years . . .[21]

The particular Cincie brought into being by Miss Jourdain, the one who accepted the 'complete cleavage between . . . the Body –

the vile Body – and the Soul'[22] and other such stirring metaphysical concepts, now vanished under the etiolating effect of the
new governess. She was Austrian, called Miss Fräulein by the
household and Squidge by Cynthia. For the next three years, until
her sister Mary moved from the nursery into the schoolroom,
Cynthia was the only pupil, and the two of the them spent many,
many hours cooped up together in the schoolroom overlooking
'the pear-tree clad backyard into which at all hours clattered the
carts of the baker, the butcher, the grocer, and the milkman'[23]
(the latter bringing the milk for the feverishly awaited elevenses
of milk and biscuits).

Sadly, the teaching Cynthia received during these years was
almost directionless. Squidge was amiable but 'bird-witted', being
quite happy to teach entirely by rote; she had a heart but no
mind. Dates were memorised, as were strings of towns, rivers,
imports and exports. Learning poetry by heart was encouraged,
thus paving the way for a ritual which Cynthia returned to in
adult life. But as for an 'overall view', a theoretical approach to
education, or anything even approaching the metaphysical, there
was none, with the result that apart from the factual knowledge
that Cynthia's excellent brain managed to hold on to, she learned
nothing.

She did, it is true, grow familiar with, 'gabbled through', the
classic works of Racine, Corneille and Goethe. By the time she
was sixteen she was fluent enough in French and German for this
to be useful later on and 'I do at least owe her the not inconsider-
able debt of having been allowed to read the whole of Shakespeare – not even *Titus Andronicus* was left out – during lesson
hours'.[24] Yet the irony of Cynthia's development as a 'free weed
instead of a wired flower'[25] is that whereas Mary would fret about
her children when they were tiny and look forward to their
coming out or leaving Eton, where her daughters were concerned
she gave rather little thought to the years in between. Cynthia,
and her sisters were supposed to be contentedly aimless,
sponging up a little knowledge and waiting, bud-like, to unfurl.

'All the valuable part of my education was out of school hours'[26]
was Cynthia's verdict. She was kept busy enough, but there was
none of the competitive element she would have enjoyed so
much, no sense of achievement, no goal; 'for a girl to go to a
university was a deviation from the normal almost as wide as
taking the veil, or, by a stride in the other direction, going on the
stage'.[27] It was axiomatic that to educate the female beyond a
certain point was to damage her marriage chances: when Cynthia
was allowed to have some Ancient Greek lessons in the autumn

of 1905 Mary made the condition that no-one was to know about them. Thus her proper education, her knowledge of the world and her insight into the culture in which she was brought up, was acquired 'downstairs' at Stanway or on visits to other houses.

·····➤· Chapter 6 ·◄·····
Gosford, Lord Weymss, Dresden: 1903

Compared with Stanway, the house seemed so bleak – so without atmosphere, like a handsome person without charm. The rooms were airless and except with the aid of a long hooked pole, it was impossible to open or shut any of the heavy windows. Out of doors I missed the mossy drowsiness, the green leafiness of Stanway with its great over-spreading beeches. Here, dwarfed and twisted, the trees were cut by the wind as though by a razor.[1]

This was Gosford, the house that Cynthia used to visit most often apart from Stanway and Clouds. It was the home of Hugo's father and Cynthia, once she was six and emerged from babyhood, usually went there every September.

Gosford is a very large house a few miles east of Edinburgh. It had, and still has, a rather lowering feel, inducing what the family called 'Gosforditis', an indefinable sense of homesickness, not for anything specific, but for a sense of homeliness which was there so lacking with the huge drawing-rooms, the marble hall and staircase, an imposing Roman eagle on a pedestal and the fierce winds that swept in from the Firth of Forth. The house had originally been built to the design of Robert Adam. Then, in the late 1880s, there was a major enlargement and remodelling. After 1914, when Hugo inherited it upon the death of his father, it was lived in spasmodically by him and his mistress, Lady Angela Forbes; for a while they tried to run it as a hotel. In 1939 it was requisitioned by the army and during the war there was a fire which left the east wing roofless and the middle partly uninhabitable. Today the west wing is lived in during the warmer months. But there is quite enough of Gosford left for the visitor to be able to grasp how vast it must have seemed to a child of six – and how inhospitable.

Cynthia's grandfather was welcoming but imposing.

> Lord Wemyss was extremely deaf. His Dundreary whiskers almost met under his chin; he surveyed the world with a singularly piercing glance, over the high bridge of his aquiline nose. Opposite him sat Lady Wemyss in glacial silence. Their eldest daughter, Lady de Vesci, sat on her father's right, looking like a beautiful queen of tragedy, saying nothing.[2]

Anne, Hugo's mother, was indeed rather glacial, and was described by Mrs Humphrey Ward as upright, rather alarming, always dressed in black, deeply religious and very moral.[3] She was also famous for her passion for equality – what kind of equality is unclear for her life did not appear to proceed on especially democratic lines. When she died in 1896 Lord Wemyss, by then over eighty, caused a family fluster when he married a woman called Grace Blackburn who was much younger than himself and rather pretty.

Lord Wemyss was founder of the Volunteer movement and the Liberty and Property Defence League and the inventor of the Elcho boot, the Elcho bayonet and the Elcho military shovel. He never held high political office because his temperament was too independent but he was active in the House of Lords for over seventy years. He collected paintings, and ignored all attempts by the art-historian Berenson to convince him that his Botticelli and Mantegna should merely be 'attributed to' these artists. He sculpted, hunted, took a great interest in military matters. His son Evan observed that

> he had many more convictions than opinions, and these seemed to keep him eternally young. He held them in the face of all argument and opposition, and as the result not so much of reason and thought as of temperament and tradition. If he ever had doubts he never showed them, if he saw any force in his opponent's arguments he never admitted it.[4]

He was notoriously abstemious: 'gambling filled him with horror, and, as if by a malicious irony, fate developed in his sons a vicious tendency to harass him in this respect.'[5] He wrote his memoirs, which got as far as being printed but were never published. They

49

seem on the one hand to have been too opinionated ('He seems to start from the firm vantage ground that everyone is wrong except himself and that what happened to him, in his youth, is the only way'[6]) and on the other too gossipy. The Earl of Crawford wrote in his diary, having presumably had a glimpse of them:

> I confess I should regret any publicity being given to Lord Wemyss's recollections. Their style is too colloquial, the anecdotes though capital much too frequent, while there is a strain of personalities running through all the volumes which would not give pleasure. Moreover these pages – and there must be 300 or more – fail to represent the charm, the dignity, the independence, and above all the great courage of the old gentleman. Moreover there is no attempt at systematic record of his considerable activities . . .[7]

Although she had such a plethora of relations, Cynthia saw some much more often than others. She did not stay very often with either of her Wyndham aunts Madeline and Pamela or with her Charteris aunts Lilian and Hilda; but she stayed frequently with her other Charteris aunt Evelyn de Vesci (after whom she was named). Evelyn's home Abbeyleix in Ireland was almost as familiar to her as Clouds and Gosford, and more welcoming than the latter. Evelyn, whose marriage had been childless for seventeen years, eventually had a daughter named Mary who, although eighteen months younger than Cynthia, became her closest friend. Mary came to Stanway, Cynthia went to Abbeyleix, and their shared childhood experiences ensured a loyalty which lasted well into adulthood; then, with the premature death of her husband Aubrey Herbert, Mary embraced Catholicism and the countryside just at the time when Cynthia was becoming more urban and more cynical – and the two women grew apart.

In many ways Mary Vesey had always been Cynthia's opposite. Although adored by her family, and especially her mother, she remained quite unspoilt and was never interested in her own beauty; whereas Cynthia minded above all about her looks and spent a lot of time worrying about whether she was or was not 'in good face'. When Mary became eccentric in that way which suits Englishwomen so admirably (tweed skirts, freezing houses, a passion for gardening) Cynthia deplored all these characteristics and was worried by Mary's painful shabbiness.

In her adolescent years, however, Mary conformed, although her dark, strong-charactered looks (she was not unlike Vita Sackville-West in appearance) were always to set her apart from her contemporaries. She and Cynthia encouraged each other's latent serious-mindedness; one can imagine them at Oxford together had they been born a few decades later and had they been able to persuade their families to send them. During her visits to Abbeyleix, Cynthia shared English teaching with Mary's governess and very much enjoyed her cousin's companionship and rivalry.

There were more friends during the London season (May, June and July) for it was the custom for girls like Cynthia to exploit the fact of their being in London (Mary and Hugo opened up their house at 62 Cadogan Square just for this period, keeping it shut up the rest of the year) in order to be taught subjects which were outside the scope of a country schoolroom. Various memoir-writers remember perching stiffly round a long table at Miss Wolff's, Monsieur Roche's or the Duchess of Sutherland's, with the governesses and nannies sitting round the walls – as at dancing class – and the girls trying to answer questions correctly to save their own teacher losing face. (Joan Poynder, a younger friend of Cynthia's, remembers the Duchess setting essays and the governess writing them for Joan to copy out.)

Cynthia attended French and Italian classes and also, when she was a teenager but not yet 'out', went to McPherson's Gymnasium in Sloane Street twice a week. 'Exhilaratingly clad in blue serge tunic, a belt fastened with metal clips shaped like a snake, knickers and rubber-soled shoes, we marched, wielded Indian clubs, brandished dumb-bells, swung on parallel-bars, and vaulted over a contraption called the "Horse".'[8] She went, too, to Mrs Wordsworth's at the Portman Rooms in Baker Street for dancing; she was a terrifying woman who was large and domi-neering and whose black-satin bosom was never forgotten by those she taught. It seems an irony that it was to this tartar that the upper classes gave the important task of teaching their daughters how to behave in the ballroom – and what, when it came down to it, was 'behaving' if not man-trapping, a skill which was imparted by a bawling haridan and not, for some reason, by a gentle beauty?

When she was fourteen, Mary decided that Cynthia should experience the atmosphere of a girls' school. She consulted Balfour as to which subjects he thought appropriate (he advised French Literature) and sent her once a week to Cheltenham Ladies' College which had been founded twenty-five years previously by Miss Buss and Miss Beale. Cynthia made the twelve-mile journey in a tiller-steered De Dion Bouton: this was probably Balfour's car, since the Elchos did not own one, and was driven by Mills, Balfour's notorious chauffeur. It broke down a good deal and

51

needed the rope-pulling power of Mills and two helpers to re-start it; meanwhile Cynthia and Squidge sat in state in the back.

During the Spring term of 1902 Cynthia learnt physiography (a mixture of science and geography), history and drawing, drop-ping the first subject for the half of the Summer term that was allowed her before she went with the 'babies' to Abbeyleix while her mother awaited the birth of her seventh baby (Irene, always known as 'Bibs', was born on 31 May). She had enjoyed her scattered days at Cheltenham but took away the impression that a proper education was appropriate only for those who were going to earn their own living. For those who would marry rapidly and suitably it was enough to be able to make conversation at dinner and hold one's own at word games.

Over the half-term holiday of the term she was at Cheltenham, in February 1902, Cynthia went to stay with Miss Jourdain at Marlborough and had lessons with her two pupils. Mary was told:

> She was very keen and interested and threw herself into everything. I thought her exceptionally quick in understanding. She gathered up what was said and summarized it in a few words. She says her difficulty is in remembering – of course that didn't show in the few days . . . I allow the reasonableness of Fraulein's [sic] but I miss Cincie every day of my life and I'm very glad you let her come here.[9]

It was at this time that Mary told Balfour, 'poor Cincie has become a woman – and inherited Eve's curse – I weep to think of her young shoulders with that burden on them'. In October she spent some time in London in order to attend confirmation classes. These were held for some half a dozen girls at a time in a house called No. 2 Amen Court near St Paul's Cathedral. It was the home of Cosmo Lang, then Bishop of Stepney and a future Arch-bishop of Canterbury. In January 1903 Mary took Ego, Guy and Cynthia to Madeira for eight weeks; the confirmation ceremony was in the crypt of St Paul's Cathedral a fortnight after they returned. Then, over the summer, Cynthia spent a month at Gosford and it was on this occasion that she was drawn by Violet Granby, later Duchess of Rutland, 'virtually the portrait artist by appointment to the Souls, and also to their children'.[10] In the drawing Cynthia still looks solemnly Pre-Raphaelite, with a fat plait hanging down her back, and she has not lost the chubbiness of a schoolgirl. For she was spending more hours in the school-room with Squidge: she was further to improve her German since in October she was to go to Dresden.

This was *the* place to go to be 'finished', and for various reasons: the English were great admirers of Germany post-Bismarck; it was clean, efficient and upstanding and had the right moral values (unlike the primitive Italians or the feeble and feckless French). As has been remarked by D. H. Lawrence's biographer for 'the British intelligentsia . . . Italy was overdone and France decadent . . . Germany, clad in shining armour, but *gemütlich* with beer and a warm heart, was the vogue.'[11] Then, the Kaiser was part of the royal family, there was a court at Dresden (that of the King of Saxony); and there were famous art galleries full of pictures by Veronese, Tintoretto, Holbein, Giorgione, Titian, Correggio and so on. Then, too, there were the literary associations with Heine, the lure of Meissen porcelain and, above all, the musical influence of Weber and Wagner and of the opera. And the city itself was beautiful. Dresden was the nearest many girls of the period ever came to the community feeling of a school or university. Friendships formed here often lasted for life, and as one of Cynthia's contemporaries (Mrs Claude Beddington) said, 'there is a freemasonry among those who studied in Dresden when young'.[12]

Some girls were at schools but most lived in small hotels or pensions; Cynthia's was the Pension Wagner (Reichsstrasse 28) and from here she sallied forth after high-tea supper (black bread and *leberwurst*) to take the clanging, lurching tram to the Opera. Here the atmosphere was almost sacred, the Germans treating the occasion as seriously as a church service, the English school-girls often being irreverent, removing hair pins from the coiffure of the girl in front or aiming cherry-stones across the auditorium using thumb and forefinger as a sling. Opera was not to be one of Cynthia's adult pleasures (she preferred plays and, not being musical, liked spoken not sung language) but she liked it when she was young. When she was in her early twenties she wrote that she had 'loved the opera last night and almost though not quite fell under the old Dresden operatic spell when one used to lose all sense of being a mere spectator'.

The atmosphere was the pleasure: the gilt plasterwork, the red velvet seats, the rustle of silk, the smell of powder and leather. And, as well, being with friends of her own age – Eileen Wellesley, Stella Campbell, Mary Vesey, Violet Asquith, all of them shrugging on their cloaks as they came out into the frosty air and walking arms linked back to their pensions, boots echoing on the cobbles and the feeling of being unleashed from the years of nanny, governess, nursery tea, bucket and spade holidays and good deportment.

Cynthia went to Dresden with her brother Guy, who had been forced to leave Eton owing to illness; he was the only boy among a crowd of girls. The mornings were spent in learning to draw and, as at Cheltenham, hours were wasted while Cynthia stared at busts of Roman emperors and tried to translate their features onto paper, an occupation she was never even to try in later life since her imagination was so much more verbal than visual. She did not even decorate her letters with hearts, leaves or cherubs in the charming way that came naturally to so many of her female friends and relations.

The afternoons were filled with *Kunstgeschichte* – tours of the art galleries under the direction of a guide. Sometimes there were day trips into the surrounding countryside. And twice a week Cynthia kept up the German she had learnt with Squidge. Before the Dresden experience, Cynthia's life had been dominated by comfortable precepts: a childhood in the country surrounded by siblings, a love of literature and ignorance of science, the unspoken acceptance of the idea that the boys would shine and their sisters would reflect their glow. Now, in the winter of 1903, Cynthia became aware of all kinds of other possibilities: the Asquiths were, to her, their embodiment.

Cynthia met Violet first. She had had a similar upbringing to Cynthia, although her life had been both more urban and more urbane. But she too had been well-educated by a good governess, and had enjoyed dancing lessons, long holidays in the country, good conversation carried on by highly intelligent grown-ups, and so on. Like Cynthia she was witty, opinionated, sensitive and beautiful (although her beauty was in her extremely characterful and lively features, and her unruly hair, rather than in any classic qualities). In addition both girls were still being regarded as children who, not having yet come out, were de-barred from grown-up life.

Then, in December, she met two of Violet's brothers who had come out from England to be with her for Christmas. When Cynthia left Dresden in May 1904 she was in love with the whole family, even with the idea of their father and step-mother whom she had previously only met when they were guests of her parents. But it was the boys who had captivated her. She had met other young men but not young men like Beb and Oc Asquith.

····➝· Chapter 7 ·↜····
Asquiths

Their name has, in the twentieth century, developed a glamorous, almost aristocratic resonance. But a visit to St Catherine's House, repository of birth certificates, is a reminder that, in Yorkshire, it is a well-used surname. There are numerous Asquiths in Dewsbury, Wakefield, Leeds, Bradford – as well as in Morley, one of the small West Riding wool towns where Herbert Henry Asquith was born in 1852. His father was a wool-trade worker, 'pious, agreeable, and somewhat lacking in business initiative',[1] and the family lived in 'simple comfort'[2] in a squat, grey Yorkshire-stone building called Croft House. It was a life of puritan traditions, chapel on Sundays before roast beef and the afternoon walk, and, lessons every day with Mrs Asquith, 'a woman of wide interests, considerable cultivation and unusual conversational powers'.[3]

When H.H. (as he was often to be called, having first been called Herbert and then Henry) was eight his father died and the family, after two years of living with their grandfather, came south. The two brothers went to London and the City of London School for Boys, their mother and sister Evelyn made their home at St Leonards-on-Sea. They were to nurse their health in the soft seaside air, the boys were to make their way in the world. For them it was a life of straitened circumstances and hard work, of travelling every day from their 'digs' (first with their uncle, then in Pimlico and then in Liverpool Road, Islington) to Cheapside, of letters home and brief holidays by the sea. H.H. excelled academically and won one of two annual classics scholarships to

55

Balliol College, Oxford: 'this was the proudest moment of my life'.[4] His career here was distinguished, though less so than his sons' careers were to be, and he decided to read for the Bar.

During the year he went up to Oxford, while staying with his mother, he had met a Manchester girl called Helen Melland. She was only sixteen and it was not for another four years that they became secretly engaged. They married three years after that, in August 1877; H.H. was not yet twenty-five. It was hardly the action of a man with his eye on the main chance, even though Helen did have a small dowry, and his mother must have wondered whether her son's romantic, domesticated temperament would harmonise with the ambitions she had for so long been inculcating in him. But she had also nurtured steadfastness in her children: Helen was Asquith's first 'real' love and 'I showed the same constancy wh. has since been practised by my sons, and waited from about 18 to 25 (hardly ever seeing her in the interval)'.[5]

The couple settled in Hampstead; Margot Asquith was to remark cuttingly of Helen that she 'was no wife for [H.H.]. She lives in Hampstead, and has no clothes'.[6] Eton House, where the Asquiths lived, was a cream-coloured, double-fronted Georgian house surrounded by gardens in what was then John Street and is now Keats Grove. The house where Keats lodged, and the descendant of the tree under which he wrote 'Ode to a Nightingale', were across the road from the Asquith home. Hampstead in the 1880s was then, as now, a part of London that enjoyed a measure of rural peace and yet was unsuburban in feel. It has always been a favourite of artists, writers, lawyers, of those who have enough inner resource to want to escape from the city centre but are not pastoral enough to want to leave it altogether.

Three sons were born in John Street, Raymond, Herbert (in 1881) and Arthur; a fourth brother was to be born in 1889. Herbert was at first known as 'Bertie' and later as 'Beb', Arthur was always called 'Oc'. (When young the four Asquith boys were called Rub, Beb, Oc and Cis, but Raymond was never 'Rub' after he went to Winchester; the others clung to their diminutives.) In 1887, after the birth of Violet and in order to have more space, the Asquiths moved to the other side of Hampstead, to 27 Maresfield Gardens. No one was very happy about the change. Beb was to write:

The first momentary excitements of exploring the new house were soon tempered by regret at leaving the old one: the new house had a garden, but it was not so large or so wild as the orchard of John Street; like the house, it was new, and contained no pears or apples,

Beb in 1918.

Simon c. 1922.

Basil Blackwood.

McEvoy's oil painting of Cynthia done over 33 sittings 1917–18. 'The canvas, from continual over painting, begins to look pipe-clayed.' Owner unknown.

Cynthia in the late 1920s.

Beb in the late 1920s.

Nanny Faulkner and Simon mid-1920s, his
pullover appears to be an everyday version of
the Peter Pan costume.

Cynthia, Michael and Simon in 1921; note
Michael's medieval tabard.

and no timber of any merit; the turf of the lawn was unseasoned by the years; there was no mulberry tree, young or old, and the seductive scent of mulberry jam no longer floated up the stairs from the kitchen.[7]

Summer holidays continued to be spent as usual at Allan Bank, a house at Grasmere in the Lake District that had once been lived in by the poet Wordsworth and his sister Dorothy. Then, in 1891, when Cyril ('Cis') was eighteen months old, for 'an isolated experiment, a momentary change'[8] the family decided to rent a house on the Isle of Arran. With the change came disaster. Helen, gentle, kind, quick-witted and understanding, caught typhoid two days after Beb was laid low by it and, after three weeks of mixed optimism and despair, died on 11 September. When Asquith returned to Maresfield Gardens with the five children life had dramatically changed.

Helen may have appeared unworldly to the obtuse, a Natasha only interested in the colour of her babies' napkins, but she was a great deal more intelligent and percipient than most people realised; Asquith genes on their own could not have produced *five* clever and successful children without the necessary quota of some remarkable Melland characteristics. She had taken a great interest in her husband's work both as a barrister and, after 1886, as Member of Parliament for East Fife, and a regular feature of the children's life in the John Street years was their parents' evening walk beneath the apple trees while they discussed the day. Helen was, too, more than a mere listening-post: 'at Maresfield Gardens my mother's small dinner-parties increased in number and among her guests were Augustine Birrell, Haldane, John Morley, Mr John Roskill, who was working with my father, and Cyril Flower'.[9]

Yet Asquith's horizons had expanded while Helen

entirely unselfish in her nature, had little desire for the obvious prizes of the world, little care about her own position, no taste whatever for personal fame; her ambition was not for herself; her main desire was that her husband should fulfil his powers, and that his life should have a background of amusement and happiness remote from the dust of its conflict.[10]

Beb, in writing this passage, had his mother's critics in mind, the Marys who could not understand her preferring hearth and home to 'who's in, who's out'. He must also have been defending her against his father's slightly ungenerous posthumous assessment: H.H. wrote a year after her death that 'what has happened to me lately' (his social and political successes) 'would have given her little real pleasure . . . She was the gentlest and best of companions, a restricting rather than a stimulating influence'.[11]

It is mere speculation to suggest that, had she lived, Helen would have blocked Asquith's career. She would have preferred to be in the background; there would have always been a female confidante to whom Asquith wrote letters; but there is no real evidence that he had begun to find her calm Hampstead aura, her 'still centre', irksome rather than soothing. The point needs to be made because it has so often been suggested that the Asquith children only shone because of the *entrée* into society they were given by their step-mother – that under Helen's influence they might have subsided into bank clerks and schoolmasters (as did their Uncle William who, although intellectually able, was 'only' a Clifton schoolmaster all his life). Yet Raymond was a mere six months away from his Winchester scholarship when she died, Beb had acquired her calm, her wit, and her love of poetry, and the other three had an independence of outlook which owed as much to Helen as to Margot.

But, without his first wife, Asquith's more ruthless qualities at once began to predominate; the days of cricket on the lawn and low-key suppers were over. Also, without Helen, the famous Asquith reserve came to the fore: the deprivation first of a father, then (in the everyday sense) of a mother and then of a wife encouraged the aloofness which a happy family life might have fended off. H.H.'s biographer has commented that 'his austere classicism of expression now suggests a certain want of feeling. But there is no reason to suspect this. A Roman reserve was always natural to Asquith'.[12] This is true, yet Helen might have ensured that, with his children at least, he displayed some of the hidden emotions. In mitigation, Asquith could not have known that a large reading-public was going to be unforgivingly critical of his failure ever to write to his sons when they were fighting in France or that all the details of how he presented the idea of a second wife to his children (in a word, callously) were going to be made public.

In the months before the disastrous autumn of 1891 H.H. had begun to widen his circle of friends and had got to know some of the Souls. No longer a junior at the Bar, he did not have to bring briefs home every evening and, with his widening political contacts, his love of success was growing fast. He had straight-away determined on a career in politics and had enough abandon in his make-up to allow him to take risks, for example 'taking silk' very young. 'It was in the same spirit that when in the 1880s he had by some means saved about £300 [£7,500] he went out and spent almost the whole of it on a diamond necklace for his wife.'[13]

Back in Hampstead in the autumn of 1891 Beb had his final term at Miss Case's school at 96 Heath Street, a pretty cottagey building overlooking the trees of the Heath at the back. He had been going there since he was six; his teacher (a sister of the Janet Case who was to teach Greek to Virginia Stephen, later Woolf, a decade later) 'had once acted the part of Clytemnestra in the Agamemnon of Aeschylus, a role that seemed scarcely in harmony with the rare gentleness of her own disposition'.[14] Then in the New Year he started at his prep school; his father had written to the headmaster only eight days after Helen died asking whether he could take 'Bertie' in January.

The school was called Lambrook at Bracknell in Berkshire and Beb was to stay here for two and a half years. His father kept all his Sunday letters with their weekly repetition of 'Dear Father I am sixth this week' or 'Dear Father, I am first this week' or 'Dear Father, I do not yet know my place for this week' and then the details of cricket matches. (All Beb's black-edged letters are dated '91 as though he was wishing himself back to the previous year.)

It is rather touching to read that on his first night at school he was allowed to sleep in Raymond's dormitry (sic), rather less touching when he writes:

> I am glad to hear Miss Margot Tenant is a decent person; I expect she is the same one whom Rub said chucked her hankerchief into the court when Piggot* was being tried. I am 2nd this week. I hope you get a decent house somewhere. It was very wet yesterday. Goodbye from your loving son H. Asquith.[15]

Or (three days after his father's re-marriage in 1894): 'Is Mells Park† a decent place? In one of the papers I saw a reproduction of that sketch of Margot of yours. I don't know where you'll put all your presents'.[16]

---

*He meant the Tranby Croft Case (1891), the famous baccarat scandal. He was muddling it with the Parnell Commission of Enquiry 1888–9, also involving both his father and Sir Charles Russell, after which the forger Piggott killed himself.
†Mells was the home of Sir John and Lady Horner where his father and step-mother spent the first part of their honeymoon. Raymond was to marry Katharine Horner.

Asquith had met Margot Tennant* at a dinner party in the spring of 1891. She was twenty-seven. Neither beautiful nor charming, she was electrifying. Her need to dominate made her overbearing and she successfully elbowed her way onto centre stage in the way that foreigners often love (and feel compelled) to do; she was Scottish but, at first, felt as excluded from London society as, say, a dynamic Australian does nowadays. She was the perfect egoist, yet she had enough charisma and spunk and intelligence to carry it off. Initially she appealed to the side of Asquith that had been suppressed by the hard-work ethic of his youth and by the gentle self-effacement of the Mellands. He was interested, too, in the similarity (given the aristocratic circles in which they both, by this time, moved) of both their fathers living on their own not inherited money. And he admired Margot's acute political antennae.

She, having always pursued notoriety as though it was an end in itself, was astonished that Asquith was not mapping out his career with more energy; with Margot's help Asquith set about it, and he raised his social aspirations still higher. As another biographer has remarked: 'His modest upbringing, while never repudiated, was effectively transcended, especially after his second marriage . . . he obtained admission to the *salons* and country houses of the high born and the well bred. Once he arrived, he had no reason to recollect his point of departure'.

Margot quickly contrived to meet Helen and found her calm placidity and lack of self-centredness almost incomprehensible. Wanting to see what the Souls would think of someone who *preferred* staying at home with her children to going about with her husband, she asked Ettie Grenfell to invite the Asquiths to Taplow for the weekend. Margot alleged (for her diaries and autobiography are colourful but not always truthful) that Helen had told her that she had enjoyed herself at Taplow but 'would not care to live in the sort of society that I loved'.[18]

Asquith and Margot began exchanging letters as soon as they met: if Helen had not died, Margot might only have been the first in a line of half-a-dozen female confidantes, women (of whom Venetia Stanley was to be the most notorious example) with whom he was to be – intellectually – in love. By the end of July

---

*Margot, the daughter of a very wealthy Scottish businessman, had been captivating London society for nearly a decade. Her sister Charty's marriage to Lord Ribblesdale marked the family's move into high social circles and their spreading fame.

1891, just before his departure for the Isle of Arran, Asquith was writing to Margot: 'You have made me a different man and brought back into my life the feeling of spring'.[19] After his wife's death Asquith, being a practical man who liked to get things sorted out, was able to propose to Margot with rather indecent haste. By December he was writing to her: 'You tell me not to stop loving you, as if you thought I had done or would or could do so' and by next summer was declaring 'I can conceive of no future of which you are not the centre'.[20]

Before the announcement of their engagement Asquith took Margot to meet his children who had been living since the end of 1892 in Surrey, cared for by a nanny and a housekeeper – first in a house on Box Hill and then in Redhill. Their father lived in a flat in London and visited them when he could. The first meeting with their new step-mother was rather stiff. She once wrote, 'I always tell everyone of temperament *never* to be a step-mother'[21] but some of her difficulties might have been avoided with only elementary precautions. It does not seem quite good enough to announce a forthcoming marriage by letter ('I am glad to hear Miss Margot Tenant is a decent person'), nor to leave the children on the sideline during the marriage ceremony, nor to remove them, curtly, from Redhill and everything connected with their old life to the new house in Cavendish Square in a manner that Raymond (at least) was to resent all his life, to such an extent that there was always to be something of a rift between him and his father. Asquith admired his eldest son but did not like him that much (he liked Oc best) – and the feeling was mutual.

But temperament was at the root of it all. In future Asquith had to be loyal to his wife, yet the difference between Tennants and Asquiths was almost insurmountable, the relationship being a question of conciliation and compromise; others (children-in-law in particular) became adept reconcilers. Margot summed it up brilliantly in her *Autobiography* (1920):

Whereas Tennants made scenes, stormed and over-reacted, Asquiths believed in the free application of intellect to every human emotion; no event could have given heightened expression to their feelings. Shy, self-engaged, critical and controversial, nothing surprised them and nothing upset them . . . Perfectly self-contained, truthful and deliberate, I never saw them lose themselves in my life and I have hardly ever seen the saint or hero that excited their emotion.[22]

Asquiths did not get up when someone came into the room, were oblivious to clothes, disliked hunting (Margot's passion) and enjoyed word games. In short, they did not suffer from 'nerves' and were sensible about their health (Margot's notorious miscarriages, although sad, were at least partly caused by her refusal to take care of herself *for the sake of the baby*). 'All Asquiths sleep like hogs' she wrote, famously, in her diary, trying later to change the 'h' to 'l', for to her insomnia was a virtue that was at one with sensitivity and depth of feeling; to this day Asquith descendants are extremely late risers. Finally, Asquiths tended to be careful with money whereas Tennants, because they liked making a splash, liked spending it. It was just as well that Tennant *père* settled £5000 a year on the newly-weds (£150,000 a year in today's money).

All these character clashes made Beb's adolescence rather unsettling; not that one would know this from the bland eloquence with which, in his memoir of his father, he alludes to his schooldays at Winchester and his career at Oxford. But it is likely that the intense volubility of his step-mother induced him to withdraw more and more into himself, that the extreme peak of emotion upon which she lived her life caused him to adopt the qualities of 'benign detachment' and 'mellow fatalism'[23] which he had so often observed in his father. Raymond did the same, appearing (in the words of his friend John Buchan) urbane, scornful of obvious emotion and (that word again) detached. Yet to his friends he denied nothing, for one of the most admirable Asquith characteristics was their loyalty to their family and to those they loved. These very English traits are sometimes confused with flippancy by the obtuse. They are, however, mere shields; Cynthia was to try to pierce them all her life.

····ᢒ· Chapter 8 ·ᢒ····
Coming Out, Northlands:
1905

Cynthia was sixteen and Beb twenty-two in the winter of 1903–4. He was in his last year at Balliol where, after Winchester, he had gone to read Greats. His university career was quietly successful but always second-best to Raymond who, the previous year, had followed his First in Greats with an All Souls fellowship, having won some of the scholarships – such as Craven and Ireland – which are so prestigious. Nor did Beb do as well as Cis was to do a decade later (Cis's academic career was to be even more outstanding than Raymond's). Yet Beb had 'a sweet and gentle nature and much originality'.[1] Being self-effacing and introspective he was not conspicuous (except for his good looks), nevertheless he gave an impression of depth and solidity which was easy to admire; one result was that 'somewhat to my surprise, I was elected President of the Union'.[2] Beb seems to have been the one of the five children who was most like his mother: she too would not have spoken unless she had something to say. And in this respect Beb and Cynthia's first meeting in Dresden was laughably 'typical':

> I suddenly found myself being swiftly propelled over the frozen waters by a tall young man on skates. Not a single word did he say, and it was not for me to break the silence, but I remember a sense of momentousness out of all proportion to the event.[3]

They did not meet often for the next couple of years. Beb, after

Schools, began to read for the Bar. Cynthia's life took its expected course. She returned to Stanway after her six months in Germany and resumed lessons with Squidge. The time dragged: neither child nor adult, there was a feeling of life beginning but being as yet rather empty. But Stanway life was as busy as ever. There were visits to other houses and occasional treats such as a visit to Ego in Oxford where, in the autumn of 1904, at a lunch party in his rooms, Cynthia, Mary and Squidge were introduced to some of his friends. A few months later Cynthia, then nearly eighteen, listed her favourite young men as Jack Mitford, Edward Horner and Frank Adlard.

At the end of May 1905 Mary took her to Paris for six weeks. 'We did the usual things: the Opera, the Louvre, Chartres, Versailles, Fontainebleau, etc.'[4] Then, much sooner than she had planned, Mary had to return to Stanway to cope with a domestic crisis (Bibs was only just three) and Cynthia was left in the charge of a maid and a daily French governess. She was abandoned to a régime of morning walks and shuffles round the Louvre, but managed to persuade the governess to take her to the Morgue so that she could find out for herself if Svengali's description of it (in George du Maurier's *Trilby*) was realistic. It was.

In early July 1905, on her return to England, Mary decided that Cynthia should be presented at Court. This was not because she was the requisite age – she would not be eighteen for three months – but because Mary had promised to present the daughter of the Stanway vicar and did not want the bother of presentations two summers running. Cynthia made her curtsey along with the eighteen year-old débutantes, went to a ball given for Eileen Wellesley (she was gratified to be asked to dance by the 'best dancer in London'. 'Had I known he was destined to be the father of Joyce Grenfell I should have gazed at him with even deeper respect'[5]) and there encountered Beb, with whom she danced twice, and then returned to Stanway for the summer. ('Do you mean to say she's not finished *yet*?'[6] Hugo asked.)

Any more education was not contemplated, which Cynthia regretted not so much because she had academic aspirations as because she longed to read widely. However 'the sight and thought of my mother, so exhaustingly over-occupied with family and household cares, made it impossible for me ever to read a book in the morning without a positive sense of guilt'.[7] All the young men she knew were allowed the indulgence of 'reading parties'; for Cynthia to have gone to Oxford would have been to risk the appallingly derogatory label of 'highbrow'.

But it was agreed by Mary that, 'as a concession, and provided it was kept more or less secret'[8], and if it was combined with more French and German and two mornings hunting a week ('pure ecstacy'), Cynthia should be allowed to learn Greek with Guy's tutor. After Dresden, Guy had gone to be coached by the Reverend Allen, an amiable Cotswold character known as 'the Priest' because he looked so unlike one, an ex-headmaster who had early on fallen into financial difficulties. Since 1904 he had lived modestly at Didbrook as curate, taking up to six pupils at a time; an inspired if unusual coach, they remembered him with great love. He remained a close friend of everyone at Stanway until his death in 1950.

For a few weeks Euripides and the Greek alphabet, in that order, made Cynthia's life far more satisfying. And it was, perhaps, the Priest's high opinion of his only female pupil that made Mary decide to send her to school, albeit that it was for the two terms *after* her presentation at court. Mary Vesey had recently been sent to a school at Englefield Green in Berkshire called Northlands and her mother had bought a house nearby called Clonboy so that Mary could be a day pupil. Here Cynthia went to live and to have her only experience of a proper school. Squidge finally left (and went to teach another Cynthia, namely Curzon, and her two sisters).

Northlands was not an orthodox establishment. It had been started by Sophie Weisse, always known by the formal Miss Weisse, as a 'Dame' school for the children of some of the Eton masters. Molly Warre-Cornish, later MacCarthy, born in 1882, whose father was Vice-Provost of Eton, described the school as 'musical, comfortable, dignified'[9] in that order. Music had always been an important part of the curriculum even before the day in 1879 when the four year-old Donald Tovey begged to be allowed to attend the Northlands singing class with his elder brother. Later Miss Weisse recorded that 'thenceforth my life was devoted to the care of what was a very delicate child, in whom I recognised an unusual mental endowment and an almost incredible musical talent'.[10]

Thenceforth, too, the school became an even more musical one. The usual subjects were on the curriculum, but the presence of the child prodigy Tovey, who was nominally at school at Eton but largely at Northlands, ensured the strongly musical bias. A couple of years after she had left, Cynthia described the school to Beb:

It is a sort of Rambouillet – a meeting place of musical geniuses, unwashed minor poets and uncouth Professors, there were real 'subject' conversations at every meal, in the morning we had a lecture on 'Poitree' [poetry] and in the afternoon one on Musick. Mercifully Painting was omitted. I don't feel quite at my ease there as the familiar atmosphere relegates me to the schoolroom and I'm afraid of being asked to write an essay or sing a scale . . . Miss W. always makes me feel I am a fritterer.[11]

Cynthia was the only pupil not learning an instrument (Hugo had once put a stop to her practising the piano because he could not stand the noise). Nevertheless Miss Weisse taught her a good deal. She cared much more about the urge to learn than about achievement, and abhorred competition between pupils; the concept of 'personal best' prevailed. She also emphasised the importance of learning methods. Tovey was taught at a very early age the art of practising for a short time regularly and often. To Cynthia she imparted the habit of learning, or meaning to learn, something by heart every day; her lifelong ambition to know by heart every poem in the *Oxford Book of English Verse* originated with Squidge, but began to be realised with Miss Weisse.

Northlands was 'an excellent incubator for the appreciation of music and literature'[12] but would not have been a success for girls who were going on to earn their living and needed qualifications (they were better off at Cheltenham); but since the school was fashionable and idiosyncratic there were few of these. The atmosphere was, too, somewhat exotic, due partly to the presence of a budding genius and partly to the excitement of frequent musical events, for example the Northlands Chamber Music Concerts which took place in the beautiful music-room. Cynthia continued to be fond if frightened of Miss Weisse ('I felt all the old tremor on driving up to the door'[13] she wrote in 1916) and enjoyed an atmosphere which was occasionally somewhat histrionic. Miss Weisse moved from being passionately attached to Tovey to being single-minded about him, interfering in every aspect of his life. Her possessive feelings were to be harshly tested in 1916 when Tovey married – from the tone in which Cynthia mentions this crisis in her diaries it would be difficult for the uninitiated to know whether she is describing the tribulations of deserted mistress or mother; Molly MacCarthy once remarked memorably that 'visiting Miss Weisse was like seeing King Lear very badly acted'.[14]

During Cynthia's Christmas holidays from Northlands Ego's coming of age was celebrated. There was a dance for the tenants and some neighbours. Next day there was a dinner for all the two hundred labourers on the estate; this took place in the Tithe Barn. Finally, on 30 December, the estate mothers and children were entertained to tea and a Punch and Judy show. 'Our children got very wild with excitement. Music and fireworks were followed by meat-pies.'[15] The night before Ego's return to Oxford he escorted Cynthia to the Broadway Ball; 'Cincie seemed to enjoy herself and made much more progress with Jack than I did wih Joan'. (Jack was one of the three listed by Cynthia as her favourite young men; he was Lord Redesdale's fourth son who was then nearly twenty-one and had led an idle life since, on being expelled from Eton, he had been stopped from entering the diplomatic service. He was to gain notoriety in 1914 when he married the daughter of a German 'Coal King' and was divorced by her after ten weeks for 'masculine indolence and an unbearable selfishness'.[16]) On his return to Oxford Ego very much appreciated the peace after his 'harassing and strenuous Christmas'.[17]

In May Cynthia officially came out. She was eighteen and a half and this was nine months after she had been presented at Court; Mary's contemporaries were rather critical of this muddled way of doing things but (and this was the main thing) it did not seem greatly to affect Cynthia's chances, and that, after all, was what the Season was all about. In any event, coming out had changed greatly since the 1880s, when a girl's performance determined her whole life. As Mabell, Countess of Airlie, formerly Mabell Gore, observed:

Unless a girl was quite exceptional – which I was not – her fate was decided by her first impact on society. Anyone who failed to secure a proposal within six months could only wait for her second season with diminishing chances. After the third there remained nothing but India as a last resort before the spectre of the Old Maid became a reality.[18]

In 1906 this was no longer so. Marriage may have been the only predictable future but it did not depend on the Season.

All summer Cynthia appeared at London dances. She also went to Commem Week at Oxford. At the Trinity College Ball 'Hugo, for the procession into supper, was asked to take in the Chinese Ambassadress. He offered his arm to the Chinese Ambassador. In their lovely flowing garments they were indistinguishable'.[19] (This incident was used in a novel by the Edwardian novelist Harry Graham.) Then, at the end of July, Cynthia went to stay at Castle Ashby in Northamptonshire. This was a memorable occasion and Cynthia kept a diary, unfortunately now lost, which she used to get out and read aloud for the amusement of family and friends. This was not merely for the fun of it; it was also a reminder of a former life, of an atmosphere so delightfully gay and carefree that the whole occasion came to be an image of unfettered pleasure.

The three-day long festivity was held to celebrate the twenty-first birthday of William Compton, then heir to the Marquess of Northampton; he had just come down from Balliol. There were about fifty people there, all under twenty-five and most of them Cynthia's friends – only a few 'non-conductors' as she put it. There was an air of romance, even of eroticism, which affected everyone. Clementine Hozier, later Churchill, became engaged to someone called Lionel Earle and had to be brave enough to break it off a month later. Cynthia 'quoted' from her diary in her memoirs (but she must have edited the original a great deal):

> Tuesday. Arrived at station just in time to catch the Special. . . . We were met by several enormous brakes, into which we were packed like bank-holiday-makers. Arrival at this extremely 'stately Home of England' somewhat alarming. Descending in hordes, we were greeted by . . . the two official chaperones imported for the occasion. . . . Before long I wanted to be shown my room, to have time to 'rest my face' before dressing for dinner. No such luck. We all paced the superb garden in THREES. . . .
> Wednesday. At half past nine a ladysmaid appeared with invitation from Violet Asquith and Hilda Lyttelton to have breakfast with them. Relieved at chance to escape ordeal of public breakfast. . . . Venetia Stanley and Clementine Hozier came up from dining-room breakfast and gave us all the news. . . . Watched several games of golf. Went with Oc, Ego and Guy to see accommodation improvised for the men of the party – lovely tents far more luxurious than most bedrooms, each hung with tapestry and rigged up with electric light.
> Thursday. Danced like Dervishes. Everybody went rather mad, dressed up, and to annoyance of the professional band made hideous noises on improvised musical instruments. . . . To sleep at about five.
> Friday. Oc and I fled, and went on the river. . . . Dancing again after dinner. Sat out in the churchyard with Oc . . . Venetia, Violet and I foolishly went on talking until nearly six o'clock. . . . After two hours' sleep, descended, bleary-eyed, to extremely gloomy dining-room breakfast. Up to London by the special train. Violet, Beb, Oc and I, all feeling much the worse for wear, travelled together.[20]

At Stanway that summer visitors came and went, neighbours came over for lunch (Liffords, de Navarros, Millets, Noels, Andrews, Sargents, von Glehns, Barnards), there were walks and tennis and expeditions and arrangements. Some of Ego's Oxford friends came to stay; his closest one was Robert Smallbones (of whom it was said that the Oxford Proctor of the day would not believe that his name was authentic until it was spelt out for him over and over again). He had a pleasingly unusual background – his Scottish father lived in the romantic Schloss Velm in Austria – and had been conducting a flirtation with Cynthia which was to continue for many years. He was at Stanway for the whole of August and September because he and Ego were being coached in history by a young Oxford graduate called Edmund Curtis (who, ten years later, still had his rooms at Trinity College, Dublin 'furnished with large photographs of me'[21]).

It was from now on that there are references, the merest glimpses, to the depression that was to feature in Cynthia's life. Some of its cause was genetic – Hugo was prone to deep glooms, his sister Evelyn looks, in her photographs, gaunt rather than serene, while his eldest brother Francis (Franko) killed himself at the age of twenty-six. Melancholy was, as well, part of the *zeitgeist*. Part of it is easily comprehensible. Who would not feel gloomy on a wet Saturday at Gosford? Or indeed at any country house organised and peopled by servants when there was nothing to do except kill birds or kill time before the dressing bell went and the day itself could be killed off in eating and drinking? ('From five o'clock to eight is on certain occasions a little eternity' observed Henry James on the first page of *Portrait of a Lady*, one of Cynthia's favourite books.) Melancholy was also an occupation. Margot suffered months of depression after a still-birth: not for her the brisk practicality of her more stalwart mother; the 'life must go on' attitude was not always part of her over-sensitive mien.

But it was very much part of Mary Elcho's. Cynthia watched over her mother being harassed by the demands of her household, never having time to read or draw, obsessively recording arrangements in her diary, and then having to retreat to a *Kurhaus* to try to put on weight. And it does not take a great deal of imagination to guess at the acute strain imposed on her by the necessity of juggling ('arranging') Balfour, Hugo, Stanway, financial anxiety, friends, children, servants, nannies and governesses. It is hardly surprising that she was only forty-three when Raymond Asquith described her as 'worn and faded but I think one would always jump among lions to redeem her glove'.[22] Stanway may have been run by servants, the Elchos may have been cushioned from any real financial difficulties, but someone had to be the pivot of it all. And Cynthia, determined to help all she could and always the loving daughter, was sure that when the time came she would not want to be so pivotal.

····➤· Chapter 9 ·◄····
Raymond: 1906–7

For the moment Cynthia was waiting. Waiting for what? she must often have wondered. She was not submissive enough to find the 'babies' preoccupying. The young men she knew were reading for the Bar (Raymond, Beb, Harold Baker), in the Diplomatic Service (Ego, Smallbones, George Vernon, Charles Lister) or banking, soldiering or spending a private income. Despite the example of Sir Charles Tennant, none of them wanted to have anything to do with industry or to be scientists. Balfour's 1908 lecture on Decadence in which he saw 'the modern alliance between science and industry' as the hope for the future would have fallen on rather deaf ears where the children of the Souls were concerned. Even the brilliant Raymond seemed to have no ambitions to *renounce* other than politics. As for the girls, Molly MacCarthy was to observe, 'our parents seemed to have no other wish for us but that we should flit for ever about their house and sit at the round dining-room table day after day in contentment with home. They have no idea of giving us any particular training to any professional end. On the other hand, we all did very much what we liked after we grew up'.[1]

Cynthia did what she liked, but within the parameters of propriety. She could not go to London on her own, she could not see friends without her parents' permission. Philanthropy would have been a diversion and it was one she thought about briefly but, not being quite sure what one did, day by day, with that bit of equipment called a social conscience, she dropped the idea.

Nor was she interested, as were her grandmother, mother and sisters, in the Arts and Crafts Movement or the Royal School of Needlework.

People, always, came first. Nothing could take precedence over a luncheon or dinner, and letters or books had to be put away at the first sound of carriage or motor-car on gravel. 'Eliza is just looming on the horizon bringing a cottage-full of Bohemians over to lunch, so goodbye'[2] she wrote, typically, to Beb in 1908. And in another letter, written the same spring, she spelt out her life of 'turnip-like rustic simplicity and clock-work domestic regularity':

> I get up at 7.30 – read or write letters till breakfast at 9 o'clock – go for a ride with my mother, sister etc, lunch 1 am, afternoon walk with Mary, Fraulein and dogs. Tea five oclock – play with Bibs, pounce [a card game like racing demon] with Mary, dinner 8 – reading aloud, bed 11 – read till 12.[3]

Apart from the 'simplicity' of Stanway and the dressmaker – dinner – dance ritual of London, there was country-house visiting. This was Cynthia's main occupation in the years between coming out and marriage (1906–10) and its conventions have often been described: the servanted comfort which meant that visitors were 'quite untroubled by any fear that my presence would mean either more work or less food for my hostess, nor did I feel any obligation to take my turn at dirtying the sink or at mislaying the table';[4] the cold, despite the luxury of a fire in each bedroom; the housemaid bringing in cans of water and trays; the trunks packed with many changes of clothes; the many-coursed dinners and the breakfasts of kedgeree and kidneys under silver lids on the sideboard. It has all become part of the mythology of the Edwardian glow that 'vanished for ever with the First World War'; and is familiar nowadays from television serials like *Upstairs, Downstairs* or films like *The Shooting Party*.

It is therefore easy to imagine Cynthia as she set off for a Saturday-to-Monday or longer visit, either to be part of a house party or to join in the daily life of a girlfriend such as Mary Vesey or Venetia Stanley (for having a friend to stay was a convenient way of occupying unmarried, brought out daughters). The journey was checked in *Bradshaw* (the timetable) and meant several cross-country trains and idle moments in waiting-rooms; the last part was completed in a brougham or motor-car. It was usual to arrive at tea-time, for the ritual of spreading catalpa tree or crackling fire, scones and jam on a silver tray, long tweed-trousered legs sprawling from wicker or chintz armchair.

The days passed in a round of meals, walks, word games and conversation. There was croquet, tennis or boating on the river, card games and song recitals, or, especially in the winter, charades and gibbets and analogies. Most country houses had common features such as many cherished and undisciplined dogs, the sacred babies' time after tea, a long-staying musician or librarian or writer in residence and, upstairs, a retired nanny (definitively described by Evelyn Waugh in *Brideshead Revisited*). No other servant was ever mentioned and there would be no clues in Cynthia's surviving letters to allow one to guess, what she briefly confirms in her memoirs, that she went everywhere accompanied by her maid Polly.

The predictability engendered its own *ennui*. Cynthia disliked shooting-parties and found that to say 'bad luck' when her 'Gun' missed or 'well tried', as if he had muffed a shot at tennis, gave offence. ('Silence seems so unsympathetic' she observed characteristically, for Mary's handed-on creed was that silence was *never* golden.) She did not always find her neighbours at dinner sympathetic and once anguishedly described a pair as 'the myopic, throttled-looking equerry of the German princeling, and that monosyllabic young man who looks like a piece of sucked asparagus'.[5] She went on (in a letter that was 'reprinted' but was in fact a very much jazzed-up version of a much briefer scrawl):

> Now it is Sunday morning. What shall we do all day? Besides feeling so ill, I've got a bad attack of social nausea. Intense distaste for self and others. Can scarcely suppress a scream when spoken to. The prospect of being nailed to the Merry-Go-Round of another Season makes me feel positively giddy. That awful *bustling* idleness! I know I shall do absolutely nothing; yet have less time to myself than a Prime Minister. [He, for the last few months, was Beb's father.]
>
> Sorry to inflict such a Jeremiad on you, but I am so utterly miserable – literally weeping with self-pity. I don't feel able to cope with life; yet death doesn't seem worth dying. I am losing my mirages without finding reality. At this moment there seems nothing to be sure of – nothing to look forward to – nothing to want. Oh, how I want to want![6]

The phrasing of this passage – 'death doesn't seem worth dying' and so on – is very similar to the tone used by some of Cynthia's male contemporaries such as Julian Grenfell; they, at least, were to have the excitement of war. The letter was (allegedly) followed by another letter two days later.

You *were* sympathetic about my wail, but of course by the time your letter came, I had completely forgotten my purely transitory suffer-ings. You must realise that I am a quite unconsecutive being. Remember that whenever I am depressed and therefore in a self-depreciatory mood, it means that something is chemically wrong. . . Today I am positively bubbling with happiness . . . Did I really say I wished I were dead? So sorry, but I must have been very ill . . .[7]

Cynthia was always to attribute depression to ill-health or, when she was much older, to the prevailing east wind. She never assumed that it was a facet of her temperament or that her life could reasonably cause it. Mary's firm insistence on being busily, therefore happily occupied ('My mother is a slave to her sense of duty'[8]), Ettie's determination to be at all times cheerful, made the more introspective Cynthia continually apologetic if she was less than 'bubbling'. Unhappiness, she believed, was something in the air, not something to be thought through or fought or rooted out. (The roots would, in any case, have to be uncovered and this a child of the pre-Freudian era would not think of doing.) When, for a brief period of the 1914–18 war, Cynthia was a nurse and loved the hard work and sense of something daily achieved, or when as a woman in her late sixties she wrote in her diary that she was only ever happy when she went to the London Library in order to make notes for her book on Countess Tolstoy, she accepted these periods of happiness as one accepts balmy days in January; they were a bonus but not a right and their source was irrelevant. Yet, weeks and weeks of her life were spent resting and eating the 'right' food and adopting a 'strict regime' in order to cure lassitude and depression; hardly a moment in trying to find causes.

It is easy enough for us to decide, bossily, that Cynthia 'should' have fought to educate herself for a profession or, even, to read seriously instead of hanging around a 'Gun'. And, since Vanessa and Virginia Stephen were, at exactly this period, 1906–8, setting up house in Bloomsbury and beginning to paint and write, easy enough to assume that all it needed was determination and money (when Leslie Stephen died in 1904 he left his children £15,000 (£350,000). But the Stephen girls were exceedingly, indeed outrageously, unconventional and were moreover orphans who happened, through their brothers, to meet young men whose ideas and opinions gave them the courage and inspiration to behave as they did. Cynthia was, *au fond*, a creature of convention. Also she loved her family and all it represented and was bound by its ideas of suitability.

The aim of the dances and dinners and country house visits,

of the periods of recuperation at Stanway, was that Cynthia should meet as wide a circle of men as possible before choosing or being chosen by a possible husband. Greek lessons or 'slumming' or unchaperoned meetings were unhelpful occupations; keeping one's wardrobe in good order or Italian lessons or meeting people of the 'right sort' were all desirable. And the whole process was of consuming interest to other people who were watching and waiting to see where the dice would fall. When she was still only eighteen Ego had written flippantly but with an edge of seriousness: 'I am going to float Cincie as a limited company, selling shares about the date of her engagement, her marriage and how often if ever she will be divorced – I am also going to liquidate a sweepstake with all possible runners included'.

Nevertheless, the strictest upbringing, and Cynthia's was not that strict by some standards, could not stop a daughter, whether dutiful or not, from making up her own mind. And it was at about this time, in the winter of 1906–7 when Cynthia was just nineteen and untouched by her first season, that Mary (who had been engaged to Hugo when she was twenty) began to realise that her eldest daughter was unlikely to fulfil the hopes she had had for her. She was being 'discriminating', and in favour of exactly those kind of people whom Mary liked to know, to entertain and to patronise (in the old-fashioned sense) but not to marry. Mary began to accept the likelihood of Cynthia choosing someone impoverished, poetic, introspective, urban and urbane rather than the heir to an estate like William Compton or George Vernon or John Manners, all of whom Cynthia dallied with. (After her next daughter also made up her own mind, in her case choosing a country squire, Mary allowed Bibs no lattitude. She was married suitably to the future Earl of Plymouth when she was just nineteen and he was thirty-two. But she was always to resent that she had been given too little chance to make up her own mind.)

Mary taxed Cynthia with prejudice and she replied (in another heavily doctored letter):

> I'm sorry you thought I was being 'cliquey' at the ball. Of course I'm not 'prejudiced against the Guards'. You might as well accuse me of being prejudiced in favour of barristers. I don't see human beings in categories. Nor is it fair to say that I only like 'clever men'. I only mind the intolerant, the aggressively stupid, who consider reading a vice and whose idea of damning someone is to say, 'He thinks he's clever' . . . I find the world only too full of people I like. You don't want me to become a sort of social glutton who likes absolutely *everybody*, do you?[9]

Of course Mary did not. But neither did she want her to like Balliol men and barristers too much: for this Cynthia had done ever since her winter at Dresden. She had been immediately attracted to the Balliol frame of mind, shrewdly defined by Asquith's biographer as 'public-spirited, but somewhat aloof; cultivated, but not necessarily cultured; earnest, but never strenuous in its exertions; and methodical, but often tinged with an unfeeling sterility'.[10]

The reason for her attraction does not have to be spelt out. The intelligence, and the disdain for the brash, and the suavity, were all qualities that Cynthia's background and upbringing directed her towards; even if her background simultaneously made her value qualities that Balliol men of this period (or the type of man which, loosely and for purposes of definition, it is shorthand to call Balliol men) were taught to despise. For example, they did not tend to *do* much. People like Raymond Asquith and his contemporaries had, in a sense, reacted against Jowett, the previous Master of Balliol; his aim had been, briefly, 'to attract to Balliol an élite of ability, to teach it to work hard, and thus to create the best training-ground in the country for rulers and administrators: politicians, educators, members of the home and imperial civil services'.[11] But Raymond's circle rejected Jowett's ideals, scorning the 'Heygates' who planned to toil away at their careers, and thereby identifying with the aristocrat with a private income. It was, alas, a very old-fashioned attitude to life and one that could not survive in the world post-1918. By then Raymond had been killed and never needed to accept that the Heygates were taking over; Beb should have accepted it but was never able to.

Cynthia liked Balliol men, barristers and, in particular, Raymond. His relationship to the children of the Souls was not unlike Arthur Balfour's to the Souls. Both were about ten years older than most of their contemporaries, and thus detached by experience from their friends; both were revered for their insight as well as their intellect. Raymond was debonair and unmistakably clever in a way that the more accessible Beb and Oc were not – the former being introspective and the latter kindly and gregarious (Cynthia was to describe Oc as 'a great dear – genial and sane to a fault'[12]). But Raymond was, as well, charismatic. Although he was not *that* much more brilliant or witty or handsome than his contemporaries, his death in the First World War appeared to have an effect equalled by only a few such as Rupert Brooke or Julian Grenfell. Without having achieved more in his life, on paper, than winning prizes and a fellowship and making a start on a legal career; and, indeed, without appearing to have wanted to achieve much more, he nevertheless had a brilliant reputation. 'There is a widespread conviction that Britain has been careering downhill since and because of the death of Raymond Asquith in 1916'[13] wrote a Fleet Street journalist recently, demonstrating that, myth though it might be, most people believe it.

It is hard to account for the charm and brilliance of someone who left no lasting memorial: one simply has to accept the accounts of others, and these all testify to the qualities that have already been enumerated. Yet Raymond was, as well, an interesting mixture of tenderness and ruthlessness. Many readers of his letters, published in 1980, remarked on his tendency to callousness: a deeper insight into the Asquith family leads one to see this as a flippancy and a distaste of betraying feeling engendered by the early death of Helen, the swift arrival of Margot and by a Winchester/Balliol education. One has to believe that there was emotion under the aloofness, although it is sometimes hard to do this. Raymond wrote to his wife Katharine after the birth of their second daughter: one cannot imagine his words would have been exactly what she was waiting for. 'I am so glad that at last your long wait is over, and the baby safely born . . . When you are a little stronger I will run over for a couple of days to see you. Probably I should be able to see more of you if I came, not next Saturday, but the one after. And the baby would be more personable by then, too.'[14] Yet it is certain that Raymond did not mean to be hurtful and sometimes he realised that his thoughtlessness was wounding. He wrote to Cynthia at the end of 1908:

> When I told Katharine that I was going to give you the little Egyptian shirt which we spoke of at Archerfield she made a great outcry and said that I had long ago given it to her – and I really believe that I did – she then said that of course if I liked I might take it away again & give it to you, & also her wedding & engagement rings, her ivory tankard, and anything else that I had ever given her. But I believe she did not really wish to part with any of these things, so I must do my best to find you something else for a birthday present.[15]

Raymond met Katharine Horner at Clovelly, the Hamlyns' house in Devon, when he was twenty-two and she was nearly fifteen. He told Harold Baker that she was very clever, and that he found in her 'many of the qualities I admire in boys – especially a combination of purity and vivacity which I am coming to fear is rarer in them than in girls'.[16] By the summer of 1904, during a visit to Avon Tyrrell, the house in the New Forest built by Lethaby in 1892 which belonged to the Horners' close friends Lord and Lady Manners ('Hoppy' and 'Con'), Raymond and Katharine had become secretly engaged – secretly because Katharine was not yet even nineteen and Raymond was still a junior at the Bar. (Since the Horners were old friends of H.H.'s they naturally approved of the match, but not of Katharine's youth.) Raymond wrote: 'I shall always love Avon because of the wonderful things that have happened to us there. I think of it more than of any other place as the cradle of our love, and it will always have a romance for me which I believe not even Mells can equal'.[17] They told no one except Con who, discussing the matter with Raymond, pronounced that 'temperaments not circumstances will be the bar to your ultimate happiness – and that is harder to overcome'. Raymond suggested to Katharine that 'perhaps it would be worth while one of us making an alteration, shall we draw lots to see which is to change the spots?'[18]

The next two years were a matter of contriving to meet ('Pamela has asked me to Wiltshire on 16th July: couldn't you insist on going?'[19]) and of letters. There were melancholy moments ('I never felt blacker in my life'[20]) and small misunderstandings ('after considering the alternatives of killing myself or falling in love with Cynthia, and finding insuperable objections to both, I was quite at an end of my resources and simply went on enduring with no policy but the dim hope of better times'[21]). But, over Christmas 1906, some sort of resolution was agreed upon: presumably that Katharine's parents should be 'tackled', and H.H. and Margot should be asked for an allowance. A month later they were engaged.

Clearly Raymond had dallied with Cynthia. And clearly she had reciprocated. Although she 'always used to say "I was in love with all my brothers-in-law"',[22] family legend has it that, rather than to Beb, Oc or Cis, Cynthia 'offered to leave Raymond her hair, of which she was inordinately proud, in her will provided he wore it, *all* of it'.[23]

By February 1907 the engagement between Raymond and Katharine was common knowledge, if not official. It was at about this time that Beb, cannily, was showing one of Cynthia's letters to his friend Wertheimer, who claimed to be an amateur graphologist. (He pronounced her vain; Beb did not break this news for a year and was then rather off-hand about it, asking Cynthia what she thought of this idea.) She had been less organised but, in her own way, was determined. In June 1907 at Clovelly, where

Katharine and Raymond had first met six years previously, Beb and Cynthia decided that they cared for each other seriously.

For a few weeks things were tentative. Then, in July, Mary made a significant note in her diary: 'Hugo said that people said Cynthia saw too much of Beb'.[24] They met whenever they could, at the kind of occasions that had been their meeting ground ever since Cynthia returned from Dresden: at Ettie's annual New Year party to which children of the Souls came in fancy dress, with, in 1907, Beb as a monkey, Cynthia 'as Ophelia, with her wonderful hair hanging down';[25] at Stanway Saturday-to-Mondays when a typical group of Cynthia's friends would have been Beb, Violet, Stella Campbell and Harold Baker;[26] or at dances during the Season: 'a long, long vista of balls from beginning of May to end of July . . . Violet Asquith and her brother or brothers, and myself and my brothers, were "swept out" of every single one'.[27]

By the end of the year, with the difficulties of contriving to meet in private having become more urgent, it was necessary to persuade someone to play pander. The ever-helpful Con invited Beb to stay at Avon; Ettie (her cousin) invited Cynthia. And so it was that Avon (the library) became the scene of a second Asquith engagement. (Raymond and Katharine had preferred the terrace, but then it was June, not December.) Again Con was sworn to secrecy; and again an impoverished junior at the Bar, having met his bride-to-be when she was sixteen and he was twenty-three, and having fallen in love three years later, was embarking (like his father before him) on a three-year engagement. Via Clovelly and Avon, via the good auspices of Con, via three years of subterfuge and letters, Raymond aged twenty-nine and Beb aged twenty-nine married Katharine aged twenty-two and Cynthia aged twenty-two. And, in the July of 1907 and the July of 1910, Avon was the scene of Asquith honeymoons. One can only conclude that, given the almost implausible synchronisation of behaviour, that if Cynthia could not have Raymond – then she would have Beb.

The day after they became engaged Beb wrote a letter to Cynthia in language which, to us, is curiously reminiscent of Barrie or Walter de la Mare but, for him, was some kind of unconscious anticipation of the future.

I hope that you slept late into the morning and that you weren't uneasy about the 'dream' when you woke up. I don't think there was any reason to be – I thought that I might repent of it, but I find that it has left me in a 'golden' frame of mind and has done an infinite amount of good in other ways, and I'm sure you won't think that I should look on your sweetness as giving me a licence to be familiar.[28]

⋯⋯⇀ Chapter 10 ↽⋯⋯
1908

A secret engagement has the drawback that if no-one knows about it, no-one is intrigued by it. Cynthia had to continue to play her role of 'popular girl' while, privately, binding herself to Beb. There was a lot of discussion about what form this binding took. Cynthia, evidently, would have liked Beb to be a bit more passionate, a bit braver. Beb, the barrister, was circumspect. 'I couldn't say I was "bound" without in a sense binding you' he wrote, and 'I am bound by it, but it would be wrong for you to be'.[1] He was always practical: 'I'm afraid sentimentality however extreme does not make as much difference as people suppose & you must remember that however much I care for you, I can't feel as though I had a claim upon you of any kind'. (There cannot be many women, eager to read words of love, who would be stirred by the phrase 'sentimentality however extreme'. But Cynthia could comfort herself that Beb, and she, had to write as though their letters might be read by their parents.)

They had not met very often over the summer and autumn of 1907, and cannot have been alone together very much. They knew that if they were to be formally stopped from seeing each other, meetings would become even more difficult; as it was, they could 'sit out' a dance or walk on a terrace or 'frowst' by a library fire during a Saturday-to-Monday. Cynthia was careful to avoid suspicion (it was important that her reputation remained unsullied) and considered a decoy-duck to be necessary. It had to be a plausible one, not a Guard or an aristocrat, for Cynthia's leanings were well-known by now, and therefore he had to be chosen from the group of Oxford men whose names turn up so frequently both at this period and for the next ten years.

Aubrey Herbert, George Vernon, Jasper Ridley, Julian and Billy Grenfell, Charles Lister, Bron Lucas, Patrick Shaw Stewart, Edward Horner, Conrad Russell, Robert Smallbones, Harold Baker – all were among Cynthia's 'set'. ('Write and tell me gossip about people. Cynthia and her admirers, the "Set", etc . . . Is the "Set" as consolidated as of old?'[2] Ego asked in 1908). And it was Smallbones 'Bones' and Harold Baker 'Bluey' who appeared to outsiders to be the most persistent. They both followed the pattern of Oxford, Foreign Office or the Bar; Bluey, the most favoured, was to go on being fond of Cynthia until the end of the First World War when he fell in love with 'Goonie' Churchill. The family legend is that Cynthia did not marry Bluey because he suggested that they sit under a tree, got out a large pocket handkerchief, placed it on the primroses and sat on it.[3]

Bones must have had a long drawn-out and rather trying relationship with Cynthia and it was probably he who proposed to her when she was fifteen since he visited her in Dresden. The pattern set with Bones was to become a familiar one – she dazzled physically and intellectually, approached, withdrew but did not back off entirely – preferring to keep her pursuer hopeful – and adopted that slightly withdrawn demeanour that young men were to think was a trait of character rather than a sign of boredom. 'Elusive' and 'squirrel-like' were words that were to be often bandied about in the next fifty years.

The summer term of 1907 was Ego's last at Oxford. The Elchos took the Norman Hall at Sutton Courtney in Oxfordshire for Commem Week, and various festivities took place, some at Sutton Courtney and some in Oxford. There is a surviving photograph which shows the guests, posing by a very obviously Norman door, after luncheon on 28 June. It shows Cynthia and Guy (but not Ego), Evelyn de Vesci and her daughter Mary, Katharine Horner, Letty Manners, George Vernon, Harold Baker, Smallbones, the Bursar of Trinity Mr Raper, and Mary Elcho and Balfour.

Raymond wrote to Cynthia to thank her for one of the Commem Week events that he had attended. He began by praising Bones's character and efficiency and went on:

Perhaps you deal more kindly with him in his position than I give you credit for; but I do feel that there is an occasion for dropping an extra lump of sugar in his cup – Please do, Cynthia. If I were he, and you didn't, I *should* be so miserable. But perhaps you do drop in lumps – when no one is looking except the owner of each particular cup – In fact I think you must. They all swill so much tannin in public – and always ask you for more. I used to think Ettie the past mistress of method: but now I put you easily first. You are the super-woman – You fight with masked batteries – It is magnificent – and it is also war.[4]

The comparison of Cynthia with Ettie is shrewd. Already at nine-teen Cynthia seems, whether consciously or not, to have been adopting 'Ettyism' as a creed – one which she was to adapt to her own style, but remain loyal to, throughout her life. It had various facets, of which the best known was a determined cheeri-ness. Ettie felt that it was defeatist, a negation of life itself, not to be happy about everything. Even tragedy could be exploited as a source of ecstacy and vitality. Mary once, memorably, defined Ettie's philosophy as her 'stubborn gospel of joy'.[5] Cynthia lifted the phrase for her memoirs and even Ettie's biographer assumed that Cynthia coined it, but, to be fair, the phrase had by then become part of Charteris vocabulary. The word stubborn contains its own side-kick, as does the word insistence in Balfour's phrase 'her deliberate insistence that everything is a success'.[6] During the war Cynthia was occasionally to analyse Ettie in her diary, for it was then that her qualities came into their own. After her son Julian was killed she was to be in a state 'not even of hysterical exaltedness, but of real immunity to grief of the ordinary sort . . . She will not break down, wears colours, and scarcely admits she is to be pitied at all. Can it last? One feels there must be a reaction to flatness and just the daily longing. The only thing is, she has got such marvellous powers of bluffing herself that she may succeed'.[7]

Ettie's creed was so definitive it was also blinkered. She refused to notice what she did not want to see and this Cynthia was to be guilty of as she grew older. But, as a young girl, the aspect of Ettyism she had only just begun to adopt was the emotional one, in particular her tentacle-like attitude to men. She adapted it to the twentieth century, but elements of it will be seen in all her sexual relationships. The twin pulls of Mary, warm, unaffected and sincere, and of Ettie, manipulative, obsessively optimistic, complacent and cold, though 'radiant' (a word that people used a good deal about Ettie) and delightful on the surface, were both to be an important part of Cynthia's life. She was to need marriage; the stability of a long-lasting *amitié amoureuse* such as Mary had with Balfour; and admirers, men who were entranced by her, who came to love her, to whom she gave lumps of sugar but kept, finally, at a distance, while holding on to them as long as she could; then, when the time for a break could not be put off any longer, she would blame her own failings so that the man would feel abject. There would never be a final rupture – Cynthia, like Ettie, remained friends with her lovers.

After Raymond was married he took Katharine to Venice. Here he saw something of Cynthia. ('Do come to Venice. Do. Do' he had written to her.) Whether she contrived it, whether it was coincidence or whether the unsuspicious Mary viewed the time in Italy as merely a delightful meeting of old friends, is debatable. Mary remembered:

> In September Cynthia, Harold Baker, Ego and I went to Venice. We stopped one night in Milan and saw the Cathedral . . . We spent a good deal of time in Venice at the melodramatic 'movies', then quite new to us. We also did all the regular sight-seeing. Katharine and Raymond Asquith were there on their honeymoon.[8]

Ego told Bones that they looked very happy. It is rather too easy to imagine the feelings of Cynthia, and her sexual fantasies and identification with Katharine as she observed this older, more debonair but so closely related version of the man that she was secretly engaged to marry.

The newly-weds had a double piquancy for her because she and Katharine were often compared with one another. Both were daughters of Souls, both had unusual Pre-Raphaelite looks (Burne-Jones drew each of them as children) and both had a reputation for cleverness. Katharine was more intellectual, her knowledge, for example of the classics, was deeper; Cynthia was wittier and sharper. Comparison of the two was a favourite topic of conversation: Venetia Stanley told Edwin Montagu that, although interesting, the topic should not be allowed to over-shadow politics, adding, 'I always like you to talk to me about these more important and vital issues in your life rather than permanently to stick to . . . whether Cynthia is nicer than Katharine or Cys cleverer than Raymond!'[9] And Margot wrote in her diary for October 1914: 'The Tennants are so tremendously vital that after them no one seems to me to have much life: when I look at my beautiful delicious daughters-in-law I almost wonder by what impulse they move at all (Cynthia is less of a spectator than Katharine). I expect my restless energies have a dampening effect tho' they worship me and I adore them'.[10] Katharine and Cynthia were to remain very close but began to drift apart during the war when Cynthia began to be known as a woman who liked the company of other men even while her husband was at the Front. Then, in the 1920s, Cynthia veered towards the literary world and Katharine towards that of the countrified Roman Catholics.

That autumn of 1907, after her holiday in Italy, Cynthia was, on the surface, preoccupied by her routine of Stanway, Saturday-to-Mondays, theatres and dinners and visits to the dressmaker in London, the enlarging and maintaining of a social circle, a few books read and poems learnt by heart. As yet she and Beb were not forbidden to meet.

Then in the second week of April 1908 H.H. became Prime Minister. In early May the family moved from 20 Cavendish Square to 10 Downing Street. And in June there was an Elcho crisis: Hugo put his foot down. It was one thing for his eldest daughter to be seeing too much of the younger son of the Chancellor of the Exchequer, quite another for her to be even imagining herself the daughter-in-law of a Liberal Prime Minister.

The fact that Cynthia was only twenty, and that Beb was the grandson of a wool-trade worker, were important factors in Hugo's attitude. But the political situation angered him most. In the past, his attitude had not been very different from that of the Horners to Raymond. Tories and Liberals may have sat on opposite sides of the House of Commons, but socially they were intertwined. H.H. met Balfour not only at Stanway and other houses but also in Scotland; Archerfield, the house the Asquiths were at this period borrowing every autumn, was close to Gosford and Whittingehame and the families often met (despite H.H.'s preference for golf and Balfour's for tennis). How intertwined they were politically is apparent from an anecdote related by Balfour's biographer. In 1898 Margot had written to Balfour asking him if he 'would use his influence with her father to persuade him to make Asquith independent of the Bar'[11] so that he could become Leader of the Liberal Party. Balfour tried but Charles Tennant refused: he was a Liberal, but he was also a stickler for seniority and he believed that Campbell-Bannerman took precedence.

The incident illustrates that in the 1890s the parties were not deeply divided. After the election of 1906 this was, however, no longer so. The Liberals gained complete dominance in the House of Commons in an electoral revolution in which Balfour detected 'a faint echo of the same movement which has produced massacres in St. Petersburg, riots in Vienna, and Socialist processions in Berlin'.[12] And the Conservatives ruthlessly used their dominance in the House of Lords to mount a campaign of vigorous opposition orchestrated by Balfour and Lansdowne.

> Both were aristocrats born in the purple. They belonged to, they led in, and they felt themselves charged with the fortunes of, a small privileged class; which for centuries had exercised a sort of collective kingship, and at the bottom of its thinking instinctively believed that it had a divine right to do so. Passionately devoted to the greatness of England, these men were convinced that she owed it to patrician rule.[13]

The inevitable result of their strategy was a constitutional crisis about the powers of the House of Lords.

From the Wemyss vantage-point Asquith's years as Chancellor had confirmed the dangers of this radical Government; his first years as Prime Minister were to be even worse. Lloyd George, as his Chancellor, promoted a series of Land Taxes 'for raising money to wage implacable warfare against poverty and squalidness'.[14] He further provoked the Lords by asking whether 'five hundred men, ordinary men chosen accidentally among the unemployed, should override the judgement – the deliberate judgement – of millions of people who are engaged in the industry which makes the wealth of the country?'[15] In this atmosphere it was as if the daughter of a Tory peer wanted to marry the son of Arthur Scargill.

Was Cynthia in love? Certainly, like every girl with nothing to do, she was far more in love with love than with Beb. Yet she loved him and he loved her, they had both met many other people, and they felt that temperamentally and sexually the omens were good. Nevertheless, there was a chasm between them and it was to affect Cynthia all her life. 'Society', the chain of connections from one person to the next, was her first love. The Asquiths, however, were not as gregarious as most of their friends and were intolerant of much that Cynthia had been brought up to believe in. She saw gregariousness as a duty, indeed a purpose. She could no sooner have sat silently at a dinner party than she could have taken her clothes off. Those who could not be bothered to 'perform' were, in her eyes, *mal elévé*, and even Raymond was not immune from her criticism. In 1909 she received a letter from him that she sent on to Beb with the comment that she thought it 'a very eloquent piece of English but don't quote it to him. It also shows how beautifully spoilt he had always been'. Raymond wrote:

How wrong you are in thinking that it was my 'capacity-for-enjoyment-pride' which was injured by the scarring experience of last week! I am not Ettie. I take no pride in enjoying things which are essentially unenjoyable – I could no more have enjoyed or wished to enjoy that party than I could have enjoyed or wished to enjoy eating soot or having leprosy. If I had enjoyed it, so far from being a source of pride it would have been a source of disgust and self-contempt. No: it is not that at all. But there is an area of one's life between 8pm and midnight which is set apart for the pursuit of pleasure; sometimes one fills it for oneself, at other times one hands over the holy hours to another.[16]

The eloquent tirade continued, the gist of it being that to host a dinner party like the one he and Cynthia had attended the previous week, composed of ugly women, dull men, bad food and still wine was as heinous a crime as any. With this point of view Cynthia did not agree, but she found it amusing. She saw the falsity of the convention that turns the dinner-party into the climax and crux of the day; but since this was how society organised itself she felt obliged to follow the rules.

No better aphrodisiac could have been arranged than to forbid Beb and Cynthia to meet; thus their courtship became especially delightful during the second half of 1908. The restraint of 'I am looking forward to seeing you again' of April gave way to 'the policy of separation as well as being melodramatic is curiously barbarous, if it is effectively carried out . . . Goodnight, dearest love'.

But it was now that meetings were suddenly simplified. Katharine had given birth to a daughter, Helen, and it became possible for Beb and Cynthia to go, separately, to 49 Bedford Square to visit her and then, as if by chance, to leave together and walk in the square (Katharine would leave the key of the square on the hall table for them). If it was impossible to do this without causing suspicion, they agreed, then they would meet at the front gate of the British Museum.

All of these plans were very reckless for a twenty-one year old girl in 1908, but Cynthia enjoyed the intrigue. Also, there was the additional *frisson* that their relationship had become sexual. Cynthia wrote, after she had been unable to go to Bedford Square, 'I am sorry not to have been able to spoil you to-night' and Beb replied, 'Will you come *every* night to Bedford Square with the *blanket*?' There was unlikely to have been more than some passionate kissing but the unsurprising effect was to make Cynthia feel guilty. She did not feel as though she would be struck down by God or the devil, for the atmosphere of her upbringing had been on the whole tolerant and free-thinking, but she was enough a creature of convention to feel it against her nature to sit on a rug in Bedford Square kissing a man she was not supposed to be seeing.

Cynthia complained of being 'enveloped in a pall'; Beb suggested reading or hunting as a cure, and wondered whether men feel the pall less heavily because they 'lose it in the mechanical processes of the day'. But he was not insensitive to the conflicts Cynthia was feeling, telling her, 'I will get the key of Cavendish Square if you can manage to come there [this, evidently, had not been given up with the move to Downing Street]. If you want to stop doing that, my darling, you must tell me and don't think it could make any difficulty between us. You must be quite open about everything like that'. When writing with real intimacy Beb and Cynthia called each other Bushtail and Rag. 'Goodnight, my love; and may Bushtail think of you' wrote Beb; 'go on loving your Rag. You don't have much chance of wearing it out' replied Cynthia.

'To-day I really feel much better than I have for some time; I think any violent dislocation of one's habits gives one a hectic feeling of health' Cynthia informed Beb after they had done a night walk at the end of December. Beb found the dislocation to his habits inspirational and began to write poetry. Cynthia was very proud of it and would make comments:' "The winged vanguard of the free" and the preceeding lines are excellent and I like the verse ending with the "heartbeat of eternity" *very* much, but I am delighted with it *all* . . . Thank you for it darling, you should write some more, I should like to "discover" a poet and I will send you a laurel wreath . . . Shall I inscribe it in my white vellum sanctuary?'

The 'sanctuary' still exists; it was a present from Madeline who was always fond of commonplace books. The vellum is dark grey now, but 'Cynthia' is embossed in gilt on the front and inside is the date March 1907. In large, firm, rather Germanic handwriting Cynthia filled the book with copied-out poems, poems cut out from a printed book and pasted-in pictures. On the first page there is a painting of the Virgin Mary and child with saints around her. (Years later Cynthia was to cut out the face and insert a photograph of herself on another similar painting, a gesture which was to cause shudders among those who failed to realise that this was done more as a joke than out of outrageous conceit or religious piety.) The poems are a predictable mixture of Keats, Shakespeare sonnets, the Rossetti sonnet that was always to be a favourite and that was to inspire a book title (*Remember and Be*

Glad) and A.E. Housman. The pictures are strongly Pre-Raphaelite with some Dürer, Fra Angelico and two photographs of Rodin's Kiss. The impression is of a young girl yearning for love: which is what Cynthia was. I, as biographer, searched for Beb's poem to see if she had indeed inscribed it in her commonplace book. None of the poems are ascribed to authors, so all I had to go on was the phrase 'heartbeat of eternity'. After reading a book-full of poems which were either Tennyson, Browning, Meredith – or Herbert Asquith (as well as Rossetti, etc) I decided that the distinction between great and ordinary-mortal poetry is not one I can really understand any more, and I never did find Beb's poem; poignantly, after fifty pages of 'I will arise now' and 'Was this the face that launched a thousand ships' and 'When thou must home to shades of underground' comes the first war poem. The rest of the book consists entirely of these. The love poetry has become a thing of the past, it belongs to the days before the war.

....≫· Chapter 11 ·≪····
Marriage: 1909–10

'Will has begun another head of Cynthia'[1] wrote Jane von Glehn from Broadway on 14 August 1908. Wilfred and Jane von Glehn (they changed to de Glehn in 1914) were friends of Sargent's and were one of the group of Broadway painters who used often to go over to Stanway. That autumn the head became a full-scale oil painting. Cynthia went to the studio at 73 Cheyne Walk and there von Glehn finished the head, the dress and the up-turned arm, and added some furniture which he used in his studio as props.

In February Cynthia went to Canada and North America for six weeks. It was thought wise to distance her from Beb and the English winter, for she had been showing signs of lassitude. Her letters to Ego, who was honorary attaché at the British Embassy in Washington, had been so unhappy that he responded:

> You write very gloomy and alarming statements in your letters, but I do not believe them, as they are not endorsed by Mama. You might possibly make a wreck of your life without her noticing, but you could not waste away with anaemia and not attract the attention of her medical eye.[2]

Cynthia told Beb that 'Mama obviously wants me to go and I think she would be rather hurt if I took up a strong line against – besides it would really be a chance it would be a pity to miss if only one felt in the mood for it.' (She was in fact never to go to North America again.)

Mary and Cynthia arrived at Quebec on 19 February. Ego joined them from Washington. Three days later they went to Ottawa where they stayed in the Governor-General's house and had a very sociable time. ('I see that *partis* are being frantically dangled before poor Cynthia's eye'[3] Ego wrote to Mary Vesey.) 'Many interesting people came to dinner'[4] remembered Mary, proceeding to list them. They went to Niagara and, at the end of March, to Washington where they shook hands with President Taft at the White House and 'were given numerous luncheons, teas and dinners'. In April they had a couple of days in New York. They dined with the Vanderbilts and went to the Opera and steamed away in the ill-fated *Lusitania*.

But Cynthia failed to be improved by her American trip, and Beb continued to be indecisive. When Cynthia was longing to be swept off her feet he urged her to expand her horizons as far as possible. 'A life of many friends . . . means constant adulation and no committal and each competitor by instinct shews his best facet . . . you should not be hedged and penned but have a free hand to see whom you like for that is the only way in which you can make the most of your youth.' Then, in early June 1909, they managed to be together for most of a week at Penrhos, the home in Wales of Venetia Stanley's father Lord Sheffield. After this week Cynthia spoke to Mary again (it was now two years since she and Beb had first declared themselves to each other) and she in her turn spoke to Hugo. Beb was to be allowed to start courting Cynthia 'in a suitable party' i.e. chaperoned by other young people.

Sargent drew Cynthia this summer, a conventional enough event – ' "How do you like your Sargent drawing?" was the conversational gambit of one distinguished diplomat to ladies he had never met before, and he claimed that it was successful nine times out of ten.'[5] Cynthia thought 'the one of me presents the foulest woman I have ever seen'.[6] It is a charcoal drawing done in two sittings and does, as she thought, make Cynthia look very square-faced. During the first sitting Mrs Patrick Campbell came to watch the proceedings and to make Cynthia laugh by telling Sargent: 'Mind you get the preposterous width between her green eyes. They're so far apart that if a fly wanted to go from one to another he would have to take a fly – I mean a cab'.[7]

In August she paid a visit to the Dolomites with Mary Vesey and Venetia Stanley. 'Have you had any difficult climbs and are you wearing check knickerbockers?' inquired Beb (she was). When she returned he was invited to Stanway. Cynthia told him, 'You must be very brave and 'nonchalant' and not look shy . . .

You will have to come through fires of embarrassment and discomfort for me'. The occasion passed off without incident – Cynthia and Beb went on a night walk, but this time it was not illicit. Two weeks later Ego and Aubrey Herbert had a wrestling match and the latter broke a bone in his ankle. Cynthia and Mary Vesey, who was also staying at Stanway, looked after him, and it was now, in the November of 1909, that Mary began to warm towards Aubrey. Cynthia told him after he had left: 'You are sceptical about my possession of a heart, but I promise you I am really very very sorry for you . . . I must take my morphia now – I am tired though not sleepy. I have promoted myself to 5 grains now and oh! the dreams I have. Thank you for giving me the key to such a paradise: you were a blessed pioneer. My real life no longer matters; one can always escape to a substitute golden sphere'.[8] (This is the one occasion she mentions this drug, popular with her contemporaries.)

She discovered another golden sphere a few weeks later: just before Christmas she acted at the Court Theatre in Sloane Square and found the experience intoxicating. To raise money for charity Alfred Lyttelton's wife 'D.D.' wrote a play centring on the Carpaccio pictures of St Ursula and the eleven thousand virgins, each thousand of them being acted by one of Cynthia's contemporaries; for each of the four performances she played St Ursula, and Diana Manners was among those who were struck by her 'radiant *quattrocento* beauty with her heavy gold hair falling to her knees'.[9] Stella Campbell, in angels' wings, visited Cynthia in bed, a four-poster exactly copied from the one in the pictures in which, for reasons of decency, she was 'discovered' rather than seen getting into. Some were nevertheless affronted: Charles Lister wrote, 'I rather agree with Elcho on the four-poster question, but then I am an old-fashioned moralist, and not always in sympathy with the spirit of my age'.[10] Ego, Guy and Yvo roared with laughter throughout the performance.

Cynthia received some fan mail after this role and, in the New Year, was asked by Maurice Maeterlinck's wife to come to Belgium to be trained to play the heroines in her husband's plays. Cynthia felt some affinity with his work, and especially with *The Blue Bird* which had opened at the Haymarket Theatre in the same month that she had appeared at the Court. This allegorical drama owed many debts not only to *Peter Pan* but also to the novel from which it derived, *The Little White Bird*, which Barrie had written in 1902. It is clear why Cynthia, at this period of her life, admired Maeterlinck. As the poet Edward Thomas observed about him in 1911:

His early plays have a melancholy, a romance of unreality, a morbidity combined with innocence, which piques our indulgence. He has no irony to put us on the defensive . . . Then his *Blue Bird* allows itself to be so presented on our stage that it rivals the celebrated *Peter Pan*, and even resembles it; it is also sentimental, indefinitely mysterious and significant.[11]

Also in the January of 1910 Cynthia received a telegram from the producer of *The Blue Bird*, Herbert Trench. He wanted Cynthia to act in a comedy called *Priscilla Runs Away* and the telegram read 'Will you play lead in new play at Haymarket, without your name and at your own terms?' Cynthia told Katharine:

After endless thought, prayer and superstitious rites I had quite decided to accept Trench's offer and boldly embark on a new chapter in my life – but my father's contribution was too crushing – after three unanswered telegrams we despatched a fourth and the only reply he deigned to send was 'Think you must all be dotty'. A furious forbidding might have been withstood but this contempt quite broke my spirit. If it had been Rosalind or any wonderful part I might have telegraphed 'Engagement already clinched – am of age – can support myself' but I was too doubtful about this play to make it worthwhile burning one's family boats.[12]

Beb thought that 'for you to have a run of 100 nights or so among a mixed company would be a terrible thing' and Raymond commented: 'I expect that you feel about Trench rather as I do when I am supplicated to become a member of Parliament – divided between a loathing for drudgery and a liking for *éclat*. I hope you will decide as I have done. You are too young to be public'. Yet Cynthia would have been an excellent actress: part of her was always acting a role and she loved the theatre, dressing up and disguise. In the event *Priscilla Runs Away*, 'a charming, romantic story of a mid-European court',[13] ran for 192 performances with the eighteen year-old Phyllis Neilson-Terry in the lead. It opened on 28 June, exactly a month before Cynthia's wedding.

Since the previous autumn Beb had been allowed to see Cynthia 'officially', although there was no respite in the constitutional crisis. In January 1910 Asquith held an election which he won. Yet, deeply worried at the mere possibility of his daughter going on the stage, in March Hugo capitulated: better his daughter marry a penniless Liberal than become an actress. From Beb's point of view it was just in time: 'I hope you haven't abandoned me altogether' he wrote, adding, 'if you keep a finger on the thread, it is enough'.

Mary and Cynthia now had a long talk and a period of haggling began. Beb told Mary: 'I think I recognise the material and to a certain extent the political difficulties' and apologised that Mary, once again, had taken on the role of negotiator. He told her that H.H. had guaranteed £1000 (£25,000) a year, including his earnings, 'but I think he expects Lord Wemyss to settle about half that amount on Cynthia.' He added that 'my father would be equally opposed on political and financial grounds, but he regards these as subordinate aspects'.

Beb had an interview with Hugo on 19 April. Hugo said he would oppose Lord Wemyss settling upon Cynthia more than £200 a year and that out of the total of £1200 they would then have, he would expect Beb to pay £300 (£7500) a year to insure his life (which seems a vast fortune by comparison with the cost of life insurance nowadays). Beb wrote to Mary: 'My own view is that Cincie ought to have at least £1500 (£37,000) a year in order to be decently provided for, and I do not understand Lord Elcho's view that he ought to oppose his father in making a small settlement upon his daughter. I think my father might be ready to guarantee £1100 a year if Cincie's family provide £400 a year . . . I am very sorry for writing you a business letter.' To Cynthia he said, 'I am sorry your mother made herself ill by her daring joust with your papa'.

On 28 April, the day which saw the triumphant passing of the Budget though the House of Lords, H.H. and Mary lunched together. All during May negotiations continued, being a little slowed up by the death of the King on 6 May. But by the middle of the month close members of the family were sending letters of congratulation. Cynthia confessed to Katharine Asquith that she had not told her of her engagement before

because I felt instinctively that you were disapproving. I am sorry about this as I should value your appreciation more than anyone's, as it is I have dreaded confessing to you more than anyone except perhaps Polly and I am more frightened of you than of any of my family. Opposition based on the Heygate objections – money and so on – though inconvenient is not embarassing because – though I am far from underestimating these drawbacks – it is quite easy to argue about that side of the question. It would be quite easy to justify myself to you if you were in sympathy with the more vital and intrinsic thing, but I know you do not like Beb and that the whole situation surprises you – and however convinced one may be oneself it is impossible for one even to try and convert any one as this kind of thing is too intangible and undogmatic to be even like an opinion – But I know you are understanding enough to be able to guess how extraordinarily different people can be in different relationships and I think this applies to Beb more than to anyone else – I simply cannot recognise him when he is with other people, and I quite understand what you feel about him. *Please* don't think I feel the slightest resentment about this – I don't in the very least – I only regret it in case it should make you like *me* less and feel at all out of sympathy . . .[14]

And she told Patrick Shaw Stewart that since they had tacitly agreed that she 'should ultimately make what is called a "good" marriage so that I might be able to provide you with glittering *gîtes*, good shooting and tiarared society, I have been riding under false colours and I feel I owe you an apology'.[15]

The engagement could not have come at a politically more sensitive moment. Although the Lords had finally passed the Budget, they had brought onto themselves Liberal proposals to curb their powers which enraged Lord Wemyss still further. In June, H.H. opened his 'Round Table' negotiations with the Tories on these proposals. That preparations for the wedding had to take place against the background of an important constitutional crisis inflamed the Montagu and Capulet situation even more; as *The Times* obituary writer was to note almost exactly fifty years later, 'at the time of her wedding political feeling was running high and characteristically the bride advised the ushers to separate the guest according to their Liberal or Conservative leanings rather than by more traditional attachments to bride or bridegroom'.[16]

But the wedding, planned for 10 July, had to be postponed until the end of the month. Cynthia fell dramatically and unexpectedly ill and her appendix was removed. Everyone thought that herein lay the explanation for her depressions ('mental anaemia' Ego called it). Raymond told Katharine that the operation 'will probably have the effect of raising her vital powers and getting rid for ever of the headaches and vapours from which she had been used to suffer. Still it seems rather hard to lose both your appendix and your virginity within a single month'.[17] Cynthia convalesced at Lympne Castle in Kent and from here, weepily, wrote many thank-you letters.

The wedding took place on Thursday 28 July at Holy Trinity, Sloane Street. It was precisely three years after Raymond and Katharine's wedding on Thursday 25 July 1907. Cynthia, like Katharine, was attended by many bridesmaids and all the trappings of a large society wedding and the details were fulsomely reported in next day's *Times*. It happened to be the issue that carried the famous report that 'the Montreal *Star* yesterday afternoon received the following wireless message from the steamer *Montrose* – "Dr Crippen, wanted London for murder Belle Elmore actress, aboard." '

····➤· Chapter 12 ·◄◄····
1910–12

After the wedding Mr Herbert and the Hon. Mrs Asquith went by train to Avon Tyrrell in the New Forest. *The Times* reported that they were going to Gloucestershire: 'Later they will go to Egypt, where Mr Asquith holds an appointment and will make their home in that country.' A correction was printed next day. Hugo and Mary must have wondered whether this was a genuine error, or a practical joke arranged by someone who knew about the events of fifteen years before.

They idled around the garden eating gooseberries. Beb drew Cynthia, she read aloud, 'two rather incompatible activities as for the former I have to take off my spectacles'.[1] Cynthia had frequent baths laced with the verbena salts given to her by Mary: the smell wafted around the garden, while Beb sat outside and got down to his correspondence. He thanked Mary for all the help she had given them, assured her that Cincie was well and asked her for some addresses: 'v: Sidney Webb, vi: Berenson, vii: Lady Herbert (Cincie has already thanked one Lady Herbert, do you know who the second one is?)' There were many wedding presents to thank for, as the list in *The Times* testifies (it remained fashionable to publish this until the 1940s). Some were utilitarian: Lady Edward Cecil gave an 'old chair', Lady Northcote a blue enamel bell push, 'servants at 10 Downing Street silver inkstand; servants at 62 Cadogan Square silver mustard and pepper pots; and tenants at Stanway blue enamel watch and chain'. Lady Elcho gave an ostrich feather fan, the Prime Minister and Mrs Asquith a diamond tiara and Mr Balfour a diamond and sapphire brooch. (Blue enamel must have been fashionable in 1910 because Mrs Winston Churchill gave a blue enamel necklet which would have nicely matched the bell push and the watch and chain.)

A few addresses proved elusive and it was the beginning of the next year before Cynthia discovered Berenson's.* He replied to her letter quite severely, unwilling to allow the Souls' love of exaggeration: 'I'm charmed to hear fr. you, but how dreadful you should have had such a time getting my address, & how absurd that you should have had me on yr. conscience. One's honeymoon is not a time for polite trifles, & one should have forgotten them before that is over. Take my advice & harden your social conscience.'[2]

But practical matters could not be ignored. The financial question had been settled with the Asquiths having an income of £900 a year, leaving them £700 (£17,500) after tax, a comfortable enough amount when 'at the outbreak of the First World War, a young professional couple starting their married life with £250 a year and a leasehold house could still afford (and secure) a general servant, who received £18 a year and "all found"'.[3] Why H. H. felt that it was right to guarantee five-sixths of Beb's income is not obvious. But, whatever his intentions, his action meant that Beb was not going to 'have' to work at a career and was to be ultimately disastrous for Cynthia. It was one thing to face a future of 'living on cold beef & bicycling to save bus-fares';[4] it was another to be aimless.

However, for the moment, Beb looked forward to a life at the Bar. When, during the period of their engagement, he and Cynthia had begun to househunt, they had fixed on a house within walking distance of Raymond and Katharine in Bedford Square and of Lincoln's Inn – 38 Brunswick Square. 'I am busily upholstering in my mind's eye'[5] Cynthia told Beb while convalescing at Lympne Castle and, during the first days of their honeymoon, they both visualised sitting on a bench in the Square; the tram clanking south along Gray's Inn Road towards Downing Street or the bus going westwards along Theobalds Road towards Marble Arch and Knightsbridge; groceries and fish delivered by boys on bicycles from Lamb's Conduit Street and Marchmont Street. Like the Darlings in *Peter Pan* (who lived in Bloomsbury) their life would be rather Bohemian, in cheerfully straitened

*Mary Elcho had met him through her new friend Edith Wharton.

circumstances, and they would nurture their intellectual and literary rather than their aristocratic and political connections.

Then, cautiously, Beb rejected Brunswick Square because his solicitor advised that, the lease being only nineteen years, the house would be hard to re-let should that become necessary. Number 38 remained empty for another year; then it became the third Bloomsbury house lived in by the Stephens, the lease being signed by Maynard Keynes. He had the ground floor, Adrian Stephen the first (one of his rooms was decorated by Duncan Grant with life-sized nude figures of tennis players) and Virginia the second. When, in December, Leonard Woolf took the top floor he was charged 35/ – a week 'to include light, coals, hot baths and service'.[6] This would have been about £450 a year for all five of them (or two-thirds of the Asquiths' income). Yet the house was considered cheap. 'The one thing that seems certain is that a house is the cheapest way of living, and if you have a house you must have servants'[7] observed Virginia who thought that 'the Sq. is like Paradise, and there are the Foundlings [Hospital] for angels'.[8]

But the Asquiths had no regrets – they could have changed their minds during the months the house lay empty – and went off to Italy in the middle of August without the prospect of a home to return to. (Three years earlier Raymond and Katharine had gone from Avon Tyrrell to Italy to 20 Cavendish Square, moving in to a house of their own more than six months after they were married – as Beb and Cynthia were to do.) Yet it was not a good omen – the exaggerated caution, the indecisiveness and the easy assumption that other homes would welcome them if they had not settled on one of their own. And, unfairly, Italy was, for Cynthia, 'the worst bit of life I have ever had'.[9] She had conceived immediately and was beginning to feel sick on their arrival in Venice. By the time they reached the Herbert villa at Portofino she was in that state of mingled nausea, depression and weariness that cannot be imagined by those who have not experienced it. Back in London, at Downing Street, she wrote to Katharine.

Oh Katharine – never dare to complain of *your* misfortunes to me again & never chide tactful little Helen – *you* had at least 6 mths of peace & happiness: *I* have had no respite at all! It is terribly improvident & I don't know how the situation is to be coped with on an income of £700 net a year; but I might be resigned if I wasn't so terribly ill – *You* were in a position to shudder at poor O's grossness in asking you if you felt sick – *I* should fall on the neck of a fellow sufferer. It will probably make you think me disgusting, but I must confess that I am sick – not only in the morning – but *all* day. It is like an eternal sea-voyage & I am never safe . . . I very nearly died at Portofino . . . You will think this a disgusting & shameless letter & it is exactly the part I resent most that every other emotion & sensation should be drowned in the consciousness of nausea.[10]

By the end of September Cynthia felt better but cannot have been pleased that the role of mother was going to give her so little time to adjust to the role of wife. There is no day by day or even month by month record of her life at this time. During the winter she was at Stanway a good deal, joining Beb at 10 Downing Street when she came up to London. 'At present I am living practically in the Cabinet'[11] she wrote to Wilfrid Blunt when thanking him for some pheasants. 'It is rather alarming as I am always afraid of blundering into a Council and I constantly run into Lloyd George on the stairs.' Every Friday-to-Monday she and Beb were away; thus, although they saw each other far more, and shared a bedroom when possible – it was to be a few years before poor Margot caused difficulties by putting the two of them in the *same* bedroom – the day to day nature of their lives had changed very little. Both of them still depended on other people to arrange and provide, and as long as they fitted in amiably they felt they were doing all that was expected of them.

In December Cynthia mentioned that 'we have taken a rather indifferent house in Regents Park after ages of dreary hunting, but there is no prospect of getting in to it for some time as the inhabitants refuse to be evicted'.[12] Actually Sussex Place is one of the most striking of the Nash terraces, its stucco fronts curving along the south-west corner of the park, the pattern of bay windows and Corinthian columns emphasised by steep octagonal domes (which, nowadays, echo the vast copper roof of the mosque some yards to the north). The twenty-six houses had a large garden between them and the road, and enjoyed a clear view of the lake beyond the railings. They look like a cross between a stage set and Brighton Pavilion, settings of which Cynthia was fond. As Pevsner observes: 'The terraces are urban, but their setting is countrified. Tenants paid the price for a three-window terrace house and obtained the illusion of living in a vast mansion in its own grounds.'[13] And Elizabeth Bowen, who was later to be the Asquiths' friend and neighbour in Clarence Terrace, described the view from the top-floor windows: 'You saw the park, with its map of lawns and walks, the narrow part of the lake, the diagonal iron bridge . . . you saw, as though in the country, nothing but tops of trees'.[14]

8 Sussex Place, 'about 3½ minutes from Baker St Station',[15] had the same green tranquillity as Stanway and Keats Grove (it was even fronted by a tennis court that the leaseholders could use one day a week); yet it had the urban feel of Cadogan Square and Downing Street. The backcloth of blossom trees and tulips and bandstand made it sensuously ravishing, yet its slightly raffish location gave it something of the maverick quality that had made Bloomsbury so attractive. 'North of the park' was always to be a slightly unusual address for someone of Cynthia's background, but the telephone exchange was suitably aristocratic – Mayfair – and the number oddly prophetic of the watershed to come - 1914.

Beb and Cynthia spent their first night at Number 8 on 20 February. 'We are actually going into the house to sleep tonight. I am so excited about it'[16] Cynthia told Madeline who, although nearly eighty, was still as passionate as ever about fabrics and furnishings and had sent Cynthia some cushions. It was an early spring in 1911 and the daffodils were just flowering as Cynthia tried to settle into a way of life to which she was quite unused and quite unsuited – ordering meals, employing housemaids, walking down to Selfridges to buy coat-hangers. Yet it all had an air of unreality because virtually every day that she was in London she dined out, had luncheon in a restaurant or asked for an egg on a tray. Marriage had not yet engendered any kind of domesticity and there was enough money to make running a house an easy matter to delegate.

Politics were quite as preoccupying as daily life, that winter of 1910–11. Just before the General Election Beb wrote to 'dear Lady Elcho' (it was to be another three years before she became 'dear Mamma') mentioning Ego's 'very low spirits about the rather precarious position of the Upper House'[17] and went on to describe an extremely political Friday-to-Monday at Pixton where Aubrey Herbert (who had been married to Mary Vesey since the end of October) was fighting the Yeovil seat for the Conservatives. Cynthia said that she was unable to go to his meetings 'as my present name prohibits my appearing on a Conservative platform' (the crowd was considered too rough to mix in). It was her name that prohibited her rather than her political stance, her Tory upbringing and Liberal marriage having formed a very comfortable coalition. But, once Aubrey became an M.P., the Tory party faithfuls began to criticise his friendship with the Asquith family and, eventually, he felt the pull: (May 1914) 'Asked to P.M.'s. Have refused. Think it is too difficult. They chatter, the women

100

do, about things of great importance, as if they were talking of daisies. They are intelligent, inconsequent, informed and partisan; and one is liable to be either a spy in their camp, or untrue to one's party.'[18]

One aspect of politics that did not interest Cynthia was the suffragette movement. She and Mary Herbert and Venetia and Violet would have placed it firmly in the daisy category and would have been quite unable to understand why so many women cared so deeply. They were not perhaps as blinkered as the 'majority of pre-war women who' (wrote the author of *The Strange Death of Liberal England*) 'lived in the past, clung to their respectable and moribund security, and dreaded even the limited independence which the Vote would assure them'.[19] But they shared H. H.'s attitude, which was that militancy was counter-productive: 'the more the women marched, the less his reason marched with them'.[20] Once, while Beb and Cynthia were at dinner with him in the window of the dining-room at Lympne, a piece of granite was thrown through it, 'scattered a lady's dress with a copious fountain of soup, and bounced off the table to the other side of the room'. H.H. 'remained unmoved, steady as a rock, regarding the scene around him with a faint sniff of amusement, while the younger members of the party rushed to the window.'[21] Yet it is sad to think that a man who so much enjoyed the company of intelligent women could be so absurdly implacable about the issue of the Vote.

Cynthia made few concessions to pregnancy. 'This is to say that we shall all three love to come to Taplow'[22] she told Ettie in October 1910, provoking the latter to scrawl 'isn't Cynthia abominable!' on the paper. Yet the previous generation had found it indecent even to allude obliquely to their condition. There is a letter at Stanway that Mary Elcho wrote to her father three days before Cynthia was born from which one would have no idea that she was pregnant. And when Blunt and Balfour met at the Clouds weekend in 1887, with Cynthia's birth only three weeks away, one can be sure that there was no fussing around with footstools or cushions for Mary's back.

Margot went on hunting during pregnancy partly out of fool-hardiness, partly out of refusal to admit that her body was making extra demands on her. Cynthia did the same. 'Please avoid hunting on Saturday if possible – though it may not be'[23] urged Beb ineffectually. Nor did she settle on a doctor until her sixth month, although this was quite usual at a period when ante-natal care as we know it did not exist. Even in this she followed the pattern set by Raymond and Katharine. 'Shall we settle on the one

Frances Horner told you about?' she asked her mother. 'Katharine swears by him and he is *half* the price of a swell.'[24]

Among the interests of that winter was Ego's engagement to Letty Manners. Mary recorded that 'we were all in various states of excitement, especially Beb, who, having recently *passé par là*, was intensely enjoying a crisis that was not his own'.[25] The night before the wedding, on 31 January, Guy gave a stag party for Ego. The guest-list testifies to the continuing closeness of the group of friends whom Cynthia had first met on her visits to Ego's rooms in Oxford: as well as Yvo and Beb there were Edward Horner, George Vernon, Jasper Ridley and Eddie Marsh. Smallbones was abroad and Aubrey Herbert probably disliked stag parties. The next night a larger group, that included Cynthia, overcame post-wedding flatness by going to a musical called *The Waltz Dream*.

Ego and Letty followed the accepted way of doing things – two weeks in England, a long holiday abroad and then some months of parcelling themselves out before moving into their house behind Belgrave Square. During May they lived in Sussex Place, Cynthia meanwhile having moved to Cadogan Square to await the birth of her baby. The birth was on 7 May in Mary's bedroom and Mary wrote it up in her diary in some detail (it was her first grandchild).

> Nurse came to me at about 8 saying 'Mrs Asquith had begun – water broke'. She had been disturbed at 2 but she did not call the nurse till 5 – I went to Cynthia and Dr was telephoned to he came at 9.30 & said it might be very slow – she had pains but not very marked ones – I put on linen coat & skirt – she rather unwillingly came down 12.30 to drawing room . . . she ate q. a fair lunch at 1300 poor thing she was glad to go up to bed. I telephoned to Beb & he motored up v. concerned C was to try & rest after luncheon & I took Beb and the dogs in the Square . . . 6–6.30 doctor came back – 2nd stage had come on & things went quickly, she was very good and brave I gave the chloroform at 8.15 head born at 8.20 a beautiful boy lay on the bed & cried lustily.[26]

Even Mary, who was given to rose-coloured spectacles, would not have glossed over a difficult birth. Later on, when the baby began to give such anxiety, it would be remembered that no forceps were used and that he 'cried lustily' as soon as he was born. (The only disquieting note is the five-minute delay between the emergence of the head and the lusty crying, but this may have been exaggerated.)

Because of John's birth Cynthia missed George V's coronation and the celebrations. There was a faint sense of anticlimax. She wrote to her mother: 'It is dreadful the whole of one's future having crumbled so quickly and become the past. I shall have to invent a new landmark now, but I'm afraid there are no new great experiences left untested and I shall have to resign myself to more vicarious excitements such as baby's teeth and Beb's briefs and my first grandchild.'[27] But by August she was leading a normal life (as far as the heat allowed, the 9th being the hottest day at Greenwich since records began in 1841) and, having only breast-fed for a short time, was appealing to Katharine for help: 'I spent an embarrassing quarter of an hour at the chemist trying to discover what I wanted but failed dismally. Could you let me know what kind of a squirt, syringe, douche or whatever it's called it is that you use? Or better still could you be a seraphim & *order* one to be sent straight to me with the bill. I should be eternally grateful to you if you would do this for me.'[28]

The Asquiths had planned to travel north in the middle of August and thought they might have to change their arrangements because of the railway strike. Cynthia was as unsympathetic to industrial action as her father-in-law: 'I am terrified – I'm sure this is the beginning of a French Revolution and I can already hear the tumbrils . . . It is so difficult to imagine one's private affairs being interfered with by public ones – they never have been. There are three thousand soldiers in my own park now.'[29] Thanks to Lloyd George, who 'employed all the cajolery, all the psychological insight, all the appeals to patriotism which Asquith had disdained to use '[30] the strike that had threatened for many weeks only lasted for forty-eight hours and meant that the journey to Gosford was possible although very slow. 'We had the longest and most crowded train that has ever puffed and didn't get here till two in the morning [they had left at 10 a.m.]. I think John minded it less than any one else'[31] Cynthia told her mother. The holiday was much needed after the great heat (something which must have exacerbated the tense industrial situation) and it was a relief for Cynthia to be looked after in someone else's house.

Gosford was something of a rest-cure. Cynthia played golf and got on rather well with her step-grandmother Grace, 'nicer than I have ever known her'. The only dramas were that her sister Bibs found the visiting cousins very boring ('she hasn't got the feeling of freemasonry I used to have towards anyone else who happened not to be grown up') and that Cynthia's former 'monthly nurse' showed her jealousy of the new, permanent nanny by declaring that John looked unwell. The doctor was sent for and 'thought him extraordinarily fine and healthy' and Nanny

Faulkner, the nanny who had come to Sussex Place in June and was to stay for thirty years, was vindicated. John seemed a very happy baby: 'It almost shocks me to see anyone laughing so much'.[32]

At the beginning of September Beb and Cynthia left John in the Gosford nursery and went to stay with the Plymouths at Hewell Grange in Worcestershire, an enormous house built twenty years before whose 'great hall' was even more marbled and galleried than that of Gosford. The enigmatic, rather melancholy Lady Plymouth had for many years been the acknowledged mistress of Cynthia's uncle George Wyndham and, she and Mary Elcho having been close friends for so long, she was therefore virtually Cynthia's aunt. From Hewell Beb and Cynthia went to stay with H.H. and Margot on their annual visit to Archerfield, spending a week in the Lake District for Beb to re-visit the scene of his childhood holidays before arriving at Stanway in October.

As the winter set in 'real life' began to intrude. Up till now nothing had been very serious – the summer had been stimulating because unusual, what with the heat, the strikes, the continuing drama over the House of Lords, the parties and other festivities. The couple without a baby can play at marriage in a rather pleasant way because they have no-one to please except themselves and although a child, for all sorts of obvious reasons, involves enormous changes, these had been staved off for a few months by the monthly nurse, the unreal heat and a round of country-house visits. But now Beb had to return to his briefs with the beginning of the new law term and Cynthia had to try and play the part of young mother. She did not find it at all easy, being, as she herself observed, 'woefully ill-prepared' for all the tedious detail involved with running a large London house and was already showing signs of finding it hard to take matters lightly. Returning home she complained that 'everything got so frightfully on my nerves – I found the chairs had been hideously covered with their legs indecently showing and altogether everything was absolute torture to me'.[33] And apologising for not having written to her mother in Dresden (where she had taken the sixteen year-old Mary) she wrote that 'the frost distracted me and then the thaw'.

The habit had immediately formed of long visits without John to Avon Tyrrell, Pixton and so on. John neither stayed with his mother nor stayed in one place, yet no-one seems to have remonstrated with Cynthia. Often he was in a strange nursery and although Nanny Faulkner was a constant, nothing much else was. Before the accepted use of 'a squirt, syringe, douche or whatever' John would have had a brother or sister within a year (George and Mary Wyndham were a year apart, so were Ego and Guy Charteris) and he or she would have provided the security that his peripatetic life denied him. Also, if Cynthia had been pregnant in 1912 her own placidity would have led her to stay at home in Sussex Place and John could have led an ordered life of walks in Regents Park, tea with other nannied children and outings to the zoo on Saturdays.

As it was, much of his time was spent away from London, for example two months at Stanway over the summer of 1912. Cynthia was very grateful to her mother ('you must promise to shoot him out directly you want his room or to relieve your servants') and, although she missed John 'terribly', continued to lead very much the same life she had led before marriage. 'I doubt whether I shall be able to tear myself away again as soon' she wrote in anticipation of the approaching month-long separation in October when she would go with Mary to Baden–Baden to take a cure but she stayed away for five weeks, and would have dismissed the idea that it would have been better for the baby if she had stayed with him; and indeed better for her health if she had stayed peacefully, if boringly, at home in London.

Beb was anxious about Cynthia's prolonged absence. Writing from Clonboy, to which John had been brought after his extended summer at Stanway, he expressed misgivings about the fact that 'J has stayed here occupying the best rooms and consuming several apple pies every day for a prodigious time'. He suggested that he be brought to London because 'it is a great waste not seeing him' and because he wanted 'a united Pepinage' (their name for Number 8, derived from Pepinetta, his nickname for Cynthia). 'I want to see you *immediately* you return and dont want you to emigrate with Jonquil [pet name for John] . . . I was glad to hear you had put on 2½ lb: I am excited to see the change in contour. I have missed you enormously, darling, and I hope this tiresome experience won't have to be repeated.'[34]

But, back in London, Cynthia lost her voice. She continued, painfully, to go out to dinner ('I squandered my last notes on Winston') and when, eventually, she went to the doctor she found that she weighed less than she had in September. The only positive aspect was her 'wasp-like waist' being displayed to good effect at dances. But the weeks at the *Kurhaus* seemed even more pointless in retrospect, nor was it a comfort to be told that the German doctors often faked the weight in order 'to satisfy foolish impatient patients who want immediate results'.

Over the winter Cynthia's health continued to decline and in mid-March 1913 she was diagnosed as a tuberculosis suspect and admitted to a sanatorium on the River Dee near Banchory in Scotland. She had been here five months previously to visit her friend Eileen Wellesley, who was still an inmate, and found the place horrifying ('I have never imagined anything so hauntingly grim and grotesque') but fascinating. Unconsciously, she willed herself to lose weight and forced her fashionable doctors – to whom psychosomatic illness was an unexplored subject – to immure her in a building not much better than an asylum where, according to Mary, 'she spent many happy weeks and read innumerable books'. Her time there was indeed a rest cure and the solitude might well, in different circumstances, have proved a balm that both healed and renewed.

But there was John. His mother's boredom and frustration, combined with the unlooked-for speed of his arrival and his parcelled-out way of life, all made this renewed separation a very difficult one for him and was to have a lasting effect, an effect that was exaggerated even further because it was planned that he should be 'given' a brother or sister. 'If I begin a baby as soon as I am well enough – I shall only have had one tennis summer out of five and if that isn't a grievance what is?'[35] Cynthia asked Katharine, not entirely in jest. But before this plan could be put into effect she and Beb had to re-start their marriage. Cynthia being loathe to leave her refuge, 'at last', recorded Mary, 'Beb commissioned me to go and heckle the doctors and bail her out, which I did, and it is a mercy she did not catch the disease'.[36]

····⤐· Chapter 13 ⤐····
1913

When Cynthia finally emerged from the sanatorium in June 1913 she went with Beb to Kingsgate, a village on the Kent coast between Margate and Broadstairs where he had taken a furnished house called Marylands. The London season was thought too rigorous, too tempting, for an invalid and Broadstairs was not, on the other hand, too far for Beb to be able to make the occasional foray for briefs. Cynthia sat on the beach with John and Nanny, walked across to Margate where she had often spent childhood holidays, and enjoyed re-reading her favourite Dickens in a place full of Dickens associations. 'John is unrecognisable' she told Katharine, 'dark-burnt skin and bleached hair all over him and absolutely *ceaseless* prattle. He talks as much as any Asquith.'[1] She was not being ironic, yet Asquiths were notorious not for their prattle but for their contemplative silences. 'Dined with A.J.B.' wrote Mary in her diary on the third night after John was born, 'and with Beb who didn't speak.'[2] And Margot once implored Cynthia to dine at Downing Street, telling her that 'you will play up – what one doesn't want is these great blocks of silent men – Bongie – Beb – Cis – they never utter'.[3]

Many friends came to stay at Marylands. Among them was Eddie Marsh who arrived for a Friday-to-Monday towards the end of July; the visit was to become well-documented for, also staying in Broadstairs, were D. H. Lawrence and Frieda Weekley, in England for a month in order to provide evidence for Frieda's divorce from her husband. Presumably the seaside air was considered good for Lawrence (he had gone to Bournemouth the year before to recuperate after illness) but why he and Frieda chose Broadstairs is unclear since Lawrence called it 'that half-crystallised nowhere of a place'[4] and described it as being full of 'fat fatherly Jews and their motor cars and their tents,'[5] in the anti-semitic idiom which was unfortunately so typical of the period. But the beach is the beach wherever you are. 'We've got a tent in a little bay on the foreshore' Lawrence told John Middleton Murry, 'and great waves come and pitch one high up, so I feel like Horace, about to smite my cranium on the sky.'[6]

Lawrence, whose third novel *Sons and Lovers* had been published in May to 'flattering'[7] reviews, also wrote poetry. Eddie Marsh had recently included a poem of his in the first volume of *Georgian Poetry* and had sent Lawrence £3 (£75) – one-seventeenth of the profits; he, when thanking him ('I call that manna') had asked Marsh casually 'I suppose you won't be Margate way?'[8] Even before Marsh had arrived Lawrence was relishing his visit, telling Edward Garnett that 'Edward Marsh is coming to see us on Sunday. He is Winston Churchill's secretary and is coming down here to stay with the Herbert Asquiths, who live at the end of the avenue'.[9] He came round to '28 Percy Avenue' on the Sunday morning, 20 July, and invited Lawrence and Frieda to join him that afternoon for tea at Beb and Cynthia's house. They 'were a tremendous success' Eddie told Rupert Brooke; Cynthia wrote thirty-five years later:

> Except the mere facts that he wrote poetry, was the son of a coal-miner, and had a tendency to consumption, we at that time knew nothing whatever about Lawrence; but the moment a slender, lithe figure stepped lightly into the room, we both realised almost with the shock of a collision that something new and startling had come into our lives.[10]

Lawrence was pleased to be able to count the Asquiths ('jolly nice folk'[11]) as friends: he was intrigued by Beb being the son of the Prime Minister; he liked feeling 'a success';[12]; and he liked being introduced to people such as Sir Walter Raleigh ('but, alas, it is not he of the cloak'[13]), 'Lord Elco [sic] (Mrs Asquith's people)'[14] and Violet and Venetia.

Lawrence's pleasure in knowing all the best people is notorious. Not unnaturally, he wished to be part of London literary society; he also 'collected' titles as far as he was able. Some found his snobbery childishly endearing, others were maddened by it, as was Cecil Gray, unflatteringly portrayed in Lawrence's novel

Aaron's Rod as Cyril Scott and therefore a not dispassionate observer. Gray described Lawrence as

the most class-conscious man I have ever known . . . his allusions to members of the aristocracy with whom he was acquainted were mealy-mouthed and more than nauseating in their class-conscious-ness. He could not resist the lure of women with titles: he would roll their names around his mouth – Baroness Richthofen, Lady Ottoline Morrell, Lady Cynthia Asquith, The Honourable Dorothy Brett, 'daughter of Viscount Esher' (in a smug parenthesis) – they were all potential ladies Chatterley to his self-imagined all-conquering game-keeper. All his books are a wish fulfilment of this *leit-motif* which he was unable to realize in life.[15]

He *was* intrigued and besotted by Cynthia's ancestry. He was fascinated, if geographically inaccurate, about her aristocratic tentacles – 'Your Stanway is a jewel on a leper's body: so near to Burslem, Harley and Stoke, and Wolverhampton.'[16] And he was also interested in her as a person: not just by her feminine beauty or her charm but by qualities in herself which she was not even aware of and which Lawrence helped her to recognise. Whether recognition made her happier is another matter, but his intuitive understanding guided her towards the beginnings of self-knowl-edge. Physically Lawrence was intrigued by Cynthia because she looked so like the Pre-Raphaelite 'dreaming woman' which was always such a potent image for him. Above all it was her eyes, the window of the soul, that he found most fascinating. When, two years after their first meeting, he used Cynthia as the basis for the heroine in one of his short stories, he mentioned his nameless heroine's eyes three times in as many pages:

She had large, slow, unswerving eyes, that sometimes looked blue and open with a childish candour, sometimes greenish and intent with thought, sometimes hard, sea-like, cruel, sometimes grey and pathetic . . . She lifted her eyes to look. They were slow, greenish, and cold like the sea . . . she lifted her eyes slowly and looked at herself: a tall, loose woman in black, with fair hair raised up, and with slow, greenish, cold eyes looking into the mirror.[17]

Initially, Lawrence was very struck by the openness with which Beb and Cynthia talked to him and Frieda (who were, after all, 'living in sin') and by their willingness to accept them both as friends. 'The English *do* seem rather lovable people',[18] he wrote two days after his meeting with the Asquiths. 'They have such a lot of gentleness. There seems to be a big change in England, even in a year; such a dissolving down of old barriers and prejudices.' It was only in the autumn that he thought to apologise to Cynthia in case she had been offended by the irregularity of his and Frieda's position: 'I took it frightfully badly, that we had appeared before you as if we were a perfectly respectable couple. I thought of the contamination etc etc and I really was upset. I'm glad you didn't mind'.[19]

Having a novelist's intuition, Lawrence quickly understood Cynthia, but it was to be a year or two before he felt enough at ease with her to begin the preaching that was to be so characteristic of many of his letters to her. Nevertheless, any shyness between them was soon dispelled by their mutual interest in poetry. In addition, Cynthia had only a month earlier been released from a sanatorium apparently cured of tuberculosis but still not free of suspicion; Lawrence had had tubercular pneumonia in November 1911 and after that was always under the threat of tuberculosis. Both were aware that there is a consumptive temperament that, despite the dangers of the illness, made sufferers temperamentally compatible and which, in Cynthia's case, swayed the diagnosis where the physical symptoms were not very marked. This was how Lawrence described Cynthia in his short story called 'The Ladybird' (1921):

So her own blood turned against her, beat on her own nerves, and destroyed her. It was nothing but frustration and anger which made her ill, and made the doctors fear consumption. There it was, drawn on her rather wide mouth: frustration, anger, bitterness. There it was the same in the roll of her green-blue eyes, a slanting, averted look: the same anger furtively turning back on itself.[20]

It was Cynthia who must have set the tone for their correspondence. In his first letter Lawrence was ordinarily polite: 'Suddenly we've got a fit of talking about you and your skirt with holes in and your opal brooch',[21] but by the third he wrote quite sharply (Cynthia had been suffering from the sickness of early pregnancy but had not liked to admit it) 'I suppose you are whining and grizzling in London, and Mr Asquith has got a longer face than a violoncello: just because he can't get somebody to squabble with at the Bar'.[22] To be on these terms after a few seaside meetings and two letters shows that Cynthia must have quickly lowered many barriers.

It is only from Lawrence's letters to Cynthia that we know that she made a fleeting visit to Venice in the autumn of 1913. 'Isn't it a bit much, to go dashing to Venice and back in a week?' he inquired, adding 'Why don't you go to Margate again'.[23] And, a month later, 'I am sorry you've got a cold. But what do you expect, after purpling in Venice'.[24] The impetus for the trip was that George Vernon ('fired, I think, by my accounts of Venice and her people'[25] wrote the then Diana Manners about this occasion) had taken a palazzo on the Grand Canal in which the Coterie could be especially 'typical'. Diana later described the:

dancing and extravagance and lashings of wine, and charades and moonlit balconies and kisses, and some amateur prize-fighting with a mattress ring and seconds, and a girls' sparring match and, best of all, bets on who would swim the canal first, Duff or Denis Anson . . . All of us, pretty and unconventionally dressed, were naturally followed and stared at by the perambulating Venetians on the Piazza at night . . . there was a general new look in everything in those last years before the first war . . . a budding freedom of behaviour that was breaking out at the long last end of Victorianism. We felt it and revelled in it.[26]

Cynthia was present, even though she preferred the more formalised pleasure of the Souls – notes slipped under the door, trysts by the canal and oblique glances from under a parasol (a Henry James novel come to life) – to these rather garish antics.

'Is Mr Asquith making heaps of money at the Bar?'[27] inquired Lawrence that autumn and, on another occasion, 'You tell Mr Asquith that man does not live by Briefs alone. But he won't believe you. It's no use us poets waving our idealistic banners, like frantic suffragettes'.[28] In fact, Beb believed him all too well and was pursuing briefs with ever-increasing reluctance. Cynthia, proud of his literary aspirations but worried about money, asked Katharine rather casually, 'Has Raymond had much work? Beb preserves an ominous silence as to his profession'.[29] But, nominally, he was still a junior barrister and when, in the spring of 1914, Cynthia decided to spent some time fashionably in the South of France she left both Beb and John in Sussex Place. She professed to have been leading a very quiet life there ('I have brought the art of living subconsciously to the highest point so that the days dribble by very quickly and I have plenty of time for reading and embroidery'[30]) but, since for years it had been the custom for both men and women to prepare themselves for the rigours of the season ahead by sunning themselves at Cannes or Biarritz, it is impossible that Cynthia's days dribbled past as peacefully as she claimed. And she was happy enough to leave 'the fat and smiling John'[31] for two months, although the first faint worries about him were beginning to be felt. Asking Katharine to take her daughters to have tea with him she added, 'I don't want him to grow too shy and savage while I am away'.[32]

Cynthia was pleased to be pregnant (this time she had planned to be) because she had a sense of purpose, particularly if, as she hoped, the baby was a girl ('Rosemary'). Writing from Biarritz at the end of April she told Katharine (who, as the mother of two daughters, was anticipating a future of regular pregnancies until she achieved a son): 'You have an active life to give up – whereas I was already a crock and of course it is happier to be a crock *with* an excuse than without one . . . it *does* give me a sense of purpose'.[33]

It is often said that Edwardian men needed a war to lend their lives the sense of direction they so fatally lacked, that many aspects of their upbringing rendered life pointless unless it eventually climaxed in militarism. (Julian Grenfell: 'I adore war. It is like a big picnic without the objectlessness of a picnic,'[34] Rupert Brooke, Oc Asquith's friend: 'Now, God be thanked Who has matched us with His hour'[35] and so on.) But many women suffered from the same feeling of objectlessness; while merely admitting to the odd twinge of *ennui* or to needing a month in a *Kurhaus* they found themselves with little to do and little to look forward to, nothing to do but *be*. And there was the unwritten rule that a woman had to be married before she could fill her days with love affairs, and that these had to wait until she had produced a son.

Cynthia's position was especially equivocal. Because she married 'out' she was a victim of the peculiar upper-class ethic that the better the marriage the more lavishly it was endowed by the bride's parents. It is naive to assume that the girl marrying into poverty might need greater riches to take with her; it did not work like that (it may not still) and it was not until Mary and Bibs became engaged to very suitable men that Hugo felt compelled to provide marriage settlements more generous than the £200 (£5000) a year he gave to Cynthia. Admittedly she did not, by aristocratic criteria, have a large house to run. Yet there were certain standards she had been brought up to expect and these she could not easily drop. She could not, for example, manage without a maid to look after her clothes: once she wrote, after she had been away for a while, including one night with Lawrence and Frieda, and had not been able to take her maid with her, 'it's rather delicious to get back to Polly . . . if one had left all one's hats on the floor they would have been there in the evening and worst of all the hairs of yesterday were always in one's brush'.[36]

Although she lacked the money to sustain it, and could not

always reciprocate others' hospitality, yet Cynthia saw social life as her *raison d'être* and was as much 'a slave to her sense of duty' as she had once accused her mother of being. And, because Beb was not as impoverished as other young barristers and therefore did not have to accept every brief that was offered to him, they were both able to accept all invitations. But it is easy to see that it was not a very satisfactory existence. Nothing was quite whole-hearted: John was mostly with Nanny Faulkner; Beb was beginning to play at being a barrister and to dream of being a full-time writer; Cynthia had a bulging engagement diary but, without openly admitting it, felt aimless.

It was, and is, one of the oldest female dilemmas in the world, although that is scant comfort to the sufferer. But at least Cynthia had intelligent friends with whom to discuss the problem. One reason why she had always admired Katharine so much was that she could read Greek; Mary Herbert was interested in Aubrey's political life, had travelled with him in Turkey and had the Pixton estate to look after; Viollet was deeply involved in her father's politicaal life, as to a certain extent was his close friend Venetia Stanley. Yet the latter also suffered bouts of aimlessness and it must either have been her periodic mood of self-disgust or H.H.'s disapproval of the whirling frivolity of her life that inspired him to write her one of his best and most entertaining letters: that of June 1914 in which he told Venetia that

Even the gruffest observer cannot withhold a reluctant tribute to the vitality and versatility which, in the course of an average summer day, can betake itself – successively or at choice – to

Fencing	Shopping	Ladies gallery-ing
Swimming	Palming	Gossiping
Tennissing	Polo-watching	Hair-brushing
Manicuring	Motoring	Dining
Lunching	Golfing	Dancing
Play & opera-going		Gambling[37]

Men, as Raymond had reminded Cynthia in his letter of 1909, manage things so that 'there is an area of one's life between 8pm and midnight which is set apart for the pursuit of pleasure'. Women have no such constraints; thus H.H., while admitting that they need enormous strength of will to lead a self-determined life, yet concluded that 'it is sad to see so much of beauty and charm, and powers that might move & raise the world, running to waste'. The well-tried solutions (slumming, motherhood and so on) were not the answer according to H.H. who recommended:

a fixed time for reading every day; a chosen preoccupation about which to think and to read seriously; the helping of others in their work; and the avoidance of trivia and gossip.

Cynthia, had she been shown this letter, which is possible since she mentions Venetia showing others to her, would have taken Asquith's words to heart. She, as much as any of her female contemporaries, was adept at filling her days with tennissing, palmistry and gambling; but she was always, as H.H. put it, 'conscious that she is not making the best or the most of her world'. Though lacking the motivation 'to give up Society and take to "Slumming" ' she had (very briefly) thought of doing so; she had once attempted to work (acting); and she had had a spell in a 'Nunnery' (the sanatorium). But she did not have quite the strength and independence of her great Souls forebears, and in any case she was without house or income. Yet, despite her disadvantages, Cynthia lacked the docility to submit to H.H.'s fourth solution, 'to fold her hands, and bow dumbly to the decrees of Destiny'.

If Cynthia had had three children under three to look after, or continual visitors, or if Beb had had to work far harder than he did, all would have been well; as indeed it would if she had had a passion for decorating her house or gardening. But Cynthia had the handicap of her brain, which was a good one; she could think logically, she was perceptive, she had a good memory and she was witty. With all this she was competitive, brave and enthusiastic. Yet none of these qualities were the slightest use to a woman in her social position born two decades too soon. Because there was so little scope for Cynthia to dominate or to shine, she felt aimless and worthless, yet despised herself for making so little use of what she had, which was after all a great deal.

Nor was her frustration only mental: it was sexual as well. It is an ominous chronology, that of five weeks abroad, instant relapse into voicelessness and weightlessness, continuing decline until a sanatorium was the only prescription (even for the mother of a young child), renewed pregnancy and further time abroad. Cynthia believed in the ideal of romantic love. But she was handicapped by growing up with the belief that marriage was an economic arrangement set apart from love and sexual excitement. And it seems likely that, like many other young married women before and since, she was left wondering whether the heightened emotion experienced by herself and Beb was meant to culminate merely in changes in contour, childbirth, douches, quarrels between the nursery staff and straitened circumstances.

She had missed the 'coronation' season of 1911 and she missed that of 1914 ('the wild tango year') for the same reason. But she anticipated many more gay, as well as tennis, summers in the future and waited quietly for her confinement, which she expected at the beginning of July. At the end of June, on the 30th, her Wemyss grandfather died and Mrs Herbert Asquith became Lady Cynthia Asquith. The funeral at Gosford was the last occasion when the family, minus Cynthia, was all gathered together. There was the quiet irony noted by Mary that 'had he lived until August 4th he would have been 96'.[38]

····≫· Chapter 14 ·≪····
1914

The baby was born at Sussex Place on 25 July. It weighed over eleven pounds and had the distinctive 'draughty' Charteris mouth. Cynthia had 'anticipated a pathetically tiny girl and was confronted with a comically large boy'. So unprepared was she for a boy that he was given John's second name, Michael and H.H.'s second name, Henry. Michael was a name that had come increasingly into fashion because of the great success of Compton Mackenzie's novel *Sinister Street*, the two volumes of which were published in 1913 and 1914 and whose hero ('handicapped by a public school and university education') was called Michael Fane (a surname which had resonance for Cynthia since it was Ettie's maiden name). Nor would she have forgotten that John and Michael were the names of the two Darling brothers in *Peter Pan*.

It was a Saturday when Michael was born and Mary was in Essex. She had been staying in London ready for the birth but had gone away for the Saturday to Monday hoping that the baby would not be born until her return to London. For her, retrospectively, the day had additional implications:

I was at Terling on the twenty-fifth of July. We were all at dinner when Natalie Ridley gave a message to A.J.B. from her father, Count Beckendorff, who was not able to come himself. The message was, 'That if Austria attacked Serbia, Russia was bound to intervene', and this would bring in our entente ally, France. We listened to these sinister words in silence, while the shadow of War crept into every-heart.[1]

Mary returned to London on the Monday morning and visited Cynthia and her newest grandchild. Then she returned to Stanway and entertained various guests the following Saturday, one of whom was Beb. On the Sunday Duff Cooper, also one of the guests, was summoned to London by the Foreign Office; 'this sudden summons was the first pebble that fell into the pool of the age-long peace of Stanway, Didbrook, and Toddington. They were still drowsy, still scarcely alarmed.'[2] The next day Beb and Evan went to Cheltenham in search of news and in the afternoon there was a cricket match. On Tuesday 4 August Mary went to London again with Beb. She visited Cynthia, 'who looked lovely in a yellow jacket, lying under her embroidered quilt'[3] that she had made in Biarritz (the only embroidery Cynthia ever did was when she was pregnant, the Souls' fierce affection for it not having been handed on to her). Mary observed that 'Cynthia deeply resented the invasion of War shattering the peace of her well-earned retreat'.[4]

Waiting for her baby to arrive – lying on a sofa or walking past the tennis court towards the lake – Cynthia felt even more than most people that war crept up unannounced. And, with all her sentimental memories of Dresden and the Germans, it was especially painful and absurd. 'For the hundredth time she regretted her own stay in Munich. Save for that happy year in the land of music, toys and Christmas trees, would she, like others, think of Germans collectively – as 'The Enemy', instead of as individuals?'[5] Yet the burst of activity which turned August from a sleepy month of cricket matches, charades and early nights into a month of plans, discussions and forebodings, was, at least, stimulating. There was no time for Cynthia to suffer from the lassitude she endured both after John's birth and (more severely) after the birth of her third child in 1919.

The day after war had been declared Mary returned to Stanway and on the Thursday Ego left to join his regiment at Gloucester. On the 15th, Mary wrote,

A.J.B. arrived for luncheon. We sat in the hut and talked about the Germans' philosophy, the cynical materialism taught by their War Party . . . then I sent A.J.B. off to play tennis. After a late tea Yvo started his first stretcher class, I watched him with great interest. August 20th: I established Cynthia in the tulip room with her new baby Michael, a fine War son.[6]

Mary took a strong personal interest in the Stanway tenants. On 29 August there was a second recruiting meeting in the tithe barn; she, Beb and Eliza Wedgwood spoke; two days later the first contingent of the 'men of Stanway' left. A week after this Michael was christened in a golden robe (embroidered with pearls) made by his godmother Diana Manners (his other godmother was Dorothy Grosvenor). Mary, who quite often censured Beb in her diary for silence or lateness (though always in very kindly tones) remarked that 'he arrived late and knocked over a whole row of god-parents and relations who were kneeling on hassocks, they went down like a pack of cards'.[7]

The first death came on 14 September when George Wyndham's son Percy was killed; George himself had died the year before. Ego spent the autumn expecting to go to France at any moment and Yvo spent his last weeks at Eton 'half mad with impatience to be away'.[8] He was just eighteen and 'naturally everyone with any "gumption" over seventeen has left and gone to Sandhurst or the Army – and I am about the oldest person here'.[9]

Beb, Oc and Cis went in September to a training course at the Public Schools' camp on Salisbury Plain ('they are liking their time very well'[10] wrote H.H. to Venetia, mentioning that Beb and Oc were brown from sun and wind.) Raymond joined the London Volunteer Defence Force and noted caustically that its advantages ranged from 'a) it is not yet in existence' to 'e) no member of it can possibly be killed till Goodwood (ie. August) 1915 at earliest'.[11]

Cynthia travelled north after her curtailed stay at Stanway. Leaving John and the baby there, she went to Harrogate to join Bibs and her mother. 'Cynthia and I took the cure (Cynthia says she has never recovered from it)'[12] remembered Mary, not meaning the sentence in parenthesis as a joke – there was, in truth, a sense in which something in Cynthia's nature never recovered from the news of Percy Wyndham's death. It was the first intimation, with the war six weeks old, that the games of toy soldiers that Ego and Yvo used to enjoy so much had nothing to do with Flanders in 1914. 'I shall never forget the look on Cynthia's lovely face as she read those telegrams'[13] wrote Mary about their time in Harrogate, a place to which neither she nor Cynthia ever returned because it was there that so many tragic possibilities had been set out before them. Cynthia, sitting in the lounge of the Royal Hotel ('lounges' were to become an all-too familiar part of her life over the next four years and the word a family joke) wrote to Katharine:

Tragedy seems to be striking most at those homes which have the greatest *culte* of family love. In some ways perhaps it is better as they have the most complete and happy memories to carry on with them and can never suffer from the remorse of having wasted and not appreciated.

At first they all seem wonderfully supported by a kind of pride and the glamour of tragedy. The worst must be later on – when the war is over and the regiment comes home and there is nothing but flat loneliness left. Isn't it curious how very little pity one ever feels for the people who are actually dead themselves? It is always for the survivors. This is especially so I think when the dead seem to belong to Maeterlink's category of the 'predestined'.

The irony of it all here! Where one sees wretched joyless beings creeping painstakingly after health having their strength eeked out by science while all the time the much further developed science of destruction is hurtling thousands of beautiful young lives away. 'Lord – what fools these mortals be!' Beb is here now – a ghastly holiday for him.[14]

This is the last extant letter in a correspondence between the sisters-in-law that had been going on since 1907. Either Cynthia's subsequent letters were lost (none of the younger Asquiths had a fixed home during the war years and possessions were thus easy to mislay) or Katharine destroyed them, feeling that Cynthia and she would never again be close. There is a hint of why she might have felt this in the letter from Harrogate; Cynthia mentions someone called Basil in the casual manner which assures his place in her life. And family folklore is clear on this point – the reason Cynthia and Katharine were never close again after the war was Cynthia's attitude to men other than her husband.

She had married Beb 'for love' and had not, before her marriage, met another man who interested her as much as him. But, for various reasons, the omens were not good. Foremost of these was their shared Souls background. It was not because of filial duty or shared attitudes that so many Souls children married each other (although these helped), it was because no-one else of their generation really understood what they had endured. The Elchos, the Manners, the Horners, the Grenfells – they were all the same in the intolerably high level of expectation that they imposed, crushingly, on their children. And it was these expectations that devastated their lives, just as much as, if not more than, the Great War.

War was the one occupation that could not be controlled by their parents: it involved no value judgements, no approval or disapproval, no inheritance of the family mantle; all they had to do was to be chivalrous and finally they would be fulfilling their parents' dreams. Raymond, Julian, Edward, Aubrey, Beb – it is not surprising that, before 1914, post-Oxford life seemed to have so little to offer. Anything they might think of doing was either part of the catalogue of Souls achievements, or was thoroughly condoned by the Souls and thus came endowed with its own millstone of responsibility, which was to do and to be and to respond as brilliantly as they were expected to, if not better. Or this is how it seemed, with daughters suffering from parental expectation just as much as sons. They were to be beautiful and intelligent (Greek was a trump card), witty and wise. They should paint or enamel or embroider, as well as ride and enjoy long walks and be thoroughly fond of dogs. They should manage large houses, servants, husbands, children, guests and lovers with ease, remaining devoted to their husband even if conducting an intense love affair.

Cynthia, however, did not bother with much of this (one reason she was so uninterested in anything artistic was that Mary's enthusiasm eventually became a bore). But she did think it axiomatic that once she was married she should have the luxury of admirers – even in war time, whereas Katharine felt that the least a wife could do for a soldier husband was to be faithful to him.

Both Cynthia and Beb were curiously lacking in self-esteem, she because her mother always seemed so perfect and her father so aloof, he because his father was equally aloof and he had lost his mother. So they needed flattery, but because Beb was diffident and Cynthia emphatic it was unlikely that they would be appreciative enough of each other. Beb, for all his charm and sensitivity, could never have been a match for someone of Cynthia's temperament who, for all her professed shyness, would not have known what self-effacement meant. At the time of her marriage, when she was getting to know Beb in a way she had never had a chance to do before, she was living on a high pitch of excitement laced with bouts of depression. She was egoistic and rather inconsiderate – in short she was a woman who needed a very strong husband if she was going to find the resources within herself to be happily married. Beb was not strong. He was calm and considered and logical, and would have loathed any form of histrionics (for example a passionate quarrel and then an equally passionate and thus delightful reconciliation). He would have liked to settle down to a conventional married life and it might have been Beb, but was in fact Raymond, who wrote: 'I confess I am soppy about the suburbs. There was a rich melancholy radiance over [Hampstead] this afternoon which gave a peculiar

Stanway House, Gloucestershire: on the roof looking up the hill towards the Pyramid.

Stanway in the 1920s from the Pyramid. Cynthia loved Stanway 'precisely as one loves a human being . . . loved it as I have loved very few human beings'.

Clouds House, Wiltshire, shortly after the fire in 1889 (p.3).

Gosford from the air in the 1920s.

Cynthia with her sister Mary and brother Yvo c. 1897.

Cynthia as a crusader c.1900 (p.31).

charm to some of the older streets and houses'.[15] Cynthia found the suburbs boring and would never have tolerated living there.

So, once married, once the novelty and initial sexual excitement had worn off, Cynthia, if war had not come, would have been bored and frustrated to an intolerable degree. War, as Lawrence was not the first to realise, is always an aphrodisiac.

> Before, as a barrister with nothing to do, he had been slack and unconvincing, a sort of hanger-on. . . Then came the great shock of the war, his coming to her in a new light, as lieutenant in the artillery. And she had been carried away by his perfect calm manliness and significance, now he was a soldier. He seemed to have gained a fascinating importance that made her seem quite unimportant. It was she who was insignificant and subservient, he who was dignified, with a sort of indifferent lordliness.[16]

With her relationship with Beb revived by his military glamour, Cynthia began the war by playing the role of camp-follower and, naturally thinking that the time-scale would be weeks rather than years, planned to play it for as long as necessary. In September she visited her Aunt Pamela at her house, Wilsford,* in order to be near Beb on Salisbury Plain. She was in London while he was training at Crystal Palace and in mid-October she did something which was to change her perception of things for the next four years: she went to France.

It was an expedition organised by Margot because she wanted Violet to 'have some real experience – at first she and Henry were discouraging and said amateurs were not wanted at the front and other conventionalities, but she went and had a very interesting and wonderful time'.[17] Violet was accompanied by Beb, Cynthia and 'a new friend of mine', wrote Margot, 'a very nice clever little Canadian' (whose very profitable business was selling horses to the French). Their official aim was to investigate the conditions in the hospitals and to collect as much data as possible about the R.A.M.C. and the Red Cross; this, because of their 'crackling theatrical passport'[18] signed by Kitchener they were able to carry out quite usefully. Mr Dunn (the Canadian 'obsessed by the fear of being taken for an American') had the use of a large motor car that had been made for, and used by, the Kaiser on his last visit to England, and in this they travelled around.

On the first day they had the whole ambulance system

---

*Wilsford was a gabled Jacobean house designed by Detmar Blow in 1906 for Lord Glenconner, Pamela's husband.

explained to them. At St Omer (where, almost as though it were Piccadilly, they bumped into Maurice Baring, 'a familiar shambling figure looking strangely militarised and efficient' who had motored in to buy a lobster for the Flying Corps) they had a 'delightful dinner' with various young officers. Cynthia's impression was of a town of 'extraordinary charm . . . the glamour of its garrison beggars all description . . . I have never imagined such a wealth of good looks and charm of face and manners as one saw crowded into this part of France'. At the enormous hospital Cynthia was much moved by the 'Philip Sidney' manners of the wounded soldiers and described their effect on her in the notebook in which she wrote up the trip.

> The journalistic idea that they enjoy war like a sport is strangely vulgarising of the truth. As a matter of fact they are so absolutely devoid of any sort of clap-trap – not *one* of all the hundred I spoke to ever said he wanted to get back to the fighting. They all said it was a ghastly nightmare and spoke of it with a real shuddering and *yet* there was never a tinge of bitterness nor a trace of resentment. No cant – no head-line imagination – not even about the Germans – and such sweetness about their fallen officers – I never heard any personal complaint, but some were very pathetic and eloquent about their shattered regiments and fallen friends. One's standards have to make a very rapid change and one finds oneself congratulating men with – what one would have considered fearful injuries – on having escaped so lightly – Their patient unpuzzled acquiescence in pain is so extraordinary that much of its horror seems diminished – but the pang which never grows blunted is the common sight of an empty sleeve and a very young face.

In the afternoon they drove to the Clearing Hospital at Bethune, seeing so many British soldiers on the way that France appeared as if annexed by England. Those few French soldiers that they did see looked sullen and bedraggled, in great contrast to the 'waving, winking gaiety' of the English. It was then 'that we realised with a thrill that for the first time in our lives we were listening to the roar of battle.' It was only three miles away and Cynthia found it more stimulating than frightening (she was to enjoy zeppelin raids for the same reason). But she was very shocked by the filthy, blood-stained condition of the wounded and could not accept the R.A.M.C.'s explanation for the lack of facilities – that maintaining active supplies to the fighting soldiers had to be a higher priority than looking after the hospital patients. 'It is very difficult to collect data – each person seems to contradict the last and of course there is unfortunately a good deal of friction between the R.A.M.C. and the Red Cross. The former are inclined to regard the latter as unpractical sentimentalists who appear to think war only exists in order to furnish them with wounded while the R.A.M.C. in their turn are naturally accused of red tape.'

Cynthia was on the side of the wounded, and saw much scope for improvement in their care. All four visitors had had the impression of bad organisation: wounded men were kept jolting in cattle trucks for as long as a week, and deaths and amputations could easily have been avoided with more and better surgeons. Upset and over-wrought, the plight of the wounded having made them forget the glamorous garrison, they returned soberly to St Omer, 'the whole sky constantly illuminated by flashes as of summer lightning followed by the thud-thud of enormous guns'.

The next day they arrived at Bailleul almost simultaneously with the whole General Staff. At the hospital Cynthia talked to some of the German prisoners – 'they were all very fine good-looking men – "blond beasts" with large *schwärmerisch* eyes' (it seems vaguely indecent that even at the front Cynthia was always so conscious of people's good or bad looks). Mr Dunn, 'who enjoys a healthy collective hatred of the enemy' was not pleased about this, but then 'our two squires (he and Beb) were wonder-fully unreassuring – excellent companions as we enjoyed excite-ment – but comically alarmist and imaginative'.

At Amiens Violet and Cynthia shared a bed in which previously General French and subsequently a German General had slept. The hospital there was run by a surgeon who looked distinguished and was covered in medals but was entirely incom-petent. 'There were no worse cases that we had seen before but it was the only place in which I had an overwhelming shudder of horror and had to go out of the ward.' Its dirt and gloom were in ghastly contrast to the American hospital in Paris, which was white and clean, full of doctors 'dressed like American dentists and all looking as if they had been sterilised . . . It is all vividly and amusingly American with a slight and perfectly harmless Selfridge touch. For instance all the extracted bullets are mounted in silver and presented to the men as lockets for their wives.'

They toured two more English and one French hospital, lunched at the Ritz and returned to Boulogne via Rouen and Abbeville. The port was now teeming with wounded, some of these they saw being unloaded off an ambulance train, 'a most haunting sight as scores and scores of prostrate forms were lifted off shelves.' As the boat left, exactly a week after they had first arrived, 'we saw a long line of union-jack draped hearses leaving the hospitals and being met by that ceaseless train of wounded still pouring out of the railway station'.

···>· Chapter 15 ·<····
1914–15

The winter of 1914–15 is the last period of Cynthia's life, barring the few odd years where the diaries have been lost, where there is no day-by-day record of her movements; for, in the spring of 1915, she agreed with Duff Cooper that they would both begin diaries and that they would encourage each other to keep them up. He ordered for her a green leather-bound volume with gilt decoration on the inside edges of the cover, the initials C.A. embossed in gold on the front and a clasp with a lock. Cynthia enjoyed writing her diary so much that she soon became an addict. It became a habit that she continued until the end of her life, broken only in 1919 when life seemed so gloomy that she could not bear to write about it (until her mother suggested that she start a less expansive, more factual version). In fact it is odd that Cynthia had never started before since Mary had kept a diary since well before her engagement. By the 1920s, by the time she was forty, Cynthia was using the same kind of diary as Mary: a page-a-day Smythsons volume containing almost no emotion or analysis but a lot of 'arranging'.

It is not surprising that Cynthia enjoyed keeping a diary. First she was conscious of her closeness to the political centre and realised that what she wrote would indeed be the *'mémoires'* she anticipated, something of an interest more lasting than a mere record of the daily life of a 'society' woman. Secondly, she very soon came to depend on the daily discipline demanded by diary writing: she wrote two to three hundred words every morning, during those couple of hours when women of leisure used to write letters or consult with cook about the day's meals before visiting the dressmaker or keeping a luncheon engagement. Thirdly, she was by nature and had been brought up to be primarily interested in herself – a useful attribute for a good diarist. Fourthly, the drama of war nevertheless gave her a lot of material, a backcloth of events, that took her attention away from herself: she felt, to the great advantage of her prose, that the stage was more important than her role on it. As Katharine Tynan put it (in her memoir of Ego and Yvo) 'self-consciousness had disappeared from that world. The letter-writers were in the midst of the great things'.[1]

Yet was Cynthia capable of unselfconsciousness? In the opening paragraph of the first volume of her diary she laid claim to being 'morbidly self-conscious', resolving, because of this, to 'try and be *un*introspective and confine myself to events and diagnosis of other people'.[2]* She did not, of course, succeed; indeed, the charm of her diary is her uninhibited fascination with herself. She may have tried to write about events and other people. But since she described her own reactions and involvement with such clarity and perception she, luckily for us, did not succeed very well.

So one is drawn to a central question about Cynthia: was she self-conscious or was she vain? Again and again the word 'vain' was mentioned to me by those who remembered Cynthia, and numerous anecdotes were rolled out to convince me that the Souls and the Charterises (the sweet-natured Mary always exempted) were vanity incarnate. And it is true that there is a great deal in her life, in her relationships with other people, in her upbringing of her children, and in her fiction, which is indicative of a vast degree of egoism and self-absorption.

But vanity, in the sense of conceit and arrogance, was less part of her character than awareness of self, consciousness of self. She had a peculiar detachment, so often commented on by her admirers, which meant that although she did find herself endlessly interesting she was at the same time observing herself in a characteristically aloof manner. When Lawrence said that 'she loved her loveliness almost with obsession'[3] he did not mean that she was confident of her loveliness – she wanted to be lovely,

---

*This was comically transcribed as 'try not to be un-introspective' in the 1968 edition of her *Diaries 1915–18*.

she was obsessed with being lovely, but she was never certain enough of it to forget about it.

Narcissism is the refuge of the insecure: Cynthia's need to feel that she was admired was the driving force of her life, and she understated the case when she wrote to Katharine 'I hope you don't like Mary better than me. I grant you that she scores on every point, but please remember that it is much more important for me to be liked because I am much more affected by other people's estimates of me'.[4] She cared deeply about what people thought of her and always, however tired or distracted, tried to make them like her; she liked people who liked her and very rarely 'dropped' them (which accounted for the great variety among her friends as she grew older); and if it appeared that someone did not like her she never gave them another thought, which often makes her diaries as revealing about the friends who are not being mentioned as it is about those who are.

It is not difficult, even if one avoids the jargon of psychoanalysis, to account for Cynthia's self-doubt, need for approval and resultant self-absorption. Her surving relations have suggested that all Charterises are vain. Then there were all those years of soul-massaging ('you all sit and talk about each other's souls, I shall call you the "Souls" '). Lawrence put the blame on the manacle of the upper-classes: 'Her *consciousness* seemed to make a great gulf between her and the lower classes . . . she could never meet in real contact anyone but a super-conscious finished being like herself, or like her husband'.[5] But the root causes are to be found in the death of the beloved younger brother, the unexplained departure of the revered governess, an exceptional intelligence subdued by years of frittering and aimlessness – and the absent and inharmonious parents who must have been so crushing for a fragile spirit. Hugo, during Cynthia's childhood, was not unlike Uncle Matthew in *The Pursuit of Love*: irascible, bigoted, remote, terrified of boredom, yet very very funny and unexpectedly gentle. Ego's diffidence, Cynthia's craving for reassurance, Bibs's anxiousness, they were all rooted in the same parent. And, while Mary's effect on her sons was only beneficial, her daughters found her very hard to live up to. Everybody adored Mary, all aspects of her nature were fulfilled by Stanway, her children, her watercolouring. She managed to have a passionate affair and an illegitimate child and yet retain her innocent beauty and, more awe-inspiring still for Cynthia, she nurtured her *amitié amoureuse* with Balfour for forty years without, seemingly, damaging any of the other facets of her life.

In the war diaries Cynthia's self-absorption is shown at first-hand, undisguised, for she did not, of course, succeed in being '*un*introspective' – what, after all, are diaries for? The diarist is expected to be interested in his soul (and, by comparison, 'each other's souls') because that is why he writes a diary. If he disclaims this interest (as did Virginia Woolf when she wrote famously that she would like her diary to show 'changes, trace moods developing; but then I should have to speak of the soul, and did I not banish the soul when I began?'[6]) then he is open to criticism on grounds of dishonesty. There has, for example, recently been a long argument between those who believe that Virginia's diaries are a straightforward and reliable record of her life, and those who believe that by leaving out the soul she left out the truth and that therefore her diaries, not her novels, are her greatest work of fiction.

Cynthia, by contrast, was so honest and direct, often naïvely so, that no-one has ever accused her of making fiction out of reality; readers have, however, been distressed by her unabash-edness. There was a kind of exuberance about Cynthia at this period of her life which made her terribly alive, and, through callousness or lack of forethought or innocence, she wrote things that most people think but few write down. Though the diaries are always interesting, they are, to many distasteful. 'One cannot really like someone', wrote one reviewer when the diaries were published in 1968, 'who writes for her own reading in this fashion: "My beau Whibley called for me to take me out to lunch. I evaded the kiss of greeting which he calmly tried to bestow and got off with only the hand . . . He talked lyrically of my beauty, which he said was 'like genius', and of his love for me".'[7] Others liked Cynthia's matter-of-factness: 'Lady Cynthia had a way of coming up with sudden truth, of looking reality full in the face'[8] observed Leon Edel.

Cynthia wrote her diary for herself, but hoped for good copy: 'My only words were "something for my diary" '[9] she wrote during a zeppelin raid. She assumed that others might read it; in the beginning she allowed Beb to read it but, after a year, must have started to hide it from him because there are so many remarks that it is unimaginable she would have made if she knew that he might read them. Sometimes she showed her diary to friends, for example she pretended to be inhibited about making a comment because 'the Hun [Frieda Lawrence] will read my diary'.[10] Overall, whether she was writing for herself or for others, she appeared to be oblivious of moral obloquy.

Unsurprisingly, the central issue for the 1968 reviewers was not Cynthia's alleged vanity, nor her indiscretion, it was whether ordinary life should go on during war-time, the issue that I call, in shorthand, 'saw Beb off to the Front, went to Harrods to buy a white suit'. Some critics, such as Leonard Woolf, very much resented 'the arrogant frivolity and futility of the aristocratic society or clique to which Lady Cynthia belonged. They seem to have had no sense of social duty. Throughout these terrible years of war they spent their time moving in droves from one great house to another'.[11] And, stupidly, he accused Cynthia of lacking any awareness 'of the social or patriotic obligation' which was sending men to their deaths. Others, such as Randolph Churchill, while calling her 'the greatest flirt that ever lived', understood that frivolous preoccupations were 'a form of self-protection both for the individual and for society. The war had to go on: life had to go on'.[12] Leon Edel made the same point in greater detail:

> It would be easy to patronize Lady Cynthia's diaries. They are often trivial; they are hardly literary; and one could be condescending about the 'highlife' they describe. By democratic standards, aristocrats aren't supposed to be human. Lady Cynthia was; and in the midst of the trivia there are serious and poignant pages, for what comes through the often humdrum story is the deep suffering, the eternal ennui of the home front; a kind of killing of time as a means of insulation against the killing one couldn't shut out.[13]

While Michael Holroyd remarked: 'To her set that horrid war was no better, and no worse, than the horrid weather . . . Yet she was not insensitive – rather the reverse. She had evolved a technique for living within the horror of war that was right for her temperament'.[14]

Although Cynthia was interested in the detail of life ('We live awfully cheaply – I know these things interest you more than eternal truths'[15] Lawrence had written in his second letter to her) she had *not* evolved a conscious technique for living, and it was unfortunate for her that she had not. She spent the four years of the war simply waiting for it to be over, and filled the days in the only way she knew, which was to be sociable. If she had had rather more money and could have stayed on in Sussex Place; or rather less and been forced to look after her children herself; or if a social conscience had impelled her into a sustained bout of nursing or running a canteen – if any of these factors had existed the days might have passed less aimlessly.

Most women, however miserable they were because of what the war was doing to their lives, felt that its tragedies and exigencies gave them a purpose. This Cynthia had denied herself. By waiting for it to be over rather than living purposefully until the return of normality she had only the gay frittering of her days to fill the gap. She would have thought it cowardly and life-denying to have sat placidly at home knitting balaclavas and dreading the telegraph boy. The best way she knew of fighting the war was to behave as though nothing had happened, in addition 'having rather enthralling adventures of one's own is the only distraction which can help to prevent one being either permanently raw or numb from this war'.[16] When, in 1919, she had to accept that something *had* happened, then her depression was acute; and because the deaths happened overseas, with memorial services instead of funerals, they were never a reality – part of Cynthia expected the nightmare to end with the armistice.

There was another reason why Cynthia did not allow the war to affect her daily preoccupations, which was that she was a woman in a man's world, and in that world men went away to school, climbed mountains, went to Balliol, became barristers – and fought wars. 'We need war, don't you think?' asks the heroine of Lawrence's story 'Glad Ghosts' (she is a mixture of Cynthia and the Hon. Dorothy Brett). 'Don't you think men need the fight, to keep life chivalrous and put martial glamour into it?'[17] All Cynthia's life the chivalric ideal had been dominant: men had to be heroic, the coward or 'muff' was beneath contempt, and 'that any one Englishman could easily overcome at least four (or was it six?) Frenchmen'[18] was the central tenet of the Stanway schoolroom.

The outbreak of war in 1914 was simply the natural culmination of all these ideals (and may well have contributed to its cause). The young men of England found that their moment had come, but it had come for their women as well. 'The chivalry of England, young, brave, dashing and handsome, line up to process to the tournament. They are filled with ardour for the fight, escorted by loyal yeomanry, and longing to do great deeds and win honour for themselves and their lady-loves.'[19] All the lady-love had to do was to act the part, and this suited Cynthia's Pre-Raphaelite looks well, as she smoothed down her shift-like dresses, smiled enigmatically from between her curtains of burnished-red hair and listened sympathetically to news from the battle-front. When men were killed they became instant legends, heroic creatures of medieval fable, and this made their death less senseless. Bimbo Tennant, Cynthia's first cousin, was 'intensely chivalrous', Ego was 'of all men the nearest to a knight of chivalry', while Billy Grenfell was described as 'riding into Valhalla', 'a perfect gallant knight', 'a young Knight who would ride into battle with joy'.[20]

As late as 1918 Baden-Powell referred to soldiers aiming 'to give the big bully a knock-out blow, so that other nations can live afterwards in peace and freedom'.[21] From the nursery, through school and university, English boys had been taught that bullies should not be allowed to get away with it – to walk away or compromise or try to see it from their point of view was not what one did. One could not hold up one's head unless one was good, heroic, unselfish, brave, kind to the weak, loving to one's mother, and so on, in short unless one remained true to chivalric ideals. Rupert Brooke meant this when he wrote in August 1914: 'All these people at the front who are fighting muddledly enough for some idea called England – it's some faint shadowing of goodness and loveliness they have in their hearts to die for'.[22]

The soldiers were against bullies, and for goodness, and if the Germans were temporarily lined up with the bullies, so be it; but that did not mean that one hated *them*, merely the ideal they represented. 'Would it be easier if one hated the Germans?' Cynthia asked herself in 1917. 'I feel them – poor devils – to be our wretched allies fighting against some third thing. The whole thing *must* be the means to some end, and that no political one.'[23] She often referred to the concept of a 'third force' (the fight against bullies) and because she saw the war in these terms she never ceased to believe in its importance.

Nor was it easy for Cynthia to hate the Germans. She had had a German governess (Squidge). Her mother and later she herself had been in the habit of taking cures in Germany and so it became associated in her mind as a place of rest and tranquillity. She borrowed German books from Frieda Lawrence and enjoyed talking German to her. When she went to the front she talked in German to the wounded German soldiers and thought it absurd that they should not be treated with the same care as the English. And, like many women of her class, she was never able to forget her schooldays in Dresden: Lawrence's description in *Lady Chatterley's Lover* owes something to Cynthia's experiences. Constance and her sister Hilda 'had been sent to Dresden at the age of fifteen, for music among other things. And they had had a good time there. They lived freely among the students, they argued with the men over philosophical, sociological and artistic matters, they were just as good as the men themselves: only better, since they were women. And they tramped off to the forests with sturdy youths bearing guitars, twang-twang'.[24]

Cynthia and Beb's trip to France in October 1914 confused their attitude to Germany still further: one wounded man seemed just like the next. Beb was given a good idea of what he was facing. Yet he never mentioned that week, either in his letters or memoirs; he would have realised that the patriotic impression made by his and his brothers' speedy enlistment ('Father's Profession, 1st Lord of the Treasury and Prime Minister' it said on his official record of service) might have been negated by a description of large motor cars, hospital inspections and eavesdropping on the noise of battle. But during his months in France he must often have thought of Cynthia's remark that 'everyone should go into battle labelled 'To the American Hospital'.[25]

She, too, never referred in writing to that week in the autumn of 1914, although she presumably did in conversation since there were no conditions of secrecy attached to their visit. But it transformed her attitudes; for one thing, at the Front, 'one's standards have to make a very rapid change'. She also acquired a rapid callousness and calmly described 'two apparently flayed men lying on a table – their wounds gaping for microbes'.[26] As a result Cynthia was far less sentimental than many of her contemporaries. The Front was a reality to her and, having a clear picture of waving English soldiers and downcast French, she did not need to fantasise about it. It was perhaps for the best that she had an image of alert, healthy men and that although she saw the wounded she never saw the mud and smells and monotony of life in the trenches. She could retain the cynical detachment of her circle without having had her emotions too much swayed. 'I agree with you about the utter senselessness of war' wrote Raymond to Katharine in the summer of 1916. 'It extends the circle of one's acquaintance, but beyond that I cannot see that it has a single redeeming feature. The suggestion that it elevates the character is hideous.'[27]

As soon as Beb joined the army the small income he had been receiving from his work at the Bar disappeared and money became a difficulty. Gone were the days when, as Cynthia had written to her mother in the summer of 1911 when offering to contribute to the Cadogan Square housekeeping, 'I can very well afford it because as a matter of fact I am the only person I know at present who has a margin of money'.[28] In early February, Sussex Place was let to a family of Belgian refugees and Cynthia, John and Michael themselves became refugees although, since they were not fleeing from anything except poverty, they called it 'cuckooing'. In order to make 7 guineas (£115) a week from letting the house, and also to save the cost of cook, housemaid and running expenses, Cynthia gave up a permanent home for herself and her children. It was Stanway, temporarily displaced by Sussex Place from 1911–14, that again became her reality and her setting and from where she so often set out on the journeys that were to become such a large part of her life for the next four years.

····≻· Chapter 16 ·≺····
John

John's birth on 7 May 1911 had been normal: 'at 8.20 a beautiful boy lay on the bed & cried lustily'. Cynthia, if she breast-fed him at all, only did so for a short while and, true to her class and epoch, considered that the employment of a good nanny was one of the most crucial tasks of motherhood. 'To be of the best use to your child it is essential that you cling to an independent life and interests and breathe a distinct atmosphere of your own with a glamour he will appreciate'[1] was the rather disquieting way in which, aged forty, she was to assess the role of a mother.

But Cynthia *did* find a good nanny: Nanny Faulkner, who was twenty-nine when she came to look after John in June 1911, was to stay with the Asquiths for as long as there was a nursery for her to preside over and was not only efficient but loving. To this day she is mentioned with affection by the Asquith family and the generation that was born during the First World War, particularly Ego's two sons, still remembers her frying sausages for supper in the nursery at Stanway and the calm, clean, orderly aura she cast over its visiting occupants. Yet any modern mother cannot help but echo the question asked by the author of the classic book on this very English phenomenon: 'How was it that hundreds of thousands of mothers, apparently normal, could simply abandon all loving and disciplining and company of their little children, sometimes almost from birth, to the absolute care of other women, total strangers, nearly always uneducated, about whose characters they must usually have had no real idea at all?'[2]

All that is known about John's very early months is that at some stage he had a serious illness and was lovingly nursed through it by Nanny Faulkner. This is likely to have been in July 1912 when Cynthia unaccountably missed the Eglinton Tournament. This was a re-creation of a medieval jousting contest, and a lavish statement of the chivalric ideal, in which many of Cynthia's friends (including Katharine Asquith and Diana Manners) took part. Only a family crisis could have kept her away.

That autumn was the one during which Cynthia was in Baden-Baden for five weeks and John was at Clonboy. Nanny was a constant, but his nursery was ever-changing. Beb wrote to Cynthia pleading for 'a united Pepinage', yet after a winter of vague ill-health she entered a sanatorium for twelve weeks during the spring of 1913. John had just had measles, so while she was away 'I have sent him to be thoroughly windswept at Margate'.[3] Here, at last, she was together with 'the fat and smiling John', enjoying his 'absolutely ceaseless prattle' and showing off her 'jonquil with the golden smile' to friends. 'Your son John is a person one does not forget' wrote Frieda Lawrence. 'It's curious that you can be a real person at his tender age!'[4] But in September she was 'purpling' in Venice and in October she had a cold and was beginning to feel sick from her pregnancy. She followed Christmas at Stanway with two months at Biarritz. From here she had written to Katharine asking her to go and see John because she did not want him to grow too shy and savage during her absence. It is hard to know whether the word savage might have been used flippantly whatever John's behaviour; or whether her jonquil, by now very nearly three, was beginning to cause serious disquiet.

Yet before the 1920s there was no concept of security or 'bonding'. It would not be an exaggeration to say that physical and intellectual health was not merely paramount – but the only kind that mattered. Psychological health was not part of the scheme of things – what a child felt, what would make it happy, what would give it emotional stability in the future, were unimportant concepts. They existed, but they were secondary. It would thus be a distortion to accuse Cynthia of being unmaternal or obtuse in her upbringing of her children. She was largely doing what everyone else did.

Cynthia, like Mary before her, would not have imagined that her children could have disliked, or been damaged by, her frequent absences. When they clung to her on her return she enjoyed their devotion, accepted it as a mother's right, yet would not have given a thought, except irritably rather as one caresses a dog, to their longings or their loneliness. They were well looked after by Nanny and the nursery-maid and that was enough for them. That John might become depressed because of his continual separations from his mother would not have occurred to anyone: the work of John Bowlby (who was to define three stages – protest, despair and withdrawal – in the life of a child suffering from maternal deprivation) was after all thirty years in the future.

As soon as she had recovered from Michael's birth Cynthia went with him to Stanway. John was already there and both babies stayed there until after Easter 1915 when they went to Brighton: 'The children went off from Broadway by the 12 oclock – I helped herd them till they went'.[5] Five days later she went to visit them – 'John very naughty' – and the next day the Lawrences came down for the night and Cynthia described the behaviour of her elder son in her diary. She had been keeping it for less than a month, and had also been keeping a separate biography of him since he was born, rather as Mary kept a journal about her children. This biography is now lost so that Cynthia's incidental diary entries are now the only source for information about John.

> Lawrences *rivetted* by the freakishness of John – about whom they showed extraordinary interest and sympathy – the ozone has intoxicated him and he is in a wild monkey mood – *very* challenging just doing things for the sake of being told not to – impishly defiant and still with his peculiar indescribable detachment.[6]

At this stage John was no more than ordinarily naughty. His 'detachment' was not the withdrawing from the world of the autistic child, rather it was the defiant 'not caring' of the child who is testing adults to the limits of their endurance by refusing to do what they tell him. He wanted to be noticed, to be reassured, to be loved *despite* what he did. Cynthia was sufficiently disquieted by his behaviour to consult Lawrence, who had at once noticed 'the revolt in his eyes – the subconscious antagonism'[7] of the sensitive, unhappy child. Lawrence told Cynthia that John should never be subjected to verbal bullying but should be left to the care of the warm, uncomplicated Nanny Faulkner.

Two days later, at Cynthia's request, Lawrence expanded his views on paper. John, he believed, was an intrinsically happy child but one who was confused by his mother's cynical detachment. He needed to be looked after by someone open, generous and confident enough in themselves to be able to love undemandingly.

Don't try to make him love you, or obey you – don't do it. The love he would have for you would be a much greater love than he would ever have for his nurse, or anybody else, because it would be a true love born of trust and confirmation of joy and belief. But you can never fight for this love. That you fight is only a sign that you are wanting in yourself. The child knows that. Your own soul is deficient, so it fights for the love of the child. And the child's soul, born in the womb of your unbelief, laughs at you and defies you, almost jeers at you, almost hates you.

The great thing is, *not* to exert authority unnecessarily over the child – no prerogative, only the prerogative of pure justice. That he is not to throw down crusts is a pure autocratic command. Not to throw down crusts because it is a trouble to nurse to pick them up, is an appeal to a sense of justice and love, which is an appeal to the believing soul of the child.

Put yourself aside with regard to him. You have no right to his love. Care only for his good and well-being: make *no* demands on him.[8]

It is unutterably sad to think that Cynthia was, of all mothers, so unsuited to carrying out these demands. She was incapable of putting herself aside, incapable of not asking for love, incapable of ignoring the worldly and materialistic in order to concentrate on her child. If her child would not come to her, i.e. bow to her will and conform to her ideals, she would not come to him. She dismissed Lawrence's letter as 'very curious', noted that he 'calls my spirit hard and stoical – a serious indictment to which I do not plead guilty' but made no comment on his suggestions about John.

If, hypothetically, she had acted on the letter, what would she have done? She would have tried not to *care* so much. She would have been calm, interested, a little withdrawn, a port in a storm giving shelter when John needed her – not when she needed him; in short she would have been more tolerant. She needed to be mature enough not to be continually self-conscious about John as a reflection of herself, but to value him for what he was regardless of the credit or discredit he did to her. She needed to love disinterestedly, not to expect returns. Above all, she needed to renounce ambition for him, whether it was replacement for her own thwarted ambition or ambition that he should shine. This was not easy on either count: Cynthia had great intelligence which she had found no use for and it was all-too understandable that she should want to exploit it through her sons. Nor could someone brought up as she had been easily give up her entrenched expectations. 'You *must* have a son sometime and the more you are his contemporary when he is Prime Minister the greater the fun for you!'[9] she said to Katherine, and she was not joking. Nor was Raymond when he asked his wife in 1916 – her third child being a boy – 'Shall we send him into the Cabinet or the Grenadiers?'[10] It was tough to be a child of the Souls, it was just as tough to be a grandchild and all of Cynthia's three children were, in their varying ways, to suffer.

For the moment all efforts were concentrated into making John normal: a child who did what he was told, loved his parents a reasonable amount but not excessively, and behaved nicely when brought down to the drawing-room at children's hour. If he could not do these things he was at fault, not the world. Only a visionary like Lawrence could see the sterility of these concepts. But, partly out of politeness, and partly because the language of mysticism came naturally to him, he expressed them so abstractly that Cynthia did not really have to confront what he was saying. He did not say: you aristocrats are so dominated by convention and materialism that you are bound to break the spirit of any child who is even normally sensitive, innocent and unworldly. Instead he told her: 'Now a soul which knows that it is bound in by the existing conditions, bound in and formed or deformed by the world wherein it comes to being, this soul is a dead soul . . . the soul of John re-acts from your soul, even from the start: because he knows that you are Unbelief, and he reacts from your affirmation of belief always with hostility'.[11]

Cynthia of course found these ideas curious and took no notice. There was no question of bending the rules to adapt to the child, and to John it must have been very confusing. Why did Cynthia sometimes spend time with him and sometimes not? Why, on some occasions, was he allowed to be 'deliriously happy with taps, doors etc' (this was at Lawrence's cottage at Greatham) and on others forced to endure a luncheon party until 3.30 in a 'tiny comic little abode' full of locked doors that frightened him? 'An absolute little Hun casting everything to the ground in impish defiance'[12] was his mother's verdict on him after this occasion, the word Hun striking a discordant note, given that one of the many reasons for John's difficulties was that he began to grow uneasily aware of the world as somewhere frightening and unwelcoming just as the war was becoming an entrenched part of life.

Sometimes John was 'very vital and talkative',[13] at others 'very silent and unresponsive'.[14] He was always entranced by mechanical objects such as musical boxes, was delighted with some picture-books of trains Cynthia bought for him and 'played the piano with wonderful technique and temperament[15] . . . It really is extraordinary how he chooses the notes and gently caresses them, all the time making most eerie Puck faces'.[16] He could recite nursery rhymes, often burst responsively into roars of laughter and most of the time behaved normally – because only naughtiness was cause for comment. Yet, later on, Cynthia was to claim that he had always been odd but that she did not realise it at the time.

It was at Gosford in the summer of 1915 that John started causing Cynthia serious worry. 7 September: 'John very mad after tea . . . It's funny having a mad husband and a mad child' (this was after Beb had been in an odd mood writing poetry); 8 September: 'John disgraced us at tea. He was wildly excited and behaved execrably. All the other children were good as gold'; 9 September: 'John very naughty – he stuffed a whole scone into his mouth at once'; 16 September: 'Struggled to make John count up to 10. He was impish and obstinate. The last week or so he has become passionately demonstratively affectionate. Whenever he sees me he says 'Will Mammie "love" John' and rushes up to me. "Love" means a tight hug'; 9 October: 'It was the little Hope boy's third birthday. John walked up the dark stairs and was suddenly confronted with a bright tea-table and a becandled cake. This proved too much for his equanimity and he behaved like a savage faery – roaring – waving his twitching arms, snatching and stuffing food – incidently upsetting a glass of milk'.

It all seems so trivial – stuffing a whole scone into his mouth, upsetting a glass of milk. During the winter of 1915–16, when John was four-and-a-half, it is hard to see him as anything more than a child who needed a great deal of love and stability, who 'showed off' if he felt he was not being given the attention he craved and who over-reacted if confronted with the unknown, and this included locked doors and becandled cakes. Yet, in these situations, once a child begins to appear acutely over-sensitive, to find his reality in the imaginative world not the material, to display his 'subconscious antagonism', then the average mother feels rejected. And the more she detaches herself, however imperceptibly, the more the child withdraws, the 'naughtier' he becomes and the more difficult it is for the mother to love unreservedly.

But how difficult it is for a child to behave 'well' when he is always being watched and commented upon and when he can not allow himself the luxury of feeling that he will be loved *no matter what*. So that a visit to the zoo, instead of being a simple pleasure that John could enjoy in his own, perhaps peculiar, way, became a fence at which he baulked: Cynthia 'entirely failed to make him even see a lion or tiger. He cut them dead. I wonder if there is anything wrong with his eyes'.[17] John would look vaguely into the distance, yet was so aware of the detailed and close-at-hand that he was obviously not blind. Deafness began to be considered as a reason for his oddity since, similarly, he often appeared not to hear.

26 October: 'Bought some "mind-developing" toys for John – he liked them but only physically not mentally'; 2 November: 'Took John out in his perambulator at about 11. He was *very* naughty and boring'. Yet a few days later at a tea party John was a great success as a buffoon, examined and touched everything, loved his drive home in the dark and 'whispered to a star all the way home'. There is something infinitely touching about this image of John whispering to a star and reminds one how akin madness is to genius and how right Lawrence was to use the vocabulary of mysticism to write about him. And a child who could enjoy himself at a tea party was not what would nowadays be deemed abnormal. Visits to other people were almost always a treat: in February 1916 there was an outing to Apperley (the house in Gloucestershire belonging to the 'comfortable' Strick-lands where Cynthia's sister Mary now lived). 'John enjoyed his outing enormously and was very sweet with sudden, strange mocking all-understanding smiles'.[18]

Cynthia was now becoming increasingly worried. She could not bear to accept that John was different from other children: as yet it had not become a possibility that he was clinically 'mad'. But he was 'undeniably eccentric' and she and Beb often had arguments about his management. It was at this stage that Cynthia began asking for advice both from friends and doctors; it did not take long for matters to get worse. There were frequent 'John talks' with members of the family. Mrs Chapin (a Glouce-stershire friend of Mary Wemyss's) thought that he was a 'case of detached absorption . . . his brain too big for his control and would therefore be very slow in developing unless he had brilliant teaching'.[19] A Dr Cantley was consulted, then a Dr Shuttleworth. 'I feel cold terror about John now more and more often . . . Oh God, surely nothing so cruel can really have happened to me myself?'[20]

She asked herself this question in May 1916, a year after Lawr-ence had first been so fascinated by John. During that year Cynthia's expectations for him had been consistently disap-pointed: she did not of course imagine that it was those expec-tations themselves that were causing his peculiarity. Many, many mothers are both ambitious for their child, and themselves narcissistic, and he or she nevertheless remains unscathed. But Cynthia, and Beb, were unable to accept their son on his own terms and, in particular, refused to bend the rules towards him in the way that Lawrence suggested. And yet they did act on one part of his advice, which was that Cynthia should not look after John herself because their personalities would clash.

> He said dry, conventional authority – verbal bullying, must never be applied to him. He considers Nurse exactly right for John's nature – but I'm afraid he thinks I am quite wrong and that there will always be conflict between us. He considers me not positive enough, and that John would see lack of conviction – what he wants is a simple positive nature.[21]

Unfortunately, because Cynthia wanted Michael to be looked after by Nanny Faulkner, she now found John a governess. At the age of just five he was to be almost always kept apart from his brother and was moved about between Cadogan Square, Stanway and a rented flat. Miss Quinn, as the new governess was called, began to teach him to read and write, which he managed quite well although never seemed at all interested. 'Somehow it gives one the impression of a performing dog' wrote Cynthia wryly after hearing him read a few sentences. But the turning point had been reached for poor John. Once he had a governess who 'said she would have a much better chance of effecting improvement if she were to have him more to herself' Cynthia saw him less. When she *did* visit him he was so over-excited by her visit, but so resentful that she did not want to see him more, and so aware, when she left, that she was returning to Michael and Nanny, that their times together were never a success. By October Cynthia was writing 'Miss Quinn brought John to see me. He didn't speak'.[22]

Any parent must find those three words heart-rending. That the two year-old jonquil who prattled ceaselessly could have become this silent five year-old is quite unbearable. Physical causes now began to be considered. 'Mary started a theory that [John] had been poisoned by his vaccination.'[23] Polly (six years after the birth) now 'remembered' that the doctor 'had been very worried about John when he was born – his head being so pressed – his forehead according to this gossip being really squashed on one side'.[24] And it is true that John did have solid, ungainly limbs ('Siegfried limbs' Cynthia called them) and a large head. But there is little evidence to show that he was in fact brain-damaged.

John should have had the constant, calm, loving attention of one person. He should have stayed in one place and that place should have been the country where he could have been outdoors, unconfined, talking to stars all day long, getting physically tired out by the fresh air, removed from the anxieties of town life. Ironically, it would have been far easier for Cynthia to achieve this way of life than for many people: there were cottages on the Stanway estate which would have suited and servants loyal to her family who would have been willing to help. But it was not an option that was ever seriously considered, even when it was suggested by Lawrence who 'said I could cure him by getting off the false unreal plane of buses, Lloyd George's speeches etc to which I was now clinging'.[25]

In July 1917 Cynthia consulted a Dr Parkinson. He said that it was 'an obvious case of deficiency and that there was *nothing* to be done . . . it wasn't safe to have him with other children and that he would probably develop cruelty etc'.[26] Still other verdicts were sought. A Dr May tried to treat the large head thereby causing nose-bleeds. A Dr Hysslop put forward a thyroid-deficiency theory. Then a Dr Forsythe put forward his jealousy theory. Cynthia wrote to her mother:

He is completely convinced that John *was* normal in babyhood – at least normal in the sense of *not* being mentally deficient . . . *he* is quite positive that the trouble is nervous-psychological and not mental . . . He is very keen about his suppressed jealousy theory – and unplausible as it appeared to me I must say he was able to rather effectually quote my own diary in refutation of the arguments I now put forward.

It is true that my last entry made during John's autocracy was that he was the happiest child I had ever seen – and that after Michael's advent I (without any consciousness of any connection) describe his sudden phase of silence – the beginning of his contraryness and his evident desire to attract attention at any cost – and altogether the setting on of an 'antic disposition.'

I remember on one occasion when I went into the nursery and only spoke to Michael – John got very red and went out of the room and I found him crying silently in the passage . . .

The obstacle in my mind is that looking backwards I can now see clearly that *before* Michael's birth . . . John was quite different to other children of his age – though perhaps not to a degree which couldn't have been accounted for by his being merely 'peculiar'. Anyhow Forsythe's diagnosis is the effect of suppressed emotion on an *abnormally* sensitive intelligent and reserved child – and as such he wishes to treat him himself . . .[27]

For a few weeks he did, and with heart-breaking dividends. 'He says the only three spontaneous remarks he [John] has made during the interview are 'Does Mummie kiss Michael more than John', 'Why does Mummie kiss Michael more than John' and 'Michael not coming to have dinner in shop – Michael going to sea-side with Miss Quinn'.[28] As she took a firmer grip on John's life his 'strange charm' retreated. But, to Cynthia, *constant drilling* was the only way he would ever become civilised (able to go out to tea without stuffing the entire scone in his mouth).

It's too much that just that particular thing – which anyone would agree was the worst thing that could happen to a woman – should be applied to me. I can't believe it. I remember my *anguish* when I was afraid he was going to die when he was little. And now if my prayers had not been heard I should be blessed in the at least *rapturous* pain of remembering that darling baby.[29]

1918 was dominated by the farce of Miss Leighton. A more unsuitable governess for John could not have been imagined. She was over-emotional, lesbian, German (very confusing for a child who had spent half his childhood in the shadow of the war) and unstable to a varying degree. She, in fact, finished John off. Her only moment of perception was when she wrote Cynthia 'pages and pages of Barriesque sentiment . . . comparing John to Peter Pan and me to Wendy'.[30] ('If only he hadn't got to turn into a human being he would be a perfect "pet" just as he is'[31] Cynthia had written in 1916.)

Miss Leighton came to look after John in Cadogan Square and her personality not only began to crush whatever normality was still inherent in him but had such an effect on Cynthia that soon she dreaded seeing either the governess or her charge. At first Miss Leighton seemed intelligent, 'if rather over highly strung', and made the sensible suggestion that Cynthia should take a cottage near London – 'she thought it so important for me to be with the child.' But all too soon she confessed 'that she felt impelled to love me by some amazingly strong external influence' and John had become the pawn in the neurotic games that Miss Leighton forced Cynthia to play with her.

31 January: Tea with John – found him fretting dreadfully because I was late. Papa came down and visited us. After John went to bed I had the most shattering interview with Leighton – she inducted me into a state in which I no longer knew whether I was mad – dead – or insensate – anyhow she stripped me of any opinion or emotion. Then she goes home saying she is going to cry all night and would

like to throw herself into the Serpentine. Is she mad with her uncanny twinkly grey eyes which seem to see through the roof and with which she tells me she sees angels or is she a real mystic? Anyhow she's uncanny . . .

The pattern rapidly set in that was to be repeated throughout 1918. Miss Leighton moaned out words of endearments *or* words of fury about Cynthia's alleged callousness, insensitivity etc. Cynthia attempted to evade her and then would write, disastrously, trying to create some kind of calm. Miss Leighton would be mollified or hysterical – for a while – before renewing the attack into which she had been led by the warped nature of her personality. Quite quickly the situation deteriorated from difficult ('any love affairs I have ever had have been a rest-cure to this') to impossible, with Cynthia oddly reluctant to dismiss Miss Leighton since she had somehow convinced herself that no-one else could handle John better, but equally reluctant to go near her and be involved in the usual distasteful and unwinnable scene. John of course saw increasingly less of his mother and was left with a woman who toppled him over into the madness from which, before, he had just been hanging back. Yet no-one perceived what Miss Leighton's effect would be because it was so gradual. At first she did seem to be making John 'improve', but eventually her continual rebuking meant that it was easier to leave her and John on their own together; Cynthia visited them less and John began an irreversible decline into abnormality.

In the summer of 1918, when she had not seen John for some weeks, Cynthia felt momentarily optimistic. 'The abdicated mother was treated quite gently' and John was eager to show off his reading. 'His expresson much better – at least he wears his best one much more continuously . . . He is very, very darling and so loving – much less hysterical.'[32] Yet Miss Leighton was, for all practical purposes, John's mother and 'insists on an entirely free hand even in his dressing. She has taken a flat from September for six months where they are to live alone'. When Cynthia visited the flat, which she paid for but did not even view beforehand, 'John looked well and was very sweet, but I see no sign of fundamental change and feel very sick at heart'.[33]

His first day at school was 1 October (he was now seven-and-a-half) and a pattern began of Cynthia thinking about him relatively little and only going to visit him, usually for tea, once a week. In the late autumn she became pregnant: she was to be very conscious of the possibility of Michael being jealous of the new baby and during 1919 her visits dwindled further to once a month. Miss Leighton had become so abusive that Cynthia came to dread seeing her; John was a secondary dread. Half-hearted attempts were made to change an impossible situation but nothing had been done by the time her diary was discontinued in November 1919. When she re-started a page-a-day one in January 1921 Miss Leighton is no longer to be heard of and John is at boarding school. It was probably some time in 1920 that the incident took place, still remembered by Ego's two sons, when John 'attacked' one of his cousins. The birth of another brother, combined with his siblings being allowed to live at 'home' with Nanny Faulkner while he was condemned to a flat with a governess, seeing his mother rarely, would have been unbearable for anyone, and especially him. Presumably boarding school was thought the only solution. Holidays were spent by the sea (in yet more lodgings) with a teacher from the school and, occasionally, at Stanway when his two brothers had returned to London. It seems that John was sent away permanently and did not even spend holidays with his family at about this time.

He was sent to a special school for backward children – St Christopher's School, Ealing. The school doctor, when first seeing him in March 1920, noted 'Primary Amentia of mild degree, active, restless, irresponsible and unstable, with marked defect of active attention and control'.[34] This was only eighteen months after the occasion at Eynsham when Cynthia had found him 'very, very darling and so loving'. He deteriorated a lot during his six years at St Christopher's. When he left the headmaster wrote a letter about him.

The Asquith family knows there is mental disorder as well as very marked deficiency & until the age of 10 years when John came to school he had had no continuity of teaching, management or control & was thoroughly spoilt & out of hand.

The change to school discipline & routine was a happiness to him & corrected much that was only due to 'spoiling' etc . . . but . . . except for reading or writing more or less mechanically he has advanced very little either in school subjects generally or in handwork & occupation.

The trouble recently has been that he shows a great deal of nervous irritation & bad temper & screams with no provocation whatever. A severe nosebleed often follows these attacks & seems to relieve his feelings. He will repeat all the bad words & nasty names he knows (which fortunately is a limited list). He would throw things & be destructive but would not he harmful to others or himself barring an accident – & I have never known him retaliate even if another child is aggressive. He has very few interests but seems to like the sight & sound of life around him. Music pleases him & motoring & he can play cricket. He walks well, talks very little, can dress & wash himself under supervision, & is no trouble with regard to food. Until the recent mental changes he could be relied on to behave well & was usually cheerful & content.[35]

The school doctor reported that 'dementia precox [schizophrenia] is supervening upon his amentia.'

John was admitted to Chrichton Royal Institution near Dumfries in August 1926. It was chosen because Cynthia had made friends with Lady Lawrence, whose elder son Henry had symptoms rather similar to John's, and she was very satisfied with the way he was looked after there. On his arrival a long and detailed form was filled in about him, starting off with psychological symptoms and ending up with physical ones such as the colour of his urine. The space for personal history had a star by it: 'His father says that he was the first baby, that the labour was difficult & instrumental & that the head was very dented after birth'. General type, appearance and condition: 'pale anaemic looking youth, childish & feeble minded. Has many mannerisms. Given to screaming at times'. His physical health appeared to be sound, his mental state 'simple & childish'.[36]

During his years at Chrichton Royal a Treatment, Progress and Termination sheet was kept about John. Reading it one is close to tears; the impression of waste and sadness is indelible. For the first weeks John was very 'noisy restless & destructive' but by October he was more settled (the sedatives were taking effect) 'simple & child like . . . occasionally reads a little' and by June of the following year he was 'much better physically, more settled & not so childish'. 1928–9 was the same, but by 1930 he was 'more enfeebled, idle, apathetic, uninterested, walks like an old man (he was nineteen) . . . masturbates. Won't speak'. In 1932 there was little change except 'much enfeebled in mind' and by 1934 he was 'demented & idle . . . cannot converse'. In March 1937 when he was nearly twenty-six he 'appears to be weaker physically . . . slight cough'. 21 May 'Collapsed this a.m.' The telegram informed Cynthia that he had died of a heart attack. She wrote: 'I can only be deeply thankful about John, it is the most blessed thing that could have happened, but inevitably it takes one back to old delights and old despair and that's what had long been frozen'.[37]

There is a coda to the story of John. In 1923 Margaret Kennedy, soon to become a popular and successful novelist, published her first novel *The Ladies of Lyndon*. It was suggested to Virago Press that it should be reprinted and in 1981 it was; in my introduction I quoted from a contemporary article in *Queen* magazine:

> The idea for *The Ladies of Lyndon* arose from a children's party where Miss Kennedy met a little boy who was considered mentally deficient. He was having a sad time with the other children, so she took him into another room and played the gramophone to him and found that he could hum perfectly all the tunes she played, though he was not more than three years old. That made her consider the possibility of a child quite different from others, perhaps with genius in his strangeness, who might be treated kindly, but in quite the wrong way, by those in charge of him.[38]

I had never heard of Cynthia then. But when I read in her diaries about John I was reminded of James in *The Ladies of Lyndon*. (The two women do not appear to have met until two years after the book was published, although there is the coincidence that Margaret Kennedy's husband had been Secretary to H.H. Asquith during the war.) James's abnormality was attributed to a brain injury when he was a motherless baby ('It must have been during the period when he lacked a mother's care the harm was done'). It had become far more obvious as he grew older: 'at twenty-one he could not be depended upon sufficiently, in the matter of table manners, to dine with the family'. He was quiet, sensitive and shy, and had been taught to read by his governess only 'after a fearful struggle. He would not fix his attention'. When Agatha, the heroine of the novel, meets him she thinks him hideous, but then

> It struck her that there was not quite the vacuity she had feared to see. Those sad eyes were too observant . . . his build was massive, though short, and very uncouth by reason of his stooping shoulders and the immense length of his arms. His head was rather too big and his large, pale face, with its prominent cheekbones, was unrelieved by the faintest suggestion of eyebrow.

While her lover, more scientifically, 'divined a degree of contra-suggestibility beyond any he had previously encountered. It was impossible to make any impression upon James. He lived in a strange world of his own, developing character, as it were, in spite of his surroundings'. But Agatha soon comes to like him and is the first person who thinks his step-mother is managing him in the wrong way ('It's been impossible to teach him civil manners') and the first to be interested in his painting – at which he proves highly successful: once he has escaped from the 'normal' world of good manners and constraint, 'that abyss of irritation, suspicion, veiled criticism, of secret conclaves, tactful hints and plain speaking'.[39] His life turns out to be very happy and fulfilled (although artistic, and in Hampstead).

One will never know whether John's tragedy was anyone's fault, whether it arose from the intolerable constrictions of the society into which he had been born (as Lawrence believed), whether he could have been cured (for example by Dr Forsythe) or whether any of his gifts (notably for music) could have made a life for him. But it is unbearable that thousands and thousands of Johns have been bundled away in institutions, sedated and half-alive, left to a fate which compassion and psychiatry and more enlightened mothering might have warded off.

····⤅· Chapter 17 ·⤃····
1915

Christmas 1914 had been a time of relative happiness: later in the war Cynthia was to call it 'our high water mark of Xmas facetiousness'.[1] Stanway was full of relations and friends: George Vernon was staying, Eliza Wedgwood came over daily from Stanton, local families like the Batemans, the Allens ('the Priest' and his wife) and the Smiths came to dine. There were 'all the time-honoured stocking jokes. In George's we put twenty-four celluloid babies; in Beb's twenty-four photographs of his father, and in Papa's tiny tips from each member of his family'.[2]

In January reality broke through. Cynthia went with Polly to live in a hotel at Southsea, a village a mile along the coast from the Naval Base at Portsmouth. Beb had gone there on a training course and was soon given a commission in a brigade of the Royal Marine Artillery. He was to embark for France as soon as the brigade was supplied with guns but for the moment had nothing to do but wait. One of the things that passed the days was growing a moustache, which turned out to be even redder than his lightly red hair – nearer the colour of Cynthia's hair.

At Walmer Castle during the second weekend in January he was observed by his father, an unusual enough event since he made no secret that Oc was his favourite, Raymond the son he admired most and Beb and Cis the also-rans.

Another rather curious figure in our party was Beb, clad in khaki, & growing an orange-coloured moustache, against wh. all but Cynthia protested (I heard Puffin [Beb's half-brother] who had been among the adverse critics, say to her in a low & sympathetic tone 'I hope I didn't hurt your feelings, Cynthia'). He is more slow in speech & undecided in action than I ever remember him, and the girls say that when I asked him at breakfast if he was going to golf, he looked musingly out of the window (it was a lovely morning) and after a long interval replied: 'My plans have not yet crystallised'. He is full of rather argumentative fads about spies, conscription &c, and, as Cis says, his 'bonnet is a regular bee-hive'. Cynthia was in good looks and very happy & nice.[3]

It was the end of April before Beb finally went. ('Quiet and unassuming. Plenty of brains' wrote his Brigadier-General on his service record.) Cynthia was as disbelieving as she had been when the outbreak of war disrupted her rest after Michael's birth: 'It is very difficult to believe that History will interfere in one's private life to such an extent. Beb going to the Front seems too melodramatic to be true.'[4] She was at Dover to see him off, and was particularly struck by his driver whom she considered almost the best-looking man she had ever seen. Still nothing seemed quite real – 'I felt strangely and mercifully numb . . . the most unaccountable almost apathetic want of terror about Beb'.[5]

Nor did she feel any terror about the children. Since the previous August they had been at Stanway but in May they went off with Nannie Faulkner to Brighton: on the principle that physical health was of paramount importance, sea air carried far more weight in the scheme of things than the familiarity of Stanway. Cynthia did not inspect the lodgings first nor did she go with them and their luggage on the journey. It would have been thought a very odd thing to do and in fact would not have occurred to her. Again and again in memoirs of the period there are references to children being sent to the sea with a nanny or governess and it was unusual for their mother to go with them: she had a much better time elsewhere. The folly of this is sometimes evident, for example Clementine Churchill sent her children to Broadstairs in 1921 in charge of a young nursery-governess. Because she did not realise in time that the two-year old Marigold's illness was serious she sent for mother and doctor too late and the child died. The following year Clemmie took a large house at Frinton-on-Sea for herself, servants and children; this was partly because she was pregnant and partly, presumably, because she wanted, this time, to stay with the children herself.

Although she did not live with them Cynthia enjoyed visiting the children in Brighton: it was a place where she felt at peace with herself ('so absorbing and satisfying do I find my life at Brighton I never wish to leave it – I'm afraid there can be no doubt that it is my "spiritual home" '6 she wrote to her sister at about this time). Nevertheless after a month she moved the boys to Littlehampton, 'a real paradise for children with huge stretches of lovely sand' (unlike the shingle at Brighton).

Cynthia did not miss the domestic minutiae involved with running Sussex Place; but disliked being dependent on the kindness of her brother Guy in Catherine Street or the Brodricks in Portland Place or even her own parents in Cadogan Square. And time after time she complained about how exhausting London was. There was shopping: 'Did various shattering shoppings together for two hours, finally killing ourselves at Selfridges . . . so far from not wanting (clothes) in War Time I think they are the one thing to distract one, and I long for lovely ones'.7 (And her clothes *were* always lovely: once someone assumed that she spent £500 (£12,500) a year on them, 'the whole of my allowance!'8)

Sometimes friends involved her in war work, for example making respirators on a machine. This she enjoyed since 'any manual labour has great fascination to me and I simply loved it . . . one felt so competitive even unrewarded'.9 Even working in a canteen was fun – 'I don't know why it's so fascinating . . . it really excited me'10 she wrote after hours of pouring out tea and doling out cakes and sandwiches. Yet she knew unarguably that she was not the type of whom good nurses are made and was contemptuous of the untrained auxiliaries who were 'only decor and trimming'. 'The dreadful thing is that instead of it being rather self-indulgent to become a nurse – it is now another imperative duty to healthy and detached women as there is beginning to be a real nurse famine'11 she wrote in a now scratched-out passage in her diary, quite pleased that her children excused her. But in her autobiographical novel about the war she provided her heroine with a poisoned hand and slightly strained heart to account for her nursing duties lasting for no more than a few weeks.

Never a lunch or dinner went by without an engagement, and inbetween there was tennis, visits to women friends, letters to write, 'arranging'; and all the time there was the need to feel needed. In the same autobiographical novel Cynthia was to write of her heroine:

A talent for relieving social situations always finds plenty of exercise, and so many people appeared to depend on her, to draw some sort of sustenance from her rather unusual combination of extreme vivacity

and great (supposed) serenity . . . At times she despised herself for
her adaptability and deplored her over-receptive mind which enabled
or rather forced her to sympathise with every sort of person, but
remain without any one compelling interest.[12]

Continually putting on a show, being receptive, is exhausting,
and Cynthia's extrovert side never allowed her introvert side any
room to breathe. In London she would write, typically, 'Went to
bed very miserable and tired. Life now is really too much – one
begins to feel raw with all one's nerves exposed . . . the combination of ill-health and poverty is really too much of a handicap
to one's life. I could contend with either singly but it is a very
formidable collaboration'.[13] (The ill-health, for which many
doctors were consulted and cures attempted, consisted of tension-
induced indigestion dubbed colitis, 'this invisible handicap'.)

In mid-June Beb came back to England for a month. He had
written often during the six weeks he was away and 'sounds
really extraordinarily happy and says it is a great holiday after
the Bar.'[14] He was with an anti-aircraft battery and 'has great fun
potting zeppelins.'[15] A splinter of shell had knocked out two
teeth – 'really marvellous escape, the sort of thing one must
congratulate oneself upon these days'[16] – so he and Cynthia
packed and re-packed between Cadogan Square, the Somersets
at Reigate Priory and the hotel at Littlehampton ('What a lot of
Lounge life I have had lately!'). Beb's bonnet was still the 'regular
bee-hive' it had been in January. 'He lisps all day long his hatred
of politicians and I agree with him' Mary Herbert told Aubrey.
'He wants to bring back an army at the end of the war and string
up his father and Bonar and all old men to lamp-posts and then
have a great and glorious army to rule England and let everyone
be democrats and soldiers together.'[17]

But the great interest at this time was Venetia Stanley's engagement to Edwin Montagu and her consequent ending of her affair
with the Prime Minister. Cynthia learnt about it from Harold
'Bluey' Baker in mid June 'in great confidence'. It is rather indicative of the way Beb, and Cynthia, were not in the forefront of
H.H.'s thoughts and affections that Violet, Raymond and
Katharine knew about the engagement by the last week of May
and Cynthia only heard from Bluey. For months to come the exact
nature of Venetia's relationship with H.H. was to be a source of
gossip. A year later Cynthia noted that 'Goonie maintains with
conviction that Venetia was actually the P.M.'s mistress but
wouldn't produce any circumstantial evidence'.[18]

When Beb went back to France Cynthia continued to move

Madeline Wyndham in 1873. On the back of this photograph is a note from Madeline to Blunt (p.37).

Mary, George and Guy Wyndham in 1874. Mary, 'a scaramouch of a girl' (p.24) is eleven. All three have inherited Madeline's sensuous mouth. The boys are wearing guernseys (p.37).

Hugo Elcho, date unknown. Photograph taken by Abdullah Frères in Constantinople.

Mary Elcho by Sir Edward Poynter 1886, a few months after Guy's birth and a year before Cynthia was born.

Arthur Balfour in 1902.

The first five students at St Hugh's with the first Principal Miss Moberly at the extreme left. Charlotte Jourdain is in the centre of the back row.

Cynthia and Guy Charteris in 1889 when she was two and he was three.

Drawing of Cynthia by Burne-Jones done in the autumn of 1894 (p.25). Original destroyed by fire in 1973.

between the seaside and London where, at this time, the climax of every dinner-party was a game of poker and her enthusiasm for it sometimes caused comment. At the beginning of August, once the children had been safely moved to Gosford, their luggage towering and toppling in the taxi ('I *did* feel sorry for the nurses'[19]), Cynthia went to Dublin to stay with Basil Blackwood at the First Secretary's Lodge. There, on 4 August, she heard about Billy Grenfell's death. Julian had died at the end of May and, although sad, Cynthia had been more moved by Ettie's bravery: 'She says she feels no sense of separation, but just consciousness of his radiance and a quite unimpaired zest for life'.[20] Billy's death was, however, different. He was the first man to be killed to whom Cynthia had been physically close. Percy Wyndham, John Manners, Rupert Brooke, Julian Grenfell – they had all been acquaintances, so the fact of their death was less painful than the image of Billy's cold and rotting body which had once, dinner-jacketed and laughing and sweet-smelling, embraced Cynthia's hair and shoulders.

Billy, who was not only clever but was a good sportsman and a great deal of fun, had had an imposing physical presence. His death was 'the first that has been much more than vicarious to me . . . it is the end of one's youth all this – soon one will hardly remember who is alive and who is dead'.[21] Billy's body was never found, having been submerged in the mud of Ypres. This did not deter Ettie who sent back Cynthia's last letter to Billy telling her that it, and a Meredith poem copied out by her, had been found in his pocket when he was killed. Perhaps if both one's sons are killed within two months of each other one should be allowed limitless poetic licence. It was in fact Julian who had had the Meredith poem in his pocket; the letter that was with it was from a French girl who signed herself *'bons baisers*, Peggy'.[22]

After Dublin Cynthia went to Gosford where her father was living with Lady Angela Forbes. The children were well, but it was 'very depressing here. The house like a great dead empty cage hanging in a tempest of misery outside. Very devoid of any lived-in feeling – a sort of no man's ground'.[22] There were visitors, including the delectable Adèle Essex of whom Cynthia was very fond and whose legs she envied so much that she felt that, if she owned them, life could hold no terrors. Hugo and Angela quarrelled and made it up again publicly and exhaustingly but they enjoyed histrionics and were to thrive on them until Hugo's death. Margot visited, leaving 'a wake of weeping, injured people. Both nurses mortally offended. She said John had no roof to his mouth and Michael looked like a Red Indian'. There was the interest of her sister Mary's engagement to Tom Strickland whose family, although tending to 'palms in brass pots' was 'so extraordinarily *comfortable* to be with'.[24] Hugo promised a dowry of £5000 (£125,000), ten times Cynthia's, having rather more money at his disposal since his father's death, and this was on top both of the Strickland's £1500 (£37,000) a year and Tom's banking salary. There were numerous letters to write and there were visits, for example to Margot and H.H. (whose calm demeanour, so powerful, yet so unconcerned, aggravated even Cynthia), to Glen, and to the house where Edwin and Venetia Montagu were staying; although pleased to see them Cynthia was perturbed by Venetia's listlessness, commenting 'I'm sure the marooned honeymoon, even if unpleasant, is really the most wholesome'. The unpleasantness would lie in the enforced loneliness: a married couple that cut itself off from the rest of the world in order to be together *was* thought unusual. Marriage was meant to accommodate itself to the confines of social life.

At the end of August Beb returned, ostensibly on short leave, but telling Cynthia that 'he thought he would get an extension as he was feeling as if he would crack up'.[25] He was to remain in England until early 1917, by which time, during the two-and-a-half years the war had been in progress, he had been on active service for two six-week stretches. Being unwell for much of the time he was in England, he would probably have had a real mental breakdown if a tinge of leniency on the part of the authorities had not permitted him to lead a 'normal' life from August 1915 to January 1917.

A large part of this normality was writing poetry. Addressing him as 'Pepinpoet', Cynthia often asked him to write 'several surprise poems' and was well-known for her midwifing of her husband; when a slim volume of Beb's poems came out at the end of the year Ego wrote to his mother: 'What a great thing for Cynthia to be married to a poet. I can imagine all the business about profits from the sale of his works and Cynthia flogging up his shy muse, driving him from the Chessboard'.[26] Which is exactly what happened, although in the early days, after the courtship poems he sent Cynthia, his poetry was written out of loneliness while Cynthia was away.

This was how his poem 'The Volunteer' came to be written. Just south of Sussex Place, where the park joins Baker Street, there is a public house called The Volunteer. Beb spent many hours there to avoid the loneliness of his empty drawing room, and wrote poetry sitting at a table in the downstairs bar. (His third son was to claim that the famous talking parrot, whose indiscretions led to numerous divorces, was a great source of inspiration to Beb.) While Cynthia was in Baden-Baden and John at Clonboy, in the autumn of 1912, he wrote his finest poem and named it after the pub. Slightly re-jigged, it was published in *The Times* three years later and people started saying that it was the greatest poem to have come out of the war. Although its reputation was quite soon submerged by other poems, it remains Beb's best-known and is still frequently anthologised. It did not, however, appeal to everyone. When it was included in the third volume of Eddie Marsh's anthology of *Georgian Poetry* Edmund Gosse wrote: 'I read him forward and I read him backward and I see nothing . . . If he were a Herbert Snooks . . . no-one would ever have looked at his verses. And people say that the 'age of privilege' is passed!'[27]

The theme of 'The Volunteer' is not so much the Great War, but the chivalric ideal; the poem was written out of frustration at the life of a junior at the Bar, working late at his pink-ribboned briefs, deprived of his family and envisaging no future but more of the same:

Here lies a clerk who half his life had spent
Toiling at ledgers in a city grey,
Thinking that so his days would drift away
With no lance broken in life's tournament:
Yet ever 'twixt the books and his bright eyes
The gleaming eagles of the legions came,
And horsemen, charging under phantom skies,
Went thundering past beneath the oriflamme.

And now those waiting dreams are satisfied;
From twilight into spacious dawn he went;
His lance is broken; but he lies content
With that high hour, in which he lived and died.
And falling thus, he wants no recompense,
Who found his battle in the last resort;
Nor needs he any hearse to bear him hence,
Who goes to join the men of Agincourt.[28]

The poetry of chivalry, which in 1912 referred to the Eglinton Tournament, could without difficulty be changed into the poetry of war.

Beb himself had not found the war as satisfying as his Volunteer. He was in poor health. In January H.H. had remarked on his indecisiveness, and the strain of life at the Front, even a few weeks of it, had inevitably made him even more reserved. On 7 September Cynthia wrote that 'Beb sat up late writing poetry and was in one of his oddest moods.' A week later he complained of dizziness and faintness and 'smashed an inoffensive vase . . . because it "wasn't pretty" '. Cynthia was upset and unhappy for him and regretted not having looked after him more carefully.

I remembered Laurence's [sic] statement that Beb's destructive spirit had been roused and that he couldn't bear 'to see a house with its roof on' and I felt alarmed. I believe the desire to smash is a recognised symptom of nervous strain from artillery work and I do so understand it only one *must* drastically discourage it for there is nothing that it mightn't lead to and his arguments when scolded were rather unhinged – 'Gallant and wonderful soldiers were being killed – so why should ugly vases survive' – Such logic might lead to the smashing of Lady Horner's face. I remonstrated with him and he became very emotional and *exalté* – talking with tremendous feeling even tears of the sufferings and gallantry of the men and officers. There is no doubt that his nerves as quite distinct from his nerve are much affected and he must be kept very quiet. I think he feels tremendously the sense of the completely different plane in which the men at the front are living – and the great gulf fixed between them and those at home – He has a tremendous feeling of reverence for the soldiers and I suppose a sort of sense that the beauty of their heroism is not fully appreciated and I think this produces sub-conscious irritation and indignation against the immunity and immobility of people and 'vases' etc at home . . .[29]

But after a few days Beb was well enough to go to Holker Hall in Lancashire. Cynthia went with him and also Basil Blackwood, who had arrived a week previously at Gosford. Their hostess, Moira Cavendish, had had a fifth daughter six weeks before, yet her 'uncanny constitution is really a serious drawback in a hostess and she rather chivies one from sport to sport leaving no gaps in the day for reading the newspapers or writing letters.'[30] Another of the guests was Basil's friend Gilbert Russell, whom Cynthia had never met before; she was to become a close friend both of him and of his brother Claud.

On their return to London Beb stayed at Downing Street for the weekend. 'London fairly gloomy as to the progress of the "Victory" was the verdict he gleaned.' After visiting the children at Gosford Cynthia joined Beb in London. They were to stay at Bruton Street since the Herberts were away. 'Sometimes this perpetual 'cuckooing' gets badly on my nerves. [Evelyn] is away and there are only two housemaids, so we can only have breakfast and tea in.'[31] The familiar London gloom set in, 'disinclination to pull wires and start people . . . I had an awful *crise de nerfs* about

London life. I always do during the first days of installation – the idea of the amount of people there are to see and the prospect of telephoning, futility etc exasperates'. But London soon took its familiar hold and the Bruton Street nest made life easier. 'It is divine occupying so central a position. We have been able to walk out to dinner twice running . . . This is a most excellent nest. We really haven't been so physically comfortable since we married.'[32]

The war could never be forgotten. In early September the news had come of Charles Lister's death (he had been born a month after Cynthia, not long after his mother Charty had been deeply embroiled with Hugo) and Cynthia observed that she was 'beginning to get quite numb, one can't go on feeling with anything like normal sensitiveness'.[33] In October two Stanway boys whom she had known since childhood were killed and she had another day of misery.

But when, on the 19th, she took the telephone call from the War Office announcing the death of Yvo she was in inconsolable agony. His character had been one of peculiar sweetness. 'I don't believe anybody can ever have made himself more loved in nineteen years.' It was after his death that 'for the first time I felt the full mad horror of the war'. Understandably, words were inadequate, nor was there any comfort in Yvo's death, 'apparently it was one of those absolute chuck aways. They were ordered to do something quite impossible and quite futile under enfilading machine gun fire. Yvo was making a "gallant attempt" and it was six bullets that did it so thank God – I think it must have been quite instantaneous. I hope there was no realisation. Mamma and I went to Selfridges and bought hats'.[34]

During the last few days of October the children came briefly to London to break the journey between Gosford and Stanway. Michael held a 'levée' (nursery tea) consisting of Lawrence, Henry Tonks and his two godfathers Eddie Marsh and Charles Whibley. The same evening Beb and Cynthia dined at Downing Street and Margot asked famously 'How *could* your mother let him go?' as she shed her tears for Yvo. 'A terrible point of view'[35] remarked Cynthia understatedly, not bothering to spell out Mary's attempts to keep him at Eton for another year. Next day came the bothersome journey to Gloucestershire, 'ghastly business getting all our luggage on to two taxis – swaying perambulators, birdcages etc, the paraphernalia of nursery travelling is fatiguing to a degree'.[36]

'It's unutterably sad here' Cynthia wrote on arrival. 'Mamma has *none* of the unnatural exalténess of Ettie'. Yet neither did Mary go to the other extreme and let herself give way to grief, as

Lawrence understood when he described her at this period of her life as 'Lady Beveridge':

> She was a little, frail, bird-like woman, elegant, but with that touch of the blue-stocking of the nineties which was unmistakable . . . so wonderful in her way, [she] was not really to be pitied for all her sorrow. Her life was in her sorrows, and her efforts on behalf of the sorrows of others . . . [She] loved humanity, and come what might, she would continue to love it. Nay, in the human sense, she would love her enemies. Not the criminals among the enemy, the men who committed atrocities. But the men who were enemies through no choice of their own. She would be swept into no general hate.[37]

Cynthia shared this admirably expansive attitude to the war, which made both of them, mother and daughter, appear at times to be not only detached but cynical. Their incapacity to hate, their determination that life had to go on as optimistically as possible, led the bigoted to think them callous. But it was with heavy hearts that they got through the late autumn of 1915, with the familiar Stanway ritual of reading, exercises, regular meals, perambulator pushing and tennis ('I enjoy tennis more and more; it gives me *joie de vivre* and a sense of swift efficiency'[38]).

Then, on 11 November, a date which had as yet no resonance, came the news of the death of George Vernon, a close friend of all the Wemyss family and 'practically another brother'. Cynthia wrote heart-rendingly in her diary: 'Oh, why was I born for this time? Before one is thirty to know more dead than living people is really hard. Stanway – Clouds – Gosford – *all* the settings of one's life given up to ghosts.'

····✦· Chapter 18 ·✦····
D. H. Lawrence

In mid-February 1915 Cynthia visited the Lawrences at Greatham in Sussex. She had not seen them since just before Michael was born the year before, and told her sister Mary:

> They are living in a very 'precious' cottage on lovely downs – which has been lent to them by the poet-patrons the Meynells – the family who discovered Francis Thompson. It was delicious – the whimsical poet dressed in corduroys cooked the kippers etc with which he fed me and his delightful ebullient German wife. They had an extraordinary young Werther [John Middleton Murry] staying with them. It *was* fun, and I did like them all and their atmosphere so much better than the Coterie.[1]

Lawrence and Frieda did not enjoy Cynthia's Greatham visit as much as she had: 'she wearies me a bit' was his comment, while Frieda wrote 'she is quite nice, but – I feel sorry for her – She is poor in feeling'.[2] Yet this was to be their only recorded negative comment about her. It is possible that Murry's presence made Cynthia uneasy and silly (he was famously difficult to get on with) and that the Lawrences were rather preoccupied with him (he had arrived miserable because of Katharine Mansfield's temporary defection to Paris and was to retire to bed with flu the next day). Murry himself commented to Katharine that when he arrived at the cottage 'inside was a lady called Cynthia Asquith – not born but married Asquith – who was rather nice of the clever kind; much better than the women the L's generally pick up, though there was a great deal too much 'Lady Cynthia' about it all. L. enjoys it a bit, himself – while Frieda almost wallows'.[3]

When, a month later, Cynthia and the Lawrences walked over the Downs to Chichester, there was no-one else present and Lawrence enjoyed Cynthia more, telling Ottoline Morrell:

> I am rather fond of her. Somewhere, in her own soul, she is not afraid to face the Truth, whatever it may be. She is something of a stoic, with a nature hard and sad as rock. I admire her for her hard, isolated courage. She has never been in contact with anyone. If is as if she can't. There is something sea-like about her, cold and with a sort of passion like salt, that burns and corrodes.[4]

And Cynthia wrote in her diary:

> I find them the most intoxicating company in the world. I never hoped to have such mental pleasure with anyone. It is so wonderful to be such a perfect à trois. I am so fond of her. She has spontaneousness and warm cleverness, and such adoration and understanding of him. He interests and attracts me quite enormously. His talk is so extraordinarily real and living – such humour and yet so much of the fierceness and resentment which my acquiescent nature loves and covets. He is a Pentecost to one, and has the gift of intimacy and such perceptiveness that he introduces one to oneself. I have never known such an X-ray psychologist.[5]

Her enthusiasm was so marked that in 1915 even her mother imagined she was in love with him, and Katharine Asquith had to have a Lawrence letter shown to her in order to be convinced 'that he is *not* in love with me – as she alleges – but only regards me as – God help him – a potential instrument in his revolution'.[6]

Cynthia's friendship with Lawrence was no more complicated than her friendship with Whibley, Raleigh, Barrie, Desmond MacCarthy, Lord David Cecil, L.P. Hartley – and so on. She liked writers and she responded to them – she knew *how* to respond to them. She may not always have been as sensitive as Lawrence or his fans would have liked ('all her references to "poor Lawrence" in her diaries are shallow and patronizing' sneered Keith Sagar) but she did read his work, reply to his letters and prove an honest, warm and loyal friend – and that was enough for Lawrence and Frieda. And it is easy enough, now, to say, 'well, who would not have loved to be Lawrence's friend?' But, when she trekked to Greatham or to Hampstead, or, promptly, took out a 2/6d subscription to *Signatures*, or, uncomplainingly, helped

Lawrence to obtain a passport, she did not know he was a genius. Nor, in truth, did she patronise in her diaries. Her response is usually one of self-deprecation that she lacks the resources to reply adequately to these passionately felt diatribes against the state of the world.

Cynthia was one of the many clever women who, quite simply, responded to Lawrence's magnetism. In June 1914 Catherine Carswell walked with Lawrence past Hampstead Parish church-yard where her dead child was buried. 'Her companion, a man she had met for the first time that day, was so sensitive to her feelings that she found herself talking to him as if she'd known him all her life.'[8] In 1918 Katharine Mansfield wrote, 'oh, there is something so lovable about him and his eagerness, his passionate eagerness for life, that is what one loves so'.[9] The poet Anna Wickham used to go for long walks on Hampstead Heath with him and commented that their 'communion was profound and exceedingly serious'.[10] Eleanor Farjeon typed for him, Rebecca West admired him, Dorothy Brett became a life-long disciple, Ottoline Morrell was deeply fond of him until he used her in a novel, and Dollie Radford (a devoted Hampstead friend) described him as 'a sweet man . . . brimful of sensibility and perception . . . [who seemed to] understand most human matters at a first glance'.[11] As his friend Richard Aldington commented in *Portrait of a Genius, But*:

> The fact that so large a proportion of his chief correspondents and warmest admirers were women has given the impression that he had a Svengali influence over them. But most of them were fastidious upper-class women remarkable for their intelligence and sensitive qualities. What interested them was his 'genius', the fine qualities which went to his making as a great artist. They were interested in him, attracted by him, not because he was 'a lurid sexual specialist' but because he wasn't.[12]

For, although the friendship between Cynthia and Lawrence went far deeper than the snobbery on his side and the lion-hunting on hers, it was neither romantic or physical. In later years Cynthia was to specialise in close, non-sexual relationships with male writers of the kind she had with Lawrence. Uninterested in either father-figures or men young enough to be her sons, she was remarkable for the number of men with whom, during the last half of her life, she was on very close terms. Nor were the men always homosexual, although what they had in common with homosexuals was a special empathy with women, a special friendliness towards them so often absent from the conventional male-female relationship. All Cynthia's close male friends, and Lawrence was no exception, encouraged the gentle cattiness which women often enjoy so much, a sharpness and perception often mistaken for malice. The conversation would cover topics of mutual interest and mutual friends (Ottoline and Margot were often discussed) but not spouses.* Yet, despite his excessive reputation, Lawrence had very little understanding of women. His vision was too abstract, he saw his characters too much as re-enactments of ideas, to want or to be able to record the details of feminine existence. As Frieda observed in a letter to Cynthia written at the end of 1915 'the idea in *The Rainbow* is *Love the ideal* as a background to these marriages which are really all failures to some extent . . . For perfect love you don't only have two people, it must include a bigger universal connection'.[14] Lawrence, mystically, understood the universal but was often oblivious of the dailiness of marriage.

Cynthia, too, was an ideal to him, although she does not fit any of the following descriptions: 'the glowing Cynthia Asquith . . . became an ideally worshipped dream woman[15] . . . Lawrence made barmecide love to her through his stories'[16] (Harry Moore); 'perhaps Lawrence was a bit in love with Lady Cynthia, and, not wishing to admit to himself that he could be impressed by mere beauty and aristocratic charm, tried to convince both himself and Lady Cynthia that she had deeper qualities. Unfortunately she had not'[17] (Keith Sagar); 'the woman of Lawrence's dreams . . . at the very darkest moments she remained for him a tenuous but firm link with social and national reality . . . He had frequent dreams in which she or her "aura" played a part'[18] (E. Delavenay).

The ideal that Cynthia represented for Lawrence was one that he had already written and thought about before he met her, so that she came to embody some already-formulated aspects of his work. In *The White Peacock* (1911) the keeper's wife Lady Crystabel ('a white peacock') was a woman who began 'to get souly. A poet got hold of her, and she began to affect Burne-Jones'.[19] While, in the same novel, Lettie's lover tells her, 'I'm not one of your souly sort. I can't stand Pre-Raphaelites'.[20] *The Trespasser* (1912) was also

---

*Although it has been foolishly assumed by E. Delavenay that Lawrence 'never tired of giving advice to Catharine Carswell, the Murrys, or Cynthia Asquith on the psychology and conduct of their respective married lives'.[13]

about a woman who belonged to that 'class of "dreaming women" with whom passion exhausts itself at the mouth. Her desire was accomplished in a real kiss'.[21] A 1912 reviewer remarked that the heroine was 'a woman who cannot lose sense of her own identity even in the supreme intimacy of love'.[22] Both these characteristics were shared by Cynthia. Miriam in *Sons and Lovers* (1913), the book published a few weeks before the Asquiths and the Lawrences met, 'was romantic in her soul . . . She herself was something of a princess turned into a swine-girl in her own imagination'.[23] And although Cynthia did not have these kinds of daydreams, she was disappointed by what life had provided for her and once complained 'of my life being so terribly unlike a Burne-Jones picture nowadays'.[24]

Lawrence was of course attracted by Cynthia's aristocratic background. After his death Frieda told Cynthia (in a sentence that Cynthia scratched out before selling her letters) 'he always quoted with pleasure that you said to him once: the aristocrat and the common people can understand each other, it's the bourgeois one doesn't like'.[25] Lawrence saw Cynthia as a symbol of excellence, feeling that if she didn't get it right then who would? He felt it was her duty to lead: 'If all the aristocrats have sold the vital principle of life to the mere current of foul affairs, what good are the aristocrats?'[26]

Ther is no evidence at all to suggest that Cynthia was Lawrence's personal ideal or that she was his muse, although she did read and comment on *The Rainbow* (1915). (She called her role midwifing but she was more of a sounding-post than critic.) Quite simply, she and Lawrence liked each other. 'I suppose there is some sort of queer, absolved relationship between you and us: abstract'[27] was his definition, and he accepted that their worlds did not overlap, even though it seems, by the frequency with which he claimed to dream about Cynthia, that he would have liked them to. Once he had a dream in which he was at an Asquith party: 'I couldn't describe you the feeling of almost sordid desolateness caused by the established presence of those other people of yours, who are outsiders'.[28]

Even though Lawrence never gave up chiding Cynthia for her materialism and for her superficiality, he did it in such a positive way that she was never offended. She knew that he believed that women had to take the lead in making the world a better place and that he was not just criticising but trying to mould her into an instigator. In any case, he pointed out faults that she was already aware of and was delighted to discuss. For example, when he wrote, 'there is something infinitely more important in you than your beauty. Why do you always ignore the realest thing in you, this hard, stoic, elemental sense of logic and truth?'[29] he was not meting out blows. Cynthia *knew* that she had a detachment, a dislike of reality, a fatal lack of self-knowledge. She did not need to be told that. What she did need, insatiably, was to talk about herself, and Lawrence, because he was a kind, responsive person and a novelist, fulfilled this need. He could provide verbal dewdrops, and these were what Cynthia craved, not physical ones.

Only once did Lawrence appear to go too far, which was in his long letter to her about John, the one that urged her to give free rein, for her son's sake, to the primeval side of her nature. Cynthia did not like his advice and backed off, to the extent of never again consulting him about John, even when he returned to the theme two years later ('he is a direct outcome of repression and falsification of the living spirit, in many generations of Charterises and Asquiths. He is possessed by an evil spirit, but it is a spirit that you have kept safely inside yourself, cynic and unbelieving'[30]). Lawrence offered to have John to stay with him for a time, a suggestion which Cynthia did not even consider. One might think that she would have had little to lose except her pride, especially as he had had great success with the Meynell's grandaughter Mary Saleeby whom he had taught for ten weeks ('he must have been a genius as a teacher'[31] was Eleanor Farjeon's comment about this episode).

Beb, too, was never offended by Lawrence, or by his fiercely anti-war stance. He would return to England after the most intense experiences he would ever have to endure – the trenches – to find that life was going on unconcerned about the ghastliness in France – and then have Lawrence declare that 'the war is the only reality to him. All this here is unreal, this England: only the trenches are Life to him. Cynthia is very unhappy – he is not even aware of her existence. He is spell bound by the fighting line'.[32] When Beb fainted at Downing Street and had to be taken to Stanway for a long rest, Lawrence informed Cynthia that 'your husband should have left this decomposing life. There was nowhere to go. Perhaps now he is beaten. Perhaps now the true living is defeated in him'.[33] While Cynthia, having endured the destruction of all her certainties, her brothers, friends and lover, was told that she too acquiesced in the war and that if she had been less tolerant she could have brought it to an end.

It speaks highly for the Asquiths' broadmindedness – borne both of Beb's cleverness and classical tolerance, and Cynthia's exposure to a great variety of people – that they, despite provocation, never quarrelled with Lawrence. Cynthia was to claim that he never gave any conceivable cause for a quarrel and that in conversation he was always cheerful and amusing; which was why she never enjoyed his novels, finding them so much more serious-minded than he was in person. Even his letters were sometimes irrelevant to their conversations: when on 16 November 1915 he wrote her a long letter urging her to leave 'this decomposing life' and join him in America, he saw her in Hampstead the next day before she went down to Stanway where the letter was waiting for her, but did not mention it as though it had no relevance to the delightful time they were having together. Then, used to this, she merely commented: 'I found amazing letter from Lawrence suggesting our coming out to America. Children well'. In writing, he often lectured her. Cynthia wrote in her diary: 'Exceptionally good morning post, including an Ego, a Lawrence, an Aubrey, and a Bluetooth. Delicious, very typical one from Ego. Lawrence's letter very long and full of bitterness and diatribe – very difficult to answer'.[34] How one agrees with Eddie Marsh when he wrote, 'I have often wished I could see the answers which people like Lady Ottoline Morrell and Lady Cynthia Asquith wrote to those interminable letters in which Lawrence urged them to demolish their mental superstructure and get down to the dark roots of their being'.[35]

The war was always the focus of conversation. Lawrence detested it, and explained his theory to Cynthia: 'that the nation doesn't *really* want it to stop – because of the nullity of life, as if in a sense it were the result of a vacuum'.[36] His initial fury and despair gave way to a weary longing for compromise at any cost; in October 1915 his view was that the Germans should be given England and the whole Empire if they wanted it, if that was the only way to save lives.* He expanded this attitude in a poem he sent to Cynthia in a letter. It was originally called 'A Plea for Peace', then 'The Turning Back'. There were all the Lawrentian themes – the greed for possession, the ghosts of the dead, the importance of love, the need for appeasement. The concluding verse of the poem was:

Let us go back now, though we give up all
The treasure and the vaunt we ever had,
Let us go back the only way is love.

Partly Lawrence was refuting, in verse, a letter Cynthia had

*If this had happened, eight million lives would have been saved.

sent him in which she declared that war did not prevent the individual from loving. This was the philosophy that kept her going throughout the war; it was a very feminine one, in the true Souls tradition of personal relationships rising above world affairs, but alien to Lawrence who told Cynthia that love 'universalises the individual. If I love, then I am extended over all people, but particularly over my own nation'.[37] 'His feet quite leave the ground' was her rather despairing response, the very human reaction of the over-stretched, whose mind is a whirl of mundanities, to the idealist, reposing in his garrett expounding abstractions. His reply showed how little he understood of the everyday life of a wife and mother. 'I never quite know where you stand: whether the inner things, the abstract right as you call it, is important to you, or only a rather titillating excursus. I suppose you've got to arrange your life between the two: it is your belief – pragmatistic. I suppose it has to be so, since the world is as it is, and you must live in the world'.[38]

His supposition was correct: Cynthia was of the world and worldly and she would not change. But it took a while before Lawrence accepted this. In the early months of their friendship he continually deplored the amount of time she wasted in being sociable; Cynthia was much struck by his and Frieda's way of life ('they make one feel rather as if one had spent most of one's life on the crust of things surrounded by blindfolded friends in masks'[39]) but did not want to change. Nor did she want to try and make her voice heard at Downing Street. Initially Lawrence appeared to have imagined that, if she did not flash his letters around at H.H.'s dinner table, she might at least expound his ideas in conversation. But she was a social chameleon and would never have introduced any radical ideas; in any case she was actually less radical than she pretended to Lawrence. She would have disagreed with his hope that 'after the war, we may have a real revolution . . . women shall have absolutely equal voice with regard to marriage, custody of children etc'.[40] She was used to her luncheon guest being at the far end of the political spectrum from her dinner guest and was happy to adapt herself from Whibley to Lawrence to General Freyberg. Only once did she question her chameleon nature ('I wonder if it is a good thing to be so fluid'[41] she asked herself after Freyberg's passion for war had followed swiftly upon Lawrence's loathing) but normally she sought the serendipity of friendship and was unmoved by Lawrence's criticisms ('You see men like Harold Baker are really no good – they've got no going-forward in them'[42]).

Cynthia's responsiveness was also broadmindedness. It is to

her credit that, when she received the manuscript of *The Rainbow* (1915), she was not more appalled than she was by its 'belly' motif. 'A strange bewildering disturbing surely morbid book. It is full of his obsessions about sex conflict (all the lovers hate one another) and the "amorphousness" of actual life. Excellent bits of writing, but still too much over-emphasis and brutality'.[43] Although Cynthia was proud and amused at 'my having godmothered the one suppressed book'[44] it was nevertheless with some misgivings that, only two weeks after she had read *The Rainbow*, she received the news from Lawrence that he had just done 'a rather good word-sketch of you'[45] in a short story.

'The Thimble' was the first of half-a-dozen stories whose heroines resembled Cynthia, and they all have the same theme, expressed most forcibly the first time: a daughter of the English aristocracy, brought up in one of the most beautiful houses in England in the expectation of wealth, ease and happiness, finds that, because of the circumstances of her marriage and changes in society, happiness eludes her without her realising it. Because of her own failures in courage and intuition she can do nothing to help herself and, behind the beauty and poise, she becomes withdrawn and embittered.

'I think some of his character hints are damnably good. He has kept fairly close to the model in the circumstances'[46] was Cynthia's reaction after she had read the first story which was about a nameless heroine (called 'my lady' by her maid) who had married in 1914, whose husband ('Mr Hepburn') 'in those excited days of the early war . . . was her comrade, her counterpart in a sort of Bacchic revel before death'. But, while he was in France, she has fallen ill and, awaiting his return, realises that she does not know him. The thimble that she finds is a symbol of their previous life; his throwing it away is a symbol of the rebirth of their marriage. Cynthia did not take exception to anything in the story (though the mention of large feet was removed before publication) and must have been pleased by the references to her beauty: 'She knew she was a beauty, she knew it was expected of her that she should create an impression of modern beauty. And it pleased her, it made her soul rather hard and proud: but also, at the bottom, it bored her'.[47]

Cynthia's next appearance was in 'The Blind Man' written in November 1918. The heroine is called Isabel (a Scottish name, Lawrence being very conscious of Cynthia's Scottish roots) and lives on a farm with her husband who was blinded in Flanders. She loves him but he is often depressed and then 'she felt she would scream with the strain, and would give anything, anything to escape'.[48] They are visited by an old friend, 'a barrister and a man of letters' to whom she is close but not in a physical sense; this is a clear portrait of Barrie whose secretary Cynthia had become a few weeks previously. The story is inconclusive, showing the wife torn between her husband's physical dependency on her and her intellectual rapport with their friend who cannot 'enter into close contact of any sort'.

'The Ladybird' (November 1921) was Cynthia's most famous re-incarnation in a Lawrence story. Lawrence scholars have decided that it is a re-working of 'The Thimble', but to the non-academic the stories do not appear to have very much in common apart from the superficial resemblance of the heroine/Cynthia having a soldier-husband and the mention of a thimble. The story opens with a clear and rather touching portrait of Cynthia's mother visiting the wounded in hospital. Then she goes to visit her daughter Lady Daphne in her flat near the park. 'She had married a commoner, son of one of the most famous politicians in England, but a man with no money. And Earl Beveridge had wasted most of the large fortune that had come to him, so that the daughter had very little, comparatively'.[49] She is beautiful but too thin and has the shadow of tuberculosis hanging over her. 'It was nothing but frustration and anger which made her ill.' There are many more details which together build up an uncannily accurate portrait of Cynthia as she was in 1918. For example, there are numerous references to the moon ('We called her Cynthia' Mary had written 'because she came out of the Clouds, like the Moon in memory of her birthplace') and to various goddesses (Aphrodite, Venus, Isis, Cybele, Astarte) which place the heroine on the semi-divine plane Cynthia often half-jokingly longed to be on.

One of the soldiers Lady Beveridge had spoken to in the hospital was a German whom her daughter had known in Saxony when she was sixteen. Daphne helps to bring him back to life (the theme of re-birth as well as that of reconciliation) and is then brought back to life herself: her husband, Basil, returns from the war and Psanek, the German, comes to stay with them in the country ('Thoresway'/Stanway is most beautifully described). Daphne has begun to be ill again, since her husband's adoration is only spiritual: 'She could tell that he shrank with a kind of agony from contact . . . Alas, she was not the goddess, the superb person he named her'. But she becomes Psanek's mistress and is made calm and happy (re-born) while Basil, too, feels something new: 'He felt that she was his blood-sister, nearer to him than he had imagined any woman could be. So near – so dear – and all the sex and the desire gone. He didn't want it – he hadn't wanted it. This new pure feeling was so much more wonderful'.[50]

In 'Glad Ghosts' (December 1925) Cynthia becomes Carlotta Lathkill (although the description of Carlotta in the beginning as an art student is based on Dorothy Brett) and again is married to a man who is dead at the centre. 'Since the war, the melancholy fixity of his eyes was more noticeable, the fear at the centre was almost monomania. She was wilting and losing her beauty.'[51] In the end she is re-born by the Lawrence/Psanek figure and, to make the moral fully explicit, has a son nine months later. (By a curiously incestuous irony Lawrence appears to have derived the name Lathkill from one of Beb's war poems named 'Glimpses of England'.)

Cynthia's final appearance in a work by Lawrence was in *Lady Chatterley's Lover* (1928). The heroine is called Constance (the second name of Cynthia's mother) and has a sister called Hilda (as did Hugo). Clifford Chatterley's brother is called Herbert. Again, and far more notoriously, the husband is sexless and Lawrence further expands the idea he had been promulgating since 'The Thimble' – that these English, upright, fastidious husbands of his Mrs/Lady Hepburn, Isabel, Daphne, Carlotta, Constance figure are absolutely no good to them. Less and less implicitly he explains that without a satisfying sexual relationship the woman will be unhappy, an unfulfilled dreaming woman. After Basil's adoring, insipid love-making Daphne 'felt weak and fretful afterwards, as if she wanted to cry and be fretful and petulant, wanted someone to save her'.[52] Carlotta needs a man to 'take her in his arms and cherish her body, and start her flame again'.[53] Connie is aware 'of a growing restlessness. Out of her disconnexion, a restlessness was taking possession of her like madness'.[54] But Mellors, the gamekeeper, is her Psanek-saviour.

Lawrence never told Cynthia directly what he saw as the cause of her difficulties. It was not an easy thing to tell anyone. In any case he had offended too many people to want to jeopardise another friendship. When he proposed dedicating a small book of poems to Cynthia she read them with interest to see if there were any personal connotations. But she found them 'mainly (thank Heaven!) *not* erotic – ironical glimpses at aspects of the war – with very little rhyme or rhythm about them'[55] (evidently the poetry lessons that Eddie Marsh had once offered Lawrence had had no effect). The poems eventually appeared as *Bay* at the end of 1919, Cynthia having taken them to the publisher Cyril Beaumont in the Charing Cross Road. (He had been a friend of

Yvo's.) Lawrence was paid £10 (£125) for them. The proof lacked a dedication: 'But now *why* did you forget to inscribe it to Cynthia Asquith? I promised it her, and I *know* she's looking forward to it.'[56] (Beaumont pasted in the dedication.)

Cynthia and Lawrence saw each other less in the second half of the war than they had in the first. In the autumn of 1917 she took him to the opera, an occasion that he wrote up in *Aaron's Rod* (1922), (where he also wrote up Cynthia's stay at Chirk Castle). Even in March 1918, nearly five years after their first meeting, 'I have never known D.H. Lawrence nicer'. Nor did he feel diffident about asking Cynthia to help him. In the October of that year he needed a job and wanted her to approach someone in the Ministry of Education – 'but now he has to come to London and sees the door through which people have to go to do their work – it materializes the project to him and seems impossible. He talked of his sick dislike of nearly everyone – very funnily – and shrieked for about five minutes about the shape of Barrie's legs . . . He said his natural love of England drove him to hate it in all its present manifestations and that the only way he could serve it was by standing out against everything'.[57]

A few days later he found a job writing articles on education for *The Times Literary Supplement*. It would have brought in £3 (£35) a week but he found it impossible to do, as Cynthia had privately predicted. 26 November: 'I gave Lawrence a 15/- lunch at Queen's. He drank a good deal of red wine and became rather truculent explaining in what manner we loved one another. He upbraided me for the amount I went out – comparing it to indiscriminate charity and denying that it was an "existence" at all. "Duffer" in fact he called me and urged a retreat into the country and the doing of my own housework'.

At the end of November Cynthia's diary records her only negative remark in all the years of their friendship: 'I felt very tired and disinclined for Lawrence – but I couldn't put him off'.[58] She was by now pregnant and the usual sickness and depression set in. Barrie became more and more enmeshed in her life, Beb came home from France and it seems as though it was Cynthia's wish that the friendship should peter out a little. They continued, throughout 1919, to exchange letters. After the baby was born in the summer Lawrence asked her: 'Are you preparing to sally forth into the "monde" as a sort of young matron? Pfui!! Ah Bah! What is the new line? You'll have to have a new line. *Mère de trois*. It's a bit of a quandary'.[59] There appears to have been one meeting in November just before he and Frieda left England, and he continued to write the occasional letter.

But Cynthia forgot to acknowledge receipt of *The Lost Girl* in 1921. Perhaps she could not agree with Lawrence when he told her 'that bee in my bonnet which you mention, and which I presume means sex, buzzes not over loud. I think the *Lost Girl* is quite passable, from Mudies point of view'.[60] In 1922 he wrote a Christmas letter from New Mexico: 'Now don't *really* go and deteriorate, J Mming and Lady's Worlding'[61] (working for J.M. Barrie and writing articles for women's magazines). When he was in England for three months over the winter of 1923–4 they did not meet, but then on 25 October 1925 Lawrence came to tea at Sussex Place. It was 'our first meeting after six years . . . He looks very ill', and a second occurred three days later. Cynthia must have been abstracted because Lawrence wrote sadly from Italy, 'thought you a bit cross when we saw you last'.[62]

Lawrence's last letter was a few weeks after this. He referred to his most recent novel *Lady Chatterley's Lover* saying 'I don't suppose you'll care for the book – your husband might . . . I'll have a few leaflets sent to you. But if you're afraid of blushing when it's too late, just put them in the fire'.[63] Cynthia, had she read the novel, would have remembered that in 'The Ladybird' Daphne knew 'a gamekeeper she could have loved – an impudent, ruddy-faced, laughing, ingratiating fellow; she could have loved him, if he had not been isolated beyond the breach of his birth, her culture, her consciousness'.[64] And it is likely that it was this link between the two heroines that made her start to deny that Daphne was modelled on her, pretending, for example, to the publisher Daniel George that she was based on Enid Bagnold and to the writer George Ford that she was based on Lady Mendl.

Cynthia did not visit the exhibition of Lawrence's paintings which opened at the Warren Gallery on 14 June 1929 (although she may have gone without mentioning it in her diary, just as she may have obtained a copy of *Lady Chatterley* surreptitiously). So she may never have seen the almost obvious portrait of herself in which she is being embraced by the Lawrence-figure who will bestow on her the sexual pleasure he had for so long been advocating. There are, too, echoes in the painting of Botticelli's 'The Birth of Venus', a painting of which Cynthia had long been fond.

After Lawrence's death Frieda, to whom Cynthia had always been friendly and kind, wrote, 'I think he realised all your outer and inner beauty & I feel it always grieved him that he could not give you a life that was fit for you in this sordid world of ours . . . How you helped us in the past & what a good friend you were! . . . You & he seemed to understand each other in a strange & wonderful way'.[65]

Chapter 19
1916

For the mothers and wives in England one of the most painful aspects of the war was that wounds and death were endured in such unspeakable circumstances. They had spent so much of their lives pampering their men – but were now helpless; and it was partly the loneliness of George Vernon's drawn-out death that tore Cynthia's heart, for she had helped to nurse him through many illnesses in 'sybarite homes' and remembered how 'lovably and childishly dependent on one he used to be'.[1] So when, the weekend of George's memorial service at Stanway, Beb took to his Downing Street bed after a fainting fit, he was moved in a bathchair to Stanway for unlimited pampering.

Cynthia, with him established in her room, tried to forget the terrible scene with Margot in which she had deplored and commiserated over Beb's alleged drunkenness. 'Beb often what I call "takes his receiver off" [ie. is very abstracted] and is very distrait, especially when bored – as he is by [Margot] – and on these occasions has an odd, almost dazed manner.'[2] Once Cis and Cynthia were to agree 'that he was the "oddest" man we knew, and compared notes as to his strange, unacknowledged moods, in some of which (as far as contact with others went) he was as though in a padded room, and one was as if hammering vainly against thick felt'.[3] (The wives in Lawrence's Cynthia stories all appear to be hammering against equally thick felt.) But Cynthia was positive that Beb was never actually drunk, although she had 'always thought he drank more than was good possibly for health and complexion'.[4] (The redness of H.H.'s face had upset her – 'If I were Margot I would whitewash the Prime Minister's face' she had observed in August, adding, 'he is so much attacked for callousness because he looks rosy and well'.[5])

While immured in his room Beb assembled some poems for possible publication. Four days after he had sent them off Sidgwick and Jackson wrote to say that they would publish them in sixpenny (65p) booklets, giving him a royalty of a penny (10p) on each copy sold. Professor Raleigh, whom Cynthia consulted in Oxford (first she attended his lecture on Crabbe), told her that the terms were good, and Beb accepted them. *The Volunteer* and other poems came out three weeks later and Cynthia set to work ordering copies at as many bookshops as she could think of. Not unnaturally, the Prime Minister's own name on a slim volume was a strong selling point and must have helped Beb's career as a poet quite considerably; for example, two days after publication day, he was offered £50 (£1250) for some verses appropriate to New Year 1916 to be published in the *Sunday Pictorial*. 'I fear Beb may find it very difficult to write to order' wrote his midwife. 'I don't know how to coax Pegasus back into his room and wonder what atmosphere is most conducive to Beb's muse. Perhaps I ought to make him unhappy on the principle of "Poets learn in suffering what they teach in song." *It must be written somehow.*' (It was.)

Leaving Beb to his poetry, Cynthia went to London for Violet's marriage to Maurice 'Bongie' Bonham Carter. 'There is something terribly grim about a pompous wedding now. It seems so unnecessary and irrelevant, and one feels so remote. This is unkind because, if one were the bride oneself, no doubt one wouldn't feel one's glamour in the least impaired.'[7] The same week, in Egypt, Mary Charteris was married to Tom Strickland who was there with his regiment. 'Isn't it strange that she should be married there?'[8] Mary Wemyss wrote to Blunt. On her return to Stanway Cynthia regaled Beb with all the London gossip, although for 'insider' political gossip they still relied on Bluey. He was not, however, always accurate. 10 December 'Very Secret: The Tenth Division has been destroyed in the Balkans', 11 December 'I had another letter from Bluetooth in which he took back the worst of his news – the Tenth Division has not been annihilated'.

'We got through our Christmas somehow, though we all felt sufficiently dejected' noted Cynthia on 25 December. But she had an enjoyable New Year jaunt to London during which she saw Basil Blackwood, played poker at a 'Hell' given for her by Adèle

Essex, gleaned some gossip from Bluey ('Conscription is clinched'), shopped at Selfridges, ordered copies of *The Volunteer* from three bookshops and lunched at Downing Street. Yet 'these occasional two days in London over excite me ridiculously. I feel so much more appetite for topical life than I ever did before – I don't know whether it's health or the threat of war'.[9] (So much for Lawrence's prescription that she should concentrate on her intrinsic reality and ignore the extrinsic.) Sometimes the 'peaceful, pastoral' life as Stanway was all she wanted, at others she noted complainingly 'how demoralising my cuckoo life here is. I don't even have to order the dinner or in any way pay my passage.' The verdict on Beb was 'still a very long way off being fit to do anything. Felt rather plan bewilderment'.[10]

They decided that she and Beb should cuckoo at the Herberts. After ten days there Cynthia (and Polly) went to Dublin for a week ('Beb didn't feel up to it') and then returned to Stanway. It was during this visit that Cynthia's relationship with Basil became a much closer one: she was 'unusually possessed by great sense of the fun and fleetingness of life'[11] and was taking a great deal of interest (more than usual) in her looks. After some time at Stanway it was back to Bruton Street which was, as ever, flustering, and Cynthia, beset by the all-too-familiar longings to be in her own house, 'had one of those thoroughly fiendish telephone mornings, so typical of London life, in which the Present is always being ruined by the necessity of having to squint at the Future'.[12]

The diary entries for the end of January are squashed together at the end of the second volume. Then, on the 28th, a third volume begins, donated by Bluey, and Cynthia's most lavish up to date. The second had been an elegant but small book, this was large and gleaming red moroccan leather with gold tooling rather grandly on the outside cover. It was a mark of his and Cynthia's renewed friendship that Bluey was allowed to buy her diary, perhaps the most intimate thing one can give someone apart from underwear.

London life was no less frivolous than it ever had been, and it was the cataloguing of so much pleasure that was to distress readers of the diaries fifty years later. There was tennis with Patrick Shaw Stewart, Goonie Churchill and Basil. There were poker 'hells', for example on 19 February with Basil, Sybil Hart-Davis, Nancy and Sidney Herbert and Clemmie (who merely watched): 'it was quite a successful party though not a financial one as far as I was concerned as I only made one shilling. Beb hated the idea of it but quite enjoyed himself'. There were many lunches and dinners and visits to dressmakers. In March, May and June there were charity revues in which Cynthia took part. 'I had lots of dewdrops and felt pleasant sensation of admiration – still like a warm bath to me'.[13]

Because of domestic ructions at Bruton Street, Evelyn decided that it should have 'a complete rest-cure', i.e. the servants were to be left in peace, so Beb and Cynthia went to Stanway where Mary was bitterly depressed and the continuing snow was not conducive to lifting the spirits.

> These days I feel very much reminded of how deeply sad one is. In London one is made to forget for bits of time with sharp reminders – here one *sucks* tragedy. I really don't know which is best, only I do wish I was more conscious of some *continuity*, and was less just made by my context. The thought of Verdun and what is happening sickens one. It has all become nauseating.[14]

Clonboy was their next perch. Although Cynthia continued to grumble about the unsettled nature of their life, she was aware that it had advantages: 'One can't get really depressed when there is no long vista – nothing but blind corners'.[15] And indeed she found it hard to settle in to the house since 'having for so long complained of not having a house to myself I now felt unprotected, exposed and rather lost. Felt incapable of making an atmosphere of my own'. She was very rattled by having to provide her own cook. 'It is an appalling thought to be ordering and paying for one's own food after so long a holiday. I interviewed before dinner and tried to be clever about meticulous war economies – 'margerine' – no lump sugar . . . quite successful dish of rice and mushrooms for lunch.' But as the weather improved so did her spirits and she was pleased that Beb, who had had another extension from the board, was so happy at Clonboy ('absolutely content without occupation'[16]). Yet the future seemed more uncertain than ever. Although Beb had been promised by his father that he would find out about a 'home front' job for him, H.H. was 'characteristically inert and nothing has been arranged . . . [Beb] appalled me by saying that even if the war stopped now he would never return to the Bar but intended to become a novelist! Cheering prospect for me. Our future is indeed on the knees of the gods!'[17]

Sometimes there were Friday-to-Mondays with friends, although not as many as there had been before the war – some houses like Avon Tyrrell had become convalescent homes, others, like Mells, did not bring the same joy that they once did ('I love Katharine but I don't think her company makes me very happy' wrote Cynthia in March, regretfully remembering the 'love-lorn moonlit remote Yeatsy' Katharine of her girlhood.) But Pixton and Bruton Street were always welcoming: Cynthia had come to the conclusion that 'Mary Herbert is the only woman with whom I have anything even approaching intimacy' and it is true that in recent years she had been seeing less and less of her former women friends such as Violet and Venetia and was relying on her male friends for intellectual rapport. However, she did make one new friend during this period, namely Horatia Seymour, a friend of Clemmie's whom she met in Brighton.

When in London Cynthia perched wherever she was offered; once or twice this meant Downing Street, but it was a last resort. 'Its atmosphere distresses me but it was the only double perch I could find' she wrote in March, always unquestioning of the fact that it was she who arranged perches, she who had to keep Beb happy, she who made all the domestic decisions. Yet the disagreements between her and Beb were, at this time, never very fundamental. Sometimes he objected to dining *à trois* with her and Bluey or Basil, sometimes he was a 'dentist breaker' when a friend called to see Cynthia (i.e. he did not leave them alone), occasionally she accused him of extravagance, and always there were quarrels over rail travel: a soldier 'was bound to travel 1st in khaki' and Cynthia very much objected to paying extra for herself to travel in what she considered pointless luxury. Also, while always defending Beb against Margot's accusations of drunkenness, she often remonstrated with him about the amount he drank (and once boxed his ears about it).

At the end of April the family was informed that Ego was a prisoner; for a while they were optimistic about his safety. At Clonboy the pleasant routine continued of a chapter of history before breakfast, poems learnt by heart, exercises, John's lessons, walks and gibbeting, which was enjoying a revival. Friends such as Stella Campbell came to stay: 'She was very pleasant, if trite, and I still think her profile superlatively pretty. Beb is happy with her'. By early May Cynthia was writing poignantly: 'We are very happy alone here and it is excellent opportunity for dedication to the children – so much easier to see them thoroughly than when staying in other people's houses'. Yet their lives were firmly in the background. 6 May: 'Remembered it was J's fifth birthday the next day so Beb and I toiled that tedious walk to the village and bought him an assortment of cheap toys at a squalid little shop'. (The children had arrived from Stanway a week before and in another week went off to lodgings in Littlehampton.)

The Season, although muted in war time, still lured Cynthia to

London. Recognising that she was happier at Clonboy, yet she could not resist the pressure to be part of a social whirl; parties and clothes were a continuing preoccupation, so was Basil, so was the unsettling effect of having no permanent home. June found Beb living at Violet and Bongie's in Dorset Street and Cynthia at Ego and Letty's house behind Belgrave Square, no 'double perch' being available. Since Michael's birth separate rooms had become the norm for them; this made cuckooing that much more of an imposition upon others. But they still loved each other and wanted to be together: 16 June (Catherine Street, a double perch) 'Oh the joy and peace and soothingness of it. I felt a completely different woman directly I got into it and knew we were alone . . . Beb and I and our relationship are all entirely changed'.

Having had himself gazetted into the Royal Field Artillery from the Royal Marine Artillery, Beb was now sent to Brighton, a financial disaster since 'instead of being safely marooned in a tin hut on Salisbury Plain, he will now probably want to reside at the Grand Hotel'. But all thought of finance or plans were submerged in the terrible news of the death of Ego. Letty was never fully to recover, and one of the most moving pieces of writing in Cynthia's entire diary is her description of her sister-in-law's reaction to the news. (It was 1 July, when 57,470 men were lost on the Somme.) Her tone is straightforward and affectionate, nevertheless in 1968 some of the family wanted the entire entry cut as being too intimate, too personal. In the end it stayed, with the exception of Letty's touching and very human remark, 'I want to have another baby so dreadfully'. Cynthia tried to remain buoyant, to emulate Ettie's positive attitude to death:

> Whatever happens, I feel more than ever resolved that sorrow must not be allowed to become gloom – if for no other reason than the treachery involved to the very ones we love, were one to allow oneself to be in any way the worse because they lived. It is cruel that they who gave such joy now must give corresponding pain, and all one can do in loyalty is never to suffer that they should be instrumental in any smallest way in spoiling one for life, and all the much that is left to one.[18]

The memorial service was at Stanway, more aloof than ever, as though belonging to the dead: 'Its spirit seems broken – lush, heavy, almost black-green midsummer everywhere, and the cricket field a jungle.' Once it was over Cynthia went to Brighton to be near Beb and the children, who were still at Littlehampton but about to move to lodgings in Brighton (which she inspected first). The weather was good and she enjoyed herself; the cheerful crowds made her feel that 'being here is strangely like being abroad'. Once she had to hurry back from a few days in London in order to 'chaperone Mamma and Mr Balfour'. Beb too was happy, despite the restrictions of army life. 'I don't think we have ever had a better relationship than we have just now' wrote Cynthia who, as on previous visits, was 'reluctantly coming to conclusion that I shall have to make my home at Brighton – I feel and look so incomparably better there'. One of its many attractions was the chance to be alone, to have 'a meal after my own heart in a shop – one whiting – one poached egg – cake coffee and raspberries'[19] and then retire to bed with a book. Yet 'how I love making friends' was her comment after one of her frequent visits to Horatia in Sussex Square.

Apart from ten days in Pixton, most of the summer weeks were spent at Brighton. Then, in September, Cynthia went to Wilsford, where she had last been two years ago for exactly the same purpose – to be near Beb while he was stationed on Salisbury Plain. Her twenty-ninth birthday was approaching and she wished it was her twenty-second: 'I am haunted by the sense of evanescence lately – feel the horizon shutting down on me – the future used to be so absolutely shoreless – like infinity'. For most of her male contemporaries there was to be no future – and on 19 September came the news of Raymond's death. 'It seems to take away one's last remains of courage . . . Now I feel I have really relinquished all hope and expect no one to survive.' The same day Cynthia sent a eulogy to Ettie about her book about her two sons. The prose is, as was the pattern for that kind of letter, sugary and cloying; yet it was what Ettie would have expected.

> It reguilds all one's youth for one and makes darling Billy so vivid and near that one expects him – as Julian said – to come 'looming into the room seraphic and benign'. Julian's letters are the most glorious ones I have ever read. I think you have an alchemy which transfigures sorrow for us all – What a divine goldenly happy childhood and youth you gave them – one feels not one day was wasted or underlived – and now you have crowned your wonderful motherhood by making them immortal. Such a record of 'golden lads' must live for ever.[20]

A week later Bimbo Tennant was killed – Madeline Wyndham's fifth grandson to have died in the war; like his cousin Mark Tennant, and like Raymond, he was killed in the Battle of the Somme.

Yet death often acts as an aphrodisiac; the sense of time running out and the sight of Beb in his uniform, purposeful instead of the grudging reader of briefs, combined to give the Asquith marriage a fillip. 'And she had really loved him, he was so handsome in uniform, well-built, yet with a sort of reserve and remoteness that suited the neutral khaki perfectly'[21] was how Lawrence put it. 'I have never seen Beb look so well and good-looking and I don't think we have ever been so happy together' Cynthia wrote at the end of September, also quite unabashed by the great happiness she had been having with Basil in recent months and the fact that he was about to go to the Front. The gaiety was short-lived, for a few days later she was writing that 'the *only* bright spot on my horizon is Michael who really is the most enchanting child'. It was the first time she had allowed herself openly to differentiate one child from another in this way, and was the result of a separation which all concerned hoped would be temporary but was to prove permanent: Michael was at Stanway with his nanny and grandmother, John was living in lodgings in Brighton with the newly-appointed Miss Quinn.

The autumn of 1916 continued as a dance between Brighton, to which Beb had returned, London and Stanway ('I am in Mr Balfour's room which I hate. Very uncomfortable bed'[22]). Once Cynthia visited Oxford and compared the gloomy stateliness of her present mode of dancing with the former Commem Ball days of 1907 and noted sadly 'at any rate we couldn't have danced with more fervour and *carpe diem* spirit, even if we had known what the near future held'.[23] With Basil at the front Cynthia soon acquired new admirers: these were Gilbert Russell and his brother Claud who were Basil's friends and who, for the next year or so, were to be her 'prop and stay'. She was, too, beginning to see something of Alex Thynne, and Bluey continued to be attentive.

Cynthia was in London and by chance dining at Downing Street on 5 December, the day the Prime Minister resigned. The reason, Beb used to tell his sons, was the death of Raymond. 'If H.H. hadn't had such appalling depression after the death of Raymond in September he would have made a compromise with Lloyd-George – but he did not want to go on' wrote Simon Asquith in 1965 opposite his mother's diary entry for 5 December which reads: 'Great luck for me to dine at Downing Street on so historic a night. The Prime Minister had sent in his resignation at 7.30 . . . His conversation was as irrelevant to his life as ever . . . Was it my last dinner in Downing Street?' (Would their allowance cease? was another question she asked herself.)

'We agreed that on *paper* my life would sound about as bad as anyone's' Cynthia had written after a lunch with Bluey in June, 'but he maintained that somehow I didn't really mind any of the drawbacks'.[24] It was the stubborn gospel of joy at work. Whatever she felt in herself, the façade was always maintained, and this was particularly so at Christmas when, at Stanway, as usual, 'with very aching hearts' she and Letty 'went through the old stocking ritual – bending over the children's cots like the best Illustrated London News number.' 'What a year' she wrote a week later. 'Will the next be better?'

····> Chapter 20 <····
Basil

The atmosphere Cynthia grew up in was imbued with both physical and emotional sexuality. Upstairs there was the sensuality of the nursery with its large towels, hair waiting to be brushed and Nanny's welcoming lap; downstairs there was the more blatant eroticism of scent, rustling dresses, meaningful glances, tears, elation and broken-off conversations. It was not something a perceptive child could fail to notice, especially when her father was an acknowledged philanderer and her mother divided her loyalty between two men while enjoying intermittent flirtations with others.

Children notoriously avoid thinking about their parents' sexual selves but in the Egyptian spring of 1895, as Mary changed from a passionately fulfilled woman to an unhappy, pregnant one, Cynthia's dreams must have become rather unsettled. She had always been slightly stolid ('Cincie's voice like a young bull her face absolutely round pink and white and her energy unlimited'[1] was how Mary had described her to Balfour two years before) but now she became solemn, as though she found the rituals surrounding her days bewildering and unpalatable.

During her years of pre-girlhood, hunched over her copybook with Squidge, the path in front of Cynthia branched out: either she could conform unquestioningly to the value of her parents' world (to Souls values) or she could demand a basis of reality for her life, developing aspirations and ideals of her own. One of the most remarkable aspects of the sons and daughters of the Souls

182

was their filial dutifulness. It is true that Charles Lister was well-known for his 'slumming' (social-conscience) instincts; and it is true that Julian Grenfell spent most of his life trying to pull away from his mother's dominating aura. But, in general, they preferred to emulate and when Violet Bonham Carter wrote

> I must frankly confess that the afterglow of the tradition of the Souls somewhat clouded my very early youth. For we were constantly told by my stepmother . . . how lamentably we fell short of all their standards – in wit, in point, in intellectual ambition, in conversational skill and social competence, yes, even in our after-dinner games[2]

she did not add, but the phrase hovers unspoken, 'yes, even in the conduct of love affairs'. Souls children conformed, and nowhere was this more true than where their sexuality was concerned.

Here, again, ritual was all, a ritual that was brilliantly and memorably evoked by Nicholas Mosley when he published his biography of Julian Grenfell ten years ago. The following passage helped to inspire my initial interest in Cynthia: it certainly holds the key to this chapter.

> The pattern for women was to dissimulate, to come and go, to be worshipped by seeming to be first one thing and then another. And this was held to be the real world, the world of gods and goddesses; while those who cooked, sewed, dug the garden, cleaned stables, were smiled on but were thought to be insubstantial. This was the world of Henry James's *What Maisie Knew* and *The Awkward Age*: when children were bemused not so much by grown-ups' lack of morals as by their inability to think of anything being real except their fantasies about keeping one another in thrall.[3]

Love affairs had their own rules, as formalised as any primitive mating dance. The 'men conks' adored and begged for favours; the woman gracefully received their worship. Breast-beating was the next step, provoked by his guilt at being so clumsy and unworthy and hers at being unable to concede to his demands. Both then felt humbled by the intense emotion aroused in them and finally, in reconciliation and equilibrium, they achieved renewed exaltation at the strength of their feelings. Things would remain on an even keel until the man became assertive again and the whole cycle ('of adoration, guilt, humiliation, ecstacy'[4] in Nicholas Mosley's words) re-started.

In the desert all the rules had been broken: with sex itself no longer taboo Mary was not the goddess, Blunt was not distraught and guilty. Yet, during 1895 and 1896, while Mary was re-filling the nursery, Egypt was never mentioned and Cynthia's 'do you remember?'s were silenced; so that, eventually, she began to see that time of sun and abandon as something not to be talked about and, by corollary, shameful. Her own mother had been made unhappy. It was something she had done in Egypt that had made her unhappy. *Ergo* that something would make Cynthia unhappy. Far better to stick to the ritual and avoid anything connected with Egypt. If love remained formalised, it was contained, manageable; in Egypt it had got out of control, something unbearable to think about. (Cynthia was not to know that as late as 1920 Mary would write nostalgically to Blunt a few days before Valentine's Day, 'the stars of Egypt are an undying memory – and footprints in the sand'.[5])

Blunt had initiated Cynthia's fear of her own sexuality; Balfour confirmed it by making her uncertain; Beb left her unaroused; Basil was to be killed before he could give her the sexual fulfilment she was beginning, tentatively, to reach out for; and Barrie was to add the final nail in the coffin of her sexuality. (By curious coincidence his name, like that of all the men who mattered to Cynthia, also began with 'B'.)

After Egypt (could you get a baby without being married? Cynthia had asked Miss Jourdain) she must have become far more aware of Balfour's relationship with her mother and is very likely to have secretly read some of his letters to her. The rifts in her parents' marriage, together with the amount of time each of them spent with other people, were hardly conducive to making Cynthia feel uncomplicated about sexual relationships. Far safer to fend them off altogether and to take refuge in the more familiar rituals she had been observing all her life.

Some young men complied with the ritual very nicely. Edmund Curtis had developed his 'romantic passion' when she was eighteen and still nurtured it ten years later. Bones was as devoted as anyone could have wished and it was not until Ego's death that it became obvious that it was really the brother he had loved not the sister. Bluey was also loyal but when he, not unnaturally after fifteen years of attentiveness, turned to one of Cynthia's married friends he could transfer much of his affection to her and her child.

Even Beb became part of the adoration, guilt ritual, although he would probably have preferred to be a little more Egyptian. But he was warded off by Cynthia's appendix scar, her pregnancy and her illness. Cynthia hardly appeared to be missing her husband of three years when she wrote from Banchory 'I am

Mary Elcho with (from left) Cynthia, Ego, Guy, Mary, Yvo and Bibs (on her lap) c. 1903.

Drawing of Cynthia by Violet Granby, later
Duchess of Rutland, 1903 (p.52).

Drawing of Beb Asquith in 1901 aged 20 b
Margot Asquith's sister, Lucy Graham-Smi

Mary Vesey, later Herbert, c. 1903 (p.50).

Harold Baker and Raymond Asquith at
Oxford c. 1896.

really not in the least unhappy and the days here melt very pleasantly and almost too quickly'.⁶ A busy social life both before and after John's birth never gave their sexual relationship a chance and although the war was sexually arousing it created a sudden not a lasting passion.

Yet, even before this brief renewal of her married life, Cynthia had met Lord Basil Blackwood whom, after his death, she was to consider the great love of her life. True to Souls tradition she had waited until she had produced a son before looking elsewhere. Beb, with the 'reserve and remoteness'⁷ described by Lawrence, was not proving a very good purveyor of dewdrops nor indeed were husbands expected to be.

At first Basil was someone whom Cynthia found attractive but his attentions did not mean much more to her than the calf-love of Billy Grenfell or Edward Horner. One of Basil's attractions was that he was the first in a line of older men that were to give her so much happiness throughout her life. These were not chosen as fathers – Cynthia after all had two of these, as well as attentive uncles (Evan Charteris and George Wyndham) and brothers. But older men are less threatening sexually because, generally, they have left rampant lust behind with their youth. They are sufficiently confident of themselves to be able to admire unreservedly. And they are knowledgeable: all Cynthia's admirers taught her about life *and* literature.

Basil Blackwood was seventeen years her senior, had of course been at Balliol and had gone to the Bar. Because he 'preferred a life of interest to a career of success' he went into the Colonial Service, and when in South Africa shared a house with John Buchan, who wrote about him at length in his memoirs, and cited him as the best letter-writer he knew apart from T. E. Lawrence and Raymond. After South Africa Basil was in Barbados, and having spent a decade abroad – the years during which Cynthia made occasional visits to Oxford, came out and did the country house round – came back to the job of Private Secretary to the Lord Lieutenant of Ireland in 1910. He was then forty: intelligent, cynical and entertaining, he was 'slight in build, with a beautifully shaped head and soft, dark, sleepy eyes, everything about him – voice, manner, frame – was fine and delicate . . . With his pointed face and neat black moustache he had the air of a Spanish hidalgo, and there was always about him a certain foreign grace'.⁸ He is still known nowadays as the illustrator of Hilaire Belloc's *Cautionary Tales* and in all his attitudes was unconventional. 'The truth is he was not the kind of man who falls easily into a groove. He was too versatile, too much in love with the coloured aspects of life, and too careless of worldly wisdom'[9]: in these phrases Buchan might also have been singling out many of Cynthia's qualities.

For most of his adult years, and that included his years abroad, he had been in love with Kitty Somerset, who had been married at about the time he met her. When he returned to Europe his mother and his friends naturally hoped he would settle both on a suitable career and a suitable wife. Although glad to be back in Europe (he had written 'inconsolably gloomy letters from the Government Offices in Bloemfontein'[10] to Hilaire Belloc) he never managed to find anything or anyone to excite him for long. When he first met Cynthia he remained aloof partly because he felt it was his bachelor duty to do so. There is an interesting passage in Cynthia's 1937 novel *The Spring House* about the heroine's guilty feelings towards her lover's mother, given that she herself was a married woman not a potential bride. When seeing her lover off to the Front she 'looked into the mother's strained eyes, and at once she saw herself through those eyes – as the intruder, the unscrupulous siren, who had robbed a desperately anxious mother of the hope of a grandchild'.[11]

In the months after they met Cynthia was ill and pregnant. Then, for Basil, 'the first hint of war was like the first waft of scent to a pack of hounds. He was off like an arrow on the old search for adventure'.[12] He joined the Intelligence Corps but in October 1914 was wounded and was out of the army for two years. In war time there was more justification for putting personal feelings before family honour and when, in July 1915, Cynthia (with her sister Mary as chaperone) went to stay at the Secretary's Lodge there was not the same restraint between them. 'Lady Cynthia has the most wonderful charm' he told his mother, adding that she was '*very* pretty though not so conspicuously so as Lady Mary, but in addition she is brilliantly witty & clever'.[13] Both tried to affect the relationship of siblings. 'Basil is as nervous about Mary and me as Ego used to be about us when we came down to Eton'[14] observed Cynthia to Ettie.

It was a time of laughter, swimming, motoring in a little Ford and 'a long walk in such delicious soft rain'. 'I *am* fond of him' wrote Cynthia. 'He has real "lovable" charm, quite apart from social charm of manner, etc.' By the end of November: 'Basil walked me home and came in and shared my Bengers. I get fonder and fonder of him, and *love* being with him'. In January 1916 she went to Dublin again and found that 'my spirits in his company are quite preposterous'. All that spring they grew closer together, playing tennis, lunching, going to art galleries, sometimes forming a triangle with Beb. Cynthia's women friends began to ask her if she and Basil were in love.

August 1916 was the month that, in years to come, Cynthia was to look back on as the peak of the love affair. On the 7th she wrote, 'I wonder what particular quality it is that makes me so extraordinarily happy in Basil's company'; two days earlier she had remarked about Beb and herself 'I don't think we have ever had a better relationship than we have just now'. But she expected to have a husband and a lover; these were permanent posts even if the incumbent changed.

In *The Spring House* Miranda meets 'Captain Marlowe' at 'Star Cross' in August 1916. She finds hersef 'talking to him with unusual freedom and ease' and 'had the sensation of dancing with her mind'. Ten days later she realises that 'all her other "friendships"', then, had been little more than makeshifts. For the first time in her life she knew the sense of the world going dead because one person left the room'.[15] Cynthia, with a quite unselfconscious sentimentality, went on to describe how Miranda felt being in love. Also, with a callous obliviousness of her real-life husband's feelings, she described a letter from Miranda's husband as 'the sliding of a heavy bolt'.

The real Basil declared himself on 28 August. After dinner at Queen's Restaurant in Sloane Square – this was to be Cynthia's favourite venue with her lovers for the next decade, ('Heaven knows what its waiters think of me'[16] she once observed wrily) – they sat in the summer house in Cadogan Square. 'Lovely night and I felt very moonlit . . . I can't pretend I'm not glad – but yet – it was all done very indirectly.' They were apart for the next week, Cynthia was in Brighton to see Beb and at a Friday to Monday in Bognor. When they dined again Basil must have felt that his avowals of a week before gave him territorial rights because the summer house was the scene for a lot of kissing. After an unreadable sentence written in hybrid morse code without the dots Cynthia wrote:

> Went home with very mingled feelings. I cannot pretend I am not glad to know he loves me, and yet I feel distressed with responsibility, and the future is difficult. How I have wondered if he really cared, and how well he has concealed his feelings! I was never quite certain. He was perfect and said delicious things and, of course, it gave me great happiness of a kind.[17]

There was more morse code next night. 'I behaved with proverbial feminine inconsistency – practice entirely divorced from theory.'

She allowed him to kiss her but would not agree to be his mistress: she was truly Lawrence's woman 'with whom passion exhausts itself at the mouth.'[18]

In *The Spring House* Miranda uses her husband's continuing affection and her mother ('Such standards . . . she would know. She always knew everything') as her excuse for not giving herself to John before he went back to France. But there was another reason apart from the pull of moral standards that prevented Cynthia from becoming Basil's mistress. She did not want to be. This he must have begun to realise, although he must have thought that time – if it were allowed him – would wear down her resistance. On 11 September Cynthia wrote in her diary (and later scratched out):

> Strange sort of re-adjustment in one's public relationship a declaration makes, Basil is easier than anyone else probably. But I'm afraid uncertainty has a great attraction for me, I feel a certain edge gone now I am sure of him. It's not a very nice trait but there is no doubt to leave things undefined is the best tactic for me.

This is a classic statement – and no wonder Cynthia deleted it – of a woman who enjoys seduction only but not the act itself. It is perhaps made less reprehensible because, when her hand was forced, she never pretended. It was thus easy for the dedicated philanderer to accept her refusal without wasting too much time, as did, for example, Duff Cooper: 28 May 1917 his 'proffers of affection successfully daunted' and he never bothered to try again.

'We had a very amusing talk about "lovers", as to how far we were "gullible" and whether it was the fact, or the reputation, we liked. I confessed it was testimonials I wanted'.[19] This is what Cynthia once told Guendolen Osborne, displaying both self-knowledge and accuracy. Basil's testimonials in the summer house had been delightful, and just what she wanted. Always before in a relationship, because it had never involved a declaration on both sides, having followed the 'adoration, guilt' pattern, she had managed to pull away in time (humiliation, ecstacy). This time she had not and she felt uneasy about not capitulating to Basil, especially as he was forty-seven and fighting in a war from which he was not very likely to return. 31 May: 'Have let myself drift into a very false position. Feel I am cheating and don't know what to do . . . I often wish we were back in the undefined phase and miss my old friend'.

But before he went to France, and during his last week of leave,

Cynthia kept him happy with kissing and unpinning her hair. 'Basil stayed for a very, very long time.' When he was killed, in July 1917, a small part of her conscious mind must have been relieved that at least one difficulty was solved. Yet she was truly desolate. He and Beb were the only two men to whom she had ever felt close. And it is likely, that had Basil lived, she might have become his mistress and found sexual happiness.

····❧· Chapter 21 ·❦····
1917

After Christmas 1916 Cynthia visited John at Clonboy, had a day in London and went to Brighton, to the 'dear Royal York' where Beb had taken rooms 'having as he said secured special terms for an officer'. But at 14/- (£12) a day each this was still too expensive and Cynthia 'irritated him by talking money at dinner. His attitude about money is difficult and tiresome. He will confuse necessary economy with stingyness – as unfair as calling hunger greed'.[1] For thirty years, until Beb's death, it was to be the same story, with Beb perversely refusing to economise and branding Cynthia as mean when she tried to. Nevertheless, her position was never a very strong one, given the money she spent on clothes. Her family continued to be generous: in the spring her mother offered her an extra £100 a year as long as the war lasted. She wondered whether it should be put towards Beb's life insurance, but Cynthia thought 'it had better be given to me. It is much better that Beb should not feel any richer – the poorer he is on paper the better'.[2]

The days passed happily enough. Once Cynthia was driven up onto the downs to see Beb's guns practising – 'Beb looked very soldierly and professional'. On 14 January she had her monthly day in bed: she had her visitor, 'Betsy', and the convention was that all engagements were cancelled. On this occasion Gilbert Russell asked if her could come up and see her. She refused. Only Beb sat in he room working on his poems.

After two weeks of 'lounge life' Beb went back to barracks and

Cynthia went to London and suffered the familiar depression about homelessness. She was staying, with Michael and Nanny, at her grandmother Madeline's house in Belgrave Square. Polly was at Cadogan Square and had to walk the short distance from one to another carrying armfuls of clothes. There were frequent lunches and dinners ('dined with Colonel Freyberg V.C. . . . I love his lack of humour – his frank passion for fighting – and his unconcealed dread of peace'[3]) and one Saturday-to-Monday with Ettie, which Cynthia found something of a pre-war anachronism while admitting to herself that she was 'really happier with the Panshanger technique than Diana's'[4] (with Ettie's rather than the Coterie's). 'The thing was to like, appreciate and delight in Diana but not to take her as a touchstone or to be affected by the fear of her thinking oneself or any of one's friends a bore.'[5]

One day she took Michael to his first dancing-class, caring so deeply that he should be admired that she wondered how she would ever get through life as a mother. She was self-conscious about Beb as well – at a dinner party that month 'Beb was very silent and unresponsive between Venetia and Nelke [Gilbert Russell's fiancée]. I feel just like a mother watching a debutante about him – vicarious self-consciousness is very agonising'.[6]

Only by the end of January, with the very cold weather, were the deprivations caused by war beginning to make themselves felt to Cynthia and her circle. 'At last we are beginning to feel the pinch of the war in material things' she wrote on 7 February. 'What a long time it has taken! It has been an exclusively emotional experience for most of us, but these last days each hostess's brow has been furrowed by mentally weighing meat, bread and sugar.' (That Cynthia's brow was never thus furrowed did not bother her; she seemed to feel no compunction about accepting but not reciprocating hospitality.) It would be another year before she remarked that 'food encroaches more and more as a topic for table talk. We are very short of butter and jam and so on, and how we all enjoy our food. So far we still press the only scone or whatever it may be on our neighbours: it will be interesting to see when this formality is dethroned by natural instinct and "after me" frankly takes the place of "after you" '.[7]

She continued to feel that the war should not be allowed to interfere with ordinary, and particularly social, life. 'My sense of duty about pleasure is strong'[8] she noted perceptively, having forced herself to search through dusty piles at Sussex Place to try and find her skates (she had been presented with a 'voucher' for the Regent's Park skating club). But it was her general sense of duty that was strong; in the absence of any other motivation she made pleasure her *raison d'être* where others made work or money or motherhood or social status. That she was not at heart a hedonist was self-evident, which is why she and the Coterie went their separate ways.

But, inevitably, hedonism was not a recipe for happiness. By the end of February, after a month of cold weather, her depression was severe.

> Generally I have snapped my fingers at the *facts* of life – and my worst unhappinesses have been for undefinable causes – subjective and morbid. Now for the first time I feel the 'fool of circumstance' and yet really all the time I know it is largely *mood* – and that were I well I could surmount all my actual worries. As it is John is a nightmare, Beb is a nightmare, Basil is a nightmare and the cumulative discomfort of having no *gîte* and 'atmosphere' of one's own – and of not knowing what I'm going to do in a week's time has suddenly got frenziedly on my nerves. One thinks these material factors – money, house etc. should not be mentioned in the same breath as the other things – but they do so aggravate.[9]

The solution, according to Mary Herbert, was a cottage in the country where Cynthia could be alone with the children, perhaps in Ashdown Forest where Beb had recently been stationed. But rural life was of no interest to Cynthia: she never could understand the pleasures of solitude or of watching the changing seasons compared with those of conversation or poker. Even though the country would have been cheaper, she was not yet reduced to it. Yet something had to be done. 'Billets' such as Bruton Street or Catherine Street were becoming less easy to find, and hotels like Brown's or the Rubens were expensive and inhospitable. Living separately from Polly was endlessly trying. While, worst of all, having no nest she had no 'atmosphere', indeed no sense of identity. The kind of women she emulated all had houses imbued with their personalities – they needed settings. Madeline had had Clouds, Mary had Stanway, Lady Horner had Mells, Ettie had Taplow and then Panshanger. They had either inherited or created a medieval/Pre-Raphaelite stage on which to perform, and Cynthia felt the lack of her own stage very keenly. For a while there had been Sussex Place with its domes and lake and well furnished drawing room; without it she felt more bereft than she had anticipated.

So, the very day Beb left for France (he had applied to go, having been in England for eighteen months – 'gone to the Front is better than going'[10] commented Cynthia) she and Mary trawled Baker Street looking for flats. Beb would not have approved, nor did he when he heard that his wife was to live in a basement in Portman Mansions costing £4 15/- (£85) a week. Since Sussex Place was let for seven guineas, the saving was hardly more than the extra £100 a year offered by Mary. Nor was it especially cheap: the rent for Lawrence's half of Byron Villas, Vale of Health, Hampstead was only 15/- a week, while Horatia Seymour also moved that year to Hampstead where she and her mother 'have a *perfect* little panelled house for £3 a week'.[11] And although Portman Mansions was an adventure, given the doubtful reputation of most of the women living in the block, it was not very suitable for a three year-old child. The initial attraction of the flat was that it had a telephone by the bed, good cupboards and was at the mouth of a tube (Baker Street). Cynthia found it rather comfortable, liked being close to her old Sussex Place haunts (Regents Park, Selfridges) and enjoyed living with Michael and Nanny, the former more enchanting than ever, the latter ('too delightful and helpful') sharing the cooking and housekeeping with Winnie. She was John's former nursemaid and had for the moment exchanged roles with Cynthia's maid Polly since she had quarrelled with Miss Quinn; the John *ménage* was at the time boarding with the Seymours in Sussex Square, Brighton at a cost of £4 10/- a week and would shortly move to a cottage at Pixton while the Seymours went to Hampstead. The complications of Cynthia's domestic arrangements continued to be preoccupying.

For the next few weeks social life flourished, undeterred by 'meatless' days at the Ritz or dining rooms so cold that they were only enlivened by frenzied word games. Cynthia's friends were becoming almost promiscuously diversified. One April day she saw Lawrence, Freyberg, Claud Russell and Duff Cooper, and very much enjoyed herself with all four. Some afternoons she put on a nurse's uniform (from Harrods) and did some work at Pamela Lytton's hospital (Lawrence reproached her for 'subscribing to the war' when she described her efforts at boiling eggs and her indulgence in pantry gossip). Once or twice she went down to Brighton ('I hate the *joins* of life – so large a part of mine seems spent on platforms')[12] but there were few Saturday to Mondays that summer. Did Cynthia imagine that these would start to happen again, once the war was over, exactly as they had before 1914? She never looks to the future in her diary, but refers so often to feelings of 'numbness' and 'nightmare' that it is easy to deduce that she implicitly regarded the war as only an interval of horror that would not last. For the present it was, however, an undeniable agony. In May, at a dinner:

There was a good deal of dancing. The music teased my heart and it seemed a mockery of an old times dance. One looked for vanished faces and winced at the mushroom growth of strange men. Letty revolved round the room with her tragic mask of a face. What a mistake the 'business as usual' attitude is.[13]

Social engagements, sittings to McEvoy both for a watercolour and an oil, luncheons or dinners *à deux* with Whibley, Claud Russell, Duff Cooper, Alex Thynne or Basil all ensured a busy time and Cynthia looked forward to a tranquil month at a house called Willowhayne near Littlehampton. She and Dorothy Grosvenor planned to live domestically there with Michael and Nanny – but it was not to be. Less than a week after they had settled in there the news came that Basil was missing after a raiding party. Desolation set in. For five years (she claimed in her diary, exaggerating somewhat) he had been first in Cynthia's thoughts.

It was he and his wonderful spirits that had done so much to carry me through these awful years – now I don't know what to do – what to think. Life seems a huge bore . . . It is the first bereavement in one's *daily* life I have known. The boys were intermittent – he was the uninterrupted serial. Everything makes me realise how I miss him – nothing which is without an association with him – a whole language gone.[14]

She spent a week in London seeing Freddie Blackwood, Basil's brother, seeing the dentist about a tooth whose ache seemed to echo the ache in her heart and seeing two doctors about John. It was, she considered, and with justification, the worst week of her life, and on Friday 13 July she asked herself, 'Why isn't my hair white? To have one's dearest friend killed and to hear the words Dr Parkinson spoke about one's own son is too much'. She returned to Sussex with Horatia, Dorothy not being allowed to travel because she was newly pregnant, and managed to make the remainder of her time there 'a great rest, because – with my odd power of detachment – I have made it into a sort of parenthesis, and got outside my own life to a certain extent'.[15] During August she went to Pixton and invited various guests such as Whibley (more amorous than ever) and Miss Weisse (more neurotic than ever about Tovey).

It was at this time that she made a decision that she was always to regret – she turned down a part in a new play by Barrie called *Dear Brutus*. Directed by Gerald du Maurier, it went into rehearsal in September and opened in mid-October. When Cynthia went to see it with Alex Thynne she wrote in her diary (and fiercely scratched out) that she would have felt a fool playing the part had she accepted it; when she saw it again in December she enjoyed it more, 'but he does make one blush along one's spine at times' (more words scratched out). Pamela Lytton, a friend of Barrie's who suggested Cynthia for the part to him, 'said it would be lucrative. Perhaps it is my duty to my children and my creditors to accept, but I refused'.[16] It was the third serious acting offer in her life: there had been Mrs Maeterlinck's after the Ursula tableau, Trench's (which precipitated her marriage) and now this – and there would never be another for Cynthia was now nearly thirty – nor was she aging well. In 'normal' circumstances she undoubt- edly would have, and she never had the problem of portliness to detract from her looks, but the combination of the war, John, Basil's death, lack of funds adequate to support the life she wanted, and three years of homelessness, all ensured that even if her hair did not actually go white her face began to lose some of its beauty. Photographs of Cynthia taken during the 1920s show someone striking and attractive; but never again was she to be so wonderfully pretty as she had been before the war. And this was one reason why, although so much in her personality would have made her a good actress (love of being looked at and of playing the *beau role*, enjoyment of hard work if it was rewarding, very retentive memory, beautiful speaking voice) the chance was never to come her way again, and she was always to be wistful about it.

H.H. was staying at Pixton that August; he was drinking less but was as unresponsive as ever – when Beb wrote over the summer to ask if a seat might be found for him in Parliament H.H. simply never mentioned it. The great topic was his sexual predilections. These were thought by Cynthia to be so unmention- able that she violently inked over all references in her diary. What he was fond of does not seem so very terrible, but perhaps it was the oddity that would have been scandalous as well as the fact that the actual mechanics of sexuality were never mentioned. H.H. liked taking women out in the motor and sucking their fingers (of one hand) in his mouth or, as it was reported to Cynthia, 'my head jammed down on his shoulder and all his fingers in my mouth'.[17] (Cynthia was never quite sure which version was correct.) It was done silently. Once Duff told Cynthia that 'what shocked him about the P.M.'s motoring habits was the reported complete lack of any verbal accompaniment – he thinks the word should be suited to the action – I agree. He gives them no cue for a rebuff'.[18] The art was to fend off without giving offence and at Pixton Margot Howard de Walden was 'proudly wearing in her cap the feather of having successfully rebuffed the old boy's advances without even having had to be rude. She claimed to have done this merely by what she calls 'Poker-back'. It shows it *can* be done and she poured scorn on the acquiescent grousers'.[19]

From Pixton Cynthia visited Katharine at Mells; when she returned she was joined by Beb, home on leave, and together they visited H.H. and Margot at The Wharf, their house on the river in Berkshire. Beb seemed fit and although conditions in the trenches were ghastly ('continually in such smells that he had to puff a pipe ceaselessly or be sick') he was 'in good spirits and I see no shadow of a return of his former illness. I think this proves it to have been the effect of one particular explosion and *not* strain and tension'.[20] But 28 August: 'Poor Beb – he is dreadfully depressed at returning to Hell. He loathes it in theory and practice, with curious reservations, and passes into a sort of ecstasy at the impressiveness of it.'

In fact, Beb's return to France was rather well timed for Cynthia to be able to start her London life undistracted by any army-wife routine – or by pregnancy: she had tried to start another baby during Beb's leave ('my form of war work') but 'to my astonishment it is not to be'. For, after a recent lull, there were frequent visits that autumn of 1917, for example to Sunningdale, to Chirk Castle (Margot Howard de Walden's house in North Wales) and to Glynde where, among other guests, Cynthia found Ivor Novello. His customary breakfast was, she discovered, 'a cup of chocolate and two peaches, which I think a triumph of exquisiteness'.[21] Anne Islington and her daughter Joan Poynder were also there, the latter, who was to be a close friend of Cynthia's for the next few years, 'gives one a wonderful impression of sterling strength and sweetness'.[22] It was Anne who was deputed to tell Cynthia, on 10 September, that the news had come through that Basil was definitely dead. Although hearbroken, Cynthia was glad to have been allowed two months rather than having no hope right from the outset. It made it easier to maintain a front to the world – instant tragedy takes the breath away and the effects are harder to disguise, whereas gradually realised sorrow gives time to build up armour. And Cynthia favoured armour: she may have voiced her misery in her diary but to the outside world she was stoical, and she tried as hard as she was able to adhere to the 'stubborn gospel of joy'. Yet she was conscious of the tension and wrote on 18 September, 'I suppose being normal with people is a subconscious strain though the sort of dinner table corner of one's brain seems to work fairly automatically'.

She was by now back in the Baker Street flat which had been
sub-let for the last three months. Life there seemed especially
dismal by contrast with Chirk Castle where things were still being
done in grand style by Margot Howard de Walden and included
a quartet from London to play to the Fortuny-clad guests. 'I
suppose it's a questionable point in war time' commented Cynthia
'whether it isn't too much of a *luxe* to pay them a hundred pounds
to come down here and play to a handful of people who could
all hear them in London'.[23] Margot may have continued to live
luxuriously; she was, however, generous with her wealth,
sending a footman to buy Cynthia (and Michael's) tickets for them
when they travelled to and from Chirk and giving her a cheque
for £200 (£3000) the following Christmas.

During the autumn of 1917 the air-raids were occasionally fierce
but Cynthia enjoyed the zest they added to life, as Lawrence had
remarked, and considered that 'the two diversions of my bicycle
and the air-raids have been my salvation these days', adding the
next day 'I *wish* I could tell Basil about it and what good pictures
he would draw'. Much of the bicycling was between portrait
sessions which were happening simultaneously with Augustus
John and Ambrose McEvoy. In early November Cynthia dined
with Pamela Lytton and met Barrie, who had been invited to see
if he could help her with her plan to 'get on the cinema stage
anonymously'. He at first threw cold water on her plan but after
she had bicycled home ('terrible difficulty with my lamp. I *can't*
keep it alight and it was a dark blowy wet greasy night') Barrie
agreed with Pamela that he *would* try and help her. But the plan
came to nothing.

The social round continued: 9 November, lunch with Lady
Salisbury, tea with Freddie Blackwood, visit to Ivor Churchill ('I
brought him *The Rainbow* to read'), dinner with Duff Cooper; 13
November, the opera with the Lawrences and Augustus John; 15
November, dinner with Sybil Colefax. On 23 November came the
news that Edward Horner had been killed. He had been almost
the last remaining figure of Cynthia's girlhood and she was beginning to realise that there were now few of her friends left with
whom she could even *talk* about the past. But 'the past is another
country: they do things differently there'[24] and Cynthia, too, was
becoming different, almost consciously turning herself into
someone more impervious, less caring than she once might have
believed possible. The human instinct for survival is so strong
that in all but the weakest this is the natural reaction: tragedies
might be happening all around but at least she would not
succumb, she would try and lead the life that so many had been

cheated of. The post-war Cynthia was, as a result, to be quite hard and un-feeling ('dried-up' she called it) but it was probably the healthiest response unless she chose the two other possible routes of religion or full-time grief. 'I felt stupefied with the thought of this new load of misery crushing down on the already broken – but so curiously dried up and sterilised myself. Have I no more tears to shed? I feel I am growing more and more detached and self-sufficient.'[25]

Unbelievably, only a day later, the grief was even worse. There had been more and more visits to doctors about John in recent months and more and more doctors. The one she went to see on the 24th was unequivocal. John was a hopeless case, it was 'not idiocy but madness'. Cynthia wrote poignantly, in one of the most moving passages in the entire diary, 'I could cry for the rest of my life about it, my darling darling little lepricorn, but it's a thing one *must* have iron self-discipline about and erect fences round it in one's mind – shut it off – but oh my heart my heart'.

The Baker Street flat was now given up and Cynthia decamped to Stanway. She found her mother still very unhappy, and nothing much had changed since Christmas a year ago when Cynthia and her sister-in-law Frances had walked along the Stanton road and 'discussed the difficulties of being helpful or even demonstrative to Mamma'.[26] But things were shortly to improve. There was a new resident at Stanway, a Miss Wilkinson ('Wilkie') who had been a governess in Cynthia's Aunt Pamela's household at Wilsford and was to stay with Mary until the latter's death, proving a practical and emotional prop and doing much to ensure that Mary's old age was happier than it otherwise might have been.

After a few frenzied shopping days in London, including frequent visits to see the Augustus John portrait on exhibition and to her favourite dressmaker called Septimus, Cynthia went down to Pixton. She and Mary Herbert were not to be alone, however, because Cynthia had invited Bernard Freyberg, the most insistent and persistent of her current suitors, to stay; with Mary retired to bed she was left very vulnerable. 'However, all was not lost – I locked my door.' At Stanway two days later the Christmas festivities were 'a melancholy milestone' and 'how my heart aches for my little John'.

····✈· Chapter 22 ·✦····
Lovers

Basil's death crystallised something for Cynthia. She felt that she would never again meet a man to whom she would respond as much as she had to him. Beb was the only man she had loved in her years as an eligible unmarried girl, and now so many of her generation were dead. Even before she met Basil she had been afraid of her sexuality. Now she buried it. In the future almost all her lovers were to be men much older than her who were, potentially, impotent. The sexless man would give her the testimonials she could not live without but he would never be a threat.

Lawrence had realised this lack in Cynthia from the beginning. When he kept telling her to find her real elemental self he was hinting over and over again that her frustration was sexual as much as circumstantial; that these Englishmen imbued with the spirit of 'silent emptiness' were no good to her and she needed a man who was 'crude but real'. Whether Cynthia had ever had a lover who *was* crude but real was a topic of endless interest to her friends. She herself believed that as long as she remained technically faithful her marriage would remain technically happy. 'Astonished to hear my marriage was much canvassed, and by many thought unhappy and detached' she wrote in April 1917. 'It bears out the theory that you cannot have any friendships with men without people drawing the inference that you are detached from your husband.' The naïvety of this would be startling if one did not see this statement as so typically Souls: the happy marriage was one where both husband and lover were happy,

199

marriage without a lover was unsatisfactory. This is why Cynthia saw not the slightest peculiarity in commenting on Beb's good looks and their shared happiness virtually in the same breath as she wondered why Basil was so dear to her. Nevertheless, her position on this point was vulnerable. Only a month earlier she had had a discussion with Dorothy Grosvenor about flirting and though trying to disagree with her proposition that 'any sort of intimacy with another man was incompatible with an *entirely* happy marriage' had to admit that 'the happiest wives are the friendless women'. But Cynthia never would have been friendless because she did not set out on her marriage intending to be. It was not that she grew bored with Beb, more that she did not imagine that he ever could be everything to her.

Usually women who need male friends other than their husbands and who are in some way frightened of a physical relationship choose homosexuals: they often understand women very well and are excellent company for them. Cynthia, because she liked the trappings of love, the admiration, the letters, the declarations, and because she liked her beauty to be appreciated, preferred men who were not openly homosexual but who admired women, if possible sexlessly. Occasionally the men were younger (Billy Grenfell, Ivor Churchill) and then it was easy to keep them adoring at a distance. But being much older than her was almost always the criterion for her lovers. Either they had already sewn their wild oats; or they were, by middle age, so frightened of the idea that they were most unlikely ever to be physically awakened; or they were mother-fixated; or they were humbled in some way through lack of attractiveness and therefore did not dare even to try and touch her; or they were fathers rather harassed by domestic and career worries who needed a little excitement but were deflected by circumstances from becoming too demanding; or they had rather bizarre sexual predilections which they had given up hope of fulfilling. Then of course there were men like Lawrence (and perhaps Antoine Bibesco comes into this category) who implied that they were more sexually potent than they actually were, who were covering up some kind of inadequancy but were not going to be put to the test and risk exposure.

The older man was likely to be better company; and his maturity would allow him to be properly interested in Cynthia. He would not, as would a younger man, need to use her as a listening or testing post. If he did not understand himself by the time he was middle-aged ('funny I should have three admirers about 45 years old' Cynthia remarked in 1917) he probably never would; in any case he was past the stage of always straining towards the leading role. This was indisputably Cynthia's prerogative; unless she was playing the lead, life had no meaning whatsoever. Nor did her ability to play it pass unremarked: many people envied her her sex appeal, what Elinor Glyn called 'It'. Enid Bagnold, who was to become a friend in the 1920s, once told Cynthia that she had modelled the portrait of 'Caroline' in *The Squire* (1938) on her.

> 'You're a love-woman,' said the squire. 'You're made to please. It's your relation with life, to please. You even please the male in me; you charm everyone; that's how you have fun. But more fun with men.'
> . . . 'I should die,' said Caroline slowly, 'if I had to admit to myself that I had finished with love'.
> . . . The wet green trees warbled with birds. 'It's exquisite,' said Caroline, thinking, as always, of herself, 'and yet it's always the same thing over again, and what do I get out of it?'
> 'Yes, what do you?'
> 'I'm a complaisant victim,' said Caroline. 'Something like that. To be asked is heaven. To consent is heaven. But to give is . . . what I pay.'
> 'If you said that to a man he would say you had no temperament.'
> 'They say that,' said Caroline. 'So then I never tell them the truth.'[1]

Like Caroline, Cynthia enjoyed the asking and the consenting; the giving she avoided if she could. This is not to say that she did not give something: she was the most loyal and faithful of friends, amusing, interested, always ready to give her energies to those that wanted them. It was just that, ultimately, she was detached; and that the final and complete giving of herself was something she did rarely.

Many of her admirers would have been appalled if she *had* fallen gratefully into their arms. Before she was married, Frank Adlard, Jack Mitford, Edward Horner, Edmund Curtis, Bones or Bluey would have thought it quite improper; afterwards any but the most serious would have been taken aback. When Billy Grenfell declared that Cynthia was 'the only woman' he did not mean her to behave as though he were the only man. When Charles Whibley fondled her too vigorously in a taxi, he was obviously glad to be able to forget about it ('I hope you have forgotten all the silly-Billy business. It has all died down, as I thought it would and left nothing behind it . . . what right had a lunatic like that to make you troubled for a moment?'[2])

Whibley has nowadays disappeared from the annals of English literature ('a chubby, middle-aged clubman with a taste for good wine, first editions and classical quotations, and a bellyful of prejudices'³ is a recent opinion) but at the turn of the century he was renowned for a monthly column called 'Musings without Method' and was considered a master of prose style. Being a friend of George Wyndham's he naturally became a friend of Mary's; she found his bigotry refreshing after the polite broad-mindedness that was second nature to her. 'One always feels that he is ready to say bluntly what everyone else is afraid to say'⁴ T. S. Eliot was to write in his posthumous assessment of Whibley (to whom he was always grateful because it was through his introduction that he was appointed to the Board of Faber). Cynthia, too, enjoyed vehemence and was stimulated by this 'master of invective'. Long before her marriage she was pleased when Whibley took on the role of literary mentor and made her read Hardy, *Urn Burial, Anatomy of Melancholy* ('the section on love-melancholy is not pretty reading, but you are one of the few women who will understand its humour'⁵), Congreve, Balzac and Turgenev. Cynthia probably planned that her sons' literary awakening would be guided by Whibley (he was Michael's godfather).

For many years Whibley behaved as the good old family friend, little different from Walter Raleigh whose exact contemporary he was and whose daughter he was to marry after the death of his first wife. In August 1916, he was still being 'very dear and dewdroppy'. A few days later he reminisced happily about his first meeting with Cynthia ('Bless him, I don't believe he knows he's a 'gnome' at all. I love talking to him') but then, alas, started stroking her hand. 'I was very weak-minded – each year of seniority and each degree of ugliness makes protest more difficult.'⁶ By not protesting, she was encouraging him to make a fool of himself. But after a while she stopped mentioning his chants of 'I love you, I love you'; evidently he was obeying the 'adoration, guilt' rules and after the 'silly-Billy business' remained mostly untroublesome. Soon events distracted him: Cynthia's pregnancy, the death of his wife, and the emergence of Barrie as a major figure all contributed to the lessening of his feelings as lover, if not as friend.

Bluey was another of Cynthia's older men, although only ten years older to Whibley's thirty. When she started keeping her diary in 1915 they had just re-started their friendship after a gap of several years extending back to 1910 when he had had to accept that she was not going to marry him. On 3 June she wrote: 'It is wonderful how entirely without *gêne* we are now; quite slipped back to the old gear, yet without any reference to the past. I must say I do think him good to talk to. I think I have always missed that relationship subconsciously.' He was an old friend, a tremendous source of gossip and, despite their past rift, satisfactorily fond of her. Less than a month after their reconciliatory lunch she noted: 'Things have reverted very much to the old gear. I do hope it won't bring unhappiness again. He told me he had never seen me look so beautiful as that night, and was very outspoken. I must say he is the most wonderful incense-burner I have ever known. An equal relationship with him would be wonderful. It is a cruel wasteful pity that he should never have succeeded in having one.' This was the general opinion. Duff Cooper 'dreaded becoming a "Bluetooth", surrounded by palliatives and missing happiness'.[7]

Bluey began to imagine that, now that Cynthia had two sons and her husband was away, she would become his mistress. But she was rather proud that she had managed to establish an amicable post-passion friendship.

> 23 July: Venetia came at one and was very entertaining. She told me more about her relations with the P.M. than I had ever heard before. She *will* figure largely in the Greville of the day and must have an interesting mountain of letters. All these last weeks while she was in the hospital at France he wrote to her twice and sometimes thrice every single day – very often from the Cabinet! At present he can't bear to see her, but she hopes on the analogy of Bluetooth and me that things may come right after an interval. [They did not.]

One of Bluey's great attractions was that he liked analysing Cynthia's character to her. Sometimes he was harsh, for example repeating Frances Horner's analysis of her as having 'no objective interest in (people), and only liking them as mirrors'. Cynthia thought this was accurate: 'I have great *appreciation* of people but, though I love the company of many people, I don't suppose I am really *fond* of many of them'.[8]

By the end of 1915 Bluey was beginning to find Cynthia rather unsatisfactory. Sometimes she 'was not very "squirrel" in taxi' i.e. allowed him to kiss her, but usually he complained of her 'camouflage' and that she was 'not being sufficiently earthy'. Ironically, he once made her feel so badly that she had to ring Basil late at night for reassurance. 'Oh the relief and ease of that *un*interrogative, undefined relationship' (this was a year before the summer house intimacies after which she was to wish that *their* relationship was still so satisfactorily undefined). As usual in these situations Cynthia remained 'elusive' and 'squirrel-like' while with her lover, promised to write a letter when she got home, and then tried to explain herself in such a way that the lover grew even fonder and more abject (humiliation, ecstacy). ʿBluey, like the others, remained abject for a year or so before growing bored; the whole cycle usually took about eighteen months. Even after Cynthia had declared to him, 'You see, I *can* be happy with this "barrier" relationship and perhaps *you* can't be?' he remained devoted and she mentions no 'difficulties' when they next see each other. By April when he came to stay at Clonboy she wrote: 'B. very nice. There has been no return to a higher gear since that uncomfortable evening after which I wrote to him'. In July he told her that she was not, as he used to think, devious, but simply naive; she attributed this to her Stanway upbringing, meaning that her rather cut-off life in the country had made her unworldly. It also made her view the world from a rather unrealistic viewpoint.

Cynthia must have regretted losing Bluey's delicious analyses of herself, but since she wrote him her long barrier letter just at the time when she was beginning to be seriously fond of Basil, it is hardly surprising (since Bluey's ear for gossip was so finely-tuned) that he would realise he had a rival. Yet Cynthia would have preferred him to go on being demonstrative. 3 January 1917: 'I should be puzzled to have to define our relations nowadays. Since the midnight letter I wrote him there has never been the slightest demonstration. Everything is comfortable and unexciting – no volcanic sensation even'. It was, however, not until February 1917 that she confided in him about John for the first time; yet she had discussed John with Lawrence at once and his 'feyness' was by this time common knowledge.

In the autumn of 1918 Bluey went to Canada on a mission for the government, but came home seriously ill and was nursed back to health at Mells. He and Cynthia met occasionally, but there was no return to their former relations. In June 1918 when he learnt that she was to be secretary to Barrie he was 'almost sick with disgust'. 'Bluetooth told me again that I was a complete non-conductor to prurient conversation – I was quite piqued at what amounted to a charge of prudery and told him it was only because he had known me in my snow-drop Maeterlink days. I am now en route from Maeterlinck to Maupassant.'[9]

Bluey was not the only one to decide that lasciviousness had no part in a relationship with Cynthia. Lord Alexander Thynne, 'Alex', decided this from the outset and ran two close female friendships at once, one lascivious and one not. In October 1916, when Cynthia began her flirtation with Alex, he was then forty-three to her twenty-nine. They had been casual acquaintances for many years, but he had not formerly been an admirer of hers: 16 February 1918 'I told him what a blighting influence his spikes had exercised over my youth'. In the years since Cynthia's youth Alex had spent some years in South Africa and had been Member of Parliament for Bath since the year of her marriage. When they first became close, in Brighton, he was very appreciative of her and 'succeeded in making me feel quite pleased with myself'. Yet she was conscious of his reputation as a flirt and observed, after one of the occasions when Alex stayed for quite a long time at the Baker Street flat, that 'Mary H. will scarcely take my word for it any longer that he doesn't make love to me' and despite sitting with Cynthia for hours 'has never so much as touched my finger'. She professed to be glad that her 'alarmingness' had inhibited him. But it is unlikely that she confessed to her pleasure when she plotted with four women friends that they all four would write to him 'on the same day saying we reciprocated his passion and having determined to face the world with him had left notes to that effect for our husbands. We agreed that one surrender of that sort would probably be enough to make him fly the country'.[10]

'I am still complimented or insulted – as one likes to take it – by his making an exception of me' commented Cynthia in October 1917 after Alex, on leave, had spent a good deal of time with her without pouncing. In February 1918 'Alex still the same to me – a song without words – tender-eyed and importunate for meetings, but never a word.' Well over a year since they first started meeting regularly, they were still not on Christian name terms.

What Cynthia did not know, although she must have suspected, was that Alex was having a serious affair with Clare Sheridan. A first cousin of Winston Churchill, she had been widowed in 1915 and had fallen in love with Alex in April 1917. She found him 'entrancing – alive – able to give a sense of purpose'[11] and, at her home Number 3 St John's Wood Studios, conveniently near to Cynthia's flat, prudery was not much in evidence. By April 1918, when Alex had a month in London because of a wound, he and Clare had grown extremely close and she was expecting to marry him. Her biographer observes that she 'longed for his wound to go septic, but too soon it healed and he rejoined his regiment'.[12] He was killed in September. Cynthia wrote:

> I was relying on him more and more – his interest – spirits – his gift
> of entering into the detail of one's life – his appreciation of Michael –
> I feel bitterly bereaved and oh so weary and bored. He had been

splendid in the war . . . Now this new bludgeoning had fallen, I wonder why I wasn't happier before. If only it could be revoked I would feel so rich now.[13]

When Cynthia had written 'funny I should have three dark admirers about 45 years old' she had meant Basil, Alex and Claud Russell (if she had included Bluey in this reckoning it would have been four). Claud she had met through his brother Gilbert, a friend of Basil's. In the autumn of 1916 she had 'lunched with my two middle-aged roués, Alex and Gilbert'. The topic under discussion was marriage and she soon realised that it would be her duty to warn any potential wife of their attitude. 'They had the highest ideal of domesticity combined with the cynic's complete trustlessness. They would not suffer any friendship with other men, and would on no account allow their wife to dine at a restaurant with a man. 'After all,' said Gilbert, 'I have never dined alone with a woman without making some sort of assault on her and why should I expect other men to be different'.[14] In fact two weeks later he met and soon became engaged to Maud Nelke. She brought a rather satisfactory dowry to her marriage but – happily – Cynthia's mock-warnings did not deter her.

At about the same time Cynthia met Gilbert's brother Claud, then forty-five. Although she had been frightened of him the first time they met, this time she thought him 'extraordinarily good-looking and almost caricaturishly wellbred'. He had gone into the Foreign Office in 1897 (and was to be knighted for his services in 1930). Although Beb disliked him, Cynthia found him comfortable to be with. By March 1917 (they had met on a number of occasions whenever Claud could get away from barracks) she was writing: 'I think he is rather in love with me. Passionate hand-kissing on saying goodbye in taxi'. By April he was becoming amorous: 27 April 'I suppose I am flirting with him atrociously but it all seems so natural and inevitable. I never feel I am exercising any choice in these matters'. Because he confined himself to kissing Cynthia's hand or foot he never offended her. 'He has a certain amount of magnetism for me; but I have no fear of its being 'fire' I am playing with.'[15] What might have seemed fiery to Cynthia, but evidently did not, was that she was enjoying this flirtation while professing to be deeply in love with Basil; once, in May 1917, Basil stayed with Claud while home on leave and the morning telephone arrangements therefore became rather complicated. Nor did she appear to mind that on the last evening she spent with Basil, when he 'stayed for a very, very long time' she wore the Spanish shawl given to her by Claud whose magnificence had caused a certain amount of comment.

Eventually Cynthia realised that Claud had rather unusual sexual predilections, including sadism. Because she still allowed him to fondle her she felt 'ineffectually, flabbily angry with Claud and myself'. She must have made her anger felt because, by November, 'either he has, or he wishes to give the impression that he has, cooled off. He isn't nearly as assiduous as he was'. By the January of 1918 the rapport between them had gone. 'He was no use to me – only made me long for Basil.' Yet, piqued by his diminished interest, she managed to woo him back and by March she had 'never known him nicer'. Nevertheless, despite her feeling 'Claud falling back in love with me' at the end of May, she was mistaken and their relationship gradually petered out. In 1920 Claud, aged nearly fifty, finally married.

One of Cynthia's admirers towards the end of the war years was the youngest Brigadier-General in the army, Bernard Freyberg. Although conscious that the Coterie would think him a bore, she liked him very much and considered him a 'potentially really great soldier – in the Napoleonic sense rather than the V.C. hero. He seems to have so many of the qualities – lack of humour, chafing ambition, and a kind of admirable ruthlessness and posi-tive self-reliance.'[16] Being badly wounded he was often visited by Cynthia and did nothing but hold her hand – until his sudden pounce.

> I don't know how it happened but suddenly there was an explosion and I found myself involved in the most tremendous melodramatic scene – like something in the Sicilian Lovers. Again I felt that strange, detached, spectator feeling and my old dumbness was as bad as ever. I blame myself bitterly for my passivity – inexplicable to me – I can only infer it was his habit of command. I found him terribly difficult to cope with, though his suit only inspired contemptible Narcissus feelings in myself . . . I don't believe he is convertible – not a possible subject for a 'sentimental friendship' – and I don't want to sever all relations with him. But it's unfair playing with fire when one knows one is dressed in asbestos oneself . . . He drove me home and I foolishly allowed him to come in, thus letting myself in for the most awful difficulties[17].

This was hardly surprising, one would think, especially as Cynthia was, as she admitted, too cowardly to give the plain, brutally truthful negative answer to 'for God's sake, tell me you do care a little for me!' Always ahead of her lay the goal of breaking hearts without losing their owners' friendship – and it was not an easy one to achieve. Yet even in Freyberg's case she managed it, spending a day in Brighton with him only two days after his explosion even though she knew it was 'injudicious'.

However Beb's return on leave soon put a stop to Freyberg's attentions; when they met he and Beb 'wailed in unison over the incompetency and senility of most of the army generals'.[18] Towards the end of the war he was wounded yet again; when he recovered he too relinquished Cynthia to Barrie's stronger hold and in 1922 married her friend Barbara McLaren. But he remained on friendly terms with Cynthia. It was one of her triumphs that she always made her admirers feel that their closeness had not entirely vanished. She never provoked a quarrel and she was never disloyal: her personal reticence extended to anyone of whom she had once been fond.

····✣· Chapter 23 ·✣····
1918

It was just after the Christmas of 1917 that Beb came on leave for three weeks. He was in good form and very voluble, 'ashamed of the way England brutally snubs every peace feeler, and reiterates that, either we should negotiate or else fight with all our might, which he says would mean *doubling* our army in the field'.[1] From Stanway he and Cynthia went for a few nights to the Connaught Hotel. Here they heard the news from Freyberg of the death of Patrick Shaw Stewart. It was the first death of 1918: Cynthia had met him at a party at Taplow in 1906 and although he considered her rather too serious-minded for his taste, they had been fond of each other and had exchanged occasional letters. Exactly a year previously he, Cynthia, Eddie Marsh, Walter Raleigh, Norah Brassey and Cynthia's Uncle Evan had all spent some days together at Panshanger. At church that week Cynthia could not join in the responses: 'I felt it was too much to be asked to express gratitude for all the blessings showered on us during the past years'.[2]

From London they went to the Wharf for a Saturday to Monday with Beb's father. The atmosphere was as claustrophobic as usual and Cynthia was mystified by H.H. who, although Beb had been at the Front for four months, did not 'address one word of enquiry to him, as to what he has been doing and where he has been . . . I think the Wharf atmosphere really hurts him'.[3] This detached attitude was especially jarring to Cynthia since her family, in the tradition of the Fitzgeralds, laid such an emphasis on family love.

It was 'almost a religion with the Wyndhams' she was to remark, while Ego had written to his mother after Yvo's death and just before his own: 'When all is said and done, we were a damned good family. Qua *family* as good as Clouds. I couldn't have had more joy out of anything than I have from my family'.[5]

Yet, once at Stanway, Cynthia was made only too aware of the difficulties of maintaining a sense of self when surrounded by devoted relations. 'The worst of loose family life is the *intense* difficulty of achieving solitude without being a curmudgeon'[6] she wrote plaintively adding, some days later, that 'the struggle against friends for leisure is as bad as ever'. But she tried always to have a book 'on the go' (during January she ordered Keats's *Letters*, Morley's *Recollections* and some Balzac novels at the library) and knew that she was 'so much happier and better when I can read for several hours'. Once she talked of her difficulties to Tonks while he drew her. 'He said he was quite deliberately *complet*, like a hotel. Didn't wish to make any new friends any more than he wanted more furniture in his room.'[7]

Cynthia was not *complet* and, when Beb had returned to France, she rejected 'the calm of Toddington' and rural pleasures in favour of the 'gloom, gaunt-cold, dirt, size and discomfort of Cadoggers'. Yet, despite the pull of friends, she managed to lead 'quite a regular life these days – exercises and cold splashes every morning – breakfast downstairs in our little basement room – quantities of Horlicks' Malted Milk and every morning, and evening from 4.30 to 6.30, dedicated to John.[8]

A month after Beb's leave Cynthia again found she was after all not pregnant: 'so surprised, and so disappointed. I had become far advanced in sentimentality'.[9] She had last had a false alarm in the September of the previous year (it was to be another few months before she succeeded in conceiving) and the thought of a baby had made her very happy. In general, her mood at this time was fairly buoyant, and the gloom which might have been the result of the last few years had not materialised. But she was very restless and rarely allowed herself time to read or indeed think: friends always took precedence. 1 March: 'I have much more time in my day since Alex's departure'. To have refused to see a friend would not have occurred to her, nor would refusing an invitation, even if her boredom could hardly be concealed. There were many musical evenings at this period of the war (or perhaps it was that Cynthia had made new musical friends since the Chirk fortnight) and, being unmusical, she was often bored. During one evening she had 'never felt so unreceptive to art – and was in a thoroughly Puckish mood – with fingers twitching to pull necklaces – tweak moustaches etc etc – God knows why – The whole party giggled at catching me scrutinising my face in my pocket glass'.[10] Yet it was hard to turn down these invitations. 'I have become much more musical since rations. Music seems to evoke the only buffets . . . All ate as though the food were just going to be swept away.'[11] Indeed, her life during the last months of 1918 was more musical than at any time since the period of her coming-out when Eliza Wedgwood used to take her to Sargent's glittering musical evenings.

As the years passed, the war seemed less not more bearable. On 22 March 'the spring sparkle in the air was wonderful – it seemed incredible that that hideous tomfoolery in France should be going on under the same sun'. Cynthia found it hard not to think about the Spring Offensive on the Somme.

> The nightmare of the battle now raging oppressed me all day like a heavy weight. I have never been so haunted by the war and, as far as I know, Beb is in the neighbourhood of St Quentin where things seem to be worst . . . I felt very sick at heart. Stayed in for dinner and read *Women in Love* . . . Surely he is delirious – a man whose temperature is 103? – or do I know nothing about human beings? It is all so *fantastic* to me and 'unpleasant' – morbid to a degree. I don't know what to think about it.[12]

But, at Stanway for two weeks over Easter, she 'slipped into my Stanway self', and it was a delight to see Michael, who had been at Stanway since Christmas with Nanny Faulkner. It was hard to be exuberant, however, even on 1 April: 'Remembered the excitement of the April Fool's Days of my childhood and felt sadly "grown-up" '. Even so, she revived an old joke of inking a face on her knee and, swaddling it in her skirt, pretending it was a baby (a stunt with which she was to appal and delight her grandchildren). Practical jokes were a Charteris tradition and Cynthia took pride in her 'Puckishness'. In old age she was to instigate even more jokes, perhaps because she had stopped caring what other people thought and recognised that jokes gave herself pleasure.

One of the delights of this period of Cynthia's life was her relationship with her father. For some months he had been unexpectedly mellow and amusing, a doting grandfather who was so wedded to Stanway that he could only be persuaded to go to London for a day or two at a time. His good humour made Cynthia even more reluctant than usual to leave Gloucestershire, first for Pixton and 'the familiar moist atmosphere' of the Somerset moors and then for the Cadogan Square 'barracks with hostile housemaids'. But before London life took its hold of her there was the interest of Oc's wedding to Betty Manners and the disappointment that, because he was feverish, Michael could not be a page. 'The bridegroom was a brilliantly topical figure, and he stood so well on his one leg, without even a stick, though it made one tired to watch him.'[13] ('He is going to get £900 down and £350 (£5000) a year for his leg'[14] Cynthia was to note later in the year.) Although very tired, she managed to gorge herself ('there were actually solid things like ham!') and enjoyed re-visiting the countryside round Avon Tyrrell so familiar to her from the days of her courtship and early marriage. Concerning Lord and Lady Manners Cynthia wrote in her diary: 'Ettie told a delicious story of Hoppy. He had gone in a state of utmost concern to Con and told her that, when inspecting Betty's trousseau, he had said, "Surely, darling, these nightgowns are rather thin?" To which she had replied, "Oh, yes, but it will be all right because I shall wear my combinations under them". What was to be done?'[15]

In May, with Michael and Nanny in lodgings in Littlehampton and John at Eynsham with Miss Leighton, Cynthia went to Stanway to begin her first stint of nursing at the hospital at Winchcombe. She enjoyed it a great deal. 'I quite understand one's liking for the human interest side of it and the absorbing, feverish desire to satisfy the Sister and please the men, but I rather wonder why one enjoys the sink, tray, Lysol, bustle side of it quite so much.'[16] The reason was that her sense of logic, efficiency and achievement was at last given an outlet: as the Sister observed, 'she ought to be head of a large institution'. Because hitherto unrecognised qualities were being tested Cynthia was 'absorbed and contented in my new *metier*' which also 'incidentally makes one *forget* the war'.[17] She even enjoyed her brief spell in London, 'frittering with a clear conscience and no misgiving as to wasting one's life'.[18] She had probably, also, been given a new insight into the larger effects of nursing by reading Enid Bagnold's *A Diary Without Dates*, a recent book about a nurse's experiences in war-time which Cynthia had greatly admired; she was to meet the author in London in the interval between her two nursing bouts, and soon they were to be friends.

She was introduced to Enid by two of her putative lovers, Prince Antoine Bibesco and Desmond MacCarthy, both of whom Cynthia had recently met through her half-sister-in-law Elizabeth. Bibesco was a Rumanian diplomat who lived in Paris and is remembered nowadays because of his friendship with Proust; he was soon to marry Elizabeth. MacCarthy was a literary critic whose delightful nature played a large part in his reputation. Cynthia had already heard about him from Violet, to whom he had for a while been devoted. Both men were dark, about forty, and were to become admirers. Their effect, combined with new friends and the interest of her nursing work, made the spring of 1918 a happy time for Cynthia, even though she sometimes 'felt ashamed of my almost indecently good spirits'.

The real cause of her happiness lay within herself: it was the dawn, for her, of self-knowledge and self-confidence. That the dawn was to be false, to be replaced by a couple of years of twilight, she did not foresee. She was enjoying all the new people she was meeting and at the same time was beginning to accept that her former friendships no longer had the same hold. 1918 was the year she stopped seeing quite so much of Bluey and Claud, Katharine and Mary Herbert, the year when, partly through death and partly through her own growing away, the surviving friends of her youth were mattering less. They made her self-conscious, it was almost as though she could not be bothered to act the role that had been assigned to her when she was eighteen. Even with Mary Herbert, whom she had once considered her only close woman friend, she sometimes felt ill at ease. 'I think it is due to the nightmare sensation of not knowing my 'part'. It makes one dread any attempt at contact or intimacy. I feel I want to be by myself *chaperoned* by a book.'[19] By contrast, one reason she enjoyed nursing was 'my entire lack of shyness with the men. It is the *only* human relationship in which I haven't been bothered by self-consciousness'.[20] Bibesco's view of this period of Cynthia's life was that 'it isn't long since I left off being a Maeterlinck woman and became a real person'.[21]

The spell of nursing at last made Cynthia realise that she was much happier when she was doing something and when, in the summer, she met Barrie again and he asked her if she would like to do some secretarial work for him, she was attracted not only by the money – £400 to £500 (£5-6000) a year was the figure mentioned – but also by the chance to have a regular occupation. It was not surprising that Cynthia noticed that she was 'in glowing looks. Have never seen myself in such brilliant face, especially by daylight'. Nor was she even having to worry about Beb: after the fierce fighting in France during the Spring Offensive he had been given an office job at General Headquarters.

The summer was the by-now familiar pattern of moving from Stanway, to 'Cadoggers', to Littlehampton to see the glowingly freckled Michael, to Pixton, to the Wharf and, finally, to Gosford. Cynthia had not been here for three years and looked back 'to that visit across what a gulf of melodrama. Then the war was still not much more than academic to me and John was a happy baby'.[22]

She enjoyed the visit to Gosford, especially the many friends who arrived for every meal, and the chance she had to see something of Bibs, who was not finding the years of pre-womanhood easy. Mary was, as always, anxious to talk about John: 'Long hair combing Leighton talk with Mamma. My last letters seem to have incensed her, and she is writing rabidly to Mamma as well as me. She really is *impossible* but also indispensable. Mamma too angelic. She is a blessed being – a witness to God if ever there were one'.[23] It was fairly reluctantly that Cynthia left Gosford earlier than she had meant in order to go to London to receive Beb who was home on a short leave. But 'we have been extraordinarily happy these days. He has never been such a darling before' was the cheerful verdict on their time together.

Cynthia now began to work regularly for Barrie. She would go to his flat in Adelphi Terrace either by underground or bicycle. At first she found her working life tiring: 'I have seldom felt so dead-alive. I am quite happy reading but at present have no appetite for *living* – even last year when I was miserable I cared acutely about what happened to me from day to day'.[24] (Her reading on the day she wrote this would perhaps have made anyone weary – Barrie's *Sentimental Tommy* and Maupassant.) But another musical week at Chirk made her feel better, and she especially enjoyed being able to put her acting technique to good use, doing one of her 'melodrama screams', then going 'moonstruck', finally acting a 'looney'. The next day she completed her acting repertoire by having 'a great success with my purring, owl hooting, seal bark, duck drinking, etc., noises'.[25]

Money was beginning to be a problem over the late summer of 1918. Beb had debts of £450 (£5,500) and Cynthia of £300 (£4,000); she planned to pay off hers by working for Barrie, but Beb had no income and was urged in heartfelt tones to 'spend as little as possible on wine etc'.[26] In September Bones, who had been in England for the summer and was just about to return to his embassy job in Norway, 'asked me how much money I thought would make me comfortable. I roughly said £3,000 (£40,000) a year and he stated his determination to make £8,000 and endow me!'[27] Despite this generous spirit Cynthia, who had had to endure long sagas about Bones's disastrous marriage, found by the end of the month that 'poor darling Bones is getting just a tiny bit on my nerves'. But her first cheque from Barrie helped Cynthia's finances – even though it was £20 (£250) for the month rather than the higher figure he had originally mentioned; and even though it was only a fraction of the £108 rent (three-quarters of a year overdue) that Cynthia had at this stage to pay for the un-tenanted and shut-up Sussex Place. 'How I hate the practical incidents of day to day life' she wrote irritably in her diary. Nor were matters made easier by Beb who 'writes gaily of country house – motor – London rooms and doesn't realise that he will be returning to bankruptcy with everything costing double what it used to and I'm sure he won't be in a state to put his nose to any grindstone immediately'.[28]

The approach of peace was not to have the revivifying effect that Cynthia had hoped. On 7 October she wrote the oft-quoted passage that appears on the frontispiece – both in her diary and to Aubrey Herbert (appropriately enough, since writing the same thing to more than one correspondent was called 'doing an Aubrey'[29]). And, after a musical evening a few days later, 'these or indeed any gatherings give me great sweeps of loneliness. I am so tired of those whom I want to see being dead – and feel impatient with the substitutes one has to talk and laugh with – I have no energy or heart now for the building up of new friendship fabrics'.[30] Another problem in these last few weeks of the war was Cynthia's 'sad lack of jingoism'. While the war was going on she had 'felt it more like some cosmic thing – a plague-like calamity inflicted on mankind rather than as what man has done to man'.[31] Her view of Germans as fellow-victims had not changed during the four years. But now that all the personal tragedies were narrowed down to a question of peace terms and frontiers the fighting seemed even more barren and futile than it had before.

The influenza epidemic had begun and the illness of friends and servants made life even more complicated ('every member of the household stricken with the blessed exception of Nannie'). John was in bed for nearly three weeks and had to be provided with a nurse during Miss Leighton's illness. She was not improved by her time to herself: 20 October, 'She ranted, shrieked and wept [about some tiny failure on Cynthia's part]. I fell into hopeless catalepsy – she wouldn't listen to any proffered explanation. When I said goodbye she flung her arms round my neck and clung to me, passionately kissing me – I expressed bewilderment and she burst into a declaration of great love – saying it was only because of that she was working for John – and on that account she got angry with me . . . '

Despite all her domestic tribulations Cynthia's life was as busy as ever, leaving little time for reading, and sometimes her diary was many days in arrears. It is a tribute to her memory and energy that she always caught up, and in such a spritely tone that it is only from the changes in ink or handwriting that one can tell that she is recalling events of three days previously. But it is hardly surprising that she often repeated what she had written in her diary when writing to Beb, to whom she had been devotedly sending letters virtually daily for all the time he had been away. In the week beginning 14 October she went to Barrie every morning, lunched with Angela Forbes, Brenda Blackwood, Maud Cunard, Adèle Essex, Whibley, Bongie Bonham Carter (in order to inspect Violet's second daughter) and enjoyed one free lunchtime because of a cancellation. She dined with Katharine, Dorothy Grosvenor, Charles de Noailles and Desmond (twice). She went to a musical party at Margot Howard de Walden's, sat to Augustus John twice, had Barrie to tea, Maud Russell and Katharine to tea also, 'tried on' at Septimus (the dressmaker of the moment) and on the Saturday 'went all the way to Hampstead on a D.H. Lawrence pilgrimage. He and Frieda are staying with a woman called Dolly Radford and her daughter in a dear little panelled house where Keats is alleged to have written Endymion. Frieda was ebullient in bed – Lawrence in good spirits'.[32] This was all combined with Miss Leighton dramas, time spent with Michael, telephoning, and letter-writing. Polly was presumably looking after Cynthia's clothes, since she is only mentioned in the diaries when she is *not* so doing – and she does not succumb to 'flu until the end of the month.

By the beginning of November Desmond was becoming 'daily bread' and he and Cynthia spent the evening of Armistice Day together; he was 'the ideal companion – touched – humorous and sensitive.' Four days later, just as Cynthia was feeling closer to anyone than she had since Basil's death, Beb arrived home on leave. He had endured some of the heaviest fighting on the Western Front (being 'mentioned in despatches') and was suffering from shell-shock and the effect of gas. Yet for Cynthia it was not enough that his life had been spared, nor would she allow a period of calm and convalescence: she insisted on being briskly practical. For this reason it was a much less happy few days than the time at the end of August (and it was not really Desmond's fault).

Felt very depressed at my prospects . . . Beb is fearfully difficult to discuss the future with – irritated by everyone asking him his plans . . . Papa has asked me rather horror-stricken whether it was true that Beb didn't intend to return to the Bar, and Whibley had

The Asquith family at Glen, Easter 1904 (all except Beb). Katharine is gazing soulfully at Raymond, Violet looks an adolescent 'handful', Edward Horner is standing next to Raymond, Harold Baker is at the back and Oc and Cis are sitting on the steps.

Guests outside the Norman Hall during Commem Week 1907 (p.81). Back row: Guy Charteris, Evelyn de Vesci, Letty Manners, Mary Vesey, Cynthia, Balfour, Harold Baker. Front row: Mary Elcho, the Bursar of Trinity, Katharine Horner, George Vernon, Robert Smallbones.

Cynthia's hair, date unknown.

Mary Elcho, date unknown, possibly 1912 for her fiftieth birthday.

Sargent's charcoal drawing of Cynthia 1909 (pp.90 and 219).

Cynthia on her wedding day with Mary and Bibs as bridesmaids.

seen the sale of his Law Library advertised. I wish he hadn't given such an impression of boat-burning – I quite understand his longing for flowers, books, summer rain etc but he shouldn't be sore and resent the natural interest and enquiries of non-combatant relations.[33]

Ironically, it was at Bruton Street during this leave that Cynthia conceived, so that the trying period of adjustment to peace time took place while she was feeling unwell. But she was enjoying Desmond's company too much to feel very depressed – there was one especially idyllic Saturday to Monday at Pixton at the end of November – and for a while managed not to be in any way downcast by Beb, who had come home for another three weeks leave in the middle of December. Despite her financial worries, Cynthia was very conscious of Beb's need to recover, and would probably have been more tolerant of his decision not to return to the Bar if he had admitted that things were going to be difficult. Instead 'Beb alarmed me by his obstinate plans for a country seat'.[34] For the moment they could not even afford to open up the 'deep in dust' Sussex Place and they blithely continued to cuckoo with Oc and Betty in Great Cumberland Place, Cadogan Square never having been able to fit both of them. Somehow the energy would have to be found for the Asquith ménage to be re-started. For the moment, Cynthia wrote at the end of December, 'I am feeling placid – a baby has that effect on me'. She had given birth to her last baby nine days before the outbreak of war; she conceived her next four days after Armistice Day.

···➤· Chapter 24 ·◄····
Painters

Being drawn or painted was, for Cynthia, the apotheosis of her beauty. Her roots were irrevocably narcissistic and hers was an era of extreme personal vanity, of an interest in oneself which nowadays seems quite indecent. 'She loved her loveliness almost with obsession'[1] (Lawrence) and liked other people to appreciate it too; she was proud of being sought-after in fashionable artistic circles; and the finished product was a delightful and lasting extra. Like her Souls forebears, who had inspired a large corpus of pictures, Cynthia considered a painter's studio one of life's touchstones, and it was only because her intelligence was more verbal than visual that her friendships tended to be with writers rather than the artists to whom her mother, Violet Granby or Frances Horner were so close. 'Sitting' became a familiar part of her activities – even if Tonks did have to explain the word's context to the ingenuous Miss Charteris: 'I mumbled something about being "perfectly happy standing, thank-you" ' she was to recall charmingly if perhaps apocryphally after he had suggested that she sit to him at one of Sargent's musical evenings. 'The last thing I wanted was commiseration. After all I was not at a *dance*. Why should I be mortified by the sympathy due to wallflowers?'[2]

Tonks was the first of many painters to whom she ruefully deplored the anachronism of her Pre-Raphaelite looks, declaring that she 'was trying to pass myself off to myself as quite up-to-date. Yes, I hoped I was looking what would now be called "Edwardian" '.[3] Writing in 1950, she considered that had Burne-

218

Jones been born five hundred instead of a hundred and sixteen years ago he 'could scarcely have belonged to an age more utterly remote from our own'.[4] Yet her long reddish hair ('the colour of the best marmalade'[5] Cynthia remembered Mrs Patrick Campbell describing it to Sargent), wide apart, slanting eyes and rather large drooping physique did give her a 'Burne-Jones' appearance and it was a sobriquet that she was not easily to shake off. (It was appropriate that he had been the first artist to whom she sat in 1894.)

When she was nearly nine, in the summer of 1896, Cynthia stayed with her uncle George Wyndham. Here Charles Furse painted her against a background of snow in a Red Riding Hood cloak (ignoring the fact that the weather was very hot, that his sitter was posed in a greenhouse, full of ferns and that she was dressed in blue). This picture has disappeared but the next to be completed, a drawing by Violet Granby, is still in the possession of one of Cynthia's grandsons.

In 1908 Cynthia was painted, apparently more than once, by von Glehn. One of the portraits was exhibited at the Royal Academy in 1909; was 'the gem of the Exhibition of Fair Women at the Grafton Gallery in May' (1910), according to a newspaper cutting kept by Mary Elcho; was exhibited at the Royal Commission of International Fine Arts exhibition in Rome in 1911; and was taken to Pelham Road, New Rochelle, New York some time after this date – it is not known why. It seems probable that one of the paintings was shown in Rome and returned to von Glehn's studio and that the other was sent to America and is still there.

Only one painting has been traced: Cynthia never owned it (or its companion), perhaps because she could not afford to buy it, perhaps because von Glehn did not consider it finished, perhaps because it was forgotten about in the turmoil of her marriage, pregnancy and move to Sussex Place, followed by four years of cuckooing. Or the canvas was 'lost' in the mass of stacked pictures in von Glehn's studio at Cheyne Walk.

Nor did she acquire the result of her next sitting. This was the charcoal drawing done by Sargent in 1909 which she thought so unflattering that she never wanted it in her own house (although it did stay in the family for more than fifty years). A drawing of which she was, however, far more fond was done by an amateur, a close friend of Basil Blackwood's called Lady Norah Brassey. Cynthia admired the result so much that she used it as the frontispiece to the first volume of her autogiography instead of any one of the portraits by well-known artists that she would have been entitled to use.*

Although Cynthia met Tonks when she was sixteen, he became a close friend only in the 1920s when they used to meet through her friend Coley; he did not in fact ask her to sit until some ten years after their first meeting, just before the outbreak of war. Tonks was by then not only a well-known painter but also an influential teacher at the Slade School of Art. Tonks did a pastel which Cynthia liked so much that she purloined it from the tenants of Sussex Place in order to hang it in Portman Mansions. Nearly four years later Tonks took two sittings to do a second pastel:

> I lunched with Tonks – a sketchy lunch of two raw eggs and some oatmeal biscuits – before sitting to him. He began a pastel of me – he claims to have entirely mastered the medium since his former effort. That was just before the war. The two would do as advertisements of 'before' and 'after' for the use of militarists or pacifists . . . Tonks was delighted with his beginning of me and, chuckling sardonically, said he hoped it would 'annoy McEvoy'.[6]

The next day 'he was pleased with his work on me, but I hope he will subdue the roses in my cheeks'. Tonks gave Cynthia the second pastel in February 1919 ('quaint as a likeness – but a most charming drawing'[7] she commented). Whether it was this or its predecessor that was hung by the Asquiths after the war is impossible to say, but there is a glimpse of one of them in a photograph of some of the rooms at Sussex Place. In an article in the December 1922 issue of *Eve: The Lady's Pictorial* (part of a series called 'Other People's Houses') the Asquith household is featured; the photograph of the upstairs drawing-room shows a drawing of Cynthia's half-profile which the caption attributes to Tonks. Neither portrait survives, one was lost and one was destroyed by fire in 1973.

The decisiveness of Tonk's methods could not have been more different from the 'pliability of mind' of his pupil Ambrose

---

*She would also have used one of the following: in April 1921 she was drawn by a Miss Noyes, in 1921, 1928 and 1936 by Katharine Shackleton (the first time for *John O' London's Weekly* and the second for *The Bookman*). In 1924, 1926 and 1929 she sat to Cuthbert Orde and in 1932 she was painted by McEvoy's widow. None of these works have survived. The surviving chalk drawing attributed to Francis Dodd may have been done in 1933, the year for which Cynthia's diary has been lost.

McEvoy. Whereas the one artist executed his work swiftly and purposefully, eschewing human contact because it distracted him (it was he who had told Cynthia that he was *complet*), the other feverishly invited both friends and criticism. While this was to the detriment of his output, it ensured that he became a fashionable painter: it was only because he *was* in demand, and dilatory, that Cynthia 'sat to him for years during which innumerable oil portraits were begun, [yet] all that survived at the end were two watercolours'.[8] (An oil did survive but Cynthia chose to forget about it.)

She had commented, after a visit to the New English Art Club in June 1916, that 'the McEvoys – *the* fashion at present – are interesting: curious smudgy *lineless* technique'.[9] When she met McEvoy a month later she found him 'a *delightful* man – eager, natural and amusing . . . I liked him *so* much and should like to make friends with him'.[10] This was never a difficulty for Cynthia, even though their next meeting was 'rather shy', and in February of the following year he asked if he could draw her one day, repeating his request next time he saw her three weeks later. Cynthia forced herself to 'be wary and make quite certain that he means at his expense, not mine' but was delighted when, a fort-night later, he booked her for a definite time, apparently making it clear that no payment would be expected. Diana, Mary Herbert, Elizabeth Asquith, Venetia, Goonie Churchill ('a most lovely one') had all been painted by him, and Cynthia could not bear to appear overlooked.

At the beginning of April 1917 McEvoy started a watercolour 'of my left (certainly my best) profile, and was enraptured with his work. I think it is quite promising – hopelessly Pre-Raphaelite though – I had rather hoped for a new version'.[11] But Cynthia was disapproving of the way the small studio in the Grosvenor Road was crammed with unfinished portraits and, even after the first of what were to be numerous sittings, condemned him for being *too* fashionable and spreading his talent too thin. After two more mornings work on the watercolour (in which Cynthia was dressed in a dark, round-necked dress) he announced himself 'baffled' by it and began an oil sketch of her wearing her Mercury (i.e. winged) hat. She thought it brilliant but after two more sittings he changed it from nearly full face to three-quarter face and finally to a 'Greek coin' or 'large postage stamp' of her profile. By mid June, two months and five sittings later, 'at last my black Mercury hat with silver wings specially made for the oil picture was finished – Picture got into very ugly phase'.[12]

Now McEvoy returned to the baffling watercolour and made it

'very lovely I thought'. He finished it in two more sittings and a month later painted another watercolour of Cynthia in 'my love-in-a-mist blue teagown, greatly approved of by him'. This picture appeared to be started and finished in one sitting because Cynthia, always accurate where these things were concerned, does not mention any more work being done on it. Ironically, given McEvoy's *penchant* for re-working his paintings, it is by far the best of the three that survive.* In November it or its predecessor was exhibited at the Grosvenor Gallery and looked 'very pretty'. 'Diana and I hang side by side, and one withering woman, in a significant voice fraught with 'Birds of a feather' innuendo, exclaimed 'Friends!'[13]

By this time, after fifteen sittings, McEvoy did not appear to be working entirely for love because Cynthia remarked of the first watercolour that the ever-generous Margot Howard de Walden 'says she will buy it and give it to me'. Somehow, as well, Cynthia acquired the love-in-a-mist watercolour. Then, after an interval of six weeks, work began again on the ill-fated oil which had by this time become 'a washout. He has taken off my hat and recommenced.' She disliked the *'utterly* Pre-Raphaelite version of me, hands uplifted in the type of clasping a crystal, a pomegranate, or even a pigeon'[14] and wished that McEvoy could perceive in her some of the modernity he found in Diana Manners, whose portrait was immediately christened 'The Call to Orgy'. All through that winter and throughout the next year he could not decide what it was that he *did* perceive in Cynthia.

At the seventeenth oil sitting (the two watercolours together having taken a mere seven) 'the picture became lovely – far better than it has ever been before . . .' And by the end of March he 'had practically finished the picture. I *do* like it now.' But it was not to be – Pamela Lytton visited the studio and pronounced it 'cruel' and, 'open as he is to suggestion, it was all in the melting pot again'. Soon Cynthia was twisted into another angle and McEvoy, saying that 'I had brought him quite a different face', painted it all over again. By the thirtieth sitting, in July 1918, 'for some mysterious reason he is pleased with my portrait in its present phase. It is infinitely less good than in any previous one – very wooden – quite unlike and quite ugly.'[15] There were to be three more sittings lasting until the end of the year; on 17

*This painting was sold at Christie's on 18 July 1984, Lot 90 of the watercolour sale; its whereabouts are untraceable. The first watercolour is in the possession of the Asquith family.

December the painting was abandoned since McEvoy 'seems to have despaired of oiling me.' Yet the indefatigable Margot bought it nevertheless and it stayed in the Howard de Walden family until 1967 when it was sold, coming on to the market again in 1981, 1983 and 1987, always failing to find a buyer. At a recent exhibition of 'Society Portraits' in London it was hung bedraggledly behind a pillar, shrinking from the full-blooded delights of 'The Call to Orgy' and Sargent's magnificent 'Portrait of the Acheson Sisters'.

In January 1919 Cynthia went to McEvoy's studio in a black velvet dress and since he had given up the oil as a lost cause he 'started a darling little water colour – quite promising – makes me look perky – smart and wicked with my winged hat on.'[16] At the second sitting the picture was still 'very delicious; I *do* hope he won't spoil it'. At the third Michael was introduced but by the fifth, at the end of March, McEvoy 'said I looked too detached from my child so my face was entirely scotched'. Although she, Michael and Beb 'were all disappointed'[17] when they went to see the final watercolour at the Grosvenor Gallery in October, it stayed in the family until destroyed by fire in 1973. The cartoon still exists: a drawing of about five inches by nine, it shows Cynthia with her hand on her hip, pouting rather uncharacteristically and wearing her hat with a large feather, and a straight-haired Michael with his hands in his lap.

Margot Howard de Walden did Cynthia many artistic and musical favours in the last years of the war. It was she who introduced her, in April 1917, to Augustus John. Cynthia liked him but felt very shy, describing him as 'very magnificent-looking, huge and bearded'. Six months later they saw but failed to acknowledge each other at the Queen's restaurant. John claimed that on arrival he was so dazzled by the lights that he did not distinguish the component elements of the blur of beauty in the corner. The next day he wrote to apologise for his 'unconscious rudeness & will you come & see my studio and sit for me? Lady Howard told me I might succeed in inducing you to it'.[18]

When, on 9 October, Cynthia went to the studio in Mulberry Road (the cold was frightful) she took some clothes on approval 'but he chose to do me in the black serge dress I arrived in'.[19] She 'is painted in an unusually subdued mood, doubtless in respect for the sitter's grief at the recent death of two of her brothers, to whom she was devoted'[20] was the comment of a Canadian art critic who saw the black dress as perhaps a more potent image than it was actually meant to be. John's working methods were far more silent and concentrated than McEvoy's, for which

Cynthia was grateful; 'he made – *I* think – a very promising beginning of me sitting in a chair in a severe pose – full face but with eyes averted – a very sidelong glance'.[21] 'Strange satyr-like charm'[22] was John's conception of her demeanour. The picture was completed in seven sittings, at the fifth Lawrence appeared to observe and to criticise ('he charged John to depict "generations of Wemyss disagreeableness in my face, especially the mouth", said disappointment was the keynote of my expression'[23]).

Not wasting a minute, John exhibited the portrait in an exhibition of his work at the Alpine Club which opened only ten days after the final sitting. 24 November: 'My portrait is very much admired. I don't quite know what I feel about it myself. Sometimes I got glimpses which I loved, and then again I would see it Chinese and freakish. I am not at all sure it isn't rather a great picture, whatever it may be as a likeness'. Madeline Wyndham was horrified by it, so was Nanny, Tonks disliked it, Claud thought it a caricature, McEvoy was enthusiastic, Margot Asquith thought it too dramatic, the *Daily Mail* thought it turned her from a young Florentine matron into a weary fish wife.[24] Cynthia, who felt the portrait growing on her – by early January she thought it had 'real beauty from a distance and a wonderful rhythm' – never considered buying it and the picture stayed in John's studio until 1933 when it was sold to the Art Gallery of Toronto for £1400 (£20,000). The curator of the gallery has noted that 'at the time of purchase, we were requested to hang it as *Portrait of a Lady in Black* and not refer to the fact that it was a portrait of Lady Cynthia'.[25] Presumably this was at her request.

While John was in France he thought rather longingly of his companionable sittings with Cynthia and wrote to her on his return in the spring of 1918 asking if he could see her. 'I am in a state of utter mental confusion but perhaps you will have the effect of restoring my stability to some extent because you are quiet and reposeful, in addition to other things of value.'[26] Sittings recommenced on 25 June. 'Oh, the agony of standing!' moaned Cynthia after a 'most promising beginning, full-length in beige-and-green stockingette suit with bright green hat' ('out-door country clothes'). At the third sitting she took her bicycle and leant on it. But John could not get along with his new element and instead began a small head 'very good, I thought – but with grass-green eyes and scarlet hair. Next time, however, he made 'a *monster* of me' and improved things very little for the next six sittings. Then, at the beginning of October, he started afresh for a third time, 'a beautiful head of me on new canvas. I *do* pray he won't spoil it – but I feel very nervous of his touching it again. I had just had a letter from him in which he wrote – "Obviously I am ill since I cannot stand *anybody* – of you alone I can think with longing and admiration – you have all the effect of a Divine Being whose smile and touch can heal, redeem and renew. I am always in terror lest you should tire of sitting especially as the results haven't been brilliant so far." '[27]

At the end of November a fourth canvas was started, with Cynthia in the same propped-hand pose as in the third. On the 26th Lawrence again came to the studio, accompanying Cynthia after she had given him lunch at Queen's. 'Between those two beards I nearly got Fou Rire. He said John made him talk Latin so 'dead' was he. He kept muttering 'mortuus est', 'mortuus est' and condoling John on the fact that the baby he had just painted was so obviously a corpse. He said my portrait was an impertinence – he couldn't bear its pipe-clay look and summed up by saying 'Let the dead paint their dead'. [28](Partly this was a reference to John's stated intention to abandon portraiture for a while in order to concentrate on his vast painting for the Canadians.)

John decided to adopt different tactics in the New Year of 1919. First he did several pencil full-length sketches, then returned to the full length canvas started six months before 're-dressing me in black velvet instead of summer stockingette'.[29] This was the same black dress which had inspired McEvoy to do his 'dashing little water colour' because on this particular day, 19 January, Cynthia sat to one artist in the morning and sat ('or rather, alas, stood') to the other in the afternoon. Soon the canvas was abandoned again because John had to go to Paris to paint the Peace Conference; he and Cynthia continued to be friends and to exchange occasional letters fixing meetings – but he never finished a second painting.

····❧ **Chapter 25** ❦····
1919

In the New Year of 1919 Cynthia and Beb left Pixton to go and stay at the Wharf. Four days before H.H. had lost the parliamentary seat that he had held for more than thirty years, yet apart from cursory expressions of regret the subject of politics was little touched upon. It was Violet who privately told Cynthia that Margot had sobbed out her remorse to her:

> Violet thought for a minute that the scales had suddenly fallen from her eyes and that she perceived the subtle way she had really injured him – by forcing him in self-defence to grow a thick hide – a kind of tortoise-shell – which has come to encase him in his public as well as in his private relations – cutting him off. But all Margot meant was that by putting a silver spoon into his mouth she had made him self-indulgent and soft. 'Your father never had a hot bath before I married him: he couldn't afford it' etc.[1]

Cynthia must have often wondered whether the attention-seeking Margot might not have had the same tortoise-shell effect on the five children. And when, some weeks later, Margot greeted her with the 'soothing tactful words of "Are you very sad at having another baby? I always prayed you wouldn't" '[2] she must have wished she had grown a thick hide too.

Once Beb had returned to France, Cynthia could again take possession of her 'bed-sitter' at Cadogan Square and start manipulating the wires of her London life. Sussex Place was still being

226

let: a brief visit of inspection had found it 'horribly deep in dust. The prospect of reoccupation is a nightmare'. It was in mid-January that things were considerably enlivened by Elizabeth's definite engagement to Antoine. He had been acknowledged as her 'rich Rumanian lover' since the end of 1917 but it was only in the first days of 1919, after both parties had been alternately 'cooling' and becoming more fond, that Antoine found he 'had the key to Eden in his hand if he wished to use it, Elizabeth having told him that she would marry him in three months if Gibson [her other lover] remained indifferent, that proviso of course meaning nothing, it was only the form in which she had to reopen negotiations'.[3] Desmond MacCarthy told Cynthia the news and the next day she went to a lunch with Antoine (fending off a brother-in-law's kiss). One of the topics under discussion was Violet's attitude. Never shy of trying to get people to think along her lines (in 1915 she had written a copious letter to Montagu trying to forestall Venetia's conversion to Judaism) she deplored Antoine's 'perverted sex-emphasis and his Hamlet moods'; Cynthia disagreed. 'I think it a great chance for Elizabeth and am all for it' though 'I must say *I* was completely bamboozled – I thought he was completely off Elizabeth – it's very funny to think how much he made love to me, how fortunate that I rejected his advances . . . I'm not sure that Antoine isn't fairly mischievous, but I do delight in him, he is a luxory [sic] as a companion'.[4] Ten days later Antoine thanked Cynthia for not having proclaimed the fact that he had 'fait la cour' to her, saying that she could thereby have broken off his engagement. (His marriage was not, in the event, to be a spectacular success: by December 1920 Elizabeth was to imagine herself in love with John Middleton Murry, necessitating a letter from Katharine Mansfield, 'Dear Princess Bibesco, I am afraid you must stop writing these little love letters to my husband while he and I live together. It is one of the things which is not done in our world'.[5])

Cynthia continued to see Desmond, Freyberg, Whibley, Antoine, Claud, and Raleigh fairly regularly. Although so many of her former male friends had been killed in the war, she was not friendless. But the spirit of the Coterie had been dissipated, so that she saw less of Katharine, Mary Herbert, Violet and Venetia, women friends who used to be such an entrenched part of her life. She began instead to see more of a different kind of woman: Adèle Essex and Anne Islington (and their daughters Joan Capel and Joan Poynder, 'the two Joans'), Nellie Romilly, Brenda Dufferin, Maud Russell, Goonie Churchill, Clare Tennyson, Dorothy Grosvenor, Margot Howard de Walden, Jeffie Darrell,

Moira Cavendish, Nathalie Ridley. These women were lively and witty but made no pretension to any intellectual leaning, were heavily titled and tended to fill their lives with lunch and dinner engagements, poker and fashionable pursuits rather than the less sophisticated, more rustic pleasures which the Souls had valued so much. Not for them the bicycling holidays in France or a deep, if amateur interest in painting or philosophy. It was almost as if the death of the children of the Souls was leaving Cynthia with no-one to turn to, for the moment, but the children of the Marlborough House Set, those who had once grouped themselves round the Prince of Wales and helped to indulge his many pleasures. The days when Beb and Cynthia had considered living in Brunswick Square, and all that stood for, were now far away. Yet although she tried, Ettie-like, to carry out the doctrine of 'le roi est mort, vive le roi', sometimes she could not help noting in her diary that 'melancholy fell over me. It seemed a mockery of the past – all the same old women – Lady Randolph West Porch bounding round the room – and no men but diplomats, Americans and boys of 17, the only old faces were Bongie, Bogie Harris and Summie'.6

The social whirl was not as hectic as it had been before 1914, but it was still busy enough. In the last week of March alone Cynthia went to four balls, given by Cynthia Curzon, the Duchess of Rutland, Ettie and Eloise Ancaster. Her position was slightly indeterminate: too young to be a proper chaperone she was too world-weary to enjoy the fun very much. That year the poker games became especially feverish, on one unfortunate occasion Cynthia joined a club and lost £50 (£750). 'Beb must never know or how could I ever again nag him about taxis etc?'7 she wrote, mindful of her spoiler-of-the-fun strictures about his February visit to Paris: 'I am haunted by visions of you swilling liqueurs and lying like a crocodile in 5 francs baths – oh dear Oh dear. "Special prices" for officers indeed!'8 But she had added helpfully, 'if you go and have tea at the Ritz you are sure to see lots of people you know'.

In early March Cynthia went to stay at 72 Brook Street for six weeks to chaperone Joan Capel at the request of her mother, Adèle Essex. She left Michael at Cadogan Square, where he had been taken after his long stay at Pixton and where it was convenient for her to visit him most days for tea. John she saw very rarely now, sometimes not even once a month: Miss Leighton always asked her to stay away, in any case visiting him made her miserable ('to see John being drilled by a very nice sergeant – Leighton was very much of a nightmare to me'9). Brook Street was so luxurious that 'a glimpse of the 60 pairs of shoes left *behind* by Adèle made me feel I had gone no better than barefoot all my life'.[10] The tone of this remark was a good deal less light-hearted than the one used by Cynthia before her marriage, when she had told Patrick Shaw Stewart cheerfully enough that 'I shall be squalidly poor (at first anyhow – I am inclined to be optimistic about the future) and you will have to bring sandwiches and caviar in your pocket when you come to lunch with me'.[11]

Although the Sussex Place tenants were about to give up the house, leaving it in a state of 'unutterable filth', with endless plumbing troubles and needing 'men with gas masks' to clear up, Cynthia preferred to re-let it over the summer rather than start re-building her nest. She had, ever since her marriage, assumed the role of the domestically inadequate so fully that she was convinced that running a large house was beyond her capabilities. 'Can't understand *what* it is Fanny wants me to do to the mattresses' she wailed during the week she was trying to make the house habitable for the next tenant, groaning at the thought of going to the agency in order to search out housemaids or, occasionally, talking to cook. In Cynthia's character Martha and Mary never had to fight it out between them – the former always retired defeated straightaway; when Cynthia went, on the same afternoon, to visit first the fashionable Ava Astor and Maud Cunard, and then the stolid 'Betty [Asquith] and Co' ('wonderful contrast in atmosphere') there was no doubt in her mind which appealed to her most.

Why did Cynthia prefer to continue her life in the cuckoo's nest rather than build a nest of her own in time for Beb's return and the birth of the baby, which was due in August? As well as shirking the domestic role, Cynthia felt subconsciously that it was only by continuing to be homeless, and accepting hospitality without ever reciprocating, that she could remain girlish, that she could crystallise in the part of the carefree, unfettered young girl. Once married she had found little happiness in the wife/mother/homemaker kind of preoccupations and preferred to escape from their *mise en scène* whenever possible. In this respect, despite her frequent complaints about the lack of a London base, the war had been a useful reason to continue a peripatetic life; now that it was over she must have dreaded confronting those aspects of her nature that would have to be created or awakened for 'normal' married life to start up again. So, for reasons of her own, she put off the consequences of Armistice Day, and was encouraged to do this by her pregnancy – 'after the baby is born' became shorthand for 'when I have to start life afresh'.

In addition, her own private war nightmare (John's deterioration had exactly coincided with the war years) had not vanished with the arrival of peace. 'The nursery should have been the one oasis throughout these preposterous years' she wrote to Desmond (discounting the fact that there had been no nursery, only a series of spare rooms and lodgings) adding, 'and the worst of it is that it makes the future towards which one would now naturally turn such an awful nightmare and I don't feel able for it'.[12] As Cynthia rightly realised, she had 'passively enduring' courage, but not the coping kind. In this respect her bravery was rather masculine, as was her determination to appear cheerful to others, to keep the flag flying: 'it doesn't matter how much it *hurts*, but one should never allow oneself to be harmed by sorrow, I mean in any sense impaired for the very very much that is always left. I should despise myself if I ever felt either bored or bitter about life'.[13] Yet the drawback to this kind of courage is that there can be no period of mourning, of frequent tears and perfectly justifiable grief; 'after the baby is born' Cynthia was going to have to build her nest *and* accept her sorrow, as well as start living within caviare-free limits. Nothing was going to be easy.

At the end of March Beb returned for good and Cynthia was officially 'off the grass'. After a few more days amidst the 'superfine linen' of Brook Street they went to Stanway for Easter, a peaceful time marred by the sadness of the Memorial Service for Ego, and by Eliza Wedgwood's deep distress because her chow Boots had bitten out the eye of 'a most provocative odious pampered little Pekinese left in her care by Sargent's sister'.[14] Cynthia was feeling perfectly well at this time, and kept being complimented on the elegance of her figure, 'it's really a pity one should look one's best with a six months baby'.[15]

But the feeling of well-being was unfortunately not to last for long. After a few days in London in order to attend the Bibesco wedding, Beb and Cynthia went to Rudder Grange at Thorpeness in Suffolk, the house which had been lent to them by Adèle. Michael had already been there for three weeks; Beb was 'delighted with having a nest to ourselves' and settled down to writing poetry ('in a perfect mood' was Cynthia's opinion of him). But she had suddenly begun to notice her pregnancy and from now on, until the baby was born, was never in very good health. Her plan was to read, learn Shakespeare by heart, play chess, give Michael lessons and even embroider (an occupation she only enjoyed when pregnant, this time she was trying to make an entire quilt for her bed and set herself the task of one embroidered flower every day). But often she was sick, she could not sleep despite being tired and she frequently endured very bad heartburn.

After a month of relatively rustic seclusion, 'the London crowd' arrived for July and the Asquiths had to vacate Rudder Grange and move to a small bungalow. 'Adèle's presence makes an astounding difference to the place. I feel as though I were at Ascot'[16] wrote Cynthia, who had thought the plain diet of sea air and early nights was what she wanted but was surprised to find how much she enjoyed the sudden upsurge of social life ('an engagement book will be necessary'). Mary Lutyens, who was then eleven and had come with her twenty-one year-old sister Barbara, and two other sisters ('all in brilliant-coloured home-made jerseys') remembered that 'as well as a number of Barbie's friends who stayed with us at our rented villas there were dozens of children. We went about in gangs and there always seemed to be a party of some kind going on'.[17] The Lutyens had rented Norah Lindsay's bungalow facing the sea. Joan Poynder had a tiny cottage, as did Nathalie Ridley. Yet Cynthia did not enjoy the merriment as much as she might and quite often 'chucked' in order to dine off Bovril and grape nuts and go to bed with a novel.

In the first week of August, during an unprecedented heat wave, the 'decayed' Sussex Place house was reoccupied by its owners after a five-year interval. 'When I arrived Beb treated me like a horse one is expecting to shy. He was dreading the fuss my own house would throw me into.'[18] And indeed Cynthia was at once very agitated, unable to sit still and extremely over-wrought about everything that needed doing to the house. For the next grillingly hot few days, before she went into the nursing-home, Cynthia counted silver with the parlourmaid, housemaid and cook, interviewed plumbers and 'spent hellish morning at Selfridges trying to find squalors – toilet services etc for servants'. She gave her first small dinner party ('appalled at expense of fruit and cakes') and wrote in her diary, only partly in jest, 'dinner good – successful mixed grill. We took £5 10/- (£75) off them [Gilbert and Maud Russell] at Bridge so got our expenses well back'.[19]

Although Beb was very happy to be back in his 'beloved Pepinage' Cynthia was not, and it was with some relief that she went off for three weeks to the Officers' Wives Maternity Home in Regents Park which, on a visit of inspection, she had found 'quite delicious – all blue and white and *private*-house looking with McAffee (matron) looking a poem'.[20] The baby was to be induced but, by auto-suggestion was born, when Cynthia was admitted, on 20 August. He was born at breakfast time; after a long night Cynthia had hoped he would arrive by dawn but 'I had a much worse time altogether and for the first time instruments were necessary and the poor little fellow got quite a nasty gash in the neck . . . The pink cot prepared for Marigold was removed and a blue one substituted'[21] for Simon.

In the morning Cynthia played a trick on her mother which was in the true Charteris tradition of practical jokes. She pretended that she had not yet had the baby and when Mary went up to the prettily decorated cot to have a look at it 'had the shock of her life when she saw the *monster* (nearly eleven pounds) lying in it'. It took some time to convince her of the truth, 'the shock made her feel quite ill' remarked Cynthia unrepentantly, in the spirit of someone who had once cheerfully made her thirteen year-old, extremely sensitive sister Bibs believe that she was a Barnardo's orphan; and who was to croon over her knee as if it were a baby without imagining that her young relations found this almost unbearably spooky. She had a toughness about jokes which she did not realise was often denied to other people.

September continued very hot – though, as soon as Cynthia arrived home, it became unusually cold. Relishing every day she was allowed to shelter under the label of officer's wife, she was very resentful that she could not spin out her three peaceful weeks to four, and liked having competent nurses to feed the baby instead of an untried monthly nurse. 'My truce with life is very nearly over', she told Desmond. 'It has been a very peaceful parenthesis, and I have felt suspended above daily life with little connection with either past or future. Now I feel slowly descending as if in a crane, Simon's arrival has bounded my horizon for so long that I have as it were the sensation of beginning to peer over a stone wall with languid wonder as to what may lie on the other side of it.'[22] She was certainly *not* a mother who longed to get home and when she did she 'felt terribly forlorn, weak and weepy'.

For the next two months, until she discontinued her diary, the pattern was the same. While in Sussex Place she found herself unable to cope and every day ended 'dinner in bed and a sleepless night from fussing over servants house etc due to weak nerves'.[23] For two happy weeks in October she went with the baby to Eliza's cottage at Stanton (it was simple but comfortable, the kitchen 'glowing with coppers and carrots'[21] and the beams in the dining-room hand-painted by Sargent) and there she followed all the old Stanway pursuits – calling on the Prews and the Allens, seizing on the newspaper which, because of the railway strike, brought news from a world even more remote than usual. But back in London she wrote 'I hate my life' and that she was 'really suicidally inclined'.[25]

The reason for her depression was something Cynthia refused to dwell on, preferring to attribute it to mere domestic difficulties. 'I am terribly fussed about the nursery. Altogether there doesn't seem a minute's peace and I am ceaselessly unpleasantly preoccupied, and all the time the undercurrent of financial terror'.[26] And to Desmond:

I am in despair about myself. I suppose it's health but the whole of life just now seems a *supplice* just made up of unpleasant details. I have been so spoilt all these years and now I am *always* preoccupied and feel as if I should never be able to enjoy the passing moments again, it's hell and I feel so ashamed because I don't suppose my life is *any* more difficult than most people's but it seems there is never a moment's peace in one's own house, I am horrified if people I love ring up and say 'when can I see you?' It's so difficult to get things in and I do resent never having time to read. I have lost the power of making any decisions, see everything morbidly and out of proportion, such things as putting a nib into a pen holder even seem insuperably difficult and I have no appetite for anything including food.[27]

But she had good cause to be unhappy, even if she would not admit it. 'The truth is I have been spoilt by five years of cuckooing' was one cause, money worries were another, Miss Leighton was finally proving herself to be too unstable even for Cynthia to endure, and Polly was leaving after nearly fifteen years (21 October: 'I have been *appealing* to Polly to stay on but I'm afraid she won't'). Four strange servants were not outweighed by the constancy of Nanny Faulkner, because her preoccupation was the children not their mother.

More importantly, the legacy of the war was a wound which had not even begun to heal. The past seemed the only reality and Cynthia had the feeling of 'having no definite event to look forward to'.[28] She never mentioned Basil in her 1919 diary, but must have missed him very much; she also missed the 'luxory' of a lover and wondered if she would ever enjoy it again. Yet she persisted in trying to forget about the war and in berating herself for not being a better manager: 'I hate myself for being braver about sorrows than about bothers' and 'I feel as though a hundred sheltering screens had suddenly been blown down'.[29] She was not suffering from 'postnatal depression' but from a multiplicity of miseries that had been held in abeyance until 'after the baby is born' and were now crashing upon her.

Beb tried to improve matters by taking Cynthia to the Royal York at Brighton for a few days where 'a gentle melancholy descended on me at seeing my old 1916 haunts' – it did not seem a very sensible choice of hotel. Simon was christened with his four godparents, Barrie, McEvoy and the two Joans in attendance; he wore the gold dress Diana Manners had made for Michael. But in the second week of November Cynthia had to return to Stanton for three weeks. In December she wrote to Desmond, who was in South Africa, 'I have been through Hell since I wrote last and am not quite out of it yet'.[30] From then until the beginning of 1921 nothing at all is known about her movements apart from the surviving letters written to her by Desmond and by Barrie and the few letters she wrote to Desmond. If it had not been for her close relationship with these two men we would know even less about her life then than we do; and if they, and Barrie in particular, had not been part of her life it would have been a very different one, because it was they who gave her the impetus to become a writer. She no longer sat at the feet of men of letters, she began to sit beside them, and the turning point in this process was 'the lost year' 1920.

···⤠ Chapter 26 ⤟···
Desmond

Cynthia specialised in men of letters and when, at dinner in the January of 1918, she met Prince Antoine Bibesco and Desmond MacCarthy she felt something of the intellectual excitement that she used to feel with Basil. It did not take long for her to decide which man she wished to claim as the serious friend. Bibesco, although alluring, had the overtly sexual attitude to women which is the mark of some French men (Fabrice in Nancy Mitford's *The Pursuit of Love* is its memorable personification). Cynthia was repelled by it, and although she was glad to be considered seductible, made it clear that she was not to be numbered among Antoine's conquests. 'He asked me what I thought of physical love and, *of course*, told me I wasn't "matured" yet – the marble was there, but the sculpture not emerged from the block . . . He wishes to undertake the job, but I'm afraid I can't oblige him.'[1] How pressing Antoine was Cynthia does not relate, and it is unlikely that he was as blatant as he was with an American literary lady called Mina Curtiss who was given visible proof by the nattily-aging but no less lustful Antoine of his instant and irrepressible desire for her.[2]

Desmond had been playing pander to his friend's literary leanings but was not always successful. Even though Virginia Woolf considered that 'the Roumanian Prince too has the most exquisite voice'[3] she stood firm against Desmond's 'pestering me with inscrutable persistence, over the telephone in letters in visits to lunch with Prince Bibesco'.[4] Cynthia was less resolute and very much enjoyed Antoine's company. But when Desmond began to press his suit she soon realised how much she preferred his gentle, witty, intelligent, half-Irish, Eton and Cambridge approach; Antoine became one of those, like Bluey, whose gossip she encouraged but whose friendship was of limited import. Having always to be 'squirrel-like' (i.e. curled up winsomely in order to fend off groping paws) became tedious. 'Funny what much better talks we have on the telephone than face to face'[5] she commented rather naïvely.

She had at once found Desmond *'delightful* – a nice, plain face – very appreciative and great flavour in his talk'.[6] It was as a conversationalist that he was most unique; yet it was his love of talk and wine and friendship, in fact his niceness, that was, from the world's viewpoint, his undoing. Aged forty when Cynthia met him, he was already recognised as a writer continually in a state of gestation, one who – when the time was ripe, circumstances propitious and so on and so forth – would bring forth a great masterpiece. It is with some justification that he has been described[7] as having something in common with the character of Bernard in Virginia Woolf's *The Waves* (1931) who knows that he will never write anything because 'I need an audience. That is my downfall', who 'cannot bear the pressure of solitude. When I cannot see words curling like rings of smoke round me I am in darkness – I am nothing.'[8]

Even Desmond's wife Molly (they had been happily and companionably married for twelve years and had three children) confessed to Virginia, at the time when Cynthia was getting to know him, that 'she finds him a little spoilt, terribly without a will, & much at the mercy of any fine lady or gentleman with good wine'.[9] Yet Virginia thought he probably had

the nicest nature of any of us – the nature one would soonest have chosen for one's own. Who is more tolerant, more appreciative, more understanding of human nature? It goes without saying that he is not an heroic character. He finds pleasure too pleasant, cushions too soft, dallying too seductive, & then, as I sometimes feel now, he has ceased to be ambitious . . . Yet it is true, & no one can deny it, that he has the floating elements of something brilliant, beautiful – some book of stories, reflections, studies, scattered about in him, for they show themselves indisputably in his talk . . . I can see myself, however, going through his desk one of these days, shaking out unfinished pages from between sheets of blotting paper, & deposits of old bills, & making up a small book of table talk, which shall appear as a proof to the younger generation that Desmond was the most gifted of us all. But why did he never do anything? they will ask.[10]

Affairs of the heart are essential occupation for someone who needs to be kept from his desk. They have the additional, and excellent, advantage that they involve letter writing, a pursuit at which the procrastinator always excels because it involves his first love, words; these, mysteriously, arrive with no effort, cudgelling of the brain or forced seclusion. When MacCarthy's letters are published they will be seen as his lasting masterpiece but, sadly, it is not enough to write good letters; nevertheless his fair, even-tempered if ephemeral reviews were excellent enough for MacCarthy eventually to be knighted.

At first Cynthia only met him with Antoine, with either Elizabeth or Horatia or Enid Bagnold making a fourth. Then, during April 1918, while Cynthia was away (she was nursing, Desmond was working at the Admiralty) letters were written and, on her return, books were lent. At the end of May they dined alone together at Queen's, sitting 'in the Square' until nearly midnight. 'You could scarcely find two men more different' commented Cynthia, 'and yet, ridiculously enough, there is something in talking to him which faintly reminds me of Basil. It is, I suppose, something in the responsiveness of thought, voice, and laugh which they have in common. Between talking to them and to others is something of the difference between dancing on a floor hung on chains and on an ordinary one'.[11]

By the end of July their friendship had progressed far enough for Cynthia to feel able to ask him to accompany her on a Saturday to Monday at Jeffie Darrell's. He 'had accepted my invitation to come on this visit with me – but to my astonishment when I telephoned to him in the morning I found he had gone away leaving no message. Either he is ill or he forgot'.[12] This is the same syndrome so beautifully described by Leonard Woolf forty-five years later:

> Here for instance was a fairly common situation in Desmond's life: he is engaged to dine at 7.30 with someone whom he likes very much in Chelsea; he looks forward to the evening; at 7 he is sitting in a room at the other end of London talking to two or three people whom he does not very much like and who are in fact boring him; at 7.5 he begins to feel that he ought to get up and leave for Chelsea; at 7.30 he is still sitting with the people whom he does not much like and is uncomfortably keeping them from their dinner; at 8 they insist that he must stay and dine with them; at 8.5 he rings up his Chelsea friends, apologizes, and says that he will be with them in 20 minutes.[13]

Virginia described Desmond's friendship as 'sunk under a cloud of vagueness'.[14] It was a cloud that Cynthia was to see a good deal of. But one of her strengths was that, as with Lawrence, she did not take offence: 'Desmond has behaved very oddly to me – I have never heard a word from him since he chucked coming to Jeffie's with me without either warning or explanation' she wrote a month later, going on to describe another delightful lunch at Antoine's, this time *à cinque* with Beb and Molly. 'There was something funny about my meeting him *with* his wife for the first time coinciding with Bibesco's first glimpse of Beb. I liked his wife and found her reported deafness not at all bad.'[15]

It is certain that Desmond, who was one of the most literate of Cynthia's entire generation, said nothing to make her feel inadequate: 'We looked at my commonplace book. I was surprised by the poems he didn't know'. 11 September: 'Told me stories of Henry James. No further ground covered in our relationship.' What ground might have been covered? Cynthia would have liked Desmond to be her acknowledged friend, one who continued to write her delightful letters and to amuse her with his good, and literary, conversation, who confessed to feeling fond but always with the qualification 'if only' (I was not married, you were not married, circumstances were different . . .). By comparison with Antoine, Desmond was so reticent physically that at first Cynthia hoped he would prove ideal for a long-lasting relationship; she saw no reason to qualify her original assessment which was that he 'was not for "luscious purposes" (as Violet would say) but he has the most agreeable mind and is extremely nice'.

It would not have been in her mind to get closer to Bloomsbury. Despite her flirtation with Brunswick Square it is no coincidence that her only close contact with the group of friends who were labelled 'Bloomsbury' was with the one of them who did not live there, who preferred the slightly more salubrious address of Wellington Square, Chelsea. This had raffish connotations but was within walking distance of South Kensington. Cynthia felt most at home here or in Regents Park, and would not have wanted to cross the cultural divide remarked upon by Virginia Woolf who was writing in her diary that autumn that 'the gulf which we crossed between Kensington and Bloomsbury was the gulf between respectable mummified humbug & life crude & impertinent perhaps, but living'.[16] The Asquiths would have been among those labelled irredeemably Kensington by Virginia, 'dressed up so irreproachably, so nice, kind, respectable – so insufferable – You remember the kind of politeness, and the little jokes, and all the deference, and opening doors for one, and looking as if the mention of the w.c. even would convey nothing whatever to them'.[17]

Desmond understood that if Cynthia had not yet been embraced by Bloomsbury she was unlikely to be so now. Once he described to her the evening when he 'slept with the Wolves, at Richmond, which always does me good. It is a pity you do not know the Wolves. I know I shall never take steps to make you meet them. It is a pity. But you ought to have known the Wolves (the emphasis in reading is on the 'have'). Now it is too late to begin'.[18] (This was the visit described by Virginia rather sharply in her diary because Desmond, characteristically, wanted to talk and 'L[eonard]'s morning wasted in the sun of his laziness'.[19]) His understanding of Cynthia's temperament made Desmond realise that 'it is too late'. He could have anticipated occasions in the future when Cynthia called in at a party of Ottoline Morell's and noted laconically 'she has one every evening. Queer fry'[20] or described a lunch party of Enid Bagnold's at which she found Clive Bell and Duncan Grant as merely 'very highbrow'.[21] (She did like Lytton Strachey on the half dozen or so occasions on which she met him, but that was because he was not unlike the men of letters she was used to.)

Cynthia found the intellectual air of Bloomsbury too formidable for enjoyment, and disliked its sexual frankness. She was made uneasy by its unconventional attitudes and continued to be an admirer of Tonks at a time when Vanessa Bell was furiously reacting against him. Even their decorative styles differed. When Desmond and Roger Fry showed her over the Omega workshop in December 1918 'the first impression is grotesque' she wrote, adding however, 'but I was conscious of considerable slowly working charm'.[22] Cynthia would, too, have felt disorientated by houses where the sofas (mattress ticking or faded pink or very elderly chintz) would have perpetually leaked their stuffing, the floors were piled with books and stacked canvases, the gardens were wild instead of ordered and the flowers were dried not florist's; while the walls were never painted cream but were instead a blue-grey wash with pinkish motifs, or even displayed the brown wrapping paper and grey corduroy curtains of which Yeats was so fond. This was all quite different from Cadogan Square or Sussex Place where the cushions were at angles, the walls were bland, hung with framed pictures, the table polished mahogany with a dumb-waiter in the middle and the polished mahogany sideboard had a neat vase of flowers on it (*never* an earthenware bowl of red and yellow peppers, tomatoes, tomatoes, carrots and mint).

Antoine Bibesco was in Paris during September and October, and Desmond and Cynthia began to dine together at least once a week. Soon Cynthia felt his sympathy so keenly that she told him about John. 'He talked about him – very tactfully and nicely. He is a delightful new friend. I feel him a real addition to my life and look forward to him . . . He has great felicity of speech – I liked "Birrell looking benevolently trenchant".'[23] By early November they were together whenever possible, to the extent of Desmond hovering under the lamp-post in Cadogan Square waiting for Cynthia to return from a dinner engagement, then coming in to sit by the empty grate for an hour. It was after this that there was a 'letter from Desmond taking deliberate stride' to 'Cynthia' (instead of Lady Cynthia) and 'your affectionate'; soon after that it was 'My dear Cynthia'.

Cynthia took Desmond to meet some of her friends: at lunch with Adèle Essex there were Duff Cooper, Diana, Goonie and Eddie Marsh. Cynthia was upset because, by Desmond's standards, the conversation seemed desultory. He, politely, said that he had enjoyed himself, but Cynthia, seeing her friends in a different light, felt 'jarred and jangled'. The same day Desmond came to see Cynthia in the early evening. He visited Michael in bed and then 'sat on and on with me. The appearance of my little egg dinner made no difference and – all unfed as he was – he stayed until ten'.[24] Among the books he lent Cynthia at this time were his wife's first novel *A Pier and a Band* containing 'a very obvious sketch of Desmond'. When, two days later, Cynthia was asked to tea by Molly she was able to express her appreciation of her writing.

> We talked of her deafness, their poverty and her fears for the future when Desmond's Admiralty job terminates. She seems to have lost faith in his capacity for bread-winning by his pen. I said *she* must go on writing novels and she exclaimed at the unfairness of marrying an author and then having to do the writing herself saying 'What do you want Desmond to do – have luncheon with you?' – but without any bitterness and I think she likes me. I do so absolutely agree and see the danger of Desmond completely evaporating into *flânerie* and *talk*. He would wilingly talk to one for 24 hours every day – I feel rather uneasy – but I suppose if he wasn't squandering his time on me it would be someone else.[25]

(Cynthia allowed herself to believe this, and that Molly liked her. But years later Molly scribbled on a letter from Cynthia to Desmond in which Cynthia described dreaming that Desmond was angry with her, 'she probably felt my distress in the night – and had a bad conscience . . . dishonourable correspondence'.)

By 10 November Cynthia was writing that Desmond 'came to

see me. He is becoming daily bread'. The next day was the climax of their relationship. They spent most of Armistice Day together and in years to come the last day of the war was to become linked in both their minds with their feeling for each other. Cynthia felt as close to Desmond as she was ever to feel; his hopes were raised and were to be dashed over the next year. It was a day described both by Cynthia in her diary and by Virginia Woolf who, in a letter to her sister, reported what Desmond had told her.

Cynthia did not wait for Desmond's telephone call to tell her exactly when the proclamation of the armistice would be but went with Hugo to Buckingham Palace where there was a dense crowd. The King and Queen came out ('like two dolls' wrote Virginia); 'they were given a splendid ovation, and one felt the lump in the nation's throat' said Cynthia, adding 'not a word the King said could be heard'. From here she went to Barrie's empty flat (he was in France) and telepathically Desmond suddenly appeared there. 'We struggled back through the swarming, shouting mob – I felt healingly touched, and *not* jarred as I had dreaded.' She lunched with Cis and his wife Anne and then went home to her writing table, but being too restless to settle to any letters splashed through heavy rain to call on her sister-in-law Frances. Desmond meanwhile, according to Virginia, wandered into a restaurant and 'found two men fighting, and tried to separate them and was knocked on the head, and then they apologized, and he led one of them off, whose nose was bleeding, and they spent some time in a lavatory; and he became rather depressed, and wandered off, and found things a little flat'.[26] In the evening he and Cynthia dined together at Queen's restaurant. Afterwards

We bussed as far as Hyde Park corner – there all buses stopped and we had to take to our feet – arm in arm slowly pressing our way through solid beaming babyish humanity – motors laden with pyramids of hooting patriots piled on the roof . . . I felt telepathised by mob feeling and a gush of humanity love in my heart. It was the most loveable crowd – so good-humoured, so spontaneous – one felt they were celebrating *Peace* so much more than *Victory* – and I think that was why it was so completely unjarring – it was also characteristically amateurish and informal – how different it would have been in Berlin had the situation been reversed – Here no song was ever sung through – no coherent sentence concluded – it was all a vague cheer a simmer of genial *soulagement*. The sheer *grin* on the soldiers' faces really warmed one's heart and the humour of it all just softened the pathos. I liked the elderly couples one saw quite formally dancing – chasséeing and reversing in the mud . . . Desmond was an ideal companion – touched – humorous and sensitive. We finally reached

Trafalgar Sq and climbed up on the monument. From there it was a wonderful sight . . . We had to walk the whole way home. It was about one I suppose. Desmond came in and raided the nursery for cake. He said 'good night darling – God bless you' and kissed my hand when he went.

When, a few days later, 'Desmond and Molly entertained Roger Fry and me to dinner at Queen's restaurant and then we sat in their house and had very stimulating Symposium talk'[27] the phrase 'Desmond walked me home' has a green cross in the margin of Cynthia's diary which means some kind of *rapprochement* happened. Five days later (they had not seen each other for this length of time while Beb was home on leave) they 'found our way through thick yellow fog to lunch with Sybil Colefax. Eddie was there – Leonie Leslie – Stephen McKenna and Osbert Sitwell – Desmond and I dawdled home together'.[28]

They had three days with each other to which to look forward. 'He had his usual large cargo of books – so I wasn't allowed to read my own – but from a large selection chose Davies's *A Poet's Pilgrimage*'[29] wrote Cynthia about a train journey to Pixton where they enjoyed long walks in the soft rain and where, during an enjoyable discussion about themselves, Desmond refused to recognise 'my real "cutoffness" from my fellow creatures' or that Cynthia had as many personalities as Elizabeth had dresses, claiming that she gave him an impression of 'Immer die alte' i.e. steadfastness and constancy. On one afternoon Desmond was in terrible travail because he had been asked by Mary Herbert to write something about Aubrey for the local paper. 'Rumpling his hair – puckering his brow he looked more wretchedly worried than I have ever seen any one – it made me feel his life as a writer must be Hell.' Cynthia read another book from the cargo, *The Philosophical Poets* by Santayana and was much impressed by its 'arguments against the wilfull fostering of illusions'. In her life, with the ending of the war and the beginning of her fourth decade, reality could no longer be staved off.

Cynthia had 'never been happier at Pixton', while Desmond told her in the taxi from Paddington that 'you have been such a dear to me – I am so wonderfully happy in your company – the only thing that worries me is that it seems so frightfully long till I see you the next time – that's the only ominous thing – that if I don't see you for four days it seems such an unconscionable time. He took my hand'. It was on this occasion, after returning from Pixton to Cadogan Square, that Cynthia was visited by D.H. Lawrence and felt too tired for him. The contrast between his irascible exuberance and Desmond's soothing charm must have been too much even for the chameleon-like Cynthia to enjoy. After seeing him she went straight on to dinner with Violet and Bongie, where Diana's engagement to Duff was being discussed. Cynthia approved, realising that she 'will be securing the luxury of a perfect *mental* companionship, she does not really need money because she has in the extreme the talent of making bricks without straw and will always achieve splash and decor',[30] a judgement which turned out to be absolutely correct.

The day after their return from Pixton Desmond told Cynthia (in a passage which she copied into her diary) that she was 'the most delighting angel of a friend, so charming and just and beautiful and sensitive and kind that when I try to distill a lucid dewdrop for you it turns, you see, into a vulgar warm shower-bath'.[31] Cynthia replied – as yet she was not having to stall – 'bless you for yourself, you will never know how much of a luxury you are . . . you have made me so so much happier during the last months and please do in the coming ones too'.[32] It was an ideal *status quo* for Cynthia but was unfortunately not to last. Two days later, after going together to a lecture by Bernard Shaw, Desmond and Cynthia had 'a milestone interview'. First they discussed his life, whether he 'ought to dig a deeper shaft into his mind and produce something more solid' (necessitating living in the country). But since Desmond believed that nothing but the best literary production was worth the sacrifice of any life or human relation – 'and he has no *conviction* that the best is in him' – it was not something he would do lightly. Then Desmond declared himself, and tried to get Cynthia to reciprocate. He called her 'angel' and kissed her hand. There are not many occasions when it is distasteful to read Cynthia's evocative, witty and heart-felt diaries, but this is one of them, as she carefully remembers, almost gloats over, Desmond's phraseology – 'You are just delicious and delightful to me', 'the worst of it is that you are so *seriously* to be loved' – since one knows that it can only bring unhappiness for Desmond.

> I was very tongue-tied and he expressed great concern at having 'worried' me – I do feel the difficulty of the situation. He obviously has real qualms as to future developments and I suppose I ought to be self-sacrificing and make him cut his losses at this early stage – I doubt whether what I could give him would make the disturbance worth while – and even from my own point of view I don't know that another indispensable friend is desirable. But the deliberate sacrifice is a lot to ask of myself. He is *such* a luxury and the only man now who makes me bubble and bloom and sparkle.[33]

The next day Desmond left a note apologising for making Cynthia feel tired, adding that 'if what I feel for you turns into *l'amour triste* I shall be no good to you at all & despise myself'.[34] Cynthia replied, copying the whole letter into her diary; and again one cannot but wonder whether this was because she had already written this letter so many times already that this time she was going to play safe: when, in the future, she needed to write to a would-be lover whom she was advising to baulk at the last fence, she would not have to think it out all over again. She wrote a four-page letter, the gist of which was, first of all, her apology for being tongue-tied, and her protestation about how happy he had made her. 'I do *loathe* to think I may only develop into something not worth while – a worry and inconvenience – just a disturbance.' She reiterates that she is a cat who walks alone, that she does not want to lose Desmond as a friend, that she understands he has a dread of *l'amour triste*, but that he has made her very happy. Desmond's reply was 'a perfect brief letter' – 'My dear – don't put my candle out', a response to Cynthia's saying 'in so far as you may be a moth and I may be a candle you can tell me to put myself out.'

'Four days abstinence from my company' was the penance Desmond set himself. When it was accomplished he took Cynthia to Hampton Court, 'a very happy afternoon – Hand captured in taxi'. At their next meeting Cynthia evidently allowed a little more than hand holding (the date is embellished with a flower, in exactly the same way that Mary Elcho used to decorate a significant date in her diary). This intimacy prompted Cynthia to write a long letter, a 'jeremiad' (Souls word for a grumble) mostly about John. Desmond's reply was long and tender, 'divine gloriously long . . . perfect letter'.

> O my dear, when I think that your love of John may be – is – mingled with a terrible shrinking from him, it seems that nothing in life could make up for that for you . . . If John is going on living in a chaotic little dream world of his own, you can always be faithful to him; but it will be better if you cease to love him. Perhaps already love for him is beginning to die. For love, though it can live without return, cannot last long unless it receives some delight as well as pain from the object of it. If you do cease to love him be glad. This sounds very harsh, but it does not mean that you forsake him.[35]

The gist of this rather rambling letter was that Cynthia should go on loving John but should 'keep your heart for life' – she should have a separate compartment in her mind labelled John so that her misery about him did not make all of life miserable. The letter is magnificent in its way, yet it is an indication of why Desmond remained an essayist: beautifully written, in the most exquisite handwriting, yet throughout its seven tender and concerned pages it says little more than what is summarised by the sentences above.

After spending Christmas with the Morrells at Garsington, Desmond travelled to Pixton and, despite Beb's presence, saw a great deal of Cynthia on her own. But he was depressed, partly because he had never seen the Asquiths together before, partly because Cynthia was now in the tired-sick stage of early pregnancy. It was only after he had left and she had gone to the Wharf that she wrote to tell him she was pregnant ('this gives me a certain placidity and sense of direction'[36]). 'That is the best thing that could have happened to you I believe' wrote the kindly Desmond, expressing neither envy that this Armistice baby was not his, nor sadness that it would inevitably provide a barrier between him and its mother.

Meetings in January were quite frequent, despite Desmond's flu and exile to Littlehampton in order to work and to convalesce. At the beginning of February he took Cynthia to Box Hill, an hour's drive from London, to enjoy the clean snow and crisp air. It was to be the last occasion that they felt close to each other; a year after their first meeting, as always with Cynthia's relationships, the downward turn was beginning. On this occasion she wrote 'felt very comfortable, intimate and mutually delighted'[37] – but she was not to do so again. By the end of the month, when both of them had been at the same dinner party *chez* the Herberts, Desmond 'felt as though I had been shot away from you into – no – not into space, but into, say October 1918 as far as our relation was concerned'.[38] Cynthia, revivified, asked him to explain this remark, but Desmond could not; he did tell her that 'you had not for some time talked to me about yourself . . . as though it signified that it was no longer so natural to you to be intimate with me . . . I *know* you are a joy and a treasure to me and if I try to understand you it is that I may not lose you'.[39]

Cynthia, in reply, expressed her appreciation that at least Desmond had not dubbed her 'elusive'. 'Ever since I was five I have been bullied about being elusive and mysterious and I have no wish to be "a sphinx without a secret". If I have talked less of myself it is not due to my resolution of reticence but merely that at present I am not very conscious and feel rather in a parenthesis and in a skimming mood.'[40] Despite this protestation, there was no escape: once Desmond had declared himself the only retreat was backwards into elusiveness. It was the best way of avoiding confrontation. From now on, although she saw Desmond regularly, their relationship began to change. Her letters became shorter than ever (she rarely wrote long letters, usually covering two or three sides with a rather hurried air and often her letters began 'this is not a letter'). At the end of March Desmond wrote, 'your letter was such a humbug of a letter: folded into four inside a flimsy envelope it looked so bulky, and crackled promisingly – then, O, inside!'[41] He was gloomy ('my self-respect, some of my friendships, my income, my health all want seeing to'), Cynthia was pregnant, Beb was back, and Desmond as a would-be lover was less enticing than Desmond as an attentive, literary friend. At Thorpeness in May Cynthia remarked that 'he is afraid that he has proved a disappointment to me in the way of a 'tonic' – that he gained my friendship on a false basis and that now I must have discovered that he really belonged to the "weary and dreary" . . . I was as inarticulate as ever'.[42] And it was true that Desmond had been talking a good deal to Cynthia about money, his children, his lack of impetus to write, and having rejected the role of mistress, she must have been feeling a little like a secondary wife.

For a while both of them tried to recapture some of the mental stimulation they had given each other. Cynthia declared, 'you are articulate, so please justify me to myself. Perhaps I am a "good work" to you, like a day's slumming?'[43] Desmond replied, 'you must be fond of me . . . I shall talk to you on my walk and expect a definite assurance on that point'. But, a month later, when Cynthia was hot, unwell and eight months pregnant, he wrote a little tetchily, 'somehow your last two letters – I could see no affection in them and I thought that they showed you liked getting *a* good letter better than hearing from me'.[44] There were to be lots of good letters over the next few months because in September Desmond went to South Africa. 'He will get £800 (£9000) for it', Cynthia had noted 'and it will only absorb 3 months of his life. Amongst his duties he has to build a house, help Paley to write a book and write one himself'.[45] On 21 September 1919

Desmond came to say goodbye for really the last time. He exhausted me poor dear – I felt he wanted me to rise to the occasion and say something emotional. I failed dismally and as usual must have resource to my pen. He lingered and lingered over his goodby clinging to my unresponsive hand and looking abjectly miserable. I kept getting a confused impression that he was going to the Front. As a matter of fact those awful goodbyes were generally slurred over – this which after all is only for three months was very much dramatised.

While Desmond was away Cynthia became very depressed. When he came back she was beginning, slowly, to recover from her unhappiness. But, whatever efforts he made, he was unable to be lover-like ever again; in future they would be close friends (on V.E. Day 1945 Desmond asked her 'do you remember sitting on the paw of a Trafalgar Square lion on November 11th 1918?') but the excitement and intimacy had gone. In a last, splendid letter Desmond analysed the reasons. Bemoaning their lack of time alone together, he referred to their lack of physical relations.

> Then, I have made great efforts in our relation to sink the He & She – because – for complex reasons, in which fear and the more respectable motive, the idea that there was more room for me in your life if I did, played parts. But in doing so, I extinguished that ardour which is best able to melt reserve and make even 10 minutes to bear fruit in intimacy; even between such people as you and I. And I was disturbed by the thought how easy it might be for any one who did *not* put that restraint on himself to reach you and give you (though you might not value it more) a better time.

He went on to deplore his own restraint and dullness, for waiting for the right moment (which never came). And he observed that he had begun to realise that in the part of Cynthia's life to which he had confined himself he now had a rival. Generously, unhappily, but without bitterness he concluded thus: 'In Barrie you had that kind of loving, considerate, intimately appreciative friend, and not only could he be far more useful but he had oceans of time in which to make you aware of what he was to you and you to him. No woman *needs* two Barries or two Desmonds, though she may hate losing one of them'.[46]

·····ᕬ· Chapter 27 ·ᕬ·····
Barrie

A Dulcinea is a necessity to Barrie. Sentiment is only irritating to an onlooker, and when it is combined with playfulness and real kindness and springs from a cold detached heart, it is a delicate tactful thing delightful to receive. Barrie, as I read him, is part mother, part hero-worshipping maiden, part grandfather, and part pixie with no man in him at all.[1]

Desmond MacCarthy, when he wrote these words to Cynthia, had only known her for a short while. Yet he was intuitive enough to realise that a Barrie was what she had been searching for. It would be no exaggeration to say that her life had been leading up to her involvement with J. M. Barrie, (who was, when she met him, one of the most famous men in England). In so many ways her life became smoother and happier once it had become entwined with Barrie's – a large part of her life's search was over.

Barrie was born in 1860 (three years after Cynthia's father). His family was Scottish and lived near Dundee, at Kirriemuir, further north than Gosford. He was the seventh child of a family of eight and, like Cynthia, he had lost a beloved brother when he was very vulnerable. To Barrie's mother her dead son remained a boy of thirteen who would never grow to manhood; her grief was described by Barrie in *Margaret Ogilvie* (Scottish women kept their maiden names). One of her characteristics was her reluctance to give up games. 'The horror of my boyhood was that I knew a time would come when I also must give up the games, and how it was to be done I saw not (this agony still returns to me in dreams, when I catch myself playing marbles, and look on with cold displeasure); I felt that I must continue playing in secret.'[12]

By the year of Cynthia's birth Barrie had been in London for nearly three years and was a successful journalist, writing articles for numerous publications: before he was thirty he was an established man of letters. Despite his early rise to fame he continued to harbour very complicated feelings about his family background, and would pretend that it was severely impoverished when in fact it was merely straitened middle-class. Nor did his appearance add to his self-confidence: with sallow skin, sunken eyes with shadows round them and a height of five foot three and a half inches he knew that he would never be conventionally good-looking and instead established a *persona* based both on charm and moodiness. Although he could be witty and entertaining he was often implacably silent, and Cynthia, who had already seen a few parallels to Mr Darling in her father, now found something of him in Barrie, especially his sulkiness. All her life she had been a practised 'cajoler' and with Barrie she was going to need all her resourcefulness.

At the age of thirty-five he had become a successful novelist with a wide circle of literary and theatrical friends, and soon he had also become a playwright. And he was married, to an actress named Mary Ansell who, on her honeymoon, bought a St Bernard puppy called Porthos on which to lavish the love that Barrie could not reciprocate. Courtship by letters he certainly was capable of ('the emotional frankness with which Barrie could always write but never speak'[3] was his friend A. E. W. Mason's summing up) but verbal or physical courtship he was not. Barrie found women very far from distasteful, but his marriage was a mistake. Before and after he met Mary he was attentive to women, particularly to the leading ladies in his plays; but if she had seen a notebook he had kept while at Edinburgh university she might have held back.

Men can't get together without talking filth.
He is very young looking – trial of his life that he is always thought a boy.
Far finer and nobler things in the world than loving a girl & getting her.
Greatest horror – dream I am married – wake up shrieking.
Grow up & have to give up marbles – awful thought.
Want to stop everybody in street & ask if they've read 'The Coral Island.' Feel sorry for if not.

Want to go into shop & buy brooch for child, but don't dare.[4]

Lawrence understood Barrie's nature when he described him as Bertie Reid in 'The Blind Man', a short story written in November 1918 just after Cynthia's life had started to become enmeshed with Barrie's.

> Bertie was a barrister and a man of letters, a Scotchman of the intellectual type, quick, ironical, sentimental, and on his knees before the woman he adored but did not want to marry . . . He was a bachelor, three or four years older than Isabel. He lived in beautiful rooms overlooking the river, guarded by a faithful Scottish man-servant. And he had his friends amongs the fair sex – not lovers, friends. So long as he could avoid any danger of courtship or marriage, he adored a few women with constant and unfailing homage, and he was chivalously fond of quite a number. But if they seemed to encroach on him, he withdrew and detested them . . . He was ashamed of himself, because he could not marry, could not approach women physically. He wanted to do so. But he could not. At the centre of him he was afraid, helplessly and even brutally afraid. He had given up hope, had ceased to expect any more that he could escape his own weakness. Hence he was a brilliant and successful barrister, also litterateur of high repute, a rich man, and a great social success. At the centre he felt himself neuter, nothing.[5]

It was not until the end of 1897, when he was nearly forty and she was just thirty-one, the same age as Cynthia would be in 1918, that Barrie met Sylvia Llewelyn Davies and discovered his life's obsession: the worship of mothers and their children. He had already made friends with Sylvia's three sons in Kensington Gardens. Walking Porthos, he would meet up with the boys, George and Jack (Peter was still a baby) and entertain them with games and stories. Now that he had met their beautiful mother (like Cynthia she had a charmingly upturned nose and wide-apart eyes) he could entertain her too.

Sylvia was one of the daughters of George du Maurier who wrote *Trilby*, the novel that had inspired in Cynthia a desire to visit the Paris Morgue. She was the middle one of five, being younger than Trixie and Guy and older than May and Gerald, and had been brought up in Hampstead. Her husband was a moderately successful barrister; they were not well off but were very happy together ('there never was a simpler happier family until the coming of Peter Pan'). Sylvia and Arthur's sons were, at least in their photographs, most unusually lovely children, and the family had five and a half years together before the New

Year's Eve dinner party at which Barrie and Sylvia met. 'If only I hadn't accepted that invitation to dine' bemoans Mr Darling to his wife on returning home to find that his children have flown away to the Neverland with Peter Pan. 'It was shortly to become Arthur's cry too' commented Andrew Birkin astutely in his classic biography *J. M. Barrie and The Lost Boys*, adding that 'in the Davies family he had found what he had been searching for all his adult life – a beautiful woman who embodied motherhood, a brood of boys who epitomized boyhood – and he did not mean to let them go'.[6] The essential ingredient for Barrie was that Sylvia was happily married. Thus he could adore her without feeling physically threatened. He could also adore her boys.

As is well known from Birkin's book, Barrie insinuated himself into the Llewelyn Davies's life to a distasteful extent. Sylvia was an exceptional person, charming, dignified and brave. Although rather fastidious and self-contained she was adored by her children. She would not have known how to be rude to Barrie and it was soon accepted that he was inextricably bound up in her life and in the life of her family; whether he cushioned her life with actual gifts of money is not known, but he certainly made it much easier. For, admirably, he was never parsimonious – when his agent was prosecuted for embezzling his money in 1906 (£16,000 – half a million pounds – is the reputed sum involved) Barrie always felt very much to blame because he simply had not *noticed*. Allegedly his total earnings that year had been £44,000 (over one and a quarter million pounds).

In the August of 1899 Barrie and the Llewelyn Davies's rented seaside homes near each other. On the beach Barrie continued to entertain the boys with stories that were later to reappear in *Peter Pan* and with the games that he had played as a child. Soon, at his country cottage, they were to play games based on pirates, red Indians and desert islands. The model was Barrie's favourite book as a boy, *Coral Island*.

Fifty years later, when Peter Llewelyn Davies wrote *The Morgue* (an informal history of his family's involvement with Barrie compiled through reminiscences and letters), he asked his former nanny: 'Did J. M. B's entry into the scheme of things occasionally cause ill-feeling or quarrellings between mother and father?' She told him that 'the Barries were overwhelming (and found your mother's help, grace & beauty a great asset in meeting the right people, etc) – aided by Mrs du Maurier – always ambitious for her favourite daughter'.[7] For the gain was not all one-sided: Barrie certainly brought his adopted family into contact with many theatrical and interesting people.

In 1900 and 1903 Sylvia gave birth to her fourth and fifth sons, Michael and Nico. The day before the latter was born, a few days before Cynthia and Beb met on the ice in Dresden, Barrie began the first draft of what, the following Christmas, was performed as *Peter Pan*. The new baby was only a month old, and the play still in draft form, when Arthur, at last, decided it was time to remove his family from Barrie's reach. Two years earlier the latter had moved north of the park in order to be nearer the Llewelyn Davies's in Kensington Park Gardens. Now, ostensibly to live more cheaply and to be near a good school, they were to move twenty-five miles outside London.

But Sylvia could not, by now, do without Barrie. As Andrew Birkin observed:

> She had, in Peter's words, an 'innate and underlying tendency towards melancholy, a constant awareness of the *lacrimae rerum*', counterbalanced by an appetite for luxury that Arthur neither shared nor could hope to satisfy. She once teased his sister Margaret's socialist principles by exclaiming, 'I should love to have money. I should like to have gold stays and a scented bed and *real* lace pillows!' Barrie was in a position to gratify those whims. Denis Mackail wrote, 'He was rich; in a way he was extraordinarily innocent; and if Sylvia Davies used him – which she was undoubtedly doing by this time – as a kind of extra nurse, extremely useful fairy-godmother, or sometimes even errand boy, it wasn't in her character to resist that amount of temptation. More, for her, never existed'.[8]

Sylvia's only drawback for Barrie, was that she was not an aristocrat by birth, even if she was one naturally. However quite soon Barrie began to make the acquaintance of enough duchesses to satisfy that side of his nature.*

But Arthur had not acted quickly enough. Two years after the exodus from London, he was found to have cancer of the mouth and was operated on in a nursing home in Portman Mansions. Barrie's role as a friend came into its own with Arthur's illness and no praise was great enough for his acting out of the role of comforter and organiser. 'Mr Barrie is our fairy prince, much the best fairy prince that was ever born because he is *real*' Sylvia

---

*He became a close friend of Millicent, Duchess of Sutherland. She had aspirations both as a novelist and social reformer and had a daughter called Rosemary who was so like Cynthia that one had 'actually been mistaken' for the other. He was also a friend of Aubrey Herbert's cousin Lord Lucas, of Pamela Lytton and of Brenda Dufferin.

wrote and told Michael. And it was after Arthur's last illness that Barrie's place in his family became unquestioned. Peter wrote in *The Morgue*: 'How strange the mentality of J. M. B., whose devotion to Sylvia seems to have thriven on her utter devotion to Arthur, as well as on his own admiration for him. It would be misleading to call his devotion more dog-like than man-like; there was too much understanding and perception in it – not to mention the element of masterfulness'.[9] (Cynthia was to encourage the masterful element more than Sylvia. In his letters to the latter Barrie signed himself 'Your loving J. M. B.' but to Cynthia he was 'loving Master'.)

Arthur was buried in Hampstead Churchyard next to his father-in-law. Sylvia moved back to London, to a house on Campden Hill Square near Kensington Gardens. 'Very early in the proceedings J. M. B. affixed to the dining-room ceiling, by means of a coin adroitly spun, the penny stamp with which he used to hall-mark his acquaintances' houses, whether he effectually owned them or not.'[10] Sylvia's feelings in the years following her husband's death were summed up by Peter:

> That [she] found him a comforter of infinite sympathy and tact, and a mighty convenient slave, and that she thankfully accepted his money as a gift from the gods to herself and her children – all that is clear enough. I think that she laughed at him a little, too, and was a little sorry for him, with all his success, as anyone who knew him well and liked him was more or less bound to be.[11]

The actual nature of her relations with Barrie will never be known, but they proved as enigmatic to outsiders as Cynthia's were to be. In 1909, Barrie and his wife were divorced because of the non-consummation of their marriage; she was to marry Gilbert Cannan, a novelist more than fifteen years younger than her who was a friend of Middleton Murry, Lawrence and other young writers. In the week that the divorce case was heard Sylvia, who had been unwell since the beginning of the year 'suffering great pain (I think close to the heart)' was diagnosed as having cancer in that region. Arthur had contracted his cancer in the mouth, the organ with which he carried out his profession and wooed his wife: she contracted it in the organ of feeling, the seat of tenderness and of grief.

Peter, who was then twelve, 'received an impression of direness and fatality, and a sense of shocked misery and half-comprehending desolation, which has remained with me ever since.'[12] At first his mother's illness was not thought to be serious and it was Barrie's divorce rather than their sister's illness that was the main subject of discussion between May and Trixie, the latter commenting that 'I do think [Mary] deserves something to make up for what she has probably suffered in seeing J. entirely wrapped up in someone else's children when it was very obviously his fault that she had none . . . I have by the bye often heard you & Coley [May's husband] say she might be forgiven if she did seek consolation'.[13]

Just before Christmas 1909 Barrie moved into a flat in Adelphi Terrace House in Robert Street off the Strand; his departure from Kensington was curiously timed given that Sylvia, though dying, was not dead yet. She was by now very weak and was in a bath-chair; Barrie was her chief attendant and accompanied her and the boys when, in August, she insisted on taking them on a fishing holiday on Exmoor, quite near to Pixton and even nearer to Porlock. It was in their rented farmhouse that Sylvia died. She was very nearly forty-four, the age Arthur had been when he died, and had gone on living for a little more than three years after him; the desperate grief she felt at his death cannot be doubted, nor can there be any doubt that although she allowed Barrie into her life out of the kindness of her heart, she never allowed him to be anything *more* than a friend. Nevertheless, Jack claimed later that Barrie had told him that Sylvia had promised to marry him; he also told Nico, upon his marriage in 1926, that 'we would have been married had your mother lived'. But Peter wrote in *The Morgue*:

> J. M. B. was quite capable of imagining, and of coming in the end to believe, such a might-have-been . . . But it does seem to me that a marriage between Sylvia, the widow, still so beautiful in her forty-fourth year, of the splendid Arthur, and the strange little creature who adored her and dreamed, as he surely must have dreamed, of stepping into Arthur's shoes, would have been an affront, really, to any reasonable person's sense of the fitness of things. And I do not believe that Sylvia seriously contemplated it . . . Let me not be thought unmindful, in writing what I have written, of the innumerable benefits and kindnesses I have received, at one time and another, from the aforesaid strange little creature, to whom, in the end, his connection with our family brought so much more sorrow than happiness.[14]

A few weeks after Sylvia's death Peter, the third son, began his first term at Eton and was so badly teased as the 'real Peter Pan' that in later life he came to loathe his association with the play and referred to it only as 'that terrible masterpiece'. 'What's in a name?' he asked in *The Morgue*, 'My God, what isn't? If that perennially juvenile lead, if that boy so fatally committed to an arrestation of his development, had only been dubbed George, or Jack, or Michael, or Nicholas, what miseries would have been spared me'.[15] But Barrie imagined that he was doing all that was best for 'my boys' emotionally and financially: far too much was the opinion of their helpless relations, who disapproved of the lavish style to which the boys were becoming accustomed. It was his wish to help them in any way possible that led him, in 1913, to accept a title, although he had refused one five years before. This time he was offered a baronetcy, a hereditary title which no-one would ever inherit except in Barrie's dreams. And if he dreamed of handing it on to the eldest of 'my boys', two years later this dream was shattered: George was killed in a trench in France.

The strain of the war was almost greater for Barrie than for any other man or woman because he worried about first George and then Peter as if they were mother, father, lover, best friend, brother and sister rolled into one: his agony was six-fold. By the time Cynthia met him for the first time, a year after George's death, he had become the morose, silent, coughing little man that he was to remain for the rest of his life. With all her practice at coping with grunting silences, even she was disconcerted by Barrie at first. At dinner with Violet 'I sat next to Barrie and found it a sad humiliation. He destroyed my nerve for ages, so great a bore did he convince me of being. I could *not* make him smile . . .'[16] But she battled on, talking about the cinema and the red bananas that decorated the table.

In 1917 Barrie moved to the top floor of Adelphi Terrace House from which there was a wonderful view of the river on three sides. But the great attraction to Barrie was the inglenook fireplace, just the right size for him (but not anyone taller) to stand in, or sit down on the uncomfortable-looking high-backed sofa. There was a permanent pile of wood-ash in the grate, and the room always smelt of wood-smoke, leather chairs and books. In the surviving photograph the study has the same wooden panelling and rugs and slightly spartan air as Stanway (no chintz or tablecloths or William Morris wallpaper here). It is not surprising that Cynthia was to think of this room as a home from home.

Barrie and Cynthia met for a second time at the end of 1917 when Pamela Lytton invited them to dinner together so that Cynthia could discuss her cinema plan with him. Nothing was to come of it: 'I didn't really approve of it for you' Barrie was to tell her. Then, during June 1918, they again talked to each other and at dinner, this time at a dinner party given by Brenda Dufferin who 'with her unique talent for diffusing ease made shy, sad apparently morose little Barrie quite comfortable'.[17] The other guests were Summie, Claud and Letty, all people that Cynthia knew extremely well so Barrie saw her at her most relaxed. It would be unfair to suggest that since Sylvia died he had been deliberately 'trawling' for a new friend. But there can be no doubt that the sight of this close-knit group would have made him feel – as it would have made most people feel – how delightful it would be to be part of it. Cynthia, of course, as has become evident from the portrait of Sylvia on the preceding pages, was exactly what he would have been looking for – had he been looking. She was beautiful in the way he admired with a tilted nose, wide apart eyes, flowing but contained hair, a full, imposing 'figura' and a slightly melancholy mien. She was married, the mother of sons, and she had tragedy in her life, including a son who would never grow up. She also, like Sylvia, rejoiced in unsupressed admiration and, because she too was married to an unsuccessful barrister, needed money for the luxuries that straitened circumstances denied her. She was invariably polite and, through breeding and upbringing, considered it her duty to be nice to Barrie even when he was in his blackest mood. She admired literary people and liked enmeshing them into her life, one or two of them tightly. Finally, she was used to famous men, either politicians or aristo-crats or writers. One must not underestimate how famous Barrie was when Cynthia met him. When he came to stay with her at Thorpeness and found that many places were named after Peter Pan characters and that there was a path called 'Barrie Walk' he told her 'I pay in notes because I am frightened the man would say "I don't think!" if I tried a cheque'.[18]

When Barrie had mentioned to Pamela Lytton that he needed a secretary, albeit a rather unusual one, to replace Elizabeth Lucas who was doing war work, she had first suggested Goonie Chur-chill but Barrie had not wanted to pursue this idea further. But he liked what he had seen of Cynthia and when, at Brenda's dinner party, they sat together on a sofa it is likely that she told him she enjoyed her nursing or kept a diary or learnt poetry off by heart. Whatever it was, he gained the impression that she was methodical, literate, needed an income and that she might, just might, go some way to replacing Sylvia. 'Little did I think this evening was destined to be a milestone in my kaleidescopic life' wrote Cynthia the next day in an oddly weighty turn of phrase: she was not to know for months, or indeed years, that it *was* a milestone. But Private Secretary was a profession she knew about.

Basil had fulfilled the role for the Lord Lieutenant of Ireland and H.H. had had a succession of them, including Bongie and Margaret Kennedy's husband-to-be David Davies, so Cynthia was at once aware that there would be more to her duties than merely letter-writing. In any case, Barrie told her, 'I don't want "efficiency", I should dislike anybody with a typewriter who could do short-hand and there are very few people I can bear to have in the room with me for long'.[19] The hours would be at her convenience on three or four days a week, would take school holidays into account, and the pay would be, as Cynthia understood it, £500 (£6000) a year. (In fact he started her off at £250, in itself an amount she was glad to earn, but rapidly gave her an unspoken 'rise'.) 'The idea of myself as Barrie's secretary made me rock with laughter – and will amuse me until I die . . . If I act as a filter to his sentimentality, I shall ruin him as the King of Pot Boilers.'

Three days later she called on Barrie and thought that 'his room in Adelphi House Terrace is the most enchanting I have ever seen'. She even admired the 'delicious Peter Rabbit kitchen'. She poured tea and 'the little man' described what her duties would be.

I should have to cope with his correspondence (I suppose he gets hundreds of letters from silly women asking *what* it is that 'every woman knows'.) In time I should be able to act as a filter and exercise my discretion as to what could be burnt – what answered by me – and what should be seen by him. I should also have to tease him to send cheques into the Bank etc etc. He showed me his 'best' and his 'worst' drawer which I shall have to tidy – the worst containing a welter of dusty papers which had burst their elastic bands.[20]

Cynthia thought it 'a very soft job and I think it would be too silly not to accept' and told Desmond that 'the enchantment of his room made up my mind in spite of our mutual shyness'.[21] Having canvassed as many opinions as she could, among them Whibley, Sir Walter Raleigh and Mrs Pat Campbell, she wrote to Barrie to accept.

On 24 July she did an experimental morning's work. A pseudonym was discussed and she suggested the one she would have used had she become a cinema actress, Sylvia but with Greene as a surname instead of the more flowery Straite which had been her putative screen name. 'To my surprise he answered, 'No, not Sylvia, any name except Sylvia – Greene will do very

257

well'; the sexless C. Greene was chosen instead and, presumably, the first of many future jokes made about incorruptible.

From the first Cynthia realised that this secretarial job was not to be like any other. 'It would be much easier really to be secretary to a very red-tapey business man – as it is I feel *I* shall have to initiate all the method instead of merely carrying out instructions to the best of my ability.'[22] But she liked the work enough to decide to do it on a permanent basis and five weeks later, after August in Scotland, started work. 29 August was her first day of proper 'breadwinning': she worked from eleven to one, as was to become the norm. The work itself was not too demanding. Cynthia read a *précis* of his letters to Barrie and he told her how to reply. But as yet she found her role 'socially rather difficult, because undefined. I don't quite know when to go, when to talk, when silently to work'.[23] For the next week she arrived at Adelphi Terrace at eleven o'clock. Sometimes she answered letters, sometimes she tore them up (including some from Pamela and Violet) and sometimes she arranged them in box files. Soon she turned her attentions also to sorting out old prompt copies of plays and filing original typescripts, as well as to coping with royalties.* She found it all rather trying: at times Barrie would smoke, cough, and write, paying no attention to Cynthia. At others 'the little man in the black alpaca coat prowls up and down like a caged animal and occasionally addresses a remark to me. One is at as great a disadvantage as when one's dentist makes conversation'[24] or, alternatively, 'Barrie talked a lot and I *can't* hear what he says'.[25]

Cynthia imagined that once she had done the arrears there would be very little work. But the 'appalling cupboards of chaos' and dusty chests meant that this moment would be a long way off. All the manuscripts were in terrible confusion and she 'got rather exasperated fumbling amongst them'. After only a couple of weeks she realised that if she wanted to continue with the job it would have to be on her own terms. 7 September: 'Stayed in bed mixing my intellectual drinks – Barrie and Maupassant . . . My first Barrie-shirking. I telephoned and wrote to excuse myself'. From now on she was more confident about her job and was on the way to fitting Barrie into her life. By the middle of September

*In later years she was to make much of the fact that she found £350 (£4000) worth of unpaid-in cheques, changing this for the 1942 edition of Barrie's letters to £1700 (£22,000). In fact £350 was worth almost the same in 1918 as in 1942.

the job had become enough of a routine for her to write for the first time 'Barried' and 'went to work as usual'. By the end of the month *he* felt confident enough to 'give his first example of Barrie sentimentality. I had for the first time put my clothes on a chair behind my screen and he removed them saying, 'No – I must have these in my part of the room. I like to see a woman's clothes lying about'.[26]

By now he was beginning to be quite used to his secretary's presence and would talk to visitors while she was there. 3 October: 'Lorraine the actor-aviator was very anxious to get Barrie to write a new play for him to act . . . Barrie sketched several plots which are germinating in his brain – one about the three different types of woman – the bird, the cat and the cow'. By mid-October he was beginning to talk about himself. 'Barrie talked of his youth and its extreme poverty – he never had dinner at the university nor for four years after he came to London – he suffered very much from loneliness'. The next day he came to tea at Cadogan Square in order to see Michael. 'M neither looked nor was in his best form – but it was quite a success and we looked for fairies under the sofa. M was quite becomingly credulous.' By November Cynthia felt 'I am getting on to much more comfortable terms with Barrie. He told me how much he loathed going to plays either written by himself or others'.

It was at this juncture that Cynthia organised the first of the evenings when she and Brenda Dufferin disguised themselves as parlourmaids and served incognitae at a dinner party given by Barrie for Birrell and H.H.

> To my amusement I saw that Brenda's pretty face had immediately caught H.H.'s eye and the thought 'now why can't Margot get a parlourmaid like that?' was quite legible . . . I must say it was the most awful show-up of men's dinners – the conversation was neither amusing nor interesting – but just trickled on from Wilson to Pershing – casualties – influenza etc. I should have been ashamed to have had such dull talk with any other two women.[27]

The evening was repeated the following February with Olivia Wyndham as the other parlourmaid. The guests were Evan Charteris, Tonks, A. E. W. Mason, F. S. Oliver, Freyberg and Whibley. 'I felt a surge of Bolshevism when Whibley grunted away my proffered dishes, instead of saying "no thank you".'[28]

In November Cynthia managed to arrange for Barrie to go on an official visit to France as guest of the American army. She was amused when it transpired that part of her duties was to see him off at the station. 'It was strangely unlike other Charing Cross seeings-off. Barrie seems much fonder of me suddenly. He went near the soppy line talking of being seen off by a woman, was personal about my hat and leant out of the train shouting 'tell Michael not to forget me'. I was tickled by my morning's work.'[29] But she did not miss him while he was away. Although she did not dislike him, he had as yet no charm for her, and there was not the thrill of the chase – she could not anticipate ever taking him seriously as an admirer.

She did not go to the flat for three weeks over the New Year. When she did, to tackle a 'vast pile of letters', 'he made me jump by suddenly saying "You're thinner". What will he say soon and how am I to break my news to him? I think someone must write him an anonymous letter telling him his secretary has "got into trouble".'[30] In April she told him, by letter, that she was intending to spend the summer at Thorpeness ('a nice little bomb to send me on St George's Day . . . Do you remember my little kitchen? Do you remember the sticks outside my door?'[31]) And she asked Pamela Lytton to break her 'guilty secret'. 'Now I know why your eyes have fallen of late when they met my honest gaze . . . I think of writing a paper for the *Mail* entitled 'Secretaries Don't Do These Things' (a stinger).'[32]

In July, at Thorpeness, the first meeting took place between Barrie and Beb: in April the latter had refused to come up either to see the flat or to meet his wife's employer. The visit was a success, although a strain on Cynthia. Apparently Barrie was not inhibited by the sight of pregnant women and twice came to tea at Sussex Place in August, once reading aloud a dramatic version he was writing of *The Young Visiters*. (It is quite clear from Cynthia's mentions of this book that Evelyn Waugh's lifelong belief that it had actually been written by Cynthia was misguided.) Just before Simon was born he went to Scotland for a month and in October 'said he was hurt at not being Simon's godfather so I begged him to be'. At the flat that month she 'nearly died of misery there finding such confusion'. 29 October: 'Dragged myself to Barrie's. After I had muddled through a little work we had a talk. He was wonderfully sweet, sympathetic and understanding . . . I felt we were much more in communication than ever before – but what a secretary – preventing her master writing his play while he tries to comfort her!'

The play was *Mary Rose*. Deriving from an idea formulated by Barrie in 1902 that 'the only ghosts, I believe, who creep into this world, are dead young mothers, returned to see how their children fare',[33] the name of the heroine was that recently given by

Guy and Frances Charteris to their new daughter. The play, which opened at the Haymarket Theatre in April 1920, had much in common with Maeterlinck's work and its writing and rehearsing gave Cynthia an involvement in the theatre which she thought she had relinquished for ever ten years before. *Mary Rose* helped to life Cynthia out of her depression – but its emotional strenght also ensured that she and Barrie were for ever enmeshed.

····>· Chapter 28 ·<····
1920

1920, Cynthia's 'lost' year, saw her slow return to life. Her scars were not visible (if only, she thought, her war wounds had been as evident as Freyberg's) but the healing process was long. November 1919 had been the peak of her depression; by the time she returned for the second time from Stanton she had begun to improve and was able to tell Desmond, just before Christmas, that she had *been* through Hell. She was not for long the sofa-bound convalescent, companionable but inactive, to whom Desmond had rather looked forward. 'Do you realize' he asked plaintively some months later, 'that with the exception of those first few delightful evenings beside your drawing room fire, we only *once* had such a time together since my return from South Africa? The afternoon we rode for hours on a bus & landed at Shooters Hill?'[1]

For, as the New Year of 1920 became the spring, Cynthia again started to be at the mercy of her engagement book and by allowing Desmond only 'those social meetings & those snips of time, a tea, a lunch, a couple of hours, served rather to make me feel further from you than ever.' She promised that things would be different in the autumn. But they were not – and the reason, as Desmond suspected, was Barrie. In her 1919 diary Cynthia was to scrawl years later, 'Left this diary off. Feeling too ill and wretched to continue so dismal a chronicle . . . It was not until this winter 1919–20 that [Barrie and I] really swam into each other's ken, and I did not even begin a short journal until 1921.' Having become

262

an established writer, she had begun to look to the future and to realise that if she were ever to write about Barrie she would have no material on which to base a description of their early relationship.

But she did have his letters. And it is from these that we can understand what happened that year: which was that Barrie became more, and then less, lover-like, and finally consolidated his stance as a blend of father, son, brother and 'master'; and that he gripped the Asquith family with claws already sharpened on the Llewelyn Davies's, but this time neither cancer of the mouth nor heart was to deprive him of what he wanted. Yet a cancer of a sort had invaded the Asquiths' lives. Barrie's hold was so firm that not one of them was to escape until his death in 1937 – and not even then.

At the beginning of the year Barrie was still writing fairly formal letters. But by March it was Cynthia instead of Lady Cynthia and by April, when she was in Northumberland for a Friday to Monday, there was a letter with the first tinge of properly Barriesque sentiment. He had tried to draw Cynthia's empty chair 'with a ghostly occupant, but she always comes out howling like a boy'. Yet he considered this hardly likely in view of her consummate femininity. And he added, 'I am glad the dress promises well. Yes, tell them to send me the bill'.[2] It is the first clear evidence, apart from the monthly cheque of £40 (£450) (paid even when Cynthia had done the minimum of work) of the extent to which Barrie's grip was financial. Worries about money had contributed very much to Cynthia's depression. When Beb returned from France in the spring of 1919 he and she were worth between them no more than they had been in 1910, i.e. £500 a year from H.H., £200 from Hugo, £150 from Mary, and whatever Beb was earning, which had formerly been another £500. But now he was not even professing to earn, and since the cost of living had more than doubled it was hardly surprising that Cynthia should be overwrought about finance. It is not unfair to suggest that when she began working for Barrie she was desperate; that when her initial payment of £500 a year began to be augmented by sudden windfall cheques or the picking up of dressmakers' bills she was in no state to refuse. She could not live more cheaply – by moving to the country and foregoing new clothes from Septimus or managing without four agency servants – and with this self-knowledge some expediency was necessary.

Barrie was the expediency. Yet the bargain, spoken or unspoken, that he and Cynthia struck with each other during 1920 was far from one-sided. Indeed, the story of Cynthia's fourth and fifth decades is such that it appears that she had by far the worst side of the bargain, that the sacrifices she made can barely have justified the cheques. But she worked hard in her unconventional job, and at what cost in terms of boredom, sacrifice and lost opportunities it is hardly bearable to imagine.

Initially, Barrie tried to assume the role of lover, thinking, not unjustifiably, that he and Cynthia would be ideal partners in a non-physical *amour*: he was, after all, dark, balding and middle-aged. But by this time he was rather too much of a father-figure even for Cynthia's tastes; he was irredeemably short, deplorably bad-tempered and more unromantic than any man she had ever met, having all his life used his notorious sentimentality to overlay his endemic coldness. If he were ever to become 'daily bread' it would be in a different context.

Barrie, however, was rapturously appreciative of the effect Cynthia had on him. On 10 May he took her to dine at the Ritz to celebrate his sixtieth birthday, a ritual that was to be carried out for the next seventeen years. As soon as he returned to the flat he wrote her an elated letter telling her how young he felt, how invigorated and witty, and exclaimed, 'How unobservant Brown [his manservant] is – he does not seem to notice any change in me'. Three weeks later Cynthia was addressed as 'My darling Puss' and the letter ended: 'Such an adorable baby, and how proud I am of her, and how I revere her'.[3] On 6 June she was 'Dearest downy . . . I shall go on being dreary till my lamb comes back again. Your loving Master'. This was the first time Barrie signed himself thus. It was a signature that Cynthia was to see many, many times and which, curiously, she cannot have disliked since she did not censure it. She expressed disapproval of the lover-like tone, but did this gradually. There seems to have been no one unequivocal letter, on the lines of the *amour triste* one to Desmond or the many other precedents for it in which she had tried deftly to convert a romantic friendship into a lastingly platonic one. She did not, after all, want to risk a sudden break with Barrie and since she knew that a sexual relationship was an impossibility she had merely to dissuade him from using endearments. Yet she allowed him some latitude, for example to address her as Mulberry, a nickname that he chose because of a mulberry tree at Stanway and the overtones in the name of silk and luxury and rustling dresses. (Sylvia Llewelyn Davies had only been addressed by her second name of Jocelyn; nor, it appears, had Barrie's tone ever verged on the lover-like.)

Cynthia was in her old haunt of Margate during most of the summer, occasionally leaving the children with Nanny while she made a foray to London. The reason for the foray at this time was more than dinners, clothes or the hairdresser, it was to go to Adelphi Terrace to answer Barrie's never diminishing pile of correspondence. She was always much missed on her return to the seaside. 'My darling Cincie . . . It's sad my lassie is so far away though I know she is being a darling of a mother all the time. What I most admire in her is her sheer goodness.'[4] In July she and Beb toured the battlefields for three days ('it seems asking for trouble'[5]). Barrie wrote to Poste Restante, Amiens: 'I think it good for you to go, must be good for everyone to get nearer to a knowledge of what 'glorious war' really is'.[6] (Cynthia, one might think, was one person who already possessed this knowledge.) From France she went to Stanway. Barrie had long been familiar with that part of Gloucestershire because he used, like Sargent, to go to Broadway to stay with the de Navarros and had there instituted an annual cricket match. He wished he could have been at Stanway with his 'Mulberry girl' but felt that he must stay with Michael and Nico during their holidays. Instead he fantasised about arriving by train at Winchcombe; and being met

by the loveliest lady. The wind had driven all the hair pins out of her, and her glorious hair is streaming down her back. Our hero had thought that nothing could ever again surprise him, but he trembled (for the last time) as he saw her looking once more, as ever, a little more dear than he had thought.

Cynthia had said that she felt 'muffled by the past' at Stanway; Barrie interpreted her feelings to mean something different.

If I was there I'd see you running about at an age somewhere between Michael and Simon – flinging your first apples and then toppling over. Do you remember how you laughed then? So out into the garden and gather me a basketful of the laughs with which you strawed it when you were a child. They are probably still jigging about.[7]

During August, Barrie took 'my boys' to a house in Scotland which had been lent to him by Margot Howard de Walden. It was while he was there that Cynthia wrote her letter exhorting friendliness without intimacy. A slight coldness set in but was short-lived under the impact both of Cynthia's concern and of Barrie's possessiveness. It was already assumed that they would, as a matter of course, dine together on the first night they were both back in London; 'must see you on Tuesday, also'. By the autumn of 1920 life had taken on a pattern which was to last, for both of them, until 1937.

Barrie had now found what he needed. He enjoyed a close relationship with a beautiful, aristocratic woman who wished for no physical contact but was devoted, sympathetic and tolerant of his eccentricities. She was the mother of sons, one a permanent lost boy who Barrie was never to meet, one old enough already to appreciate Barrie's 'way' with children and one who had been conceived just after Barrie met Cynthia and whose childhood could be closely and proprietorially observed (as Michael and Nico Llewelyn Davies's had been fifteen years before). That Michael and Simon, like their predecessors, were beautiful and rather unusual children, was just part of the pattern; that the lake at Regents Park replaced the Round Pond at Kensington Gardens was quite satisfactory since the old haunts were, in fact, tinged with sad memories; that Beb, because of what he had been through during the war, appeared to resist 'the little man' less than Arthur certainly made things easier; and that Cynthia, because of her need to earn a living by whatever methods necessary, seemed to find their entangled lives perfectly endurable – all combined to make Barrie feel happier than he had for many years.

But did Cynthia find it endurable? There is no answer to this question because, once she no longer wrote detailed diaries, she never again expressed her true feelings on paper. Her surviving letters do not reveal more than a transient tiredness or elation, so that to understand Cynthia's character during the second half of her life it is necessary to become an adept reader-between-the-lines. And nowhere is this more true than in her diaries. Before 1919 she was interested enough in her thoughts and feelings to want to remember them. By 1921, when she re-started diary-keeping on a more concise scale, she had lost the self-absorption necessary to the detailed diary-writer (half a million words had been her output over more than four years) yet she did not want to give up a bare but useful record of the day's events. She would have claimed to have become rather less self-conscious, and in one sense she had: the diminishing of her egoism and a pervading sense of disillusion made her care less about writing down her own personal reactions.

The photographs of Cynthia during the early 1920s show that she had rather suddenly lost her looks, and it was not merely because she cut her hair. Life had not come up to expectation, she had suffered too many tragedies, and although she appeared brave, her courage had an element of desperation ('there was nothing else to be'[8] she had told Barrie when he complimented her on her bravery) rather than of guts. John, the futility of the war, the death of so many, Beb's lack of drive, the domestic difficulties she failed to overcome – it was not surprising that life had lost its excitement and her looks something of their charm. And, as she recovered during 1920, in the sense that she began to 'cope' without weeping, she found that she needed to change a good deal. It would not be too dramatic to suggest that she developed a new *persona* with which to face the post-war world. Both the Maeterlink and the Burne-Jones woman had gone for ever.

One of the facets of Cynthia that intrigued me most when I began the research for this biography was understanding what changes took place in her as the Pre-Raphaelite child of the late-Victorian sunlight became a middle-aged woman of the inter-war years. I had always been interested in social change over these two decades and I imagined that Cynthia would be their upper-class exemplar. The changes were not revolutionary. She never felt hungry, she enjoyed new clothes, she did not make her own bed. Nor can one draw large conclusions from the fact that there were fewer Saturday to Mondays in large country houses or that it was becoming an old-fashioned ritual to glide with maid and trunks from the Season, to Stanway, to Gosford for the grouse-shooting. But at another, human level the changes were very great indeed and it is the aim of these last pages to show what they were, to demonstrate how the child of the English aristocracy, hothouse reared in the schoolroom for a great marriage, became a South Kensington literary lady living in relatively modest circumstances.

It was largely her own choice, for Cynthia's nature shied away from excessive affluence. Yet she could not visualise living in straitened circumstances and thus quickly became the prisoner of Barrie's generosity: she was dependent on his money until she could find an alternative source. It was not a joke only of his making when he signed himself 'your loving Master' ('dined alone with Master' she sometimes noted in her diary). Cynthia, although she saw herself as secretary, friend, companion and helpmate, had slowly begun to dwindle into the role not only of substitute-wife and of mother, but also of servant, roles she would not be able to renounce after 19 May 1921.

This was the day on which Michael Llewelyn Davies was drowned by mischance, or possibly by suicide. Cynthia was chief comforter and as Denis Mackail was to write in his biography of Barrie:

No praise or gratitude can possibly be too great for Cynthia during these days. She spared herself nothing. She gave out everything. She shouldered an insupportable weight with faith and courage that must never be forgotten when this part of the tragic story is told. It may be said – and, indeed, it must be said – that it was she who preserved his reason, for throughout that almost unimaginable week-end there were moments of terrible danger.[9]*

Day after day Cynthia looked after Barrie who was literally groaning with grief. His feelings were also remorseful. Michael had been trying to pull away from his guardian since he went to Oxford, but his attempts to grow up had been hampered, and he was known to be unhappy. Whether he was any more 'half in love with easeful Death' than other young men or whether the loss of his parents and a decade of fettering by Barrie made him suicidal will never be known. A contemporary, Bob Boothby, was in no doubt that it was possible:

> Michael was the most remarkable person I ever met, and the only one of my generation to be touched by genius. He was very sensitive and emotional, but he concealed both to a large extent . . . (He) took me back to Barrie's flat a number of times, but I always felt uncomfortable there. There was a morbid atmosphere about it. I remember going there one day and it almost overwhelmed me, and I was glad to get away. We were going back to Oxford in Michael's car, and I said, 'It's a relief to get away from that flat', and he said, 'Yes, it is'. But next day he'd be writing to Barrie as usual . . . It was an extraordinary relationship between them – an unhealthy relationship. I don't mean homosexual, I mean in a mental sense. It was morbid, and it went beyond the bounds of ordinary affection. Barrie was always charming to me, but I thought there was something twisted about him. Michael was very prone to melancholy, and when Barrie was in a dark mood, he tended to pull Michael down with him . . . [10]

Barrie must too have remembered the phrase in Sylvia's will: '*great care* must be taken not to overwork him'.[11]

Until 1921 Barrie had had another focus of interest, his devotion to Michael ('for ever and for ever I am thinking about him'[12] he was to write six months after his death). Now, with Jack married, Peter finding freedom, as he hoped, by working in a furniture

---

*Barrie's influence spread far: although Denis Mackail was the author of several good novels, including the excellent *Greenery Street* (1925), he seems to have felt impelled to write this 1941 biography in an absurdly mawkish style.

shop and living with a much older woman, and Nico remaining good-naturedly but determinedly aloof from emotional entanglement, there was no-one for Barrie to centre his thoughts on but Cynthia. 'You are really all or pretty nearly all that is left to me' he told her. 'If it were not for you I don't see how I could go on.'[13]

And Cynthia, too, liked to be needed. When Barrie told her, 'I can't think of anyone who is so eager as you to give pleasure to other people. Your first instinct is always to telegraph to Jones the nice thing Brown said about him to Robinson'[14] or 'how dear and loving you have been all the time'[15] she *was* eager to give pleasure, she *was* dear and loving. As Cynthia's self-absorption waned and her generosity of spirit grew she was discovered by Barrie and, to a large extent, exploited by him. He had found someone who, like Sylvia, did not know how to be rude; who, like Mary Elcho, undertook friendship as a social duty. How much of a duty it was to prove she could not have anticipated.

····➤· Chapter 29 ·◄····
1920s

The pattern for Cynthia's life that had been established during 1920 was to last until she was fifty. From the beginning of 1921 we know what she did each day (except during 1933, the diary for this year having been lost) yet this detailed knowledge of her movements tells us almost nothing about what she was feeling. There are occasional glimpses ('went to Adelphi Terrace and wept there') but few explanations and on the whole the narrative of the day's activities is unrevealing. And Cynthia cannot have found her diaries very useful because when she wished to vary the tone of her memoirs by 'quoting' from her diary entries she had, unless she was drawing on material from the war years, to make them up. But this did not matter. The point of their page-a-day record was something more than their retrospective importance: they gave her days, and her life, a shape; by recording events she endowed them with more meaning, they were imbued with 'felt life'. *Cogito ergo sum* would have been re-phrased by Cynthia as 'I record in my diary therefore I am'.

What she was, the diaries themselves do not make apparent. The listings of trains caught, hair washed, dressmakers visited, lunches, dinners and nursery teas eaten and talked through, friendships made or lapsed in themselves reveal little. Nor can imagination be allowed in biography. Whereas the writer of fiction can list the diary entries and *then* explain their impetus as she will, the biographer can only draw on factual evidence for her explanations and must largely suppress the mutterings of her intuition. Thus in her novel *Mrs Dalloway* (1925) Virginia Woolf cites the external evidence – 'that network of visiting, leaving cards, being kind to people; running about with bunches of flowers, little presents; So-and-so was going to France – must have an air-cushion; a real drain on her strength; all that interminable traffic that women of her sort keep up'[1] – and then goes on to explain what lies behind it. In Cynthia's case the biographer has to rely on intuition since her subject seldom explains her actions or analyses her feelings.

In fact, a reading of *Mrs Dalloway* provides clues to Cynthia's character which are missing from the little red diaries. The voluble Desmond, obsessed with Cynthia from 1918–21, must certainly have talked about her and her circle to the 'Wolves'. The novel had begun to take shape in the summer of 1922 but had been abandoned until Virginia was given further inspiration by a visit to Garsington, when she found many of the people who were also Cynthia's friends, among them Margot, Puffin, David Cecil and Leslie Hartley.

Always intrigued by her friends' love affairs, Virginia must have wondered what drew Desmond to Cynthia and it is not fanciful to see her in Clarissa Dalloway. It cannot be mere coincidence that the names Mulberry, Sylvia, Elizabeth, Evelyn and Herbert are introduced into the novel; that one of the scenes is set in Regents Park ('looking at the pompous houses overlooking the Park'[2]); that Clarissa 'had a sense of comedy that was really exquisite, but she needed people, always people, to bring it out, with the inevitable result that she frittered her time away, lunching, dining, giving these incessant parties of hers, talking nonsense, saying things she didn't mean, blunting the edge of her mind, losing her discrimination'[3]; that she is 'the perfect hostess' who is nevertheless incurably self-conscious, 'half the time she did things not simply, not for themselves; but to make people think this or that'[4]; that she sleeps in a single bed, 'for she slept badly, she could not dispel a virginity preserved through childbirth which clung to her like a sheet'.[5]

Mrs Dalloway was a married woman whose role was to be a 'good' wife to her husband ('there she would sit at the head of the table taking infinite pains with some old buffer who might be useful to Dalloway') whereas Cynthia, who could take pains, of course, was never, ever merely a wife. What her role was she might have found hard to define: one of the intriguing aspects of this child of the 1890s adapting herself to the 1920s was that she seemed to get her roles muddled. Effectively she had not one husband but two, not three sons but two; ten years later she was also to have four aging men dependent on her. 'I seem to have drifted into an odd *métier*' she told her mother, 'sort of Nanny to four elderly charges'.[6] (She meant Beb, Barrie, 'Coley' and Algernon Cecil.) But one of the 'husbands' would perhaps have preferred to be one of the sons and the other would have preferred to be more of a husband; and one of the sons was becoming almost entirely removed from her life because she had not been able to provide the deep maternal involvement that his nature demanded; while with the other two she sometimes forgot that she was neither brother nor lover nor pedagogue and began slowly to deprive them of the independence of outlook so necessary to maturity by assuming a form of domination which has to do not with maternal love but with the need to be in control.

Cynthia had wanted to be an actress but never was. She watched herself adapting, chameleon-like, to the many parts she had to play, but often she sensed that the casting director had got it wrong and that she was failing to get inside the character's skin. Nevertheless, there were many parts which she made definitively hers, among them the platonic mistress (the two relationships she enjoyed during the second half of her life bringing her unanticipated happiness), the literary lady and the close and devoted friend of many. The most demanding role was as Barrie's helpmate. Although she still wrote his letters and cleared out dusty drawers, the purely administrative tasks had become secondary. 'If only I hadn't accepted that invitation to dine' were words that must by now have been striking a clear echo with Beb for, like Sylvia twenty years before, Cynthia could no longer do without Barrie. Yet, despite his childish moods, she grew to like him more and more. Often after they had dined together she would note that they had 'a very happy evening'. However grateful she was for Barrie's generosity there was no need for her to dine with him on the first night of her return to London, however long or short her absence; or for her to look after him during his frequent minor illnesses with as much devotion as if they had been related; or for her to telephone or write or otherwise 'keep in touch' ('a telegram would have been welcome to inform me of your safe arrival' was Barrie's occasionally expressed grievance). Her behaviour went so far beyond what was necessary that affection must have been the motive. In addition, she admired Barrie as a *raconteur* and as a writer and soon her deep sense of responsibility became embedded in her other feelings. Although he often annoyed her, she could not give him up.

She enjoyed, also, sharing her life with a famous man, and can never have felt that she lived in a backwater while she played such a large part in all that happened to him. She knew that she would be more than a mere footnote in any life of Barrie, in the same way that her mother would be more than a footnote in any life of Balfour. Both men were witty and intelligent Scots who were charismatic because of their fame; while Barrie was all cold sentiment and Balfour all cold intellect, the two were alike in being detached, self-absorbed and under-sexed. Where they differed very much was in their physical aura: Mary and Balfour made a handsome couple, but Cynthia and Barrie must have looked very odd together, and it was physically impossible for him to take her arm without looking child-like.

Cynthia must have questioned her relationship with Barrie, and often needed to justify it to herself – and to Beb, who was not always as acquiescent as Cynthia might have wished. Until the first months of 1921 there seems to have been no dissent between them: in March of that year, two years after he had come back from France, Beb started to work at Hutchinson's as a reader and, since his earnings were far from high, he could hardly object to Cynthia's money-making strategy. But in June he did protest. On the day of Michael Llewelyn Davies's funeral Barrie had gone with the Asquiths to Margate and there they stayed for a week. On their return to London Cynthia began to spend a large part of the day at Adelphi Terrace, reading aloud and talking ('wonderfully interesting but heartbreaking talk'[7]). On 10 June she wrote 'argument when we got home [from a charity ball] about Barrie's plan for taking us and children to France in August'. She was not able to persuade Beb to change his mind. 6 July: 'Sleepless night. Plan talk with Beb in morning. France must be abandoned'. Yet of Beb's reaction to the new plan that was formulated only a few hours later there is no mention. At tea-time that same afternoon Barrie 'was distressed about plans. I suggested his taking Stanway!'

It was to become the routine for the next twelve summers. For the whole of August Barrie paid Mary a substantial rent while she went to Gosford. Cynthia had the pleasure of a month at Stanway and, although playing 'housekeeper-hostess' to her own and Barrie's guests was rather exhausting, she knew she would have a holiday at the end of the summer since Beb worked on in London during August and then took Cynthia away during September. How much happiness she derived from being wifely to two successive men in two successive months is of course questionable; but perhaps her situation was only different in kind from that of other women with varied responsibilities who must often wonder whether they will ever again find the freedom and the solitude to *be themselves* instead of over-burdened and at the beck-and-call of all.

These Stanway summers became something of a legend, and the guest-list over twelve years was a long one. Barrie invited his friends and Cynthia hers, although very soon they had become mutual, with the proviso that, while Cynthia had to endure Barrie's few Scottish relations, he returned to London if someone was coming whom he did not like. Oiled by Barrie's money, the domestic wheels of Stanway ran smoothly and were naturally never alluded to by Cynthia except on one occasion in 1924 when there had been 'wild ragging after I went to bed . . . servants in hysterics over rag'.[8] She became as adept at arrangements as her mother, with no day passing without some definite plan. There was fishing, tennis, croquet and cricket (Barrie organised matches as he had once done at Broadway), shuffleboard and cards in the evening. Cynthia accompanied Barrie on at least one walk a day, tried to find time to be with Michael and Simon and to do some writing. It was not surprising that these Stanway summers proved rather debilitating. Nor did Barrie's temper make things easier. During the first summer Cynthia noted over a period of ten days, 'Barrie's guests very much on his nerves, complained to Barrie in morning and he turned over new leaf as regards behaviour to Gerry [the wife of Jack Llewelyn Davies], Barrie's nerves regarding Gerry worse and worse, quite annoyed at finding her in my room'.[9] On his return to London he apologised: 'How many things I might have done to help you that I didn't do and how often I was irritable and depressed and selfish – it is as if I was trying to see whether I could break down the patience and sweetness and loveliness of mind that go to the making of Cynthia'.[10]

But, with practice, Cynthia learnt how to keep him tolerably happy, and realised that it was the three Llewelyn Davies's who often caused conflict. Barrie could not accept that they had grown up and was never more than grudgingly tolerant of their wives. He only began to be courteous to Gerry after she had had a child and he could by-pass her in his affection for her offspring; Peter had made his escape so long ago that Barrie had long severed deep emotional ties and was content with directing his choice of career; but Nico was not relinquished without a struggle. 'Barrie in great state over blatancy of affair between Nico and James girl . . . argument with him.'[11] Yet if Cynthia managed to make Barrie a little more reasonable about 'my boys' she was not always so successful about his other foibles. He would sulk if his whim was not deferred to and once, as though he were six not sixty-six, berated his guests for choosing to play cards after dinner instead of his preferred shuffleboard. Various topics were also taboo if he were not to refuse to speak. 12 August 1930: 'All well at dinner until Bibs mentioned 'rats' and then an iron shutter came down'. Barrie loathed rats. He had also been 'very surly' with Bibs ever since the time when, having decided to commission Sargent to paint the next generation of 'The Three Graces' he had been put off the plan by her unpunctuality.[12] (Since Sargent had all but abandoned large-scale portraiture nearly twenty years before, turning instead to charcoal drawings, it was not, in 1924, a very realistic idea.)

It was not only Barrie that Cynthia had to humour, there was also Beb. Typically she 'walked with Beb. We had *crise* over whole situation here and I returned in pouring tears, doctored by Mary'.[13] But Cynthia held the trump card and until such time as Beb earned enough to support his family they would continue to be dependent on Barrie. They must both have hoped that Beb's novels, four of which were published over the next ten years, would be a financial success. Yet Beb could never have achieved Barrie's level of riches and he gradually gave up trying to change the intolerable triangle of which he was part. That he turned elsewhere for comfort is certain, having always been responsive to women, but Cynthia never expressed any jealousy. He, after all, had always accepted it when she became fond of someone else and, apart from taking care not to break the obvious social rules, she tended to ignore his feelings. But during their annual holiday together she tried to devote herself to him and to ensure it remained *à deux*. Once when the twenty-three year old David Cecil innocently joined the Asquiths in Holland 'Beb furious at continued *à trois* – absolutely jibbing at any more dinners together'.[14]

Yet Barrie generally needed more soothing than Beb. When, in 1928, Cynthia became deeply involved with her new lover, 'Coley', and, at Stanway, wanted to walk with him in the mornings, there were 'complaints from J.M.'. The following August, when the same thing happened, Barrie went to bed early to sulk. Eventually Cynthia was forced to have 'great crisis and explanation with Barrie lasting till two in the morning'.[15] The next day 'wrote another letter to Barrie – a success'. By this time she was also having to justify her actions to Coley. Since he saw her frequently in London, it would have been absurd for her to refuse to see him on his own during August merely in order to avoid bruising Barrie. When, inevitably, Barrie *was* bruised, Cynthia had to bandage him.

In many ways the two pulled each other down. Both tended to melancholy and both were too intense easily to be able to 'look on the bright side'. Often Cynthia went to Adelphi Terrace to weep not because Barrie provoked her but because she felt unhappy and, with all she was doing for Barrie, she felt justified in giving vent to her feelings. Sometimes he compounded her gloom. 30 December 1926: 'Went out a bit with Barrie after lunch. He depressed me'. Exactly what about is unclear but is likely to have been her feeling that she had enmeshed herself into a situation from which she saw no escape. Her life was not of her choosing, and yet she seemed to have no choice about changing it, especially as she had failed to escape from other entanglements before in her life (Miss Leighton being the most obvious example). But outsiders tended to see things differently. Gerry told Andrew Birkin in 1976 that 'Cynthia, of course, was merely out for what she could get out of it. She was on the make', and Nico described how

> I'd open the door of his wonderful 'study' . . . and find Uncle Jim lying prostrate on the settee. I was the only person who could get him out of these fits of despair . . . What Cynthia had been doing was crying her woes: talking of her oldest (dotty) son and her abject poverty etc. etc. etc. 'Sucking' all sympathy from him and he was a fantastic mass of sympathy (people came from miles away for his comfort).[16]

Nico attributed purely manipulative motives to Cynthia. When he found an explanation for her charm by saying that she was 'wholly wonderful company and snobbery came into it to a certain extent. And she was very, very clever at saying exactly what he wanted her to say', he was merely denigrating her for being able to make Barrie happy. Again, although Cynthia's diary entry ('argument with him') makes it clear that she approved of the affair between Nico and Mary, Nico remembered Barrie saying 'I think you're seeing a bit too much of Mary James' and added 'I'm sure Cynthia put him up to this'. In reality Cynthia persuaded Barrie to be far more moderate in his paternal approach to the still-undergraduate Nico than he might otherwise have been.

No-one will ever know the truth – a statement that would have pleased Cynthia very much since she liked to cover her tracks. The 'elusiveness' of which she had so often been accused was becoming something to be sought after, and to be dubbed mysterious was by now the ultimate compliment. She did not *wish* the world to understand the exact nature of her relationship with Barrie, and when she wrote a book about him was as anodyne and circumspect as she had been in her previous two volumes of reminiscences. She may have been described by Hugo's mistress Angela Forbes as 'alarmingly observant, which makes her super-critical even in a critical family' but she never criticised anybody in writing, almost as though it was indecent.

Cynthia found happiness of the kind she had not experienced since the summer of 1917 when she and 'Coley' realised that they were fond of each other. Edward Horsman Coles was sixty-two in 1927. He was five years younger than Barrie and five years older than Basil Blackwood would have been. He had been at Winchester and New College, Oxford, had become a barrister and had worked in the War Office from 1908 until the year of his retirement, which coincided with his wife's death. He had been married in 1897 to one of the du Maurier daughters, Sylvia's sister May. She was thought delicate, 'thin and passionate and highly imaginative'[17] and allegedly had a better brain than any of her siblings. Her husband was considered charming, a man 'whom everyone took to on sight, quiet, dependable, clever, and with a capital sense of humour'.[18] He and May had had a very happy although childless marriage and their house in Cheyne Walk, with its excellent collection of watercolours, had been popular with many painters, especially Tonks, of whom Coley was a close friend. Both he and May were sensitive, understanding – and realistic. Gerry Llewelyn Davies knew that May well understood the disastrous nature of the bond between Barrie and her mother-in-law. 'I remember being told by Aunty May . . . how, some-thing about Sylvia, Barrie said to her one day, "What champagne shall we have?" "The best, Jimmy, the best" '.[19] It had been May and Coley who had often said that Mary Ansell 'might be forgiven if she did seek consolation' elsewhere and had not hidden their criticism of Barrie's devotion to Sylvia.

Barrie saw little of the Coles's in case they tried to play a part in the upbringing of the boys, despite Sylvia's hope, expressed in her will, 'that May & Margaret would give their dear advice & care'.[20] But when May had died Barrie invited Coley to Stanway and he and Cynthia were mutually delighted with each other: for the second time she was to be the replacement for one of the dead du Maurier sisters. After Coley's next visit to Stanway they met once or twice in London for tea and a walk on Primrose Hill. The following year there was a 'milestone with Coles' and three days later 'explanation with E.C. could no longer be deferred'.[21]

On Cynthia's only day back in London, between Stanway and going abroad with Beb, she dined with Coley and 'he came in for a while. Much Hermes'. It was the first time she had used this synonym for love-making but it was to occur a few times a year for the next twenty years; it was probably derived from a dog the Asquiths once had who, although Cynthia only mentioned his shyness, must have been nuzzlingly affectionate. That Coley and Cynthia made love in the modern sense of the phrase is unimaginable; that their tenderness and their kisses were a sign of their lover-like affection for each other is certain. When she returned from France he 'came to dinner. Very very Hermes'. Presumably it was after this occasion that Cynthia again sat down to write the affectionate but repressive letter which she always did have to write at this juncture in an affair since, although there were many delightful expeditions together over the winter of 1928–9, there was no more mention of Hermes. Of course the favourite walk round Hampstead, tea at Jack Straw's and bus home from Swiss Cottage gave little opportunity, Shakespeare sonnets, *Paradise Lost*, James Elroy Flecker and other favourites from Cynthia's repertoire being the substitute. But then in the autumn of 1929 Cynthia went 'up to Hampstead with C. Lunched at Jack Straw. Long walk. Tea at Jack Straw. C and I dined at Canuto's. Back to Sussex Place. Gossamer garment'.[22]

Cynthia became happier once Coley had been drawn into her life, but not happy enough to ensure good health; Health and Sleeplessness were beginning to play important walk-on parts in her diary. 'To mention both the weather and my state of health in two lines on the same page is a treat I don't often allow myself'[23] wrote Siegfried Sassoon, but Cynthia was not so firm. She suffered from different digestive ailments and until the end of her life her diaries mentioned the more vulnerable parts of her body and the remedies that she tried out. Nor had she slept well since Simon's birth, and was never to regain the easy sleep of her younger self. Yet she could not have done without illnesss because it became a refuge, an escape from Barrie, Beb, the house, social engagements and 'arrangements'; it gave her a chance to be alone. Sometimes she enjoyed a spell in a nursing home in order to try and gain weight, surprising as this might seem since in later years she appeared stocky. Often she looked pale, especially at times of crisis, for example at the time of her sister-in-law Frances's death during a minor operation when she 'looked simply ghastly, very white with black bags under her eyes'.[24] Yet, for all this, she had such an unusual and individual character that her physical presence, though not beautiful as it had been in her youth, was impossible to overlook.

The 1920s took on a shape not so different from that established during the war years. Christmas was spent at Stanway (after the ritual family outing to *Peter Pan*) although the New Year visits to Pixton slowly came to an end after Aubrey Herbert's early death and Mary's conversion to Catholicism. Easter was usually at Stanway and there were regular visits to Bibs at Hewell, to her new friend Dorothy Wellesley and to the Peakes. In the early years Sussex Place was still let at times ('How are you, how well off? – beyond the exorbitant 20 guineas [£225] for the house?'[25] asked D. H. Lawrence) while the boys were at Stanway or in a bungalow at Margate for £2 (£21) a week and their parents were staying at Cadogan Square or, increasingly, at Adelphi Terrace. From 1924–8 Michael was a boarder at a prep-school at Kingsgate. Nanny and Simon often stayed down there to be near him; Beb and Cynthia visited.

As her writing became an increasingly important part of Cynthia's life she saw less of her woman friends. She continued to see some, such as Dorothy Wellesley and Joan Peake, but Joan Poynder she did not see after her marriage, nor did she keep in touch with friends such as Jeffie Darrell or Clare Tennyson or Eileen Orde. Even the Bruton Street period of her life vanished when Adèle Essex died there in rather mysterious circumstances. True to her earliest predilections, almost all Cynthia's friends in the second half of her life were men of letters. She still saw Whibley and Desmond. She met Lord David Cecil who, although fifteen years younger, was to be her friend for life, as were Walter de la Mare and Leslie Hartley. When Guendolen Osborne married Algernon Cecil in 1923 he also became a friend. Lawrence had rather faded out of her life: perhaps Cynthia realised that he and Barrie were so unlike that it was not possible even for her to be the friend of both.

Michael and Simon she found more interesting the older they became. She did not see them a great deal but regularly read aloud, played *l'attaque*, sent them to the seaside and tried to be with them during that hour between six and seven dubbed by Barrie the most important time of day for a mother and son: 'Heaven help all mothers if they be not really dears, for their boy will certainly know it in that strange short hour of the day when every mother stands revealed before her little son. That dread hours ticks between six and seven; when children go to bed later the revelation has ceased to come'.[26] And to John she was as devoted as she was able, which meant that she visited him at his boarding school in Ealing about once a term and tried to spend a few days with him at Stanway after Christmas, his siblings having returned to London. Once Barrie wrote (Cynthia never allowed the two to meet):

> I feel very sad without you I wish I had been at Stanway with John. I would rather have been there with him than with any others and hope this can be arranged the next time. I had a letter from him that rather went to my heart though of course his teacher was behind it. Just a schoolboy letter.[27]

Two months before he wrote this Barrie had had a dream about Michael Llewelyn Davies that he recorded in a notebook. He wrote that 'it is as if long after writing *Peter Pan* its true meaning came to me – Desperate attempt to grow up but can't'.[28] It was also the true meaning of John.

The Wemyss family in 1934. Cynthia is in the middle row, third from the left.

Cynthia photographed by Cecil Beaton during the Second World War: in the kitchen at Sullington (p.328).

Cynthia with Collin Brooks at Stratford in the early 1950s.

Cynthia with Michael and Hase in the drawing-room at Queen's Gate Gardens in 1958. A bottle of wine is being assessed for its vintage; all the details of an ordered South Kensington existence are here in evidence.

····⤐· Chapter 30 ·⤏····
Writing

At the end of 1918 Venetia Montagu had suggested to Cynthia that she write articles for Lord Beaverbrook's new paper, the *Sunday Express*. She would be paid £15 (£200) and they should be rambling and discursive paragraphs about London and people, with historical associations and anecdotes. Cynthia was afraid that social gossip was what was wanted. 'If on the other hand very light essays on topics connected with Society such as "The Post-War Girl", "The Hobble Skirt", "War Painters" etc etc would do, than I might attempt it.'[1] After a few days of thinking the proposal over, and declaring that she could not face her friends if she published *anything*, she 'retired after tea and wrote an article for Beaverbrook'.[2] As she had anticipated he refused to publish it anonymously and the matter lapsed.

Although she had enjoyed keeping a diary, and although she had spent her life surrounded by people who wrote, Cynthia had never yet considered earning money by writing. It did not occur to her that the article she wrote with such ease might be accepted by another newspaper. Then, in 1922, Marie Belloc Lowndes, who was aware of the Asquiths' financial insolvency, and knew and admired Cynthia's written and spoken style, suggested to the editor of *The Times* that Cynthia might write an article for him. 'Got letter from editor *Times* and began article on 'How to sit for your portrait' she noted on 11 April. The next day 'went on with my article' in the morning and on 13 April 'finished my article and sent it off. Went to Adelphi Terrace'. Five days later she had the 'intoxicating experience of unexpectedly finding my first article in the *Times!*'[3] It was the start of a writing career that was to last nearly forty years.

Over the next few months she wrote regular articles that appeared under the heading 'The Woman's View' and were signed 'From a Correspondent'. She was paid fifteen guineas and since she wrote very fast – a couple of one-hour sessions were the norm for 750 words – did not find it a difficult way of augmenting her income. By the end of April Mrs Belloc Lowndes was able to tell Cynthia that the Editor was delighted with her articles and in May she went to see a literary agent: 'Of course he wants me to write signed articles'. Nevertheless, two weeks later she sent three articles to him for, although he reluctantly agreed that she should go on publishing anonymously, he also decided to try and sell her articles to other newspapers. In this he was successful, and Cynthia began to feel that she was a writer.

Barrie took a master's interest in the pieces, even writing one for her to submit as her own. It appeared on 8 June as 'The "Private Private" Secretary' and Cynthia felt a little 'pique on noticing that, unlike my own, this article had not one single word cut out!'[4] To the observant it might have betrayed the unmistakable Barriesque touch, and an assurance she could not achieve:

> You must have an instinct for knowing that he does not want to lunch on Tuesday week with Lady A, but that, if the answer is left to him, he will weakly say 'Yes' and then when Tuesday comes scowl at you for not having invented an ingenious 'No'. You must know that if it had been Mrs B, and he had shouted at you (while in the middle of an inspiration) to tell her to go and drown herself, what he means is that by Tuesday he will want to attend that luncheon.[5]

Among Cynthia's articles over the next few years were Seaside Lodgings, Children and the Doctor, Telephoning, Lion Hunting, A Plea for Rouge, Children in Train, The Plot Shop (all authors catered for), Tact on Tennis Court and Other People's Dogs. They were undemanding to write and undemanding to read, of the type that use up the empty columns of a newspaper without either offending or stimulating anybody; they were perfectly anodyne and, of their type, very well done. For example, in 'The Seaside for Children' most of what she said about shrimping nets, clothes and paddling was blandly common-sensical, although few mothers or nannies can have gone in for the following: 'In the case of a baby too delicate for paddling, sea-water should be brought home in pails and warmed for its bath'.[6] The articles provided a little gentle self-satisfaction for the reader and, too, for their author, who soon found them a reliable method of 'bread-winning' since 'alas, neither poetry nor Poker, however congenial as pastimes, can be regarded as reliable means of livelihood'.[7]

Soon other newspapers took her work, such as the *Daily News*, the *Daily Express* and the *Daily Mail* (which published an article on 'Eclipse of Feet' under the signature of 'Thoughtful Woman'). She was paid £5 a time as long as she remained anonymous. 'I must say,' wrote Barrie, 'I feel dead against your writing anything with your name on it except the kind of thing that you would write for choice. Don't be led away by fifteen guineas'.[8]

Then, at the end of 1922, there was the prospect of higher earnings. A small firm of publishers named Nisbet and Co. wrote and suggested that Cynthia do a book based on *The Times* pieces about children. 'The book is mainly rather playful advice' was how she described it to Scribner's in America when offering them the book (which they took), 'offered from recollections of child-hood and observation as a grown up. It dwells on how much parents can do in the way of editing life both for increasing happiness and decreasing trouble . . . there is a considerable economy streak.'[9] It might have appeared that Cynthia was setting out to be an expert on child-care, something which had not previously been an enthusiasm of hers, but her tone was much too light for it to be taken very seriously. Not many mothers, even in the 1920s, would so charmingly have defined themselves as a cross beween a nanny-substitute and a treat:

> 'What is Daddie for?' (as I heard a two-year-old inquire) ably expresses the puzzled bewilderment of a child concerning the *raison d'etre* of anyone whose function towards himself was not apparent. Easy enough to see the object of nurse and the cook. Mother is either a makeshift for nurse or a standing treat, but what and why is this large strange being who is neither child nor servant?[10]

Fifty thousand words had to be written in three months. Cynthia soon found that the only way to work was to stay in bed in the morning and this became her regular routine when she was working on a book. By the end of January she was writing rather bemusedly, 'have never been so happy. It's dreadful to be so platitudinous and find it was work I needed all the time'.[11] By 11 February she had reached Chapter Twenty on 'Dressing Up, much disturbed by children coming in dressed as soldiers!' On 21 March she finished and, after a week of correcting, 'left my poor little book at the publishers'. She had finished just over three months after she had sent Nesbit's the outline, proving that although her prose was not very profound or original, her efficiency and professionalism would always make up for these deficiencies. Barrie ('so much more interested in this book than I let on'[12]) helped with the proofs and upon publication there were some excellent reviews and many extravagant compliments from friends. Eddie Marsh, for example, thought that 'the writing is extremely good – it is so easy & pointful, with innumerable nutshell phrases such as 'editing life', children 'in process of becoming biped' . . . in the future people will be able to realize from your book exactly what children were like, how they were brought up, what the attitude of their elders was to them, etc,etc, in the cultivated classes of England at the beginning of the 20th century'.[13] 'It really is a good book and has a hundred touches of yourself alone' wrote Barrie, adding, 'the distinction of your book is of course the poetic mind at the back of its practicality . . . a mind of virginal purity "edited" it. You seem to me to have a very virginal mind'.[14]

It was indeed Cynthia's virginity, i.e. naïvety, rather than deviousness or deliberate 'lifting', that caused the threat of a law-suit from an author whose book Cynthia had heavily plundered. Mrs Charis Frankenberg was soon to become an 'outstandingly sympathetic popular author . . . a Somerville graduate who wrote *Common Sense in the Nursery* (which went into several editions between 1922 and 1954) at a time when it seemed to her that there was absolutely nothing worth reading on the subject around'.[15] When Cynthia's book appeared only a few months after hers she went through it marking the passages which were most heavily plagiaristic and sent her father to threaten legal action. But he, as Mrs Frankenberg noted in old age, was 'overcome by her charm'[16] and instead a note was inserted in the second edition of Cynthia's *The Child at Home* citing *Common Sense in the Nursery* 'to which I should like to express my indebtedness'. Although Cynthia appeared to have copied down many phrases directly, it is possible that some of her plundering was unconscious since she had such an excellent memory; she evidently persuaded the angry father to this effect. His visit is nowhere recorded in her diary for 1923, another instance of Cynthia simply ignoring an uncomfortable truth if she could.

Although writing a book had not proved especially lucrative (Cynthia made about £200 (£3000) from the four thousand or so copies sold in Britain and America) she had enjoyed the experience. Photographs of her and the children appeared in many illustrated papers; the reviews were highly enjoyable public dewdrops; and then there were the letters from friends. In the same way that she had felt fulfilled during her brief period of nursing or was to enjoy her shift as a canteen worker during the 1926 General Strike, so she preferred the shape that was now being given to her life and found that 'I seemed to have more rather than less leisure. I believe this seeming paradox always results from having one settled purpose, the compelling claims of which seem to stretch rather than crowd the days'.[17]

At Stanway that summer Cynthia wrote a short story for children, 'my first attempt at fiction' and in the autumn she contributed a chapter on 'The Nurseries' to *The Queen's Dolls' House*, a limited edition book with chapters on various aspects of the recently completed Queen Mary's Dolls' House, now at Windsor Castle, which had been designed by Lutyens. The miniature theatre displays the set for *Peter Pan* and Barrie's influence was clear even on Cynthia's prose:

> As we gaze on the sleeping forms, the tick-tick-tocking clock strikes seven, and we are reminded of Time; Time, pitiless enemy of Mothers, for ever brandishing his scythe, uncradling children and cutting their curls, defying the nursery nest, sawing through its sheltering branches one by one, until leaves fall and cold winds come.[18]

It was the natural step from an advice book, a short story and an article about a nursery, to a children's novel. *Martin's Adventure* was written in the spring of 1924; it was published a year later by Partridge and in America in 1927. The adventures were those of a boy from his ninth birthday 'until the day he went away to school' and for this reason, while the book did quite well in England, it was not well received by the American reviewers. 'A child, one feels, would resent the false didacticism which is poured into this story. Mrs Asquith carries her definite idea of what a child should like to hear and ought to feel too far for truth or art or pleasure.'[19] Cynthia was hurt, but since she had begun something new, quickly forgot about it.

Her new venture was anthologies and it was for these that her name now started to become more widely known. She knew so many writers, and could write such charming letters to those she did not know, why not ask them to contribute to a book? The initial impetus may have come from the fact that Barrie had agreed to write something; his name was an enormous selling-point and would have been enough to initiate an entire volume. *The Flying Carpet*, an anthology for children, was published in the summer of 1925. It contained 'entirely original' stories and poems by, among other contributors, Barrie, Hardy, Chesterton, Belloc, de la Mare and Desmond, as well as two stories by Cynthia. Her delightful style of asking had met few rebuffs and she always managed to raise the financial question with delicacy, for example she asked Walter de la Mare to suggest the sum he would ask a 'proper' editior for a single poem 'and this "improper" editor will give you that and if possible more when she knows more about her budgeting, in any case I will pay promptly'.[20] In the event she paid £20 (£250) for 'Pigtails' of which she wrote, 'it's enchanting and has all my favourite words in it – comfits, cinnamon and so on'.[21] She subtly adapted her rates to the fame of the author, for example W.H. Davies only got two guineas for his poem but Hugh Lofting (the author of the Dr Doolittle books) got the same fee as de la Mare.

The anthology was a success, ten thousand copies being sold in America in the run-up to Christmas. This, from American sales alone, made Cynthia about £750 (£10,000) minus about £200 due to the contributors. She decided that this was where her talents lay, and she was right, although it was unfortunate for her that none of the subsequent annuals edited by her, either for children or adults, did so well. She found the administrative aspect very little trouble, always wrote a good letter, and had a previously undiscovered talent for editing: the children's anthologies in particular are a clever mixture of stories, poems, drawings and coloured plates of the kind that grown-ups like to give to children and children used to like to read. She knew nearly all the authors of the kind she needed to approach and if she did not know them personally knew someone whose name she could use (Lawrence recommended Oliver Onions). She also had a talent for coaxing unlikely contributions out of people: David Cecil wrote a children's poem, while Beb was eventually to produce a whole volume in this genre. As a reviewer of *The Treasure Ship* (1926) remarked, 'it is an interesting and significant fact that such collections of children's stories as Lady Cynthia Asquith has made should be able to show so brilliant a list of authors (more of them men than women) whose work has been primarily for grown-ups'.[22] It was to be the formula for six annuals over the next few years and for one further one in the 1950s.

As soon as she realised the potential of the children's annual, Cynthia had the idea of one for adults. She mentioned it to friends, including Lawrence ('discussed my 'Yellow Book' project with him')[23] and had no difficulty in assembling another distinguished list of contributors for *The Ghost Book* (1926).

Whether she visualised herself as having a greater editorial influence than with the children's volumes is unclear, but she appeared to make very few changes, considering, not unjustifiably, that coaxing the story out of an author by the set date was effort enough ('the difficulty is to keep them to their word and many reminders have to be written[24]').

But she did refuse things. She had asked Lawrence for a story in October 1925 and six weeks later he had sent her a very long one called 'Glad Ghosts'. But she recognised herself in the character of Carlotta and did not feel that another story using the same theme as 'The Ladybird' was suitable for an anthology of ghost stories, despite its title. Generously Lawrence wrote another, shorter story instead. 'The Rocking-Horse Winner' did use two aspects of Cynthia's character, namely the mother's lack of maternal instinct and her need to make money ('there was always the grinding sense of the shortage of money, though the style was always kept up'[25]), but Cynthia did not imagine that Lawrence would have been so gratuitously cruel as to paint yet another 'word-picture' in a story that she herself had commissioned when she had rejected the first. Nevertheless some Lawrentian scholars have managed to find parallels between the Asquiths and the family in the story and have identified Paul in the story with John ('Nurse gave him up. She could make nothing of him'); others have, however, assumed Lawrence's inspiration to have been a child called Leonora Brooke who sometimes placed bets on horses when left at home with the servants.

Lawrence approved of the idea of story-collections: 'I do hope the book will be a shining success. If it is, do a book of adventure stories: & a book of stories about the sun (not for adolescents this time) & a book of stories about the end of the world. It would be fun to have a sort of series'.[26] In the event Cynthia decided to bring out a book of murder stories for 1927; unfortunately it was once again Lawrence's contribution that caused her misgivings. She told Walter de la Mare: 'I am worried because Lawrence has sent me a ghost story that I really don't think it possible for me to publish. I doubt whether the publisher would. It's very long and I'm afraid he'll be furious. Another portrait of me too which makes it more difficult'.[27] In fact this time it is difficult to see with whom in 'The Lovely Lady' it was that Cynthia identified; surely not with the spinster Cecilia, nor with the warpedly egocentric mother whose death is necessary before her son can become sexually free? But there are elements of Barrie in the son Robert who is described as 'the shell of a man who had never lived . . . he was ashamed that he was not a man'.[28] Eventually

Cynthia decided not to reject the story but asked Lawrence to shorten it by a third and to change some details, for example Cecilia showing Robert her breasts in an attempt to lure him away from his mother.[29] This he quickly did and the anthology, which included Barrie's one-act play 'Shall We Join the Ladies?', appeared in the autumn of 1927 as *The Black Cap*.

After the peak of success for the first children's annual, all subsequent annuals, both for children and adults, sold between fifteen hundred and three thousand copies both in England and then in America. They provided a satisfactory if not large income. But Cynthia enjoyed doing them, made many friends and liked the usually adulatory reviews, even if she had to ignore the occasional adverse comment, such as that about the 1928 anthology called *The Funny Bone*: 'these are the least likely to cause side-splitting of any stories seen anywhere for some time.'[30]

Cynthia was continuing to write for children and in 1926 brought out a collection of short stories. But *The Ghost Book* had awakened a new interest. She had always enjoyed the macabre, humour with a twist in it, things not being what they seem, and ghost stories proved the ideal medium for this enthusiasm. She was to write more than a dozen during the rest of her life and eventually collected them together in one volume; four of them are regularly anthologised. Nor was she content with the stories and the anthologies. One summer she and David Cecil put together a book of questions demanding quotations as an answer, for example 'What is the question?', 'To be or not to be, that is the question' or 'Who is willing?', 'Barkis is willing'. Another year she did an anthology of passages from literature describing beautiful women. But in 1926, the year which saw the publication of two anthologies and her own book of short stories for children, a new project materialised: she became a biographer of the royal family.

It was suggested that she write a life of the Duchess of York to be serialised in the *Woman's Pictorial* and afterwards published as a book in England and America. The fee was to be £1000 (£15,000) and this was not all. As the literary agent David Higham wrote in his autobiography years later, 'I got my first real leg-up at Curtis Brown from inducing Walter [Hutchinson] to pay really good terms for Cynthia Asquith's life of the Duke and Duchess of York'[31] – which he did, for the advance was £500 in England and $750 from Lippincott in Ameica. This was the first of her books not to go to Scribner's; they continued to publish almost all her work, including the reminiscences in the 1950s, but evidently did not wish to launch into the 'royal' market.

The offer came towards the end of 1926 when the baby Elizabeth was a few months old and the Duchess was due to leave England for six months to accompany the Duke to Australia. The agreement was that Cynthia should write the 25,000 words 'when Her Royal Highness returns to England'. But she was introduced to the Duchess before she left and had the pleasant sensation of a large sum of money being in the offing with no work needing to be done for some months. In the July of 1927 Cynthia went to tea with the Duchess: 'She was charming and gave me many photographs but not much information. Very amiable baby came down'.[32] The material *was* rather thin, nevertheless the work was ready for the press by the autumn of 1927, the time of year which also saw the publication of *Can's and Can'ts* (the split quotation book), as well as two anthologies, *The Black Cap* and *Sails of Gold*. Since Beb's second novel *Young Orland* was by then being reprinted for the ninth time, the Asquiths were beginning to feel a perfectly literary couple.

The Duchess of York was published in book form in the spring of 1928. Characteristically, Cynthia managed to end the short biography on a note that linked in well with her reputation as a children's author. She ended with the Duchess's return from Australia and with the first meeting between the fourteen month-old Princess Elizabeth and her mother who was, to her, a stranger. But both mothers, the Duchess and the Authoress, were undisturbed by lengthy separations between parents and children and could not have imagined that anything could be amiss: which, of course, it was not.

> How will the baby receive this stranger mother?
> It is an anxious moment.
> All is well. Princess Elizabeth seems almost as pleased to see her mother as if she were quite a large crowd. Her round face breaks into a wide smile and her arms go out.
> Thus, happily reunited, we leave this enchanting pair of smiling Elizabeths. Two wishes rise in one's heart: that the daughter may grow to resemble her mother, and that for the mother the Summer of life may prove as fair as its Spring.[33]

It was to be a lucrative part of Cynthia's writing career and one which, as the notorious Pearnie, her agent at Curtis Brown, had foreseen, suited her admirably. An Earl's daughter who wrote clear, readable and unprovocative prose delivered on time and to the required length, and who needed the money, was a publisher's dream. And from the point of view of the Royal Family Cynthia was ideal in being pleasant and discreet. Yet they appreciated her incapacity for being over-formal and very much enjoyed having her to tea or, on two or three occasions, going to tea at Sussex Place. Once the Duchess and the two Princesses met Barrie and David and Rachel Cecil; one of the publishers of the 'royal' books 'nearly had a fit when I said I had had Barrie and the princesses to tea and had *not* got a photograph of them'.[33] It was partly because of this atmosphere of trust that she was asked to do the articles and books, partly because she was on comfortable terms with the Duchess and would not have wanted to criticise. But she was uneasily aware of her adulatory stance: 'To see Princesses. Both charming. Shall be accused of sycophantic gush unless I *understate*.[35]

In 1931 Cynthis earned £500 (£10,000) for writing a further 20,000 words about the Duchess of York for *Woman's Journal*. In 1933 this and the first book were combined as *The Married Life of the Duches of York;* the rather minimal advance of £75 was presumably because little new writing was necessary. In 1935 came a short book for the Jubilee called *God Save the King* and then in 1936 Cynthia, after she had finished her novel, agreed to write two books about the royal children, one for adults and one for a younger readership. The titles of both books were, because of the abdication, quickly changed and became *The King's Daughters* (for adults) and *The Family Life of Queen Elizabeth* (for children). Cynthia, on the very day of the abdication, happened to be going to 'tea with York children and governess. Cheering crowd outside. Flash-light photography. E obviously very excited: glittering eyes, twitching fingers. *Millions* of people outside. M.R. enchanting elf – "Uncle David's been such a bore – I've just learnt to spell York and now I am not to use it." Played answering questions without smiling, Happy Families and Donkeys.'[36]

It was a busy time. On 9 December Cynthia's agent had rung up 'to say *Daily Mail* would commission article on Yorks whatever the circs. – £100 [£1800] if abdication, £70 if not, so I cleared my afternoon'. Then, apart from hastily writing the two books about the Princesses, she had to amalgamate the 1928 and 1933 Duchess books for publication in 1937 as *Queen Elizabeth: Her Intimate & Authentic Life*. Again, she luckily finished this before 1937 erupted into 'the year of my life'. The royal books had proved a lucrative sideline in her writing career but, apart from the very occasional article, there was to be no call for any more books or woman's magazine features: this was partly because Crawfie's books about the Princess filled gaps Cynthia could not have hoped to fill. However, in 1953, she wrote some short items: a talk for Woman's Hour on 'Memories of the Childhood of Queen Elizabeth' and a

'Coronation article' for the *Illustrated London News* for which she received £150 (£1500).

The royal books provided little opportunity for Cynthia to write about the subject which had always fascinated her, namely herself. Sometimes she incorporated aspects of herself into her work: her 1927 story for *The Treasure Ship* has a heroine who had 'hair the colour of dead leaves that lie in the sun, and from her soft, flickering face shone great wide-apart eyes, deep grey eyes, flecked with purple'. But when Eileen Bigland, Beb's close friend, suggested that she write a novel, she could not help but be intrigued. She did not mention in her diary that there was any pact between her and Eileen but that there must have been is evident from a reading of the two novels: they both feature a house called Starcross (Eileen) or Star Cross (Cynthia). Mrs Bigland's novel has the additional curiosity that it also features a house called Clewer (which was the name of the family who lived at Lyndon in Margaret Kennedy's *The Ladies of Lyndon*). Finally, the plot of both novels hinges on the discovery that the heroine is illegitimate. That Simon had something to do with these coincidences is clear. 3 September 1935: 'Discussed with Simon whether I should write a novel as suggested by Mrs Bigland'. And whereas *The Spring House* (1936) was dedicated to Beb, *This Narrow World* (1938) was dedicated 'To Simon, who has already made a pattern for living'.

The Spring House has a Miranda (Cynthia) heroine who has one son called Pat and who is living at home at Star Cross while her husband is in Canada. When the war started her home had become a hospital and here she does some nursing, when she is not in London. She has many admirers, one or two of them persistent, and falls in love with a friend of her brother's called John (Basil). He is killed and since there had been a misunderstanding at their last meeting, Miranda's grief is especially tinged with regret – until, eventually, she receives John's last letter to her and she sits in the Spring House (the Pyramid) 'the reassurance of John's love stealing over her in gentle waves. All that large part of herself that had existed only in him need not now perish. She would always have a recurring sense of his nearness'.[37]

Cynthia sometimes admitted that her novel was autobiographical and sometimes denied it. When she noted in her diary 'started reading through my old diaries with a view to material for novel'[38] she scratched this out afterwards. But she did not scratch out a later entry when she copied out 'The Letter'. Evidently John's last letter was closely modelled on Basil's which, if true, made Cynthia the recipient of one of the most beautiful love letters ever written, additional reason for her confusion as to self-publicity or silence. If a good deal of material had not been derived from her diaries and letters, Cynthia could not have written her book so fast. But, only six months after she had begun it, and with only a short time each day in which to write, the novel was finished. Her mother wrote in her diary: 'Cynthia has finished her novel. She has laboured gloriously and bravely with it, doing many other things as well and looking calm and lovely – now that the strain is over she looks and feels exactly like a woman who has had a baby!!'[39]

Barrie read the book in manuscript in July, Mary not until it had been published, more than a week after it had been reviewed. She wrote on 1 November: 'I spent all night reading Cincie's book and I wept a lot as it took one back through the unforgettable war, I think it is beautifully written (tho' uneven) and I personally love her quotations.' She wrote to Cynthia on 2, 3 and 4 November and there seems to have been no hiccup in the harmonious relationship that had always been enjoyed by the two women. Yet Mary must have been very surprised by the fact that Miranda, who refused to be her lover's mistress because of her mother's standards, discovers, after the deaths of both her mother and lover, that she was not her father's daughter, but that of the faithful family friend who had been on close but apparently platonic terms with her mother for as long as she could remember. And Mary must have noticed that there were so many resemblances between Balfour and 'Everard'.

> A sense of bitter bereavement swept over Miranda. She had spent her life with a stranger. She had never known her mother. She had loved an imaginary person . . . She had thought her single-hearted, single-minded, with an infallible code and crystal-clear fixed values. Was it then only for outward seemliness that she had cared? And out of deference to the, as she had thought, rather rigid principles and inviolable standards of this imaginary woman she had allowed her own love to be frustrated! Yes, it *was* her mother who had stood between her and John.[40]

If Cynthia did not know, in 1936, that her sister was illegitimate, then this twist she gave her novel must have shaken her mother a great deal; if she did know then she must have wounded her deeply. It is therefore very unlikely that Cynthia did know the truth. Yet, like the child of seven who had been watching her mother's growing stomach and asked whether one could get a baby without being married, the adult Cynthia had long been obsessed with the conundrum of potential and secret illegitimacy.

Possibly, too, once her father or sister had read her book the news was broken to her for, three days after publication day, Cynthia had 'day of a horrid shock which must not be written down'.[41] There were other possible 'shocks' but the likelihood is that Cynthia discovered about her mother and Wilfrid Blunt.

Despite her private admission that she had gleaned from her diaries for her novel, Cynthia denied it to almost everyone else. She wrote in her diary: 'Infuriated to hear from Beb via Mary Herbert that Evan or Margot or both are saying the mother in my book is intended to be Mamma. Bewildering'. The ensuing family fuss was less prolonged than it might have been because the abdication crisis quickly proved so preoccupying. Soon, however, Cynthia was not bothering to deny that some of the material was culled from twenty years before, for example when Enid asked 'I imagine I am right, and that the war letters were included out of the past? Not that there was any "better" or "worse" about them, but they smelt different, like October and June, therefore faintly disturbed me'.[42] In the margin Cynthia wrote 'quite right – garnered from diary'. Yet, replying to Walter de la Mare, she wrote: 'To what degree is she the author? Except for her moody-ness (which I imagine to be shared by all other human beings) consciously or voluntarily not at all'.[43]

This was not, of course, true. Miranda is like Cynthia in very many particulars and as a portrait it is a curious exercise in the mixing of vanity, self-consciousness, lack of self-confidence, self-absorption – and detachment. Yet it was this very blend of vanity and naivety, set against the realism and quite unashamed egoism of the war diaries, that first made me want to explore Cynthia's character much more fully. In *The Spring House* vanity is, to the heroine, almost a religion, with self-chastisement being the penance; she cannot help her self-centredness, she cannot help noticing and apologising for it, and she cannot help but feel that it is perfectly justified. When her friends continually tell her 'home truths' the reader is meant to remain sympathetic to someone who is almost a victim of her own attractions: 'You only want admiration', he went on. 'You can't stand any heart-searching. All you want is a superficial, stationary relationship'[44] or 'To you people are just so many occupations – agreeable alternatives to reading or a game. You have no objective interest in them'.[45] These remarks arouse a good deal of ambivalence in any but the most imperceptive reader; yet they partly explain the complexities of Cynthia's character.

····>· Chapter 31 ·<····
1930s

Cynthia's life slowed down during the 1930s: her life had become
middle-aged. It was a ritual of Barrieing, writing, informal dinner-
parties, holidays by the sea or abroad, and increasing anxieties
about health – hers, Beb's, Barrie's, Coley's and, at Christmas,
when everyone seemed to fall ill regularly year after year, Michael
and Simon's. Yet, although for long periods there were fewer
demands upon her, she did not *feel* less busy and was frequently
rattled or suffered a 'nerve-storm'. As Enid Bagnold wrote to her
(the two women having recently become close friends, Cynthia's
new enthusiasm for the South Coast often taking her to the Jones
house at Rottingdean):

> I won't say I have not a great deal to do, but somehow I always seem
> to think I have twice as much as I have, I am sure it is what you say –
> this awful planning out beforehand. And as for you I know what the
> trouble is there. You are terrifically desirable. Everybody wants you,
> everybody wants your sympathy and your company and you keep
> giving yourself out and getting remorses that even then you are not
> doing it enough, and tear from Michael to Simon and Simon to Beb
> and Beb to Barrie and so on. Barrie is really frightfully naughty. I am
> sure he what the nurses call 'plays up'. He does just what the little
> children do when they want to be noticed.[1]

Her secretarial duties had diminished to a once-weekly session
of letter answering, and Barrie's grip would, ordinarily, have
weakened. But he at once exploited her need to be needed and

took on the role of elderly parent; since Mary had her maid and companion, Wilkie, to care for her and Hugo had Angela Forbes, Barrie was in no doubt that there was a vacancy in this corner of Mulberry's life. At the same time he cast her in the part of Margaret Ogilvie/Mrs Darling, to the extent of childishly 'playing up' when he felt like it, while continuing to write letters which borrowed the vocabulary of love. 'All days I love the sight and thought of you, whatever befall at any time'[2] was the conclusion of the last letter he wrote to Cynthia nine days before he died.

The mystery remains. Why did Cynthia continue to be so fully involved in Barrie's life that her devotion went far beyond what would usually be demanded by loyalty or responsibility? The Llewelyn Davies boys believed that her motives were mercenary; her loyal friends believed in her shining goodness of spirit, in the need to cherish which was a legacy of Miss Jourdain; nor must the forces of habit and inertia be discounted. Yet the truth was two-fold. After the Great War some spark had died in Cynthia, and her depression in 1920 had left her with the kind of fatalism which both allowed Barrie to ensnare her and made her want him to do so. Whereas some reacted to the ghastly legacy of the war by creating the 'gay twenties', Cynthia did the opposite. It was as if her suppressed grief spurred her on to greater self-sacrifice, whatever form this happened to take. In a sense the death of Ego, Yvo, Raymond, Basil, Alex *et al* had stopped her ever caring very much again about what life held for her. At least she could look after those who were alive to need her; and she could face the 'long vista', which she had avoided looking at until after the war, by being continually busy.

In addition, a normal sexual life having never been of interest to Cynthia (the occasional bout of 'Hermes' being gracefully endured but not initiated by her), she had by now channelled her sexuality into this almost masochistic devotion to Barrie, the nature of which was so similar to that bestowed by Mary upon Balfour. His behaviour to his 'dearest one' or 'Mulberry girl' increasingly became that of the hypochondriacal melancholic, merciless in the way he exploited those who did remain loyal. Often he was impossibly difficult ('Barrie went back to bed – furious because sheets were linen instead of cotton – had them taken off. Soothed him down a bit'[3]), moody ('scene with J.M.B. Couldn't stop crying so wasn't able to come down to luncheon'[4]) and manipulative (Elizabeth Bergner, Barrie's last theatrical love, once agreed with Cynthia that 'what gave him most pleasure was if we pretended to be jealous of one another'[5]). But Cynthia's devotion continued, despite the increasingly rare occasions on which the old charm and wit were displayed.

What had begun in 1918 as a job, had become a cornerstone of her life. Yet financial gain had long ceased to be the motivating factor. The £1500 (£25,000) a year given by Barrie (in the form of £500 salary, and reliable birthday and Christmas gifts) was very gratefully received yet did not make them rich. They entertained modestly and infrequently, had four servants in a not very lavish house and, while Beb had begun to indulge his interest in Chinese porcelain, Cynthia was becoming far less interested in spending money than she ever had been before. It is certain that without Barrie's money they would have been poorer; but their way of life would not have changed. Nor did it once he died, for they moved to a relatively modest house in the country which cost much less to run than Sussex Place.

In many ways Beb began to emulate Barrie as he grew older and became increasingly assertive – though his nature was never capable of being tyrannical. His health began to deteriorate further during the 1930s and in 1932 failing eyesight necessitated a long stay in a clinic in Zurich where he was under the care of Professor Alfred Vogt, the specialist who had saved James Joyce's sight in 1930. His publishing job with Hutchinson became increasingly part-time and he devoted his days to his women friends, his Chinese porcelain and his dog. After his fourth novel was published in 1932, he did publish one more book, a memoir of his father called *Moments of Memory*. Since he had been bitterly hurt when Cis had been chosen instead of himself to co-author the official two-volume Life he was especially pleased when his work was a success.

It was at this time too that he formed a close friendship with Eileen Bigland, with whom Cynthia had compiled *The Princess Elizabeth Gift Book* in 1933 and who encouraged her to write *The Spring House* in 1936. She was an unhappily married writer of popular biographies who was once described as possessing 'a roguish eye, a ready wit, and a raised glass: I think of her always with this last property as if, like her merry laugh, it was a regular attribute'.[6] It was his friendship with Eileen that gave Beb the reputation of being often to be found 'in poetic travail in the Eiffel Tower in Percy Street'.[7] Like his father before him, his fondness for wine never diminished.

The balance of the Asquith marriage was in no doubt. As Lawrence had foreseen when, in 'The Ladybird', he described Basil as worshipping his wife rather than loving her as an equal, Cynthia had become the dominant partner. The ineffectual streak that Beb had displayed before the war, that was aggravated by ill-health and the after-effects of shell-shock, was something Cynthia had long grown to accept. She looked after their finances, organised day-to-day life and made all the arrangements. Beb fitted in with these if he wished. Often they made separate plans, for example Beb never went to Rockbourne to stay with David and Rachel Cecil ('David always seems to put him off his stroke'[8]) but left Cynthia to go on her own, or accompanied by Simon. This separateness suited both of them, and it was not their friends, mutual or otherwise, that caused rows but, as always, Barrie. 30 August 1932: 'Beb disturbed me after dinner having just got wind of Barrie coming to Brighton while we are at Saltdean'. 6 March 1934: 'Fuss with Beb about dining with Barrie. Really too trying. Wrote him long letter. Dined with Barrie'. 5 August 1934: (Peacehaven) 'Barrie turns up unexpectedly. Beb very annoyed. Old cry of 'no family life'.

There was a family life but, as with Arthur and Sylvia, it was a life in which Barrie had to play the *beau rôle*. He came on holiday with the Asquiths, and when they, or Cynthia, were away without him he had to be written to nearly every day. His life was Cynthia's constant concern and worry, and this was when he was in good health. For then of course there was illness. Barrie was by now becoming unspecifically ill more and more often: doctors, nurses and sick-bed visits were an all-too familiar part of Cynthia's life, and if she was going away Barrie naturally managed a temperature. Beb, too, was often in bed, either with a minor complaint, or, as the end of 1932, with a serious one – he temporarily lost his memory and was for some weeks delirious in bed 'commanding a battery in action etc'. Time after time Cynthia would go to Adelphi Terrace to cope with the panoply of illness which was necessary in the days before antibiotics. Then she would have to repeat the ritual at Sussex Place. It never seemed to have occurred to any of her *entourage* to be brave and soldier on – at the first glimmer of illness they sank gasping into bed, thermometer on the bedside table and starched nurse in action. So often did this happen that it is clear that for both Barrie and Beb illness had become a legitimate method of returning to the mother-dominated years of which both had been in some way deprived. One happy summer, 1934, Cynthia was ill with pleurisy for six weeks and, despite the pain, was very happy – 'I loved the rhythmic serene day'. Barrie was kept away while she was at her worst; when she improved he started to visit, often and inconveniently.

Barrie was too old now to be able to replace Cynthia with

anyone else. Elizabeth Bergner, to whom he became deeply devoted and for whom he wrote his last play *The Boy David*, eschewed all maternal feelings in regard to him, being simply another in the long line of actresses with whom Barrie had enjoyed flirtatious friendships throughout his life. Nor were the Llewelyn Davies boys an important part of his life now. He did not see them very often (Cynthia did not see Nico once during the five years following his marriage) and it was Peter, of the three, who kept most closely in touch since he did not marry until 1931 and he was in the habit of lurching from one financial crisis to another.

Barrie never replaced 'my boys', but he became very fond of the Asquith children. As soon as he was at all responsive 'Barrie spent hours playing with Simon and pronounced him the most beautiful baby he had ever seen'. (He was to admire him even more once he had grown his 'lovely head of *tight* marmalade-coloured curls'.) 'Barrie became increasingly devoted to him' and 'Simon's adoration for Barrie grew all this winter' (1922).

Simon and Barrie's mutual devotion continued. They had wonderful games of make-believe – riding in aeroplanes, motors and ponycarts and going to what Simon called 'the Isle of You and Me'. There were many morning bed-room visits. One morning Simon stood over him while he dressed saying firmly 'I want to see your tummie'.[9]

By the time Simon was three and Michael eight the latter was trying to monopolise his attention, 'owing I think to sub-conscious jealousy. Michael: "Do you love James?" Simon (hurriedly and rather frightened – like a lesson learnt by rote): "Yes, but I must love brother most." '[10]

In the mid-twenties had come the possibility, swiftly abandoned, that Simon should play Michael in a Hollywood film of *Peter Pan*, Cynthia Mrs Darling and her brother Guy Mr Darling. But 'my brilliant castles in the air collapsed and I felt terribly flat and sulked'.[11] However fancy-dress parties always provided a good opportunity for Simon to dress up as one of the characters from *Peter Pan* and soon, for Simon's sixth birthday, Barrie wrote the first of his plays for him. It was called *Six Years Old Today* and was acted on a small stage in the hall at Stanway. The following Christmas came *Where Was Simon* written for the two Asquith boys and their six cousins, and in 1927, at Easter, the eight children acted in Barrie's *The Wheel*, 'of which we gave three performances to packed houses. It was the greatest strain keeping all eight children well and up to the mark. The rehearsals were onerous and the company occasionally mutinous'.

Barrie's influence on Simon was marked. It was partly at his suggestion that he did not go away to school but went to Wilkie's, like the Llewelyn Davies boys. Then, after Westminster, Simon won a closed scholarship to Christchurch where Michael Llewelyn Davies had been. 'An enchanting child and he has given a good deal of radiance to some days in my life' wrote Barrie to Cynthia, adding, 'He is rather the boy "who wouldn't grow up".'[12] But Simon's love for Barrie was lessening as he became closer to his Wendy figure, his cousin Mary Rose, who had lost her mother in 1925 when she was six and as a result was often at Sussex Place. 'At parties they were quite inseparable' remarked Cynthia. 'Once a little boy asked her to dance with him. 'No' shouted Simon. 'You *can't*, she's mine. I'm her lover.'[13] But their affection was definitely Barriesque rather than precocious and many were the times that they acted out the parts of Peter Pan and Wendy. In retrospect it was unsurprising that neither of them ever managed to escape the aura of the play or their being treated as though they were in some way set apart ('I *am* the Asquith' replied the young Simon when asked if he was related to H. H. Asquith, meaning what he said).

The concept of the child, and childhood, was central to Cynthia's life and affected all its aspects, from her over-protective (childhood-prolonging) treatment of her sons to what she chose to write about. It was not surprising that her lasting friendships, the ones that consolidated when she was in her forties, were with men and women who were, too, in some way or another obsessed with childhood.* Walter de la Mare was world-famous for his children's stories and poems; Leslie Hartley's classic novels of childhood *The Shrimp and the Anemone* (1944) and *The Go-Between* (1953) were prefigured in some of his earlier work; Enid Bagnold was writing *National Velvet* (1930) and *Alice and Thomas and Jane* (1935); Elizabeth Bowen was writing the novels in many of which

---

*The contributors to the 1927 children's annual *The Treasure Ship*, for example, consisted mainly of Cynthia's closest friends: Eddie Marsh, David Cecil, Walter de la Mare, Barrie, Kathleen Tynan, her aunt Pamela Grey, her cousin Denis Mackail, Galsworthy, Belloc, Lady Margaret Sackville, A. P. Herbert, P. G. Wodehouse, Compton Mackenzie, A. A. Milne, Algernon Blackwood, Mary Webb, Adelaide Phillpotts, Beb – as well as herself. Among the artists were Rex Whistler, her cousin Stephen Tennant and Hugh Lofting.

the theme of childhood plays an important part, especially in *The House of Paris* (1935) and *The Death of the Heart* (1938).

It was with her friends that Cynthia found her greatest happiness. She had by now developed into a most outstanding speaker, both in public and in conversation. It was in this un-recapturable art form that she showed glimmerings of genius – a genius that (before the days of tape-recordings) died with her. From Hugo she had inherited wit, quickness, a teasing spirit; from Mary warmth and responsiveness; from her Fitzgerald, Campbell and Wyndham ancestors the other myriad characteristics which together create an outstanding conversationalist. Although her voice has been preserved on several BBC recordings, they are (since she was reading a prepared talk) not indicative of a great deal. Yet they are testimony that her voice had that deep, imposing quality so characteristic of upper-class women of the period, and the careful pronunciation.* And although none of her friends left descriptions of the way she spoke, David Cecil did define, after her death, why she was such a valued friend. Referring to her gift for friendship he wrote, 'it was unobtrusively in the *tête-à-tête* interview and the private correspondence that her friendships flourished. They were singularly lasting and untroubled, for Lady Cynthia's character was faithful, discreet, even-tempered and unpossessive. Although too intelligent to be unaware of her own attractions, she was also too wise to presume upon them'.[14]

Cynthia's friends understood the art of conversation, which is to listen as well as to provoke (unlike Yeats whom, when Cynthia met him at Penns-in-the-Rocks when she was staying with Dorothy Wellesley, she found 'impressive . . . but he is not comfortable. Must be given his conversational head entirely at meals'[15]). Her friends were not gossips and they were not dull; nor were they sharp, snobbish or competitive. They were perhaps somewhat old-fashioned, somewhat vague and definitely conservative. Some of their characteristics were regrettable and the bigotry of Whibley and Chesterton was laughed at but not deplored by Cynthia; nor did she think it necessary to rid herself of her anti-Semitic feelings which continued to flourish even during the Second World War.

She was consistently loyal to her friends, as they were to her.

---

*Cynthia sometimes sat on the notorious BBC Advisory Committee on Spoken English which met twice a year to discuss pronunciation. 7 December 1937: 'Tremendous discussion margerine with soft G versus hard G.'

As her looks faded (and after the mid 1920s she could no longer be deemed 'a beauty')* her friendships deepened, proportionate with the lessening of her love relationships. Yet she could not do entirely without some form of love: Desmond had capitulated to Barrie, Barrie to Coley and Coley was eventually to give way to Cynthia's last lover Collin Brooks. This need to be always in the throes of some kind of love affair was what fascinated Enid Bagnold who, years later, reminded Cynthia that 'you said, sitting on the sofa, "I couldn't do without love". By which you meant "in love". You said that sentence. And from that sentence, which I never forgot, for it rang a bell in me, I evolved the love-woman in *The Squire'*.[16]

Although Cynthia needed love, conversation was her adrenalin. This had been the attraction of Basil, of Desmond ('how few plays have ever enchanted one half so much as Desmond's small talk'[17]) and of Barrie. It was because of their conversation that she was so happy with people like David Cecil or Elizabeth Bowen or Walter de la Mare who, as a memoir of him commented, built much of his conversation around questions, topics being suggested by free association. His talk was highly idiosyncratic and was in fact a soliloquy for two, and in this form it could not survive in a large company. His favourite themes were poets, words, time, memory, childhood, dreams, apparitions, horror, death and the mystery of life:[18] all subjects of passionate interest to Cynthia who always very much looked forward to the 'usual delightful plunge into metaphysics'[19] with Walter; 'never see him without feeling recharged and sense of general enhancement'.[20]

Because intimate, thought-provoking conversation gave Cynthia so much more pleasure than the chitter-chatter of parties, she went to these less and less, increasingly preferring the fireside chat to the less intimate arena of the crowded room or the dinner party. She still saw Desmond regularly; Leslie Hartley was by now a close friend (he dedicated his third book to her in 1932) and would become closer in the 1940s; Elizabeth Bowen often came to tea, or Cynthia visited her near Oxford, and after 1935 she too lived in one of the Nash Terraces overlooking Regent's Park. She and Ettie Desborough were the two women whose

---

*However, Galsworthy told Cynthia that he had modelled the character of Dinny in his 1933 novel *Maid in Waiting* on her, and described her as having 'a Botticellian mouth, eyes cornflower blue and very widely set' and so on. Cynthia copied the passage about Dinny into her 1934 anthology *She Walks in Beauty: A Description of Feminine Beauty in English Prose and Poetry*.

company Cynthia enjoyed best. She often stayed with the latter at Panshanger in the winter or Taplow in the summer (from where she could visit Walter de la Mare nearby). If her Saturday to Monday with Ettie was during October a great deal of mental arithmetic had to take place since Ettie refused to abandon summer time until November. Monday 15 October 1934: 'Owing to Ettie's tricks with clock left at 10.30 and arrived London same time – very convenient'. She was always lyrically happy staying with the Cecils ('I don't know when I've enjoyed anything so much as staying with them'[21]) and was during the 1930s becoming much closer to Algernon Cecil whom, since the death of his wife, she saw more often; sometimes she and Beb stayed with him in Bryanston Square for three-month stretches while Leslie Hartley's parents rented Sussex Place. A friendship with Lytton Strachey was beginning to develop: when Cynthia met him at Panshanger she 'found him quite delightful. So kindly and concentrated. Like a drawing of God by Blake'.[22] And one can imagine that, although she was quite unlike Carrington, with whom Strachey shared his house, the two might have become close, for he shared many of the characteristics of Cynthia's existing friends such as being literary, a witty conversationalist, liking women if they did not threaten him sexually and responding to many of the same things as she did. But it was not to be: he came once to a 'Poker Hell', once to dinner at Sussex Place (with Mary Wemyss and Algernon and Guendolen Cecil) and three months later he was dead.

Some of her old friends Cynthia did not miss. When David and Rachel Cecil took her over to Augustus John at Fryern Court she was 'very interested to see *ménage* but glad I didn't live there'.[23] And indeed the evocative description by John's biographer does make it seem rather alien to the Asquith standards of comfort. (It is here being compared with John's former home): 'The same smells of beeswax, pomanders and lavender, wood- and tobacco-smoke, coffee, cats; and the same amiable disorder, spontaneously thrown together, of vegetables, tubes of paint, nuts from the New Forest, saddles, old canvases, croquet mallets, piles of apples'.[24] Although much about this would have appealed to her mother and maternal grandmother; Cynthia's style remained resolutely South Kensington; and although she kept in touch with Augustus John, it was Simon who inherited the mantle of friendship.

D. H. Lawrence, Whibley and Balfour had all died in the first days of March 1930 and Cynthia mourned all three. Lawrence's death affected her most since Aldous Huxley at once began to prepare an edition of her letters and Cynthia spent some time bowdlerising hers before lending them. She was impressed by Huxley's passionate enthusiasm: he 'thinks there is no writing in English like Lawrence's.'[28] After this trio of deaths there were none that affected Cynthia until 1937 and in that year her life entirely changed.

The year did not begin auspiciously, even though, in January, a clairvoyant on Brighton Pier had said that 'this is to be the year of my life'. (Later, in blue biro, Cynthia added two exclamation marks.) At the end of the previous year there had been the strain of the failure of Barrie's play *The Boy David* which had its first night in Edinburgh in November and in London in mid-December. Since the London premier was three days after the abdication of Edward VIII and ten days before Christmas, success was unlikely for circumstantial reasons. Yet Barrie's gloom was black and Cynthia had to cope with this while hurrying to meet the deadline on her royal books.

He was not at all well after the failure of *David*, but nothing was specifically wrong with him. One of his doctors thought his case 'largely psychological' and in March a new doctor, Horder, rang Poole, his solicitor, 'to say it was pure hysteria'. He did develop pleurisy and although he was not that ill 'I felt him weighing me down to very depth'.[26] He had become preoccupied with thoughts of death and in early April was 'bothered about having to do his will with lawyer'. Cynthia, in a state of exhaustion, arranged a week in Paris for herself, Beb and Simon. She went to Adelphi Terrace just before leaving 'in terror he might stop my going' but managed to get away safely.

When she returned to England Barrie was thin and agitated, Michael was not at all well and in very low spirits, and at Stanway 'Mamma looked alarmingly thin'. Like Barrie, Mary had no obvious symptoms (both must have been suffering from undiagnosed cancer) and although she had been in a nursing home just before Cynthia arrived this had not helped her. On 21 April Mary wrote:

> Dr Todd came and gave me final marching orders – he is very grim and severe and I fear though very clever and *sincere* that he has the nature of a fanatic and therefore may be very dangerous to old people with spirit but worn out bodies, nerves, digestion etc . . . Got to Beloved Stanway – me a shattered wreck and skeleton – about five.

Two days later, having bravely carried on with her duties as hostess (she took a party over to visit John Masefield) she wrote the last touching sentence in her diary of more than fifty years –

'Miss Hassall was brought by her two artist friends and she was shewn to my room and I talked to her and advised her to go out into the golden sunshine'.[27] She died on 29 April, having never regained consciousness after an emergency operation.

Hugo had not been present at Mary's death and Cynthia's first action was to drive with Bibs to Sidmouth to break the news to him. Then there were arrangements and letters and the Memorial Service at Stanway and at St Margaret's Westminster. Barrie, despite his professed sorrow at Mary's death, was in a bad state. Cynthia wrote, 'Despaired. He was worse than I have ever known him. Quite extraordinary. Really crazed. Unrecognisable. Went back in despair. No doubt it will pass but it is hard to bear'.[28] Yet the next day 'most incredible metamorphosis. "Exalted". Never known him sweeter, nicer, in every way at his best. Staggering suggestion. He says he wants if it is possible to buy Stanway for me!!! And, four days later, dining at the Savoy to celebrate his seventy-seventh birthday 'he announced intention of doing a sort of "King Lear" in regard to me'.

In mid May, after the Coronation and after a 'terribly sad aching day, turning over all the poignant little personal belongings and trying to allocate them to relations and friends',[29] Cynthia's sister Mary was very ill at Apperley. On the day she recovered a telegram came to say that John had died of a heart attack. Cynthia had not visited him for four years and the grief she felt was a re-awakening of past sorrow rather than fresh sadness. She and Beb travelled to Dumfries and saw John lying in his coffin. He looked so much like Michael and Simon that Cynthia was shattered. 'I felt so much long-since frozen thawed, and wept and wept and wept'.[30]

In London again, she began to make plans to go to Elizabeth Bergner's house in Cortina with Barrie and with Beb. 'Beb and I had planned to go to Switzerland alone together, and change had to be broken to him very gently – I did it by note in his bedroom that night.'[31] Then, in early June, the night before Michael's final exams at Oxford, his long-standing girlfriend Didy Battye disappeared. She was found after five days, having evidently lost her memory, but the house was besieged by the Press ('usually about ten reporters in the hall'). The strain of this, after all that had happened in the past weeks, made Cynthia long to get away and she wrote to Barrie to tell him that she had been 'ordered' a complete rest. And he acquiesced placidly with his doctor's suggestion that he should go into a nursing home to be kept under observation for a while.

But the psychological effect of the move to the nursing home was disastrous. Over the weekend that the Asquiths were in Cornwall he declined drastically; Peter Davies (he alone of the three boys had dropped the Llewelyn) telephoned Cynthia and she decided to drive to London overnight, arriving in London at dawn. It was a journey that was to be made much of by the Llewelyn Davies boys who saw the dawn dash as evidence that, for mercenary reasons, Cynthia was so determined to get to Barrie before he died that she stopped at nothing, even driving through the night. But the drive was completely in keeping with her behaviour over the previous eighteen years. If Barrie needed her she went; if he needed her urgently she went at once; and if he was as seriously ill as Peter had described, she went overnight. Although she did not say so in her diary, she would have very much enjoyed her night drive: she , Beb, Bibs, and more recently Simon and sometimes Coley, had instigated a tradition of annual night walks when they would leave Stanway at midnight and return for a late breakfast. If Cynthia had some writing to finish she would sit up until four working, and always liked the feeling of being the only one awake in a sleeping world. The drive from Cornwall would have been no more tiring and certainly more interesting than yet another railway journey.

When Cynthia arrived Barrie looked very ill, 'he knew me but was occasionally wandering'. It was on this day, Monday 14 June, that the will was signed. Cynthia made no mention of this in her diary, although over the previous months she had once or twice mentioned Barrie fretting about his will or Poole, his solicitor, talking to her or to Barrie about it. She knew that Barrie had reputedly never been to a dentist or an oculist, that he never bought himself any new clothes, that he had a fanatical dislike of the kind of domestic forethought that most people consider a tedious but necessary part of life. She also knew that he was more frightened than most people of dying, that he had drawn up a will, but that he had always baulked at signing it.

Nico believed that the reason Barrie had not signed the will before was that 'in the cold light of remorseless reason he thought it would be wrong' to leave Cynthia the bulk of his fortune rather than 'my boys'. According to him, on 14 June Cynthia 'got hold of surgeon Horder and solicitor Poole with will . . . Horder gave an injection and sufficient energy was pumped into Uncle Jim so that he could put his name to the Will that Poole laid before him'.[32] Cynthia's diary during those days when Barrie was dying does not mention the will at all, but Nico was very persuasive on this point and made many people believe that Cynthia coerced

Poole and Horder into giving an injection so that his feeble hand could find enough strength to write his signature.

But there is no evidence at all for this story. Cynthia did often scratch out little phrases in her diary but she changed nothing for those days. Nor can I believe that she would have demeaned herself in this way: it would have been out of character. Cynthia was naïve, and she was capable of self-deception; she was not scheming or mercenary. It was surely Poole who longed for the already-drafted will to be signed. Since solicitors are only too aware of the difficulties that ensue if someone wealthy dies intestate, he must have wanted the will signed very much indeed. He had seen a great deal of Cynthia and little of the three boys, and he knew that Barrie had drafted a will largely in her favour. That he had not signed it was another facet of his childishness and that he should sign it was in Poole's interest also.

Barrie died on 19 June with Cynthia, Nico and Peter by his side. Again Cynthia had to deal with the myriad of chores that are necessary when someone has died, the letters, the funeral, the possessions to dispose of and in Barrie's case the large and complicated estate. Peter and Cynthia were named as Barrie's executors. Cynthia was to receive £30,000 (half a million pounds), Peter £6000 (£100,000) and Jack and Nico £3000 (£50,000) each. There were various other bequests (Katharine Asquith, with whom Barrie had occasionally stayed at Mells and who sometimes visited him, received £2000, as did Elizabeth Bergner) but Cynthia received all the rights in Barrie's plays, excluding *Peter Pan* since at Cynthia's suggestion the rights had in 1929 been granted to The Hospital for Sick Children, Great Ormond Street. Barrie's possessions, including his manuscripts and papers, were to be divided as they wished between Cynthia and Peter.

Peter was 'terribly distressed and embarrassed at being put on so entirely different a footing from his brothers'.[33] And all three were distressed at having been put on so different a footing from Cynthia. Although they contemplated a law-suit on the grounds that Barrie was not in full possession of his faculties when signing the will, once they had consulted a solicitor they abandoned the idea, realising that although Barrie had not signed his will before his last illness he had indisputably drafted it, and even tinkered with it in the way that is common to people who brood on the idea of death. For example, he had added the adjective 'loved' before Elizabeth Bergner's name on the day he left for the nursing home, putting it in, according to a note in Cynthia's diary, 'because he wanted to please her because he thought she was hurt at his not coming to Cortina without us'.[35]

Barrie's death caused Cynthia far more distress than either Mary's or John's had done. Nearly a month later she wrote, 'continue to torture myself for having left James that last weekend, and thinking how different I would have been to him all the last months if the doctors had not said it was Hysteria and warned me'. Despite Barrie's despotism, Cynthia felt no relief at his death: 'Curious how the gathering fog of worry and weariness over-hanging the last phase lifts and one remembers only the best and happiest time'.[36] But she did not have time to brood. On 12 July Angela telephoned to say that Hugo had died in his sleep. There was another Memorial Service, more letters, more arrangements. In her fiftieth year, over a period of ten weeks, Cynthia had lost both parents, her eldest son and her 'Master'. It seemed a cata-clysm at the time but was to prove a release.

Not long after this latest death Beb and Cynthia went abroad. It was the first time for nearly twenty years that they were able to go away either without Barrie or without wondering whether he was all right without them. They stayed away for six weeks, for most of the time with Elizabeth Bergner and her husband at Cortina, both women mourning yet recuperating. On their return they faced more piles of letters and domestic difficulties, chief of which was the question of Barrie's royalties and whether Cynthia should merely hand half over to Peter. She was dissuaded from this course of action by Poole, but realised that she had thereby destroyed any chance of an easy relationship with 'my boys'.

In December Simon won his scholarship to Christchurch and everyone regretted that Barrie had not lived to enjoy this success. Cynthia visited Adelphi Terrace for the last time and, deep in thought, 'unintentionally walked the whole way home'. On 22 December Michael and Didy formally announced their engage-ment – they were to be married in February. And on 30 December Cynthia, Beb, Simon and Simon's friend Robert Cleveland Stevens set out for Egypt. She never mentioned that she had been there before. But her departure day in 1937 was the very same one as it had been in 1894 and, because they travelled by the same route (overland to Marseilles and then boat), they even arrived on the same day, 4 January, that Cynthia had arrived in 1895. The first step of the newly-freed woman of fifty was to return to the one part of her childhood she did not understand.

····➤· Chapter 32 ·◄····
1940s

There is no reference in Cynthia's diary to her three months in the countryside outside Cairo as a fat-plaited rather solemn little girl; but there were several expeditions to the pyramids and perhaps the taxi driver was privately asked to make a slow detour past Blunt's former house. The likelihood is that she only learnt about her sister's illegitimacy when her novel was published a year previously. Although she must have long suspected it she had not given the possibility much thought. After all, given the moral climate in which she had been brought up most of her contemporaries were potentially illegitimate. When Charles Lister was killed she would not have thought, he might have been my half-brother, nor would she when the newspapers reported the bankruptcy of the Duke of Leinster; neither would she have wondered whether the rising politician Anthony Eden was her first cousin (his mother had had a long affair with George Wyndham and there was a clear resemblance). She would have been interested in that typically Edwardian conundrum of things not being what they seem and no-one ever really knowing the truth; and it was a conundrum that concerned herself – Balfour or Hugo?

That she did think about the implications – the ironies, the possibilities, the long-drawn out deception – is evident in her novels, since the revelation of illegitimacy is the hub of both of them. And when she found, after the first novel was published, that one of her sisters really was only a half-sister it was an intriguing shock. There was also the question of sexual passion. Cynthia had never experienced a fulfilling sexual relationship but her mother had, the mother whose standards she had been brought up to revere but who had evidently abandoned these standards in the desert. Cynthia had a good deal to think about during her private *recherche du temps perdu*. She was perfectly aware that, by curious coincidence, 1937 had concluded many things for her; but she had to make her peace before allowing the future to take hold.

Refreshed by her holiday, she returned to face a new crisis with Michael and Didy. They had been unofficially engaged for so long ('it's a great bore to be in love at school'[1] Michael had told his mother in 1932 when he was not yet eighteen) that their apprehension in the days before their wedding had become palpable. Eventually, after the usual complications to do with pre-nuptial nerves, the Dress, the invitations, the present of jewellery to the bride and so on, they were married in February 1938. Cynthia was exhausted afterwards, unable to sleep and beset by minor domestic difficulties (a maid presented her with a note 'as from a Cabinet Minister, beginning "I wish to tender my resignation",' then the 'new morning housemaid arrived. Trouble over who was to do doorsteps'). In March she went to Stanway for a week, where she already felt like a visitor since so much had died with her mother. Barely days after the funeral she had told Walter de la Mare that 'this place begins to appear no more than a golden dream'; a year later she saw her infrequent visits as mournful farewells, even though no definite decision as to Stanway's future could be taken until the legal complications consequent on Hugo's death had been sorted out. By the time war broke out it had been let for use as a girls' secretarial college.

Beb and Cynthia were now better off, although not nearly as rich as the readers of Barrie's will in the newspapers, the writers of begging letters, seemed to believe. The capital was invested for the Asquith boys; the income from royalties was about £300 (£3500) in a typical year, far less than the £1500 (£17,500) that Cynthia had been used to receiving; nevertheless they were able to buy a Tang horse and a car and, above all, they could make plans to live in the country. Where they lived mattered to them less than the feel and the situation of the house. Once they looked at something on the coast near Weymouth and another time drove down to Kent to look at the house lived in by Vita and Harold Nicolson before they moved to Sissinghurst. Cynthia thought that 'the situation, country, garden *lovely*, house though lovely in its way, to me depressing – too "ye olde" and quaint and timbered and mullioned and dark'.[2] She added, 'can't stand Vita's extreme period furnishing', which was unsurprising since her allegiance to the white walls, pale wood and chintz with which she was familiar was unwavering. Then in April 1939 Beb went to see a house belonging to the novelist A. J. Cronin and at once took Cynthia down to see it. 'Beb was wildly anxious for me to decide to buy it. I DID for its situation in best part of downs. Not a single building or person to be seen. Very exciting. Beb came back with shining eyes – like a lover just accepted'.[3]

Sullington Court (now the Old Rectory) was part of a small hamlet called Sullington, near Pulborough in Sussex. It was built in 1803 next to a beautiful Norman church, an old farmhouse (formerly the manor) and a tithe barn reputedly little older than the church. The buildings huddle on the edge of the South Downs a few miles inland from Worthing. Although the colours and the atmosphere of a little Sussex village are quite different from a Cotswolds one, nevertheless the resemblance of Sullington to Stanway must have struck Cynthia at once – there is a 'big house', a church, a tithe barn, all bordering beautiful unspoilt country-side, and a feeling of life having gone on unchanged which is not found in many places, even in England. Sullington is still miraculously lovely today, whether the garden and downs are scattered with daffodils or bathed in a low mist from which the sheep emerge mysteriously. After nearly thirty years of Sussex Place the Asquiths had no doubts.

The possibility of war had nothing to do with their decision. Once Barrie had died, Stanway had been deprived of Mary's radiance, Michael had married and Simon had gone up to Oxford, then there was nothing to keep them in London (or their 'country' allegiance to Gloucestershire) and they would have moved what-ever the political situation. Beb, the poet, had long wanted to be able to potter about the countryside with the dogs and he knew that he would have Cynthia to himself far more if he removed her from London. She was weary, suffering from various minor ailments, and needed a change, one that she hoped would be permanent. ('To place where we shall probably be buried. Lovely little churchyard'[4] she noted after a pre-move reconnaisance.)

The entire Sussex Place household, including Nanny Faulkner, moved on 4 August 1939. Beb was ecstatically happy from the first moment. Cynthia suffered from headaches and indigestion, yet it was barely three weeks before she was writing in her diary, 'I could not have believed I could so quickly have come to love a place as I do this'.[5] All their visitors (Coley was the first, followed by Algernon) were enthusiastic, and soon Cynthia resented even going to the Hamlyns at Clovelly to see Simon act Shylock in an amateur performance of *The Merchant of Venice*. On her return she could ignore the political situation no longer and tried to distract herself by shopping for enamel mugs for the expected evacuees, dead-heading roses, walking up to the top of the downs or playing word games. On 30 August she and Simon attempted a night walk but were forced home by mist. Distraction *was* difficult and she wrote in her diary: 'I am haunted by the line in *Antony and Cleopatra*, 'the bright day is done And we are for the dark'. On 3 September

> After so long holding one's breath the time to clench one's teeth came. I went to Church – nice bewildered old Vicar prayed to 'Merciful *and* Almighty God' and when I came out we were at War. Listened in to Chamberlain's statement with Beb . . . We had lovely long walks together. What can one say? Listened in and *Attaque*.

For months Cynthia had retreated from the possibility of war. Once she met Harold Nicolson at lunch with Sibyl Colefax and he recorded in his diary that 'Cynthia, like all women, is so terrified of war she would surrender everything'.[6] 'It all links up', she wrote, 'and twenty-one years seem only an Armistice. I am, I suppose, an incurably 'wishful thinker' so I never really could believe in so ghastly an encore'.[7] Her preoccupations in the next few weeks were two-fold: the role that her sons (now aged twenty-five and twenty) were to play in the war and the removal of the last of the furniture from Sussex Place. Van loads of possessions arrived and had to be stored in the old stables (where most of them were to remain for seven years). 'We remain here in our new little quite unequipped home' Cynthia wrote to Ettie, mentally comparing the size of Sullington to Taplow or Panshanger, 'in which we were caught just camping for a month – intending to do it up in October'.[8] It was perhaps fortunate that she was too busy to fret about the house being 'uncarpeted, unpainted and uncurtained'; and had never been very interested in interior decoration.

At the first possible moment, only a month after they had arrived in Sussex, Cynthia had volunteered to do night shifts at the ARP (Air Raid Precautions) post, to be on duty at the First Aid Point, to help the WVS and to do some nursing for the Red Cross; Beb, meanwhile, became a stalwart of the Sussex Home Guard. Having a definite occupation suited Cynthia and meant that although she occasionally became overwrought ('worried to death by Sussex Place things . . . the chaos here is appalling') in general she felt a sense of fulfilment. Nor was there any time to mourn the past. Very soon she was telling Walter de la Mare (in a letter written at the ARP post, where she now tackled all her correspondence) how much she enjoyed 'seeing the year round in a new place. I had no idea what the falling of the leaves would reveal in new vistas. I find I infinitely prefer living in the country'.[9] And by 1940 she was writing, 'there must be something very morbid about my constitution because never in all my life have I felt so well'.[10] Beb too told Cynthia that, despite the war, the first year at Sullington 'had been the happiest year of his life'. Their only real worry was the boys. Michael was to register as a conscientious objector and this was to cause distress to his parents, especially to Beb; Simon was passed unfit for active service, it appeared because of damage to his hearing when, as a child, he had had a mastoid operation (over one of the Christmas holidays at Stanway that were so regularly beset by illness).

Cynthia had quickly settled into country life. Whether it irked her that she had to manage without the feudal array of servants that had surrounded her as a child she did not record. She had certainly assumed, when she left London, that Sullington would be run by two maids, a gardener and Nanny. But after a while one and then both of the maids departed for a munitions factory and Nanny, who had not liked developing into a housekeeper, had decided to leave. Even Cynthia could no longer pretend that Simon, now at Oxford, needed a nanny. Yet it was not a decision that was, after thirty years, made lightly and there was the usual Charteris/Asquith night-time letter writing: Nanny Faulkner wrote Cynthia a long letter and 'I wrote her an immense one'. Finally, in February 1940, Nanny Faulkner moved into a cottage on the coast, under an hour's walk away from Sullington, where she could look after her elderly mother and have the children of friends to stay for long stretches. The person who missed her most when he came home was Simon and he often walked across the downs to spend the night with her, dodging sentries on the way. Coming so soon after the gutting of Sussex Place ('it is very sad to think of the dear old nursery broken up') Cynthia felt very regretful for the boys' childhood and even after Simon married in 1942 wrote sadly from Cornwall, 'I wish I could find Simon on the sands back in green oilskin paddlers again, and wielding a spade the size of a dessert-spoon'.[11] Nor did she cease to mourn her mother, and it was little comfort that her friends missed theirs. At her friend Viola Meynell's one day 'I found Gladys

'North Sea' by D.H.Lawrence, one of thirteen of his 'obscene' paintings seized by police on 5 July 1929 (p.171). The woman bears a clear resemblance to Cynthia. The painting was owned by Aldous Huxley and is thought to have been destroyed by fire at his home in the 1950s.

Michael and Simon in 1932.

Drawing of Barrie by Sir Thomas Monning[...]
1932. 'Unpleasing result of fuzzy techniqu[...]
made him old, bleary, unshaven. More lik[...]
Hardy than himself.'

Barrie, Beb and Cynthia in Switzerland 1936.
28 August: 'Barrie and I were dining alone but
a plot to photograph us was discovered so we
took Beb to chaperone us.'

Huntington there. We all cried. Found cold and war news was lowering our resistance and we were all missing our mothers!!!'[12]

With the logistical difficulty of seeing her friends, Cynthia became an even more conscientious letter-writer during the war years. Her letters were both characterful and delightful, and always expressive of her personality, being direct, light-hearted and fond without being intimate or gushing. But they were invariably quite skimpy and were little different in form from the days when she used to tell Beb that 'this is not a letter'. Nevertheless, David Cecil valued them enough to dub Cynthia the equal as a letter-writer of women like Dorothy Osborne, Mrs Carlyle, Emily Eden or Lady Sarah Lennox. When publishing an essay on these women as letter-writers he was asked by *Vogue* whom he would choose among modern women. He replied, 'My unhesitating choice is Lady Cynthia Asquith, who over a period of years has written me letters as amusing and charming and individual as any I have read by famous letter-writers of the past'.[13] This extravagant dewdrop, although it gave Cynthia a great deal of pleasure, might be thought unwarranted since there is no *one* letter by Cynthia to which one can point and say '*that* is magnificent'. Yet none of Cynthia's letters, whether they were to old friends or to Scribner's about Barrie copyrights or to Simon reminding him to join the Oxford Union and have seven hours a sleep a night, can ever have failed to reveal her spirit and her sense of fun. It is a pity that she had too little belief in her own immortality to think it worthwhile writing longer, more thought-out letters which could have held their own beside the letters of the women that David Cecil mentioned; or that few of those she did write (such as the standard one pleading for a platonic relationship) have survived. All her scrawls are potentially memorable, none of them actually were; which is why, although her war diary is a literary masterpiece, none of her letters are anything more than ephemeral.

Apart from the friends with whom she kept in close touch by letter (Coley, Algernon, David, Desmond, Walter de la Mare, Leslie, Enid, Mary Herbert, Ettie) there were three women all living within a few miles of Sullington who were to give Cynthia a great deal of happiness during her Sussex years. There was Enid Bagnold, of course, whose house it was possible to reach by bus and who was not only her usual invigorating self but was also a helpful critic of Cynthia's work. Then there was Gladys Huntington, with whom the Asquiths used to dine in Hyde Park Gardens during the 1930s and who now lived permanently at

Amberley.* Her daughter Alfreda was the same age as Simon and for a while there was a close friendship between the two. Finally there was Viola Meynell at Greatham. 1 October 1940: 'Felt a little embarrassed at being seen again, as in published letters of D. H. Lawrence he wrote "Viola Meynell thinks you the most beautiful woman she has ever seen" '. But this compliment of twenty-five years previously did not spoil a friendship which had added so much to Cynthia's life that when she moved to Bath in 1946 she wrote, 'Last day in lovely Sullington . . . lunch with Viola. I wonder how many times I've been. It's what I've most enjoyed in neighbourhood . . . Saw view for last time through swimming eyes'.[14]

The Asquiths also made friends with neighbours such as the Hecks's, who lived at the farm at Sullington, and the Courciers who lived nearby, and others of the Sussex gentry whose names might have come out of an Agatha Christie novel: Colonel Ravenscroft at the Abbey, Mrs Fox at Brook House, the Staceys at Lee Farm. Cynthia was very popular with everyone, was not considered arrogant, merely as someone who rightly knew her own worth; even today she is remembered for the way she would 'set people alight if she was talking because she had that absolute capacity for bringing the best out of people – and you were always hoping to hear her lovely laugh, like a bell, turning into a giggle, totally irresistible'.[15]

Beb and Cynthia were quite content with their restricted circle and did not leave Sussex with any alacrity, Beb in particular being more and more reluctant to go away even for a night or to allow Cynthia to depart. But she, despite the difficulties of wartime travelling, liked to go to London to visit Coley. Beb was not always *complaisant* about this: 'Sad homecoming. Beb unaccountably objected to my having stayed with C. at Oxford and was at his most difficult'.[16] (It clearly made no difference that Coley was by now seventy-five and Cynthia fifty-three.) She also continued to visit Ettie who was, for her, 'so linked up with Mamma and everything in the past as well as so vividly understanding of the present',[17] and Katharine at Mells and Mary Herbert at Pixton. Here she was always somewhat bemused by the 'pyramids of books on every table – dogs' dinners on sofa etc'. The house had become increasingly shabby, cold and uncomfortable and Mary,

---

*A few years later she was to write her very successful *Madame Solario*, a novel about a group of leisured Edwardians and the undercurrents that ran beneath the surface of their ordered lives.

by now 'a magnificent, imperious stag by Landseer, perhaps an eagle, is masterful and very clever. She is full of opinions and Catholic prejudice'.[18]

Some friends came to Sullington: 19 May 1940 'Sybil [Colefax's] torrent of information and accounts of intimate contact with everyone one has ever heard of quite astounding'. Yet since Cynthia was so happy with her walks, knitting and 'listening in', the day after Sybil had gone she mentioned the 'pleasant feeling of relaxing in my little back-water since Sybil left'. Because of petrol rationing they saw few people and considered each visitor to be a treat. But it was not a deprivation and they were aware that, despite the dog fights in the air above, they were so much better off than the inhabitants of London ('awful devastation in suburbs and people looking exhausted and bewildered' was Cynthia's comment in October 1940).

In the early months of the war Cynthia was preoccupied with Denis Mackail's biography of Barrie, for which she had had to 'race through old diaries' making notes, and which had to mention her as little as possible for fear of annoying Beb. It was staunchly reviewed by Leslie, Desmond etc. (when it came to book reviews Cynthia's friendship with most of the leading men of letters in England proved invaluable) but it was criticised by some not only for its 'chatty, arch style' but also for its 'almost Freudian analysis'. Cynthia was, too, 'miserably haunted by the sense of how much Barrie would have minded so much probing, peeping and analysing'. Yet she found it 'remarkably evocative of charm and of all the *weather* in his temperament, and the astoundingly strong flavour of personality'.[19] As soon as the biography appeared, Cynthia suggested to Viola Meynell that she should edit an edition of Barrie's letters. The brief was delicately to bowdlerise them so that the letters to Cynthia could appear loving but not love letters. Then, early in 1941, Cynthia decided to write another novel. '*Not* for the sake of others, nor with much hope of profit but just for the experience. It makes me feel so much more alive.'[20] Yet she felt a little half-hearted about it and 'having just read posthumous V. Woolf, anything I could possibly write seemed too dowdy to be worthwhile'. She also, at this time, read Gladys Huntington's 1915 novel *Carfrae's Comedy*, 'I am amazed by its merits'.[21]

One Sparkling Wave took much longer to write than *The Spring House* and made Cynthia realise that she was not destined to be a novelist. Yet it is a well written book which must have given many readers a good deal of pleasure. Its heroine has long since been nick-named 'Available' since this is what she always is to the three women who live up at the 'big house'. They are a Lady Wemyss/Ettie figure called Lady Glade, her daughter Daphne and her grand-daughter Lark. They have all three become dependent on Available as friend, companion, listening-post and so on. She is also very close to her widower father who is the local doctor and a man of charm and character. By the end the three women need Available as much as ever, about which she is glad since her father has died and she has rejected her one elderly suitor. 'She felt a benign sense as of a blessing shed upon her – a humorous blessing. "Well, well!" she said. "Which is it to be? Which of the three? Whom do we go to, Perks? Which one?" '[22] The twist in the plot comes when Lark's lover will not declare himself because, since there is madness in his family, he feels he can never marry. But then 'it appears that I'm not my father's son. No condolences, please. I'm bearing up splendidly'.[23] Again Cynthia had betrayed which topic was of real fascination to her. As with her first novel, the plot of this second one hinged on the concept of things not being what they seem, a secret being kept for thirty years, a person's character and happiness depending on an instant in time so many years ago, a mother's capacity for deception and a father's capacity for self-deception or ignorance: themes which in themselves would be material for an entire novel if Cynthia had allowed herself to write it.

That she had not exhausted her interest in the topic of marriage and what lay behind the public façade was evident from her next choice of subject which was neither fiction nor short story nor royal memoir but a book to be called *Wives of the Great*. The year before Enid had 'talked of my writing – thinks I have not yet found right vehicle'[2] and it is likely that she suggested to Cynthia that she might be best suited to write non-fiction and that she suggested this title. But it was never to be used because Cynthia's first choice in the category of wife to the great was Sonya Tolstoy, and she found her so interesting that she had soon decided to write only about her. Simon's friend Raymond Carr took her to the London Library to help her get out more Tolstoyana and a few weeks later she was 'suddenly seized with insensate ambition to write a PLAY about the Tolstoys . . . got in frenzy of excitement'.[25] A mere three weeks later it was finished.

If Cynthia had known that it was to be more than three years before *Tolstoy's Flight*, later called *No Heaven For Me*, was produced on stage, and that she would spend so much time re-working and re-writing, she would probably have abandoned it as soon as it was finished. But she persevered, soliciting her friends' advice, sending it to theatrical agencies, having it re-typed and finally, in 1946, having it accepted by the Little Theatre at Bristol, where it was produced in September. She had not exorcised her obsession with the Countess Tolstoy and wrote to Coley:

My whole object was to take neither side, but show how hard it was for both and how love still survived. But I cannot understand anyone not feeling sorry for her. Very few women could have stood a tenth of what she had to suffer without leaving him or committing suicide. Thirteen children in itself (three finished me), the work of at least four professional secretaries, three housekeepers, a hospital nurse, a gardener and a hostess (on a scale unimaginable to us). All the odium of his evasion of the property issue by the farce of handing it over to her, and living on her. And so jealous was he that even when she was sixty-five he would not let her have an old musician he thought she had affection for come and play the piano to her. So inconsistent that he would forbid the servants to do his room, and then, forgetting, with his own hands flog a serf because he found the room *undone*. All very amusing and lovable to read about, but to live with when you had a constant headache![26]

Cynthia did not forget Sonya and was, in ten years, to write a book about her (her swan-song).

The play was written at the beginning of 1943. The previous autumn another phase of Cynthia's life had come to an end when Simon married Vivien Jones, then just nineteen. Her father was, suitably, an Eton and Balliol barrister and her mother was the daughter of the Governor-General with whom Cynthia had stayed in Canada in 1909. Being so young and beautiful she was ideally cast in the role of a lifelong Wendy and Simon soon had his own nursery with a girl and two boys (Michael, by this time, had the same). Cynthia told Walter de la Mare, 'she is lovely I think in a special and very varying way – grace and quality and meltingly young . . . there seems no sense in deferring happiness these days. Besides, it is nice to be near *contagious* happiness and I like the way she cannot take her starry eyes off his face'.[27] A year later she added, 'she is a delicious blend of nymph and nanny and can scarcely make any pretence of listening when any other than he speaks'.[28]

In some ways Cynthia's sons had been a disappointment to her. Neither of them had been the brilliant undergraduates she had hoped for ('sad to feel I shall never have son at Oxford again, and both times disappointing: one spoiled by Venus, the other by Mars'[29]) and neither appeared to be pursuing the kind of career which, as inheritors of a great tradition, she had envisaged for them. But the weight of her expectations was, in itself, crushing, as was the depth of her interest. For the last twenty years of her life, while her sons were mature, married adults, she continued to encourage them to take up this or that career; to remember an engagement; to read a particular book. But her concern went beyond what most mothers think suitable and the result was not happy. The boys had been brought up to believe that they were something quite out of the ordinary, that the world was theirs for the asking. When it was not, and when their mother continued to assume that it was and that they only had to cut their hair or write a good letter for it to be so, they retreated.

By the 1940s Cynthia was beginning to regret that she had been an indulgent mother, and realised that she had not made it easy for her sons to struggle towards independence. Yet she still felt, as she had twenty years before when she wrote *The Child at Home*, that it was not good for a child always to be 'with the *same* loved and loving person. It should never be *one* person all the time – bad for both'. She was also, by now, castigating herself for allowing the excellent and invaluable Nanny Faulkner to be such a permanent fund of love and tenderness. She wrote to her daughter-in-law, who was successfully bringing up her daughter according to the modern precept that no child could have enough love or enough attention from the mother/nanny figure:

> I have now no shred of doubt that I was very mistaken and am to blame for going the way of least resistance and not forcing Nanny to go away on holidays. That perpetual greenhouse of love, understanding and preferential treatment was *damaging*. I've long fought against this melancholy conviction but can no longer do so. Mea Culpa. Take care that in avoiding one ditch you don't fall into the one on the other side of the road.[30]

Curiously, Beb's last poem, written just before his death in 1947, was on this theme. It began, 'Strive not to make too much your own The child whom you will ne'er possess'.[31] Rather too late he and Cynthia had realised that by loving a child too deeply, loading it with expectation, making it feel that any failure was a betrayal and then failing to allow it to walk free – all of these things would lead to unhappiness.

A child's difficulties were, in addition, inevitably compounded if it was surrounded by an atmosphere that was less than open. It was not that Cynthia was deceitful, she was not even the kind of parent who was always saying 'not in front of the children'. But her determination to evade the disagreeable often led her to evade the truth. Just like her late-Victorian and Edwardian ancestors, she believed that it was easier and pleasanter not to mention the unpalatable rather than to confront it: 'the stubborn gospel of joy' unto the next generation. Her diary is full of instances of her skating over the distasteful as if by doing so it will magically disappear. When Dr Cameron, who for years had been treating her, and latterly Michael, committed suicide because his medical practices had come under suspicion, she noted merely 'very sad to hear of Dr Cameron's death'[32] (ignoring the fact that the newspapers had made much of this drama and that his deadly injections had caused the death of Lady Ottoline Morrell.) It was not for nothing that all her life her favourite game had been 'breaking the news'.

But avoidance of the unpalatable truth rarely leads to happiness and although Cynthia appeared cheerful she suffered, as she had always done, from switchback moods and did not always have the excuse of an east wind or exhaustion to explain them away. 5 November 1939, 'a day of ghastly depression', was followed by 6 November, 'a happy day. Could not have believed I was same woman. Why am I so utterly unstable?' It was a tribute to her self-control and generosity of spirit that it was rare for anyone to notice her unhappiness, however often she recorded it in her diary, as she knew when she noted on one occasion, 'day of mental HELL . . . have never felt so deranged and for once it was apparent to others'.[33] Her attitude to melancholy was the same as that of her Souls forebears: she expected to feel melancholy, and indeed to indulge it, but she knew she would quickly recover and that it was something one hid from others.

Her depression as the war came to an end was not something she could hide altogether successfully. But she recovered, and once she had done so, and once she and Beb had had time to assess their situation after six happy years immured in Sullington, they came to the conclusion that they must move. The diaries for 1944 and 1945 are lost, so it is unclear whether it was she or Beb who first felt disenchanted with the Old Rectory. But she was nearly sixty, Beb was older and in poor health, they lived in a large house ten minutes walk from an infrequent bus and they found it increasingly difficult to find anyone to help them in the house. By early January 1946 Cynthia was telling Walter de la Mare that 'much as we love this place we have come to the conclusion that old age is wiser faced in a town and are going to live in Bath which is a lovely and civilised city'.[34]

They bought a house on Bathwick Hill called Claverton Lodge, 'the most lovely house and best situated I have ever seen . . . there are seven acres, wealthy orchards, charm, supremely lovely view.'[35] But leaving Sullington was painful. 'I felt as though committing a slow murder: deliberately day by day destroying destroying [sic] a lovely home where in spite of the war I have been almost discreditably happy'.[36] She and Beb stayed in hotels in Bath and London, their possessions in store, while the tenants slowly vacated Claverton. Once they had moved in she realised how difficult it was going to be to run such a large house in post-war England – very little easier, in fact, than Sullington would have been. Although 'the night view down on to the lights of Bath far below is a Dream of Beauty' they both missed the downs, and the chaos in which they lived during the freeze-up of early 1947 was debilitating to both of them and, eventually, fatal to Beb's health. In late May he became seriously ill; he alternately rallied and weakened but at the beginning of August 1947 he died.

····⋟· **Chapter 33** ⋞····
1950s

It was a death that had been for long expected. During his six months in Bath, Beb had spent many of the days in bed and Cynthia soon realised that Claverton was not an easy house in which to carry trays. And although she had partly moved in order to be near Leslie and Algernon, both then settling in Bath, they were not quite the balm to the spirit or the practical help that women friends would have been. She did ask friends to come and share the house – Stella Campbell came until there was a quarrel, so did Eileen Bigland, Fabienne Hillyard (a friend from Sussex) and the invaluable Ursula Codrington (who was to be not only a friend and companion but also to do much of Cynthia's typing) – but the calm that these very English ladies created came too late for Beb and, in a sense, for Cynthia.

To dwindle into a Bath widow was not what she wanted. Although she did a certain amount of meeting friends for coffee at the Gay Heart, or tea at Fortts, or buying light bulbs and elastic at Jolly's, she felt, as so often before, that she was acting a part which did not suit her. And without Beb dependent on her she was free to look for another. During 1947 and 1948, while nominally at Claverton, she was often away, either in London or by herself at the seaside or staying with friends such as the Courciers near Sullington. And it was on one of these occasions that she met Collin Brooks. It was not for nothing that Enid had made the Squire tell Caroline, the 'love-woman', that 'you are a woman meant to walk from man to man and never to look back'.[1]

When Collin and Cynthia met, at the end of 1947, he was fifty-four and she was sixty. Their relationship made a slow start since he was married with four children and Coley, although eighty-two, was still very much alive and as witty and literary as ever. But he died at the end of 1948. By the time Cynthia re-started her diary for 1949 (she either did not keep diaries for the two previous years or they have been lost) she and Collin are very close. They call each other Swan and Edgar in private (a reference to Cynthia's lifelong fondness for swans, and a pun on the name of a famous London store), meet for lunch at 'dear old Canuto's' and talk happily about each other's work. Collin had had a long and successful career as a writer and journalist, having worked as a financial economist on many papers and having, since 1940, edited a then well-known magazine called *Truth*. He was also the author of many novels, thrillers, books on economics and even poetry. That he had become a pupil in a firm of accountants rather than going to Balliol would not have been at all evident from his self-assured, charming and literary demeanour.

During the last years of her life Cynthia had numerous friends and few of them met, or even heard about Collin: he was, after all, married. But, exactly thirty years after Basil's death, Cynthia had fallen in love again; it was the second great love of her life. All the happiness and intellectual stimulation she had enjoyed with Beb, Bluey, Desmond or Coley, and the joy with Basil, all came curiously together in this new relationship. Again Cynthia had managed to find a lover who loved poetry, Dickens, Jane Austen as much as she did; who made her laugh and *think*; and who was deeply *sympathique*. It was not surprising, since she had so much warmth and mettle left in her, that she did not want to spend the days plodding down Bathwick Hill into Bath for coffee.

She and Collin were both implacably right-wing and had in common certain prejudices such as a firm anti-American stance. In this he was, for Cynthia, the inheritor of a tradition of which Belloc, Chesterton and Whibley were part, one with which she felt comfortable but which is hard to admire. For example, the anti-Semitism which had long flourished among the English upper-classes, and which was nastily evident in the letters Whibley wrote to Cynthia during the First World War, still flashed through the letters she wrote during the Second. 'I begin to feel tolerant of almost any degree of intolerance towards the race'[2] she had written to the gentle, civilised (yet obviously receptive) Walter de la Mare after entering the underground shelter at the Cumberland Hotel, thereby renewing her claim to a place in this odd little mafia of bigotry.

As she was aware, the mafia included few women. Since it had its origins in 'a serious dining club composed partly of Parliamentarians and partly of journalists, all of a Tory cast of mind'[3] she would have been debarred by sex and status. Yet many of the members were her friends, and they were loyal, for loyalty was an old-fashioned virtue of which they approved. It was not a coincidence that Whibley had recommended T.S. Eliot to Faber, that Collin recommended to Eliot's future second wife that she apply for the post of his secretary, that Eliot gave the address at Collin's memorial service and, having mentioned the dining club, explained that there had been a temperamental and political affinity between the two of them. (It was clear that Cynthia would have liked to explore this affinity further; she several times mentions reading 'East Coker' to friends in the hope that they could explain it to her. They never could.)

Despite his being 'on the extreme right wing of the Tory party to put it charitably'[4] (in the words of a journalist who worked with him) Collin was very much liked by everyone. Eliot, in his address, referred to his integrity, his incapacity for pretence, his devotion to principle. And Michael Foot, who worked with him at the end of the '30s, remembered him as charming and delightful and remarked that 'he wrote things that no-one else would have dared to say and wrote them better than anyone else'[5] (a coincidental echo of Eliot's 1931 comment about Whibley that 'he is ready to say bluntly what everyone else is afraid to say').

Cynthia had found someone with whom she was in tune, who was intellectual, verbal, charming, who loved poetry – and who loved her. As described by Eliot, Collin must have had such a zest for living that it is impossible to imagine him loving feebly and ineffectually and he would not have tolerated an *amitié amoureuse*. When she met him Cynthia must have imagined that, given her age, no other sort would be possible. But, by June 1949, after they had frequently lunched or dined, and after Cynthia had rapidly written her book, there came a 'High Water Mark'. Three days later, after another dinner at Canuto's, she wrote 'Safe from Life and Life's alarms'. In July she twice noted 'pond', a word that (like Hermes with Coley) was to denote physical love of some sort. In their case it referred to two swans on the water. 8 November: 'Edgar came to dinner. Crescendo continues. Amazing'.

It was partly because of Collin that Cynthia left Bath. In addition, she had been away so much after Beb died that she never thought of it as home; although the auction particulars were to describe Claverton as 'completely modernized and labour saving to the last degree' it was hard to heat and absurdly large for a basic household of one; and she found it wearying, since she could hardly claim that she had no room, to have continual visitors. For a while she dithered, cancelling the planned auction in the spring of 1949 as soon as the bulbs came up in the garden and, instead, leaving the running of the house to Eileen. 'The thought of upheaval grew more and more of a nightmare as it approached. Also, apart from the deliciousness of the house and its civilisedness, I'm not sure that even from purely financial point of view, the house is not the safest asset.'[6] But eventually the house was sold in the summer of 1950 and Cynthia 'left dear, lovely Claverton for ever' at the beginning of September. For the last time she walked through the garden and across the meadow to the cemetery where Beb was buried: a few months earlier she had planted some juniper trees round his grave.

For a while Cynthia continued to cuckoo. She was, by now, rather fond of hotel life and was not someone who relied on having her 'things' around her or who needed somewhere homely in order to play the part of grandmother. This was not in any case a role that appealed. Although she was fond of her six grandchildren she never quite knew how to approach the under-twelves outside the sacred Edwardian children's hour. Kip, who spent a lot of time with Nanny Faulkner after Michael and Didy had amicably separated, remembers that he and the five other children who lived with her used to call Cynthia 'the choccy lady' because she always brought sweets when she came down to visit them and how she would sweep in in her flowing clothes, soft rusts and aquamarines made by a dressmaker in South Audley Street, and the homely atmosphere would be subtly, and sometimes embarrassingly, re-charged.[7] She meant well, but a child of the Souls did not adapt well to nursery supper round the kitchen table.

She rented a flat in Queen's Gate. It was, in every sense, a return to South Kensington. Then, tiring of this, she stayed in various hotels in the neighbourhood or at her favourite Paddington Hotel. But finally, in the spring of 1951, she bought a flat on the first floor of 15 Queen's Gate Gardens and here she was to live for the last nine years of her life. She was very happy here. The flat was warm in winter and compact; she liked being able to walk about with no clothes on, and the chore of having to make her own supper quite made up for the absence of draughts, stone corridors and other people for whom she was responsible. So fond of her own company had she become that she had chosen a flat with no spare room. The only person she consented to have to stay with her was her much-loved grand-daughter Annabel, and that was on the sofa in the drawing-room.

But it was not a retiring life, for she continued to have many committments. In 1948 she had bought a shop in New Street, Brighton. She perhaps hoped that Michael or Simon would manage it, but it was not to be and she entered into some rather unsatisfactory partnerships before, a couple of years later, Cynthia Asquith Ltd was sold. It was an antique shop and Cynthia told an interviewer for *Queen* magazine, 'It is such a good excuse for my pet self-indulgence . . . You see, I love buying things'.[8] But she did not love it enough (and in fact had never been very acquisitive) and was soon to try another venture. She had been approached by Barrie's nephew Jimmie and it was for his firm that she had agreed to write her reminiscences. Eileen, who had introduced them, and Jimmie both thought that she would write a good book (their confidence was justified when it was chosen as a Book Society Recommendation). But, wanting to help one of her sons to support himself, and feeling that her invested capital was only nominally hers rather than Barrie's, she suggested to Jimmie that she invest £3000 (£30,000) in his firm and that he employ Simon. It was a very small amount of money compared with the large sums Barrie had invested in Peter Davies Ltd, but to a not very successful publisher it was almost a fortune. That Simon was neither by temperament nor by inclination suited to publishing was neither Cynthia nor Jimmie's fault.

The shop and the 'firm' were only two of Cynthia's interests in her South Kensington years. She attended meetings of, among others, the Dickens Fellowship (her passion for him never diminished), the Bibliophile Society, the Jane Austen Society and the P.E.N. Club. From 1946–8 she was Vice-President of the Pedestrians' Association, having become more and more antipathetic to motor-car traffic and especially outraged by drunken driving. She gave quite frequent lectures (sixteen in 1956 alone), at first on the well-worn topics of ghosts and feminine beauty in literature and then, as her reminiscences began to be published, on Barrie or 'Three Personalities' (her Wemyss grandfather, Lawrence and G.K. Chesterton). Sometimes she wrote book reviews and, in June 1953, was impressed by Barbara Pym's *Jane and Prudence*. Once or twice she appeared on a 'Brains Trust' but, although she did a dozen or so broadcasts on subjects to do with her reminiscences, she never appeared 'live'. (Collin was frequently, and memorably, on 'Any Questions'.)

Cynthia and Collin were, when they could be together, very happy, and she was evidently enjoying, rather than just submitting to, a physical relationship. But they could not meet more than perhaps once a week, and then only for dinner. There were no more walks to Hampstead, as in the Coley days, or lunches or long telephone conversations. But there were letters and although none of them have survived a visitor to the Cecils during the 1950s remembers finding a book left behind by Cynthia on the bedside table. Opening it, he found an almost embarrassingly passionate letter. It could only have been from Collin and it appeared to the startled peruser of this intimate document that, after nearly fifty years of being a 'love-woman', Cynthia had found what she was looking for. Certainly her diaries for this 'swan-song' period of her life (only 1951 is missing) rarely record depression; although there is a good deal about the weather, the dentist and, dread subject for biographers, digestion. (Since her late twenties Cynthia had consulted doctors on the subject of what she vaguely defined as her digestion and over the years there is frequent mention of her caecum, gall-bladder and other similar organs and as well of the need for 'w.o.' (presumably wash-out or enema). But not even once does she mention food, or imagine that her internal disturbance might be diet-related.)

Although Collin brought great happiness, he did not play a very large part in Cynthia's life. She spent far more time preoccupied about her sons' inability to settle to a career and their consequent financial difficulties; about her work; and about her friends. Few elderly widows, of the type that are most at home within a twenty-minute walk of Harrods, can have had as many friends as Cynthia. Her friends loved her dearly, and they mourn her still. It was a tribute to her capacity for listening and for giving, to the extraordinary warmth with which she made each person feel unique, that those who have survived her each speak of her as though *they* were her very closest friend. Robert Cleveland Stevens with whom she had been in Egypt, Diana Westmorland's son Julian Fane, her agent Joan Ling, a professor at Bristol University named August Closs, (she had met him through 'the Bath set', Algernon, Leslie and Sir Orme Sargent), the excellent and invaluable lady who 'did' for her, Freda James, Ursula Codrington who loyally continued to type, Thea Townsend who sometimes came in to cook, Mary Treadgold whom she met on a P.E.N. conference and who became a close friend, as did Daniel George; the list could be four times as long, but the point would be the same – that Cynthia made each of these people feel that she was *theirs*. She may not have excelled as a wife or mother but all her life she had played the part of friend with brilliance and distinction; now that she could shed the former role, she could flower in the one that suited her best.

It was at this period of her life, too, that her writing flowered. The three books she published in 1950, 1952 and 1954 are written in an excellent and unique style which, it is apparent, Cynthia had been struggling towards for thirty years. The style is very direct and mellifluous, coming across best when read aloud, thereby making the reader feel that he is part of a private conversation; which he was, because Cynthia tried not to forget that she was writing *for* someone, and used frequent questions, snatches of conversation and disarmingly intimate turns of phrase. Her descriptions, whether of her childhood, her relations or 'country house visiting', were delightfully written and never dull; unsurprisingly, *Haply I May Remember*, *Remember and Be Glad* and *Portrait of Barrie* all made a rather respectable amount of money both for Cynthia and Jimmie Barrie. That the line between autobiography and fiction became blurred is almost irrelevant. Most of the reviewers contented themselves with comments of this kind, *The Spectator's* 'I have never read any reminiscences in which the impact of the writer was more immediate or the egoism more attractive' being typical of them all. And there was the 'no moaning at the bar' review (quoted on the frontispiece) which Cynthia must have enjoyed, especially when it contrasted her approvingly with a Russian aristocrat.

It was unlikely that the reviewer knew that she had written a play about Sonya Tolstoy, but she would have well understood why Cynthia identified with her subject. Sonya was married to a great man; she was also, like Mary Elcho, holding together something that was beginning to disintegrate. And Cynthia found that she could not forget Sonya, and when she had finished her book on Barrie and her third anthology of ghost stories (*The Second Ghost Book* had appeared in 1952, the first twenty-five years before) she returned to the topic that had preoccupied her in the closing years of the war. 2 January 1956: 'Started to skirmish with Countess Tolstoy. Have condemned myself to write another book, thereby consigning myself to a Hell, but the best Hell I've yet found. Intend to write two hours every morning whatever else I may have to do'.

'The necessity to earn one's living is the only protection from people' she had remarked to her mother in the 1930s (adding, 'and dogs eat up the scraps of time left by friends, children and servants'[9]). It was still the case that writing, for someone as much in demand as she was, provided a refuge, an acceptable bridge between her need for friends and her longing for solitude. The days in Queen's Gate Gardens had a comfortable routine. She still woke early and would work in bed or at her (Barrie's) desk. When Mrs James arrived, as she did every morning for the nine years that Cynthia lived in London, she would go back to bed for breakfast. If she was not having one of her Thursday lunch parties, or if she had not arranged to go out, she would lunch off a tray. Often Mrs James would also leave supper. Cynthia, who was always mockingly to complain that she had never understood what one did with the duster once *it* was dusty or how one washed a hairbrush, very much enjoyed her electric toaster, and her grandchildren's privilege when they visited 'Granny Mo' was to make numerous pieces of toast to accompany their cold chicken and salad lunch.

Within certain limits she continued to be sociable, even if she admitted to few that her quiet evenings with her (new and cherished) television set or listening to her favourite Saturday Night Theatre were among her most enjoyable. But she had a never-diminishing group of friends who longed to see her and she made new ones all the time. She still went to stay with friends, even visiting Elizabeth Bowen in Ireland three summers running, and organised an annual visit to Stratford for herself, Collin and Leslie and other varying Shakespearean enthusiasts such as Eileen, Katharine Asquith or Simon and Vivien. Sometimes she saw old friends such as Antoine ('in every way utterly HIMSELF!') but she was not a great 'keeper-upper' with people from the past and found family weddings rather a melancholy reminder of the past; in general she preferred to forge ahead rather than look back and would not have been pleased by Cecil Beaton's remark in his diary, written after a 'farewell to No 10' party given by Churchill, that she was 'looking sadly stolid instead of the Pre-Raphaelite sprite that she always will be remembered as'.[10] (Cynthia had never quite seen the 'point' of Beaton, even though she had been so fond of Rex Whistler and still liked seeing her cousin Stephen Tennant; perhaps because he had once been brought to Sullington by Enid and the photograph he took of his hostess made her look both stolid and unprepossessing.)

Her life was a literary, South Kensington one and although, as a child of the Souls, she would not have envisaged it, she was both happy and fulfilled. But then, towards the middle of the 1950s, it began to crumble. Collin, whose health had not been good for a while, was diagnosed as having Parkinson's Disease. In 1953 Cynthia was distressed because Leslie Hartley rejected an

offer of £500 (£5000) from the 'firm' and allowed *The Go-Between**
to be published by Hamish Hamilton. It was the same year that
James Barrie was threatened with liquidation and that Dos
Palmer, who had shared her house with Coley, invested £10,000
(£100,000) in it. Cynthia was very worried by this turn of events.
'I do hope Jimmie made it plain that it might very well all be lost.
Don't know what to think. It saves us from immediate horror,
but may be only prolonging suspense and strain . . . Telephoned
to Dos. She said, "I'm doing it for Coley and you"!!'[11] It *was*
prolonging the strain and two years later Jimmy himself was made
nearly penniless and Cynthia and Dos both lost their investments
of £10,000.

Worse than either of these events was Cynthia's deteriorating
relationship with Simon. As she once wrote to him, in one of her
letters fretting about his lack of employment and consequent lack
of funds, 'I got more happiness out of your childhood and
boyhood than from anything else in my life (*no* reflection on poor
Michael because *he* was sent away) and I do not want the last
phase to be shadowed and spoilt'.[12] Part of the trouble was the
refusal of both mother and son to be honest with each other:
Cynthia would not admit how disappointed she was that her
golden lad seemed to be coming to nothing, Simon would not
admit that it was now too late for him to pull himself up and that
Cynthia's constant concern was only an irritant. In addition,
Barrie continued to cast his spell. Having consigned Simon to a
Never-Neverland it might have seemed, when he died, that he
was providing the funds for him to stay there. But Cynthia
sensibly, yet (to her son) enragingly, would not comply. Although
she was continually generous in every possible way, she refused
to hand over large chunks of capital nor, for example, would she

---

*Some of the details of *The Go-Between* may have derived from L.P.
Hartley's friendship with Cynthia. The life of the Maudsleys ('a very
devoted family') at Brandham Hall had much in common with that of
the Elchos. The hero, Leo, is thirteen on 27 July 1900, while Cynthia was
thirteen on 27 September of that year. The M.M. of Marion Maudsley is
a curious echo both of the C.C. of Cynthia Charteris and of the names
of Madeline and Mary. Ted Burgess's surname begins with the 'B' that
was so persistent in surnames of Cynthia's friends and lovers, while
Marion's fiancé's name Hugh Francis Winlove is reminiscent of Hugo
Wemyss and of the eighteenth-century 'wicked Colonel' Francis Charteris. Finally, and most important, the events of July 1900 had a lasting
effect upon Leo's life that was not dissimilar from the lasting effect of
the trip to Egypt upon Cynthia's.

pay for the thirty-six year-old Simon to begin to read for the Bar. Subconsciously, Simon felt that Cynthia's money was not really 'hers' and should therefore be his. And the resentment he felt, and the subsequent misery she endured, are in their way as great a tragedy as Sylvia's death in 1910, Michael's death in 1921 and as Peter's death was to be in 1960. Barrie had helped to create Simon; but his early death at the age of fifty-four was to be Barrie's doing as well.

Since Cynthia had such a chameleon-like capacity for adapting herself to different people, she had many friends who never even knew of the existence of her other friends (and would have had no idea about her worries over Collin, Simon and 'the firm'). By compartmentalising her life she could lead a full one, but she continued to be thereby enigmatic because she kept much of herself hidden. Thus, in the last years of her life, she used sometimes to organise dinner-parites at which she appeared wearing a band round her head with the front and back of an arrow positioned to look as though there was an arrow straight through her head. This remarkable object had been brought from the funfair at Coney Island by her friend and doctor Patrick Woodcock. She adored it, but part of the joke was that no-one referred to its being on her head. Cynthia's love of practical jokes had not diminished; yet there were others of her friends who would hardly have been aware that she was fond of them. Nevertheless, every one of her friends knew that her insights and sometimes stinging wit were never meant to be cutting. Some people were offended by her but many have said that Cynthia's dinners were the most amusing they have ever been to.

Her laughter would peal out as gaily as it had ever done. And when, in May 1954, she was courier to a party of Americans on a three-week tour of England, the laughter was what they remembered. For Cynthia, too, it was an odyssey. She had been billed in the brochure as being 'on intimate terms with the owners of many of the great houses of Britain' and conducted her 'ladies' to many places with which she had once been very intimate: Bath, Stanway, Chirk ('had not been there since I stayed with Howard de Waldens in 1917'), Kirriemuir ('disconcerting reception at Birthouse by newspapermen and battery of cameras'), Haddon Hall ('moved to tears by the beauty of Violet Rutland's sculpture of her dead little son'[13]), Stratford, Oxford, Pulborough and Brighton among others. She was paid £900 (£7500) for this jaunt and had to remind herself when the ladies became querulous that she was earning her living far more rapidly than by writing.

But, in the spring of 1957, she earned even larger sums by

appearing on the '$64,000 Question'. This was one of the American format quiz programmes put on by the new Independent Television. Cynthia told the *Daily Mail*, 'if I can win a thing like this on television I can earn as much as I would in three years' writing', and chose as her special subject something already very familiar to her, the novels of Jane Austen. She had long been a 'Janeite' and had given a talk to the Jane Austen Society in 1954. Now she set herself to read through the complete works four times in a month – a book a day.

She enjoyed the concentration and competitiveness very much, despite the embarrassing preliminary chat ('what would Lord Oxford and Barrie have thought of my doing this? etc'). She especially enjoyed the poker-playing element, and declared to a reporter, 'I love a gamble. And I look on this as a most exciting personal gamble with everything depending on me.' After four preliminary heats during which she doubled her winnings from four thousand shillings, or £200, through to £1600, she won the final and sixty-four thousand shillings, or £3,200 (£25,000). She was, briefly, a celebrity, with pictures of her being kissed by the question master Jerry Desmonde in all the papers and taxi drivers telling her 'You've got a face wot no one can't never forget.' A few weeks later she competed again but had to retire after the fourth round (having won another £1600) after her partner 'when asked what Mr Bennet promised to take Lydia to, if she was good for ten years, answered Play instead of Review, and as it was, of course, a *military* review, they could not spare her.' For the second time in Cynthia's life the British public imagined that she was suddenly rich. But she announced that apart from giving a donation to the Jane Austen society, £50 to each of her grandchildren and £100 (£750) to four poor friends she would use the rest of the money to pay off her overdraft. (In the event, some of it was also used to pay for Michael's second wife Hase's extended stay in hospital after a major illness.)

In 1958 Cynthia endured a major but successful gynaecological operation, watched Collin deteriorate, and struggled with her book. He died in the spring of the following year and it was partly to try and forget about this grief that she asked Robert Cleveland Stevens to take her to Russia to see Yasnaya Polyana where the Tolstoys had lived. Her biography of Sonya was nearly finished (it was to be published posthumously) and it was a pilgrimage she had long wanted to make. There is no written record of the six-day trip, which included two days in Moscow and one in Leningrad. But there is a ciné film, taken by Robert, of Cynthia pacing around the grounds of Yasnaya. She looks surprisingly tall and stately.

At the end of the year during which Collin had become unbearably incapacitated she had written, 'I'm not going to write a diary any longer but just keep engagement books as records. At least that is what I feel at present. But it is of course possible that I may change my mind! May the coming year be an improvement on the outgoing one!'[14] It was not. In a surviving scrap of a letter to an unknown correspondent she wrote:

When he first ceased to be able to come (was it about two years ago?) I missed him so agonisingly that it has, I'm afraid, for ever put me off my flat. (I can scarcely go into the drawing-room.) When he died, at first relief was uppermost – relief that he was not to suffer longer and worse, and dread of the future with its hideous menace. Some relief even for myself; for going to see him had become rather torture; and as I could never talk to him alone, I did not feel I could be of any help. Now, of course, the missing has come back and I seem scarcely to know *who* I am, let alone why. I really have no existence apart from as I see myself through the eyes of certain individuals; and of those, no eyes . . . [15]

The next page is missing. But, curiously, it was Cynthia's eyes that were the first intimation that her life was coming to an end. After a winter spent suffering from recurrent bouts of flu, she told Ursula Codrington in early 1960: 'I'm in a hideous trough of depression . . . complete inertia, apathy . . . I haven't even minded not reading for a week. (I broke a blood vessel in my eye and looked a Horror Comic) . . . Will it pass? Or have I entered the last black tunnel?'[16] And to David Cecil she wrote, more analytically, 'I'm afraid my real rouble is Self-Pity over my AGE, to which I cannot resign myself – a grief for which I'm afraid I must not expect much sympathy'.[17]

At the end of March she went to stay with Didy and her second husband at 'Eliza's cottage', a mile across the fields from Stanway; she had planned to spend the following weekend with Roger Fulford and his wife in Westmorland. But she collapsed and in a nursing home in Oxford she died from what was apparently meningitis. It was on the eve of April Fool's Day. Nearly a month later, on 28 April, the Memorial Service was held at St Martin's-in-the-Fields. Among the guests there were two, Freyberg (by now a Lord) and his wife Barbara, who also attended another memorial service on the same day. It was for Peter Davies. Five days after Cynthia's death he had thrown himself under a train at Sloane Square. It was as if he could not imagine being left behind while Cynthia went to join Barrie in the Never-Neverland: 'Peter Pan commits suicide' announced the headlines in Fleet Street. As Daphne du Maurier, Sylvia's niece, envisaged their meeting in an afterlife:

> Let them have it out with Uncle Jim telling them both where he himself got off (and he has had plenty of time to find that out) and then to the huge relief of Granny (who would hate any unpleasantness) both Cynthia and Peter shake hands, everything settled at last, and Cynthia evaporates to her own clan, and Peter rushes to Aunt Sylvia's arms, because really it was about time he did, having regretted them for about fifty years.[18]

····⊁· Afterword ·⊰····

Cynthia's last two books were published after her death – her life of Sonya Tolstoy and the edited version of her war diaries. She had not envisaged publication of the diaries and would have disapproved on principle; in her opinion Sonya's published diaries did her reputation a disservice, and she wrote 'nearly all have been published; some, thanks to the deleting of certain passages, with a definite bias against Countess Tolstoy'.

Deletion also caused bias against Cynthia when her diaries appeared in 1968: the effect of cutting half a million words by half was to remove much 'dailiness', much maternal emotion (especially about John), much anguish about the war. By concentrating on the passages which concerned personalities or were amusing, the editors made Cynthia appear harder and flightier than she really was. Nevertheless, the war diaries are her greatest achievement and have been widely read, quoted and culled for source material about the period. She would have enjoyed the renewed interest in herself that happened with publication – it was not for nothing that she had looked after her diaries so carefully for forty years.

Cynthia's almost abstract interest in 'herselfness' (the word Mary Treadgold has used to define her particular brand of self-awareness) had led her to be careful about all her private papers. She kept letters in neat packets, photograph albums with punning captions, press-cutting books, and a diary which, although it revealed little about her feelings after 1919, at least provided a record of her everyday life. There must have been a horde of

334

personal material which, in its comprehensiveness, would have resembled her mother's.

After her death her possessions were either sold by her sons or divided between them. The Lawrence letters went to Texas and the Barrie letters to Yale. There may be other items that I have been unable to trace. But the less saleable items were kept in their homes by Michael and Simon. By great good fortune it was Simon who stored the little red diaries and who, in the late 1960s, lent them to Janet Dunbar when she wrote her life of J.M. Barrie. Her account of Barrie's last years were largely based on these diaries – and she returned them to Simon.

In 1973 Michael stored his possessions in a warehouse while he went to Spain for the summer. The warehouse was destroyed by fire, the circumstances being somewhat mysterious. For example, a child discovered various letters burning on a bonfire 'somewhere in the South of England'. They were eventually acquired by a Bournemouth bookseller who sold them as a collection 'Letters to Lady Cynthia Asquith'; quite a number were sold to the Lilly Library in Indiana. Each letter has a corner missing, suggesting that they had been stuck into a scrapbook, which is very likely since all the letters are from well-known figures, the majority being in response to Cythia's request for contributions to her anthologies.

It is not clear what else was destroyed in the fire, although the Burne-Jones drawing and the Tonks watercolour appear to have been. Luckily Michael had not stored all of Cynthia's papers, so that the war diaries survive, as do items such as two press-cutting books (for the 1950s), two vellum commonplace books, and some letters from correspondents such as Whibley, de la Mare and Enid Bagnold. All Cynthia's letters *to* de la Mare, over three hundred of them, are in the Bodleian. The correspondence between Desmond MacCarthy and Cynthia has survived in its entirety because his letters were being typed for possible publication at the time of the fire, and hers were safely with the MacCarthy Papers. There are inexplicable anomalies among the surviving material, for example there is a large bundle of Cynthia's letters to her mother from 1911–12 and for 1932–7 but for no other years.

Simon's widow moved a few years ago and Cynthia's remaining papers were moved from one attic to another. Some remain lost, others have come to light, for example Beb's letters to his father from prep school, a few letters from Cynthia to Mary Elcho, the single sheet of notepaper touchingly explaining how Cynthia was never happy after Collin Brooks died. The little red diaries were not by this time among Simon's possessions because Michael had acquired them.

For a while I was convinced that Cynthia would not simply have abandoned the detailed diary she kept from 1915–19, and worked on the assumption that the little red diaries were a reduplication of longer ones. I no longer believe this, yet it is still possible that longer diaries may one day be found. The 'quotations' from her diary in her two volumes of reminiscences must either have been made up or the originals were lost. The former explanation is perfectly likely: Cynthia was so vague, or careless of accuracy, when writing about herself that she even cited 10 July as her wedding day instead of 28 July.

So the process of research for this biography has not been straightforward, or rather has not been a question of reading through piles of photocopies – there have been rather few of these. I have had to use a myriad of other methods, such as reading the material relating to other people (it was not until I saw the relevant Blunt Papers at the Fitzwilliam that I realised that Cynthia had been in Egypt, in the next tent, for the full three months), talking to those who knew her, even using the services of a graphologist and an astrologer.

From the former I learnt that Cynthia, through her handwriting, was revealed as charismatic, articulate, poised, self-motivated, witty and vivacious (to pick out some of the adjectives used in the report). I was (at first) disconcerted to be told to ask myself 'how truly loving she really was, and indeed, how sincere?' My graphologist wondered whether, with her analytical nature, 'she was ever self-sacrificing or capable of experiencing passion in any depth'. The astrological report told me less, but was intriguing in its observation that Cynthia was 'probably a writer, perhaps detective writer' and 'had a fight with her creativity or found a lot of restrictions'. And that she could be cutting, although unconscious of it, was a romantic at heart but had a less than straightforward emotional life.

Cynthia, liking palmistry, fortune telling and so on, would have approved of my less conventional research methods. She might not have cared about accuracy as much as I have, and would have laughed at the errors in her published war diaries (of which the change in the opening paragraph of 'try and be *un*introspective' to 'try not to be un-introspective' is only one of many examples). She might have been pleased that the lack of 'straightforward' sources has made the writing more impressionistic and less chronological than it could have been. And would have hoped, as I do, that this book answers the question (it is the one that

comes after my gentle explanation that 'no, she was not Margot')
'well, who was Cynthia Asquith anyway?'

·····➤· Acknowledgements ·◄·····

My greatest debt is to Cynthia Asquith's son Michael Asquith who allowed me to write this biography and granted me access to the Asquith Papers. My other important debt is to the editor and publisher of the 1968 edition of Cynthia's *Diaries 1915–18*. Not only did this book first introduce me to Cynthia, it has proved an endlessly useful reference tool. I must also thank my husband Chris, and Mary Willis, the best of babysitters; my agent Gill Coleridge and my editor Penny Hoare; those without whose help I could not have written this book: Andrew Birkin, Lord Charteris of Amisfield, Charlotte Gere and Lord Neidpath; those too numerous to mention who have helped in small but useful ways such as bothering to answer my letter even if the reply had to be negative, or such as putting me in touch with other people; and the following, whose help has been, in some way or another, invaluable – I thank them all and in particular:

Alison Adburgham, Lady Altrincham, the Hon. Betty Miller Jones, (Betty Askwith), Lady Annunciata Asquith, Conrad Asquith, Hase Asquith, Ivon Asquith, Kip Asquith, Luke Asquith, Vivien Asquith, Jimmie Barrie, Lady Beit, Lord Bonham Carter, Raymond Bonham Carter, Sue Boothby, James T. Boulton, Henry Bristow, Sir Raymond and Lady Carr, Hugh Cecil, Virginia Charteris, Robert Cleveland Stevens, Professor August Closs, Ursula Codrington, John Charmley, the Hon. Artemis Cooper, Rosemary Courcier, Martin Crabbe, the Hon. Iris Dawnay, Lady Margaret Douglas-Home, Dame Daphne du Maurier, Gabriel Dru, Janet Dunbar, Delilah Dyson, Honor Ellis, the Hon. Julian Fane, Rachel Fletcher, Avis Foley, Michael Foot, Veronica Gandy, Martin Gilbert, Ruth Gorb, Oliver Hawkins, Didy Holland-Martin, Michael Holroyd, Lady Howie, Freda James, David Jarrett, the Hon. John Jolliffe, Timothy Jones, Karen Knox, Philippa Lavell, Brendan Lehane, Joan Ling, Lady Mary Lyon, Laura, Duchess of Marlborough, the Hon. Fionn

Acknowledgements

Morgan, Stanley Olson, Helen Oppenheimer, Leonée Ormonde, The Earl of Oxford and Asquith, Frances Partridge, Irene, Countess of Plymouth, Judith Robinson, W. Samengo-Turner, John Saumarez-Smith, George Scott, Anne Sebba, Joyce Sharpey-Schafer, Peyton Skipwith, Margaret Sweeten, Barbara Tebbitt, Mary Treadgold, The Earl of Wemyss, the Hon. Richard and Alice Windsor-Clive, W.W. Winkworth, Dr Patrick Woodcock, Francis Wyndham, Vin and Fran Yorke. I also acknowledge the help of the late Lord David Cecil, Lady Diana Cooper and the Hon. Stephen Tennant.

I should also like to thank the following institutions: Balliol College Library, Oxford; Barrie's Birthplace, Kirriemuir; BBC Sound Archives; the Beinecke Library, Yale University; Bodleian Library, Oxford; the Ladies' College, Cheltenham; Collins Publishers; Curtis Brown; Haymarket Theatre; Highgate Literary and Scientific Institution Library; Houghton Library, Harvard University; University of Illinois at Urbana-Champaign; John Rylands Library, University of Manchester; the London Library; the University of London Library; Lilly Library, Indiana University; National Portrait Gallery; Art Gallery of Ontario; Phillips Auctioneers; Princeton University Library; Public Record Office of Northern Ireland; Royal Artillery Institution; St Hugh's College, Oxford; Scottish Society for the Mentally Handicapped; Harry Ransom Humanities Research Centre, University of Texas at Austin; State Historical Society of Wisconsin.

I am especially grateful to the following for allowing me access to the papers in their possession, and for allowing me to quote from them: Lady Mary Lyon for the Apperley Papers; the Syndics of the Fitzwilliam Museum, Cambridge for the Blunt Papers; Hertfordshire Record Office and Lady Ravensdale for the Desborough Papers; Lawrence Pollinger Ltd, and the Estate of Mrs Frieda Lawrence Ravagli for the Lawrence Papers; Laura Duguid and Andrew Birkin for the Llewelyn Davies Papers; the heirs of Michael and Dermod MacCarthy and of Lady David Cecil for the MacCarthy letters among the Asquith Papers; the Earl of Oxford and Asquith for the Mells Papers; the late Margaret FitzHerbert for the Pixton Papers; Michael Shaw Stewart for the Shaw Stewart Papers; Lord Wemyss and Lord Neidpath for the Stanway Papers.

····➤· Source notes ·≪····

I have abbreviated the source references cited in full in the preceding acknowledgements: thus the papers in the possession of Michael Asquith are referred to as Asquith papers; the papers kept at Stanway House, Gloucestershire as Stanway Papers; and so on. In the case of institutions the first reference is in full, e.g. Beinecke Library, Yale University, but subsequent references are abbreviated, e.g. Beinecke. In the first reference to a book the details of title, publication and so on are given in full. Thereafter I abbreviate either by title or author. Thus Cynthia Asquith *Haply I May Remember* James Barrie 1950 is cited by title but *H.H. Asquith, letters to Venetia Stanley* edited by M. and E. Brock becomes Brock. All dates on their own, e.g. 7 December 1916, refer to Cynthia Asquith's unpublished diaries. If they cover the period 1915–18 the quotation may be found in the published *Diaries 1915–18* (Hutchinson 1968, Century Hutchinson 1987). The version as given here will always be the accurate one, since the published diaries are a necessarily abbreviated, and occasionally inaccurate, version of the unpublished ones.

⋯⟫ Notes ⟪⋯

Chapter 1: Clouds, Stanway, Colin's death: 1887–92
1 Mary Elcho's diary, Stanway Papers
2 Mary Elcho's diary about the children 1889–93, Stanway Papers
3 Mary Elcho's unpublished essay on the Souls, Stanway Papers
4 W. R. Lethaby *Philip Webb and His Work* O.U.P. 1935 p 99
5 ibid.
6 Elspeth Huxley *Nellie: Letters from Africa* Weidenfeld 1980 p 9
7 quoted Jill Franklin *The Gentleman's Country House* Routledge 1981 p 103
8 Cynthia Asquith *Haply I May Remember* James Barrie 1950 p 4
9 Edward Marsh *A Number of People* Heinemann 1939 p 200
10 Philip Ziegler *Diana Cooper* Hamish Hamilton 1981 p 41
11 Cynthia Asquith *The Spring House* Michael Joseph 1936 p 14
12 quoted Franklin id. p 81
13 Mary Elcho's diary about the children op. cit.
14 ibid.
15 ibid.
16 ibid.
17 ibid.
18 ibid.
19 Mary to Hugo 10 January 1893, Stanway Papers
20 Mary Elcho's diary about the children op. cit.
21 *Haply I May Remember* op. cit. p 136
22 ibid. p 123
23 ibid. p 122

Chapter 2: Hugo, Mary and Balfour
1 *Haply I May Remember* op. cit. p 129
2 Blanche Dugdale *Family Homespun* John Murray 1940 p 72

3 Laura, Duchess of Marlborough *Laughter from a Cloud* Weidenfeld 1980 p 12
4 J. M. Barrie *Peter Pan* (1911) Puffin edition 1982 p 30, 31, 35, 14
5 Nancy Ellenberger *The Souls* University of Oregon unpublished thesis 1982 p 104
6 Angela Thirkell *Wild Strawberries* Hamish Hamilton 1934 p 40
7 Angela Thirkell *Love Among the Ruins* Hamish Hamilton 1948 p 106
8 Cynthia Asquith *Remember and Be Glad* James Barrie 1952 p 9
9 Francis Wyndham interview with author 22 November 1982
10 Dugdale id. p 73
11 *Remember and Be Glad* op. cit. p 6
12 Mary to Hugo 29 April 1887, Stanway Papers, quoted Ellenberger id. p 244
13 John Jolliffe *Raymond Asquith*: *Life and Letters* Collins 1980 p 98
14 Maud Wyndham to Ettie Desborough 3 March 1944, Desborough Papers, Hertfordshire Record Office, quoted Ellenberger id. p 244
15 3 February 1985, Blunt Papers, Fitzwilliam Museum, Cambridge
16 quoted Ellenberger id. p 244
17 31 July 1883, Stanway Papers, quoted Ellenberger id. p 216
18 16 December 1886, Stanway Papers, quoted Ellenberger id. p 201
19 2 March 1938
20 August 1887, Stanway Papers, quoted Ellenberger id. p 201
21 Mary to Balfour 14 February 1905, Stanway Papers
22 H. G. Wells *The New Machiavelli* (1911) Ernest Benn edition 1926 p 332
23 Norman and Jeanne MacKenzie ed. *The Diary of Beatrice Webb* Volume 3 Virago 1984 p 52 16 September 1906
24 Miss Jourdain to Mary 13 November 1894, Stanway Papers
25 Walter Raleigh to his wife 10 June 1908, Asquith Papers
26 11 February 1895, Blunt Papers
27 Mary to Balfour 29 July 1898, Stanway Papers
28 ibid. 14 July 1898
29 Balfour to Mary 30 August 1897, Stanway Papers
30 Harry Cust to Mary 4 January 1887 quoted Ellenberger id. p 130
31 undated note made by Mary on copy made by her of Balfour's original letter, Stanway Papers
32 copy made by Mary of Balfour's original letter, Stanway Papers

Chapter 3: Miss Jourdain, Egypt: 1895
1 Cynthia Asquith *The Child at Home* Nisbet & Co. 1923 p 11
2 *Haply I May Remember*, op. cit. p 120
3 Lucille Iremonger *The Ghosts of Versailles* Faber 1957 p 73
4 BBC Talk 28 March 1950
5 *Haply I May Remember*, op. cit. p 210
6 ibid. p 207
7 Elizabeth Longford *A Pilgrimage of Passion* Weidenfeld 1979 p 310
8 *Alms to Oblivion* Part III Chapter 2, Blunt Papers

9 ibid. Part V Chapter 3
10 ibid. Part V Chapter 4
11 ibid.
12 *Secret Memoirs* 15 August 1892, Blunt Papers
13 Miss Jourdain to Mary, Stanway Papers
14 Longford id. p 307
15 *Haply I May Remember*, op. cit. p 83
16 Mary Wemyss *A Family Record* privately printed 1932 p 57
17 9 January 1895, Blunt Papers
18 ibid. 14 January 1895
19 ibid.
20 ibid. 25 January 1895
21 Mary Elcho's diary for 1895, Stanway Papers
22 Miss Jourdain to Mary 1903, Stanway Papers
23 Longford id. p 312
24 10 February 1895, Blunt Papers
25 ibid. 15 February 1895
26 Hugo to Mary 26 February 1895, Stanway Papers
27 *Remember and Be Glad*, op. cit. p 7
28 27 April 1895, Blunt Papers

Chapter 4: Madame de Genlis, Fitzgeralds, Campbells, Wyndhams
1 4 June 1895, Stanway Papers
2 *Haply I May Remember*, op. cit. p 21
3 E. M. Delafield *Consequences* Hodder & Stoughton 1919 p 74
4 quoted in Mark Girouard *The Return to Camelot* Yale University Press
   p 206
5 *Remember and Be Glad* op. cit. p 58
6 Evelyn de Vesci to Miss Jourdain October 1896 copy of original,
   Stanway Papers
7 *Haply I May Remember* op. cit. p 210
8 ibid. p 205
9 Miss Jourdain to Mary April 1899, Stanway Papers
10 C. A. E. Moberly in the *St. Hugh's Chronicle* 1929 p 26
11 Joseph Turquan and Lucy Ellis *La Belle Pamela* Herbert Jenkins 1924
    p 468
12 Violet Wyndham *Madame de Genlis* Andre Deutsch 1958 p 68
13 Katharine Tynan 'Two Brothers: Lord Elcho and Yvo Charteris' in
    The Cornhill Magazine March 1917
14 Violet Wyndham id. p 189
15 Edith Olivier *Four Victorian Ladies of Wiltshire* Faber 1945 p 86
16 ibid. p 91
17 photograph of Madeleine 1873, Blunt Papers
18 Charles Gatty *George Wyndham Recognita* John Murray 1917 p 9
19 J. W. Mackail and G. Wyndham *Life and Letters of George Wyndham*
    Volume I Hutchinson 1925 p 27
20 *Haply I May Remember* op. cit. p. 43

21 Jane Abdy and Charlotte Gere *The Souls* Sidgwick and Jackson 1984 p 95

Chapter 5: The Souls, Squidge
 1 Violet Bonham-Carter 'The Souls' in *The Listener* 30 October 1947
 2 Walter Raleigh to his wife 19 December 1907, Asquith Papers
 3 Barbara Tuchman *The Proud Tower* Macmillan edition 1981 p 19
 4 Margot Asquith to Mary Wemyss 14 August 1930 quoted Ellenberger id. p 19
 5 Mrs Humphrey Ward *A Writer's Recollections* Collins 1918 p 199
 6 *Wild Strawberries* op. cit. p 40
 7 Dugdale id. p 75
 8 Walter Raleigh to his wife 20 December 1907, Asquith Papers
 9 *Remember and Be Glad* op. cit. p 108
10 Ellenberger id. p 38
11 21 April 1909, quoted Jeanne MacKenzie *The Children of the Souls* Chatto & Windus 1986 p 90
12 15 September 1915
13 Ellenberger id. p 85
14 23 September 1915
15 *Remember and Be Glad* op. cit. p 118
16 8 April 1916
17 1 May 1915
18 13 January 1918
19 Margot Asquith *Autobiography* Eyre & Spottiswoode edition 1962 p 118
20 William Rothenstein *Men and Memories* Volume I Faber 1931 p 258
21 Mary to Balfour 19 January 1900, Stanway Papers, quoted Ellenberger p 12
22 *Haply I May Remember* op. cit. p 207
23 ibid. p 206
24 BBC talk op. cit.
25 *Haply I May Remember* op. cit. p 211
26 BBC talk op. cit.
27 *Haply I May Remember* op. cit. p 228

Chapter 6: Gosford, Lord Wemyss, Dresden: 1903
 1 *Haply I May Remember* op. cit. p 63
 2 Dugdale id. p 148
 3 Mrs Humphrey Ward id. p 311
 4 *A Family Record* op. cit. p 11
 5 ibid. p 13
 6 Mary to Balfour 20 January 1906, Stanway Papers quoted Ellenberger id. p 61
 7 John Vincent ed. *The Crawford Papers* Manchester University Press 1984 p 222

8   *Haply I May Remember* op. cit. p 218
9   Miss Jourdain to Mary February 1902, Stanway Papers
10 Abdy and Gere id. p 50
11 Richard Aldington *Portrait of a Genius, But* Heinemann 1950 p 109
12 Mrs Claude Beddington *All That I Have Met* Cassell 1929 p 62

Chapter 7: Asquiths
1   J. A. Spender and C. Asquith *Life of Lord Oxford and Asquith* Volume I Hutchinson 1932 p 15
2   H. H. Asquith *Memories and Reflections* Volume I Cassell 1928 p 3
3   Roy Jenkins *Asquith* Collins 1964 p 11
4   H. H. Asquith id. p 13
5   M. and E. Brock ed. *H. H. Asquith, letters to Venetia Stanley* O.U.P. 1982 p 443
6   Stephen Koss *Asquith* Allen Lane 1976 p 15
7   Herbert (Beb) Asquith *Moments of Memory* Hutchinson 1937 p 55
8   ibid. p 60
9   ibid. p 57
10 ibid. p 49
11 H. H. Asquith to Mrs Horner 11 September 1892 quoted R. Jenkins id. p 56
12 ibid. p 55
13 Spender and Asquith id. p 38
14 *Moments of Memory* op. cit. p 20
15 Beb to H. H. Asquith undated, Asquith Papers
16 ibid. 13 May 1894
17 Koss id. p 2
18 Spender and Asquith id. p 98
19 quoted Brock id. p 7
20 R. Jenkins id. pp 80 and 81
21 quoted Brock id. p 10
22 Margot Asquith id. p 200
23 *Moments of Memory* op. cit.

Chapter 8: Coming Out, Northlands: 1905
1   Margot Asquith id. p 208
2   *Moments of Memory* op. cit. p 123
3   *Haply I May Remember* op. cit. p 225
4   *A Family Record* op. cit. p 84
5   *Remember and Be Glad* op. cit. p 62
6   *Haply I May Remember* op. cit. p 228
7   ibid.
8   BBC talk op. cit.
9   Molly MacCarthy *A Nineteenth Century Childhood* Heinemann 1924 p 82
10 Mary Grierson *Tovey* O.U.P. 1952 p 4

11 Cynthia to Beb November 1908, Asquith Papers
12 *Haply I May Remember* op. cit. p 231
13 23 March 1916
14 27 November 1918
15 *Family Record* op. cit. p 89
16   David Pryce-Jones *Unity Mitford* Weidenfeld 1976 p 27
17 *Family Record* op. cit. p 92
18 Mabell, Countess of Airlie *Thatched With Gold* Hutchinson 1962 p 40
19 *Family Record* op. cit. p 93
20 *Remember and Be Glad* op. cit. p 81
21 1 February 1916
22 Jolliffe id. p 130

Chapter 9: Raymond: 1906–7
 1 Molly MacCarthy id. p 83
 2 Cynthia to Beb 1908, Asquith Papers
 3 ibid.
 4 *Remember and Be Glad* op. cit. p 163
 5 Cynthia to Beb, Asquith Papers
 6 *Remember and Be Glad*, op. cit. p 131
 7 ibid. p 132
 8 Cynthia to Katharine Asquith 22 August 1908, Mells Papers
 9 *Remember and Be Glad* op. cit. p 128
10 Koss id. p 8
11 Jolliffe id. p 29
12 quoted Brock id. p 630
13 W. B. Hepburn in *The Sunday Telegraph* 4 May 1984
14 Jolliffe id. p 173
15 Raymond to Cynthia 14 October 1908, Asquith Papers
16 Jolliffe id. p 80
17 ibid. p 151
18 ibid. p 118
19 ibid. p 128
20 ibid. p 148
21 ibid. p 149
22 Sue Boothby in interview with author 23 March 1984
23 Letter John Jolliffe to author 18 November 1985
24 Mary's diary July 5 1907, Stanway Papers
25 Ettie Grenfell *Pages from a Family Journal* quoted Angela Lambert
    Unquiet Souls Macmillan 1984 p 98
26 Stanway Visitor's Book entry for early 1906
27 *Remember and Be Glad* op. cit. p 73
28 Beb to Cynthia, Asquith Papers

Chapter 10: 1908

1 Asquith Papers. All subsequent quotations in this chapter from letters between Cynthia and Beb are from the same source and are not separately cited.
2 *Family Record* op. cit. p 118
3 Luke Asquith interview with author 28 March 1983
4 Raymond to Cynthia July 1907, Asquith Papers
5 Mary to Balfour 2 August 1904, quoted Ellenberger p 161
6 Balfour to Mary 13 September 1911, ibid.
7 11 June 1915
8 *Family Record* op cit. p 97
9 Brock id. p 5
10 Margot Asquith's unpublished diary, courtesy of Lord Bonham Carter
11 Kenneth Young *Balfour* G. Bell & Sons 1963 p 169
12 ibid. p 255
13 R. C. K. Ensor *England 1870–1914* O.U.P. 1936 p 387
14 John Grigg *Lloyd George: The People's Champion 1902–1911* Eyre Methuen 1978 p 192
15 ibid. p 225
16 Raymond to Cynthia 3 February 1909, Asquith Papers

Chapter 11: Marriage: 1909–10

1 De Glehn Papers, Boston Public Library, courtesy of Stanley Olson.
2 *Family Record* op. cit. p 111
3 undated letter, Pixton Papers
4 *Family Record* op. cit. p 132
5 J. Lomax and R. Ormond *John Singer Sargent and the Edwardian Age* Leeds Art Gallery 1979 p 71
6 9 June 1916
7 *Haply I May Remember* op. cit. p 89, elaborated by Charles Merrill Mount in his 1955 biography of Sargent p 226
8 Cynthia to Aubrey November 1909, Pixton Papers
9 Diana Cooper *The Rainbow Comes and Goes* Rupert Hart-Davis 1958 p 78
10 Lord Ribblesdale *Charles Lister* T. Fisher Unwin 1917 p 26
11 Edward Thomas *Maurice Maeterlinck* Methuen 1911 p 2
12 undated letter, Mells Papers
13 N. J. Macqueen-Pope *Haymarket: Theatre of Perfection* W. H. Allen 1948 p 364
14 27 April 1910, Mells Papers
15 Cynthia to Patrick Shaw Stewart 7 June 1910, Shaw Stewart Papers
16 *The Times* 2 April 1960
17 Jolliffe id. p 172

Chapter 12: 1910–12

1 Cynthia to Katharine Asquith 10 August 1910, Mells Papers
2 Bernard Berenson to Cynthia 19 February 1911, Lilly Library, Indiana University
3 R. Lewis and A. Maude *The English Middle Classes* Phoenix House 1949 p 252
4 Cynthia to Katharine Asquith 3 May 1910, Mells Papers
5 Cynthia to Beb 6 July 1910, Asquith Papers
6 ed. Nigel Nicolson *The Letters of Virginia Woolf* Volume One The Hogarth Press 1975 p 484
7 ibid. p 480
8 ibid. p 484
9 Cynthia to Katharine Asquith September 1910, Mells Papers
10 ibid.
11 Cynthia to Blunt December 1910, Blunt Papers
12 ibid.
13 N. Pevsner *The Buildings of England: London (except the Cities of London and Westminster)* Penguin 1952 p 346
14 Elizabeth Bowen *The Death of the Heart* Gollancz 1938 p 54
15 Elizabeth Bowen to Virginia Woolf 1935 quoted Victoria Glendinning *Elizabeth Bowen* Weidenfeld 1977 p 92
16 20 February 1911, Stanway Papers
17 7 December 1910, Asquith Papers
18 quoted Margaret FitzHerbert *The Man Who Was Greenmantle* John Murray 1983 p 103
19 G. Dangerfield *The Strange Death of Liberal England* Constable 1936 p 128
20 Roger Fulford *Votes for Women* Faber 1957 p 184
21 *Moments of Memory* op. cit. p 158
22 Desborough Papers
23 Asquith Papers
24 ibid.
25 *Family Record* op. cit. p 155
26 Stanway Papers
27 Asquith Papers
28 August 1911, Mells Papers
29 Cynthia to Mary Elcho, Asquith Papers
30 R. Jenkins id. p 260
31 Asquith Papers
32 ibid.
33 Cynthia to Katharine Asquith, Mells Papers
34 2 November 1912, Asquith Papers
35 Mells Papers
36 *Family Record* op. cit. p 220

Chapter 13: 1913

1   19 June 1913, Mells Papers
2   10 May 1910, Stanway Papers
3   7 December 1916
4   *The Letters of D. H. Lawrence* Volume II Cambridge University Press 1981 p 62
5   ibid. p 37
6   ibid. p 46
7   ibid. p 47
8   ibid. p 35
9   ibid. p 41
10 *Remember and Be Glad*, op. cit. p 133, originally in *The Listener* 15 September 1949
11 *Letters* op. cit. p 48
12 ibid. p 49
13 ibid. p 48
14 ibid. p 51
15 Cecil Gray *Musical Chairs* Home & Van Thal 1948 p 138
16 *Letters* op. cit. p 380
17 D. H. Lawrence 'The Thimble' in *The Mortal Coil* Penguin edition 1982 pp 198–200
18 *Letters* op. cit. p 47
19 ibid. p 107
20 D. H. Lawrence 'The Ladybird' in *The Complete Short Novels* Penguin 1982 p 210
21 *Letters* op. cit. p 62
22 ibid. p 109
23 ibid. p 89
24 ibid. p 107
25 *The Rainbow Comes and Goes* op. cit. p 104
26 ibid.
27 *Letters* op. cit. p 89
28 ibid. p 109
29 31 March 1914, Mells Papers
30 ibid.
31 *Letters* op. cit. p 63
32 31 March 1914, Mells Papers
33 25 April 1914, Mells Papers
34 quoted Nicholas Mosley *Julian Grenfell* Weidenfeld 1976 p 239
35 *Rupert Brooke: The Collected Poems* 1918, Sidgwick and Jackson edition 1958 p 146
36 Cynthia to Mary Charteris 19 February 1915, Apperley Papers
37 Brock id. p 79
38 *Family Record* op. cit. p 183

Chapter 14: 1914

1 *Family Record* op. cit. p 239
2 ibid.
3 ibid. p 240
4 ibid.
5 *The Spring House* op. cit. p 9
6 *Family Record* op. cit. p 241
7 ibid. p 242
8 ibid. p 257
9 ibid. p 256
10 Brock id. p 228
11 Jolliffe id. p 191
12 *Family Record* op. cit. p 242
13 ibid. p 243
14 28 September 1914, Mells Papers
15 Jolliffe id. p 193
16 'The Thimble' op. cit. p 196
17 Margot Asquith's unpublished diaries
18 Cynthia's unpublished diary for week of 25 October 1914, ditto all subsequent unreferenced quotations to end of chapter

Chapter 15: 1914–15

1 Kathleen Tynan 'Two Brothers: Lord Elcho and Yvo Charteris' op. cit.
2 15 April 1915
3 'The Ladybird' op. cit. p 248
4 June 1911, Mells Papers
5 'The Ladybird' op. cit. p 265
6 ed. Anne Olivier Bell *The Diary of Virginia Woolf* Volume Two The Hogarth Press 1978 p 234 19 February 1923
7 Alan Pryce-Jones in *The New York Times Book Review* 23 February 1969
8 *Saturday Review* 22 March 1969
9 13 October 1915
10 14 June 1915
11 *The Listener* 25 April 1968
12 *The Spectator* 3 May 1968
13 *Saturday Review* 22 March 1969
14 *Book World* 6 April 1969
15 *Letters* op. cit. p 89
16 15 April 1915
17 D. H. Lawrence *The Complete Short Stories* Volume III 'Glad Ghosts' Heinemann 1955 p 663
18 *Haply I May Remember* op. cit. p 212
19 Mark Girouard id. p 289
20 quoted ibid. p 287
21 ibid. p 282

22 Rupert Brooke id. p cxxiii
23 8 July 1917
24 D. H. Lawrence *Lady Chatterley's Lover* Penguin edition 1981 p 6
25 25 October 1914
26 ibid.
27 Jolliffe id. p 274
28 25 June 1911, Asquith Papers

Chapter 16: John
1 *The Child at Home* op. cit. p 12
2 J. Gathorne-Hardy *The Rise and Fall of the British Nanny* Hodder and Stoughton 1972 p 19
3 Cynthia to Ettie Desborough April 24 1913, Desborough Papers
4 Frieda to Cynthia October 1913, HRC, University of Texas at Austin
5 5 May 1915
6 11 May 1915
7 20 April 1917
8 *Letters* op. cit. p 337
9 Cynthia to Katharine 25 April 1914, Mells Papers
10 Jolliffe id. p 259
11 *Letters* op. cit. p 336
12 6 June 1915
13 11 July 1915
14 14 August 1915
15 16 April 1915
16 22 August 1915
17 23 October 1915
18 14 February 1916
19 undated letter Mary Wemyss to Cynthia, Asquith Papers
20 13 May 1916
21 12 May 1915
22 14 October 1916
23 3 August 1917
24 6 May 1917
25 20 April 1917
26 12 July 1917
27 31 October 1917, Asquith Papers
28 20 November 1917
29 12 July 1917
30 15 January 1918
31 21 August 1916
32 20 July 1918
33 19 September 1918
34 Dr Tredgold to Dr Easterbrook 9 August 1926 quoting notes for March 1920, courtesy of the Scottish Society for the Mentally Handicapped

35 Headmaster St Christopher's to Dr Easterbrook 6 July 1926, courtesy SSMH
36 Chrichton Royal Clinical Records, courtesy SSMH
37 21 May 1937
38 Margaret Kennedy *The Ladies of Lyndon* Virago Press edition 1981 p xii
39 ibid. pp 15, 23, 33, 38, 217

Chapter 17: 1915
 1 24 December 1916
 2 24 December 1915
 3 Brock id. p 371
 4 17 April 1915
 5 23 and 27 April 1915
 6 August 1916, Apperley Papers
 7 7 May and 26 April 1915
 8 31 January 1916
 9 31 May 1915
10 14 July 1916
11 17 April 1915
12 *The Spring House* op. cit. p 148
13 8 and 15 May 1915
14 31 May 1915
15 Cynthia to Patrick Shaw Stewart June 1915, Shaw Stewart Papers
16 14 June 1915
17 *The Man Who Was Greenmantle* op. cit. p 155
18 28 May 1916
19 30 July 1915
20 11 June 1915
21 4 August 1915
22 Nicholas Mosley id. p 254
23 12 August 1915
24 24 October 1916
25 31 August 1915
26 *Family Record* op. cit. p 364
27 Ann Thwaite *Edmund Gosse* Secker and Warburg 1984 p 451
28 Herbert Asquith *Poems 1912–1933* Sidgwick and Jackson 1934 p 69
29 17 September 1915
30 28 September 1915
31 12 October 1915
32 18 October 1915
33 4 September 1915
34 22 October 1915
35 28 October 1915
36 30 October 1915
37 'The Ladybird' op. cit. pp 207, 210, 206
38 26 December 1915 ·

Chapter 18: D. H. Lawrence

1 Cynthia to Mary Charteris 19 February 1915, Apperley Papers
2 *Letters* op. cit. p 289 and p 288
3 ed. C. A. Hankin *The Letters of John Middleton Murry to Katharine Mansfield* Constable 1983 p 40 16 February 1915
4 *Letters* op. cit. p 339
5 11 May 1915
6 22 July 1915
7 Keith Sagar *The Life of D. H. Lawrence* Eyre Methuen 1980 p 91
8 Ruth Gorb in *The Hampstead and Highgate Express* 19 July 1985
9 E. Delavenay *D. H. Lawrence: The Man and His Work* Heinemann 1972 p 251
10 Ruth Gorb id.
11 Delavenay id. p 250
12 *Portrait of a Genius, But* op. cit. p 169
13 Delavenay p 284
14 Frieda to Cynthia 1915, Texas
15 Harry Moore *The Priest of Love* Heinemann 1974 p 187
16 Harry Moore and Warren Roberts *D. H. Lawrence and his world* Thames & Hudson 1966 p 42
17 Sagar id. p 91
18 Delavenay p 289
19 D. H. Lawrence *The White Peacock* Heinemann edition 1969 p 150
20 ibid. p 85
21 D. H. Lawrence *The Trespasser* Heinemann edition 1976 p 23
22 Atheneum 1 June 1912, quoted R. P. Draper *D. H. Lawrence: The Critical Heritage* Routledge 1970 p 45
23 D. H. Lawrence *Sons and Lovers* Penguin edition 1967 p 177
24 16 October 1918
25 19 March 1930, Texas
26 *The Priest of Love* op. cit. p 510
27 *Letters* op. cit. p 527
28 ibid. p 587
29 ibid. p 368
30 *The Letters of D. H. Lawrence* Volume III Cambridge University Press 1984 p 118
31 quoted Paul Delany *D. H. Lawrence's Nightmare* Harvester Press 1979 p 104
32 *Letters* Volume II op. cit. p 359
33 ibid. p 438
34 18 August 1915
35 *A Number of People* op. cit. p 234
36 17 October 1915
37 *Letters* Volume II op. cit. p 424
38 ibid. p 431
39 11 May 1915
40 *Letters* Volume II op. cit. p 368
41 23 April 1917

42 *Letters* Volume II op. cit. p 369
43 11 October 1915
44 10 November 1915
45 *Letters* Volume II op. cit. p 418
46 31 October 1915
47 'The Thimble' op. cit. p 198
48 D. H. Lawrence 'The Blind Man' in *Selected Short Stories* Penguin 1982 p 302
49 'The Ladybird' op. cit. p 209
50 ibid. p 272
51 'Glad Ghosts' op. cit. p 666
52 'The Ladybird' op. cit. p 247
53 'Glad Ghosts' op. cit. p 671
54 *Lady Chatterley's Lover* op. cit. p 21
55 9 March 1918
56 *Letters* Volume III op. cit. p 465
57 13 October 1918
58 25 November 1918
59 *Letters* Volume III op. cit. p 395
60 ibid. p 517
61 5 December 1922, Texas
62 19 November 1925, ibid.
63 5 April 1928, ibid.
64 'The Ladybird' op. cit. p 264
65 Frieda to Cynthia 18 March 1930, undated, 15 October 1950, Texas

Chapter 19: 1916
 1 11 November 1915
 2 15 November 1915
 3 13 December 1916
 4 15 November 1915
 5 23 August 1915
 6 19 December 1915
 7 30 November 1915
 8 E. Longford id. p. 411
 9 31 December 1915
10 5 January 1916
11 30 January 1916
12 17 February 1916
13 21 June 1916
14 8 March 1916
15 4 March 1916
16 3 April 1916
17 22 March 1916
18 8 July 1916
19 24 July 1916
20 Cynthia to Ettie Desborough 19 September 1916, Desborough Papers

21 'The Thimble' op. cit. p 196
22 16 November 1916
23 26 October 1916
24 8 June 1916

Chapter 20: Basil
1   Mary to Balfour 21 January 1893, Stanway Papers
2   *The Listener* 30 October 1947
3   Mosley id. p 51
4   ibid. p 143
5   Longford id. p 419
6   Cynthia to Ettie Desborough 24 April 1913, Desborough Papers
7   'The Thimble' op. cit. p 196
8   John Buchan *Memory Hold-the-Door* Hodder and Stoughton 1940 p 105
9   ibid. p 106
10 A. N. Wilson *Hilaire Belloc* Hamish Hamilton 1984 p 113
11 *The Spring House* op. cit. p 272
12 Buchan id. p 106
13 13 August 1915, Public Record Office of Northern Ireland D. 1231/G/5/282
14 3 August 1915, Desborough Papers
15 *The Spring House* op. cit. p 197
16 3 May 1918
17 14 September 1916
18 *The Trespasser* op. cit. p 23
19 3 May 1916

Chapter 21: 1917
1   3 January 1917
2   7 February 1917
3   22 January 1917
4   23 January 1917
5   22 February 1917
6   30 January 1917
7   16 January 1918
8   3 February 1917
9   20 February 1917
10 27 February 1917
11 31 August 1917
12 20 March 1917
13 12 May 1917
14 6 and 18 July 1917
15 26 July 1917
16 1 August 1917
17 3 September 1916

18 14 May 1917
19 6 August 1917
20 20 August 1917
21 9 September 1917
22 8 September 1917
23 21 September 1917
24 L. P. Hartley *The Go-Between* Penguin edition 1961 p 7
25 23 November 1917
26 30 December 1916

Chapter 22: Lovers
 1 Enid Bagnold *The Squire* Virago edition 1987 pp 96 and 192
 2 Whibley to Cynthia undated, Asquith Papers
 3 John Gross *The Rise and Fall of the Man of Letters* Weidenfeld 1969
    p 155
 4 T.S. Eliot *Selected Essays* Faber 1961 p498
 5 Whibley to Cynthia undated, Asquith Papers
 6 26 August 1916
 7 3 April 1917
 8 28 August 1916
 9 21 September 1918
10 2 September 1917
11 Anita Leslie *Cousin Clare* Hutchinson 1976 p88
12 ibid. p90
13 17 and 18 September 1918
14 29 October 1916
15 13 May 1917
16 23 January 1917
17 29 November 1917
18 5 January 1918

Chapter 23: 1918
 1 31 December 1917
 2 6 January 1918
 3 ibid.
 4 *Remember and Be Glad* op.cit. p 192
 5 quoted 3 July 1916
 6 12 January 1918
 7 2 February 1918
 8 10 February 1918
 9 21 February 1918
10 23 February 1918
11 28 May 1918
12 23 and 24 March 1918
13 30 April 1918
14 16 December 1918

15   29 April 1918
16   12 May 1918
17   Cynthia to Desmond MacCarthy 13 May 1918, MacCarthy Papers
18   29 May 1918
19   24 April 1918
20   20 June 1918
21   1 June 1918
22   30 July 1918
23   23 August 1918
24   19 July 1918
25   26 September 1918
26   Cynthia to Beb 25 July 1918, Asquith Papers
27   6 September 1918
28   10 October 1918
29   *The Man Who Was Greenmantle* op.cit. p 214
30   9 October 1918
31   18 October 1918
32   19 October 1918
33   15, 18 and 21 November 1918
34   17 December 1918

Chapter 24: Painters
 1   'The Ladybird' op.cit. p248
 2   *Haply I May Remember* op.cit. p91
 3   ibid.
 4   ibid. p83
 5   ibid. p90
 6   1 February 1918
 7   23 February 1919
 8   *Haply I May Remember* op.cit. p101
 9   17 June 1916
10   26 July 1916
11   5 April 1917
12   20 June 1917
13   14 November 1917
14   30 October 1917
15   17 July 1919
16   19 January 1919
17   17 October 1919
18   Augustus John to Cynthia 5 October 1917, in private collection
      whereabouts unknown, courtesy of Michael Holroyd
19   9 October 1917
20   caption in exhibition catalogue 'Another World: Salon and
      Academy Paintings c.1805–1925' at Art Gallery of New York
      University January–February 1976
21   9 October 1917
22   Augustus John *Chiaroscuro* Jonathan Cape 1952 p86

23 1 November 1936
24 *Daily Mail* 26 February 1918
25 Curator of the Toronto Art Gallery to Michael Holroyd 28 April 1969
26 Augustus John to Cynthia 31 May 1918, in private collection op. cit.
27 3 October 1918
28 26 November 1918
29 19 January 1919

Chapter 25: 1919
 1 2 January 1919
 2 25 April 1919
 3 16 January 1919
 4 16 and 17 January 1919
 5 Katharine Mansfield to Elizabeth Bibesco 24 March 1921, quoted *The Life of Katharine Mansfield* by Antony Alpers Jonathan Cape 1980 p 329
 6 30 January 1919
 7 31 March 1919
 8 Cynthia to Beb 7 February 1919
 9 28 March 1919
10 5 March 1919
11 7 June 1910, Shaw Stewart Papers
12 Cynthia to Desmond 30 November 1919, MacCarthy Papers
13 ibid.
14 23 April 1919
15 21 April 1919
16 6 July 1919
17 Mary Lutyens *To Be Young* Rupert Hart-Davis 1959 p57
18 2 August 1919
19 6 August 1919
20 7 February 1919
21 19 August 1919
22 Cynthia to Desmond 4 September 1919 MacCarthy Papers
23 13 September 1919
24 Cynthia to Desmond October 1919, MacCarthy Papers
25 Cynthia to Desmond 1 November 1919, ibid.
26 20 October 1919
27 Cynthia to Desmond 21 October 1919, MacCarthy Papers
28 Cynthia to Desmond 12 October 1919, ibid.
29 Cynthia to Desmond 1 November 1919, ibid.
30 Cynthia to Desmond 13 December 1919, ibid.

Notes

Chapter 26: Desmond

1   20 March 1919
2   Mina Curtiss *Other People's Letters* Macmillan 1978 p84
3   ed. Nigel Nicolson *The Letters of Virginia Woolf* Volume Two The Hogarth Press 1976 p 215 29 January 1918
4   ed. Anne Olivier Bell *The Diary of Virginia Woolf* Volume One The Hogarth Press 1977 pl50 28 May 1918
5   9 January 1919
6   25 January 1918
7   John Gross id. p243
8   Virginia Woolf *The Waves* The Hogarth Press 1931 pp125 and 144
9   *The Diary of Virginia Woolf* Volume One op.cit. p156 17 June 1918
10 ibid. p241 18 February 1919
11 31 May 1919
12 27 July 1918
13 Leonard Woolf *Beginning Again* The Hogarth Press 1964 p136
14 *The Diary of Virginia Woolf* Volume One op.cit. p 241
15 26 August 1918
16 *The Diary of Virginia Woolf* Volume One op.cit. p 206 23 October 1918
17 *The Letters of Virginia Woolf* Volume Two op.cit. p 291 11 November 1918
18 Desmond to Cynthia 17 April 1919, Asquith Papers, courtesy of the heirs of Michael and Dermod MacCarthy and of Lady David Cecil
19 *The Diary of Virginia Woolf* Volume One op.cit. p 267 20 April 1919
20 8 July 1925
21 8 December 1932
22 9 December 1918
23 20 October 1918
24 4 November 1918
25 5 November 1918
26 *The Letters of Virginia Woolf* Volume Two op.cit. p 297 19 November 1918
27 14 November 1918
28 20 November 1918
29 23 November 1918
30 25 November 1918
31 Desmond to Cynthia 26 November 1918, Asquith Papers
32 Cynthia to Desmond 27 November 1918, MacCarthy Papers
33 29 November 1918
34 30 November 1918
35 Desmond to Cynthia 17 December 1918, Asquith Papers
36 Cynthia to Desmond 2 January 1919, MacCarthy Papers
37 3 February 1919
38 Desmond to Cynthia 23 February 1919, Asquith Papers
39 Desmond to Cynthia 9 March 1919, ibid.
40 Cynthia to Desmond 11 March 1919, MacCarthy Papers

41 Desmond to Cynthia 28 March 1919, Asquith Papers
42 30 May 1919
43 Cynthia to Desmond 3 June 1919, MacCarthy Papers
44 Desmond to Cynthia 21 July 1919, Asquith Papers
45 29 January 1919
46 Desmond to Cynthia 1 August 1920, Asquith Papers

Chapter 27: Barrie
1 30 June 1918, original letter lost
2 J.M. Barrie *Margaret Ogilvie* Hodder and Stoughton edition 1938 p 33
3 quoted Andrew Birkin *J.M. Barrie and The Lost Boys* Constable 1979 p 231
4 ibid. p 12
5 'The Blind Man' op.cit. pp 303 and 312
6 Birkin id p55
7 ibid. p 66
8 ibid. p 122
9 ibid. p 142
10 ibid. p 162
11 ibid. p 177
12 ibid. p 181
13 ibid. p 182
14 ibid. p 192
15 ibid. p 196
16 14 April 1916
17 23 June 1918
18 Barrie to Cynthia 13 June 1919, Beinecke Library, Yale University
19 23 June 1918
20 26 June 1918
21 Cynthia to Desmond 29 June 1918, MacCarthy Papers
22 24 July 1918
23 29 August 1918
24 2 September 1918
25 31 August 1918
26 30 September 1918
27 28 October 1918
28 14 February 1919
29 8 November 1918
30 11 January 1919
31 23 April 1919
32 7 May 1919
33 J. M. Barrie *The Little White Bird* Hodder & Stonghton 1902 p 40

Chapter 28: 1920
1 Desmond to Cynthia 1 August 1920, Asquith Papers
2 Barrie to Cynthia 28 April 1920, Beinecke

3 Barrie to Cynthia 4 June 1920, ibid.
4 Barrie to Cynthia 18 June 1920, ibid.
5 Cynthia to Desmond July 1920, MacCarthy Papers
6 Barrie to Cynthia 10 July 1920, Beinecke
7 Barrie to Cynthia 7 August 1920, ibid.
8 Barrie to Cynthia 27 April 1921, ibid.
9 Denis Mackail *The Story of J.M.B.* Peter Davies 1941 p560
10 quoted Birkin id. p282
11 ibid. p189
12 Barrie to Cynthia 1 September 1921, Beinecke
13 Barrie to Cynthia 4 October 1921, ibid.
14 Barrie to Cynthia 23 December 1920, ibid.
15 Barrie to Cynthia 7 September 1921, ibid.

Chapter 29: 1920s

1 Virginia Woolf *Mrs Dalloway* Penguin edition 1967 p 86
2 ibid. p 82
3 ibid. p 87
4 ibid. p 12
5 ibid. p 36
6 Cynthia to Mary 18 November 1933, Asquith Papers
7 25 May 1921
8 30 and 31 August 1924
9 15, 21 and 25 August 1921
10 7 September 1921
11 28 August 1924
12 25 August 1924
13 1 September 1923
14 13 April 1925
15 18 August 1929
16 Nico Llewelyn Davies to Andrew Birkin 29 November 1975, Llewelyn Davies Papers
17 Daphne du Maurier *Gerald* Gollancz 1934 p27
18 ibid. p79
19 Gerry Llewelyn Davies in conversation with Andrew Birkin 20 March 1976, Llewelyn Davies Papers
20 Birkin id. p189
21 13 August 1928
22 25 October 1929
23 Siegfried Sassoon *Diaries* Faber & Faber 1981 p 168 8 June 1922
24 Lady Mary Lyon unpublished diary 10 November 1925
25 D.H. Lawrence *Letters* Volume III op.cit. p518 7 May 1920
26 *The Little White Bird* op. cit. p 5
27 undated letter (about January 1923) Barrie to Cynthia, Beinecke
28 Birkin id. p297

Chapter 30: Writing
1 28 December 1918
2 3 January 1919
3 18 April 1922
4 *Haply I May Remember* op.cit. p183
5 *The Times* 8 June 1922
6 ibid. 25 May 1922
7 *Haply I May Remember* op.cit. p179
8 Barrie to Cynthia 22 September 1922, Beinecke
9 Cynthia to Scribner's 13 February 1923, Princeton University Library
10 *The Child at Home* op.cit. p51
11 29 January 1923
12 Barrie to Cynthia 7 April 1923, Beinecke
13 Eddie Marsh to Cynthia 1 July 1923, Asquith Papers
14 Barrie to Cynthia 25 June and 3 July 1923, Beinecke
15 Christina Hardyment *Dream Babies* Jonathan Cape 1983 p164
16 Private note by Mrs Frankenberg, courtesy Christina Hardyment
17 *Haply I May Remember* op.cit. p184
18 ed. A.C. Benson and Sir Laurence Weaver *The Book of the Queen's Dolls' House* Methuen 1924 p121
19 *New York Herald Tribune* 6 March 1927
20 Cynthia to Walter de la Mare 14 October 1924, Bodleian Library, Oxford
21 Cynthia to de la Mare, 26 February 1925 ibid.
22 *New York Herald Tribune* 24 October 1926
23 25 October 1925
24 Letter Cynthia to Scribner's 13 December 1926, Princeton
25 D. H. Lawrence 'The Rocking-Horse Winner' in *Selected Short Stories* Penguin 1982 p 444
26 Lawrence to Cynthia 15 April 1926, Texas
27 Cynthia to de la Mare 19 February 1926, Bodleian
28 D.H. Lawrence 'The Lovely Lady' in *Selected Short Stories* Penguin 1982 p484
29 cf. Brian Finney 'A Newly Discovered Text of D. H. Lawrence's "The Lovely Lady" ' Yale University Library Gazette January 1975
30 *The New York Times* 30 December 1928
31 David Higham *Literary Gent* Jonathan Cape 1978 p167
32 11 July 1927
33 Cynthia Asquith *The Duchess of York* Hutchinson 1928 p217
34 21 July 1936
35 11 November 1936
36 11 December 1936
37 *The Spring House* op. cit. p 365
38 5 October 1935
39 Mary Wemyss's diary 22 July 1936, Stanway Papers
40 *The Spring House* op. cit. p 291
41 22 October 1936

42 Enid Bagnold to Cynthia 29 October 1936, Asquith papers, courtesy
    of Timothy Jones
43 Cynthia to de la Mare 16 November 1936, Bodleian
44 *The Spring House* op.cit. p 23
45 ibid. p 49

Chapter 31: 1930s
 1 Enid Bagnold to Cynthia 17 June 1935, Asquith Papers
 2 Barrie to Cynthia 10 June 1937, Beinecke
 3 6 February 1935
 4 19 August 1932
 5 23 November 1936
 6 Derek Stanford *Inside the Forties* Sidgwick & Jackson 1977 p 227
 7 Michael Holroyd *Augustus John* Penguin edition 1976 p 536
 8 23 May 1935
 9 Cynthia's unpublished diary about the children, Asquith Papers
10 ibid.
11 21 August 1924
12 Barrie to Cynthia 24 June 1928, Beinecke
13 Cynthia's unpublished diary about the children, op. cit.
14 entry in *Dictionary of National Biography*
15 2 November 1935
16 Enid Bagnold to Cynthia 8 November 1943, Asquith Papers
17 Quentin Bell *Virginia Woolf* Volume Two The Hogarth Press 1972
    p 82
18 Russell Brain *Tea With Walter de la Mare* Faber 1957 p 16
19 17 June 1935
20 15 February 1939
21 17 May 1934
22 13 June 1931
23 5 January 1936
24 *Augustus John* op. cit. p 625
25 7 May 1930
26 30 March 1937
27 Mary Wemyss's diary 23 April 1937
28 5 May 1937
29 15 May 1937
30 24 May 1937
31 28 May 1937
32 Nico Llewelyn Davies to Andrew Birkin 29 November 1975,
    Llwewlyn Davies Papers
33 21 June 1937
34 27 June 1937
35 2 July 1937

Chapter 32: 1940s
1 Cynthia to Mary Wemyss 15 August 1932, Asquith Papers
2 22 May 1938
3 26 April 1939
4 15 July 1939
5 28 August 1939
6 Harold Nicolson's unpublished diary 3 December 1938, Balliol College Library, Oxford
7 Cynthia to Ettie 13 September 1939, Desborough Papers
8 ibid.
9 Cynthia to de la Mare 19 November 1939, Bodleian
10 Cynthia to de la Mare 21 June 1940 ibid.
11 Cynthia to de la Mare October 1942 ibid.
12 10 April 1941
13 *Vogue* September 1957
14 26 March 1946
15 Rosemary Courcier, in conversation with author 10 November 1984
16 28 October 1940
17 Cynthia to Ettie 26 August 1942, Desborough Papers
18 James Lees-Milne *Ancestral Voices* Chatto & Windus 1975 14 April 1943
19 Cynthia to Ettie 27 April 1941, Desborough Papers
20 16 January 1941
21 25 January 1941
22 Cynthia Asquith *One Sparkling Wave* Michael Joseph 1943 p 212
23 ibid. p 181
24 31 January 1942
25 18 February 1943
26 Cynthia to E. H. Coles 9 September 1946, Asquith Papers
27 Cynthia to de la Mare 21 August 1942 Bodleian
28 Cynthia to de la Mare 27 December 1943 ibid.
29 24 February 1942
30 Cynthia to Didy Holland-Martin undated letter (?mid 1940s)
31 unpublished poem Asquith Papers
32 27 April 1938, cf. Sandra Darroch *Ottoline* Chatto & Windus 1976 p 285
33 28 April 1940
34 Cynthia to Walter de la Mare 9 January 1946, Bodleian
35 2 May 1946
36 Cynthia to Walter de la Mare 30 March 1946, Bodleian

Chapter 33: 1950s
1 *The Squire* op. cit. p 188
2 Cynthia to de la Mare 13 September 1940, Bodleian
3 Address by T. S. Eliot at St Bride's Fleet Street 1 May 1959, published by *The Statist*
4 Letter to author from George Scott 19 February 1986

Notes

5 Telephone conversation with author 7 October 1986
6 Cynthia to Simon Asquith 1949
7 Kip Asquith in conversation with author 9 April 1984
8 *Queen* 21 December 1949
9 Cynthia to Mary Wemyss 19 September 1933, Asquith Papers
10 ed. Richard Buckle *Self Portrait with Friends*: The Selected Diaries of Cecil Beaton 1926–1974 Weidenfeld 1979 p 287
11 29 April 1954
12 Cynthia to Simon Asquith 15 October 1955, Asquith Papers
13 11, 17, 23 May 1954
14 23 December 1958
15 undated letter to unknown correspondent May 1959, Asquith Papers
16 Cynthia to Ursula Codrington 2 February 1960
17 Cynthia to David Cecil 14 March 1960, MacCarthy Papers
18 Daphne du Maurier to Nico Llewelyn Davies 12 April 1960, Llewelyn Davies Papers

The pictures that should have been placed:
opposite p.24/5 are those opposite p.152/3
         p.56/7   p.120/1
         p.120/1   p.184/5
         p.152/3   p.216/7
         p.184/5   p.24/5
         p.216/7   p.56/7
         p.280/1   p.312/3
         p.312/3   p.280/1

····≻ Picture Sources ≺····

When no other credit is given, photographs come from the *Asquith Papers*.

Madeline Wyndham in 1873. (*Fitzwilliam Museum, Cambridge*)
Mary, George and Guy Wyndham in 1874. (Life and Letters of George Wyndham *by J. W. Mackail and Guy Wyndham, Hutchinson 1925*)
Hugo Elcho.
Mary Elcho by Sir Edward Poynter 1886. (*The Earl of Wemyss*)
Arthur Balfour in 1902. (*BBC Hulton Picture Library*)
Charlotte Jourdain at St Hugh's College. (*St Hugh's College, Oxford*)
Cynthia and Guy Charteris in 1889.
Drawing of Cynthia by Burne-Jones. (*Reproduced from* Haply I May Remember)
Stanway House, Gloucestershire. (*Country Life*)
Stanway in the 1920s from the Pyramid.
Clouds House, Wiltshire shortly after the fire in 1889. (*Geoffrey Houghton-Brown*)
Cynthia as a crusader c. 1900.
Gosford from the air in the 1920s. (*Reproduced from* A Family Record)
Cynthia with her sister Mary and brother Yvo c. 1897. (A Family Record)
Mary Elcho with Cynthia, Ego, Guy, Mary, Yvo and Bibs c. 1903.
Drawing of Cynthia by Violet Granby 1903. (*Kit Asquith*)
Drawing of Beb Asquith in 1901 by Lucy Graham Smith. (*Reproduced from* Remember and Be Glad)
Mary Vesey, later Herbert, c. 1903. (*Pixton Papers*)
Harold Baker and Raymond Asquith at Oxford c. 1896. (*Oxford Union Society*)

Picture Sources

The Asquith family at Glen, Easter 1904. (*Lord Bonham Carter*)

Guests outside the Norman Hall during Commem Week 1907. (A Family Record)

Cynthia's hair, date unknown.

Mary Elcho, date unknown, possibly 1912 for her fiftieth birthday.

Sargent's charcoal drawing of Cynthia 1909. (*HRC, University of Texas at Austin*)

Cynthia on her wedding day with Mary and Bibs as bridesmaids.

Cynthia in 1915, drawn by Norah Brassey. (*Reproduced from* Haply I May Remember)

Sylvia Llewelyn Davies c. 1900 photographed by Barrie. (*Laura Duguid*)

Cynthia and John in August 1913. (*The Earl of Oxford and Asquith*)

Cynthia c. 1918 in her winged hat.

Oil painting of Cynthia by Augustus John 1917 (*Art Gallery of Ontario, Toronto: Gift of Reuben Wells Leonard Estate, 1933*)

Beb in 1918.

Simon c. 1922.

Basil Blackwood.

McEvoy's oil painting of Cynthia 1917–18. (*Owner unknown*)

Cynthia in the late 1920s.

Beb in the late 1920s.

Nanny Faulkner and Simon mid-1920s.

Cynthia, Michael and Simon in 1921.

'North Sea' by D. H. Lawrence. (*Laurence Pollinger Ltd. and the Estate of Mrs. Frieda Lawrence Ravagli*)

Michael and Simon in 1932.

Barrie, Beb and Cynthia in Switzerland 1936.

Drawing of Barrie by Sir Thomas Monnington 1932. (*National Portrait Gallery, London*)

The Wemyss family in 1934.

Cynthia photographed by Cecil Beaton. (*Sotheby's*)

Cynthia with Collin Brooks.

Cynthia with Michael and Hase in 1958.

·····≫· Index ≪·····

For a variety of reasons, such as marriage or succession to titles, people in this book are sometimes referred to by different names at different periods. The entries in the index are the names by which they were most commonly known, and cross-references are included as necessary. For example, Lady Diana Cooper (née Manners) is indexed as 'Cooper' whether she appears in the text as Cooper or Manners, and there is a cross-reference under 'Manners'.

Index

Index

Index

Index

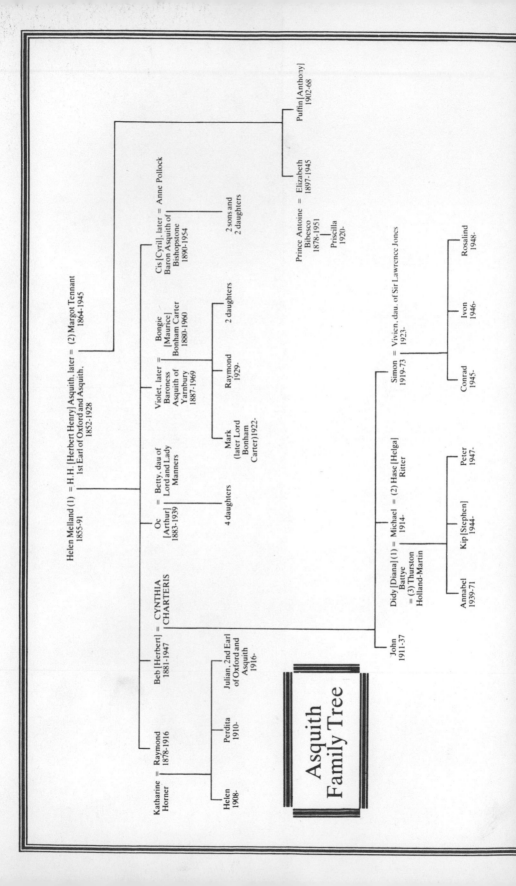

Asquith Family Tree

Helen Melland (1) = H.H. [Herbert Henry] Asquith, later = (2) Margot Tennant
1855-91   1st Earl of Oxford and Asquith,   1864-1945
     1852-1928

Raymond = Katharine Horner
1878-1916

Helen
1908-

Perdita
1910-

Julian, 2nd Earl
of Oxford and
Asquith
1916-

Beb [Herbert] = CYNTHIA CHARTERIS
1881-1947

John
1911-37

Didy [Diana] (1) = Michael = (2) Hase [Helga] Ritter
Battye   1914-
= (3) Thurston Holland-Martin

Annabel
1939-71

Kip [Stephen]
1944-

Peter
1947-

Oc [Arthur] = Betty, dau of Lord and Lady Manners
1883-1939

4 daughters

Violet, later = Bongie [Maurice] Bonham Carter
Baroness   1880-1960
Asquith of
Yarnbury
1887-1969

Mark
(later Lord
Bonham
Carter) 1922-

Raymond
1929-

2 daughters

Cis [Cyril], later = Anne Pollock
Baron Asquith of
Bishopstone
1890-1954

2 sons and
2 daughters

Puffin [Anthony]
1902-68

Prince Antoine = Elizabeth
Bibesco   1897-1945
1878-1951

Priscilla
1920-

Simon = Vivien, dau. of Sir Lawrence Jones
1919-73   1923-

Conrad
1945-

Ivon
1946-

Rosalind
1948-